PROLOGUE
Aubrey

The advertisement was pinned on a bulletin board, just between last week's coupons and a poster for a lost puppy. It was the kind with pull tabs at the bottom, three of them already taken.

The grocery store was mostly quiet that morning, with just a few people milling around. I still made sure to look around twice before grabbing a tab, careful not to be seen by anyone. Once I had it, I stepped back from the board as if it caught fire. I crushed the paper in my hand and held it there as I continued to grab a cart.

The usual boy stocking shelves smiled at me as I chose a loaf of bread. His eyes watched as I continued down the aisle and turned the corner. I shivered his gaze off my skin and took a deep breath.

His attention made my skin crawl, so I hurried through the aisles, only pausing once to grab a box of tampons. I arrived at the checkout with only two things off my list, something I would pay for later. The girl smiled at me and asked if I found everything okay. With effort, I smiled back. The piece of paper was damp now, sticking to my palm. I assured her that, yes, I found everything just fine.

The bag boy offered to carry my bag to the car. I declined. It's policy, I knew, but I still wondered if there was a different motive at play. It was just one bag and I managed it easily, dumping it in the backseat before taking my spot behind the wheel.

Ice snaked through my body, causing shivers I couldn't control. I wasn't sure if it was the cool fall morning, or my fear. My right hand was shaking too hard under the weight of the paper, so I used my left to turn the key in the ignition. Hot air hit my face, the vents on full blast from my morning drive. To pass the time, I double checked the locks on the door and made sure my phone didn't have any missed calls.

While I waited to warm up, I listened to Pink Floyd and counted the cars on the road. Only four passed by before the song ended. The shaking hadn't stopped. It was fear, as I suspected.

The radio was suddenly too loud, so I turned it down. Classic rock soothed a lot of things but that moment wasn't one of them.

I scanned the parking lot again. I had cursed living in a town with a minute population before, but at that moment it was convenient. Almost a blessing, if I believed in such nonsense. I took one final, cleansing breath. Ready or not, it was time. If I continued to hesitate, my phone would be lighting up with a call. Grocery shopping, especially for only two out of all the needed items, shouldn't take this long.

It takes a considerable amount of effort to uncurl my fingers. The paper was smaller than my palm. Since I had been pressing it so firmly into my sweaty skin, the ink was bleeding. Thankfully, I could still read it. Using my elementary school teacher's advice, I read it seven times and hoped it would stick like it was supposed to. Just to be safe, I closed my eyes and repeated it from memory seven more. Then I rolled down my window and threw it out. On the drive home, I continued to repeat it.

Self-defense classes. First session free.
Call Rob @ 555-8102.

By the time I pulled into a parking space at the apartment complex, the information was braille on the buds of my tongue. I hoped, when he kissed me, that he would not be able to read it.

CHAPTER ONE
Caden

She looks just about ready to take on the world. No one notices her, which is surprising in a gym so over-populated with guys. Jason surveys his clipboard with a cocked smile, like he's in on a secret, then turns to the girl and begins speaking. Even though my water bottle is full, I head to the fountain so I can eavesdrop.

"Make yourself at home," Jason wraps up whatever he was saying and gestures to the open gym.

The girl lifts her chin and surveys the area. I can't imagine how the place must seem to her. The sweat soaked air and obnoxious grunting is probably enough to send any pretty girl running. Hell, it's almost enough to send me running most days. Yet, she's smiling.

I give up the act of filling my overflowing water bottle and openly watch her make way through the stations of equipment. The guys all start to stare. With each step, she seems to grow taller.

Settling herself in front of an older heavy bag, she begins strapping on her gloves. Despite never being here before, she's right at home.

"Who is that?" I ask in my best *not that I care* voice. It takes a second before Jason blesses me with an answer.

"She's our new fighter." I raise my eyebrows but keep my mouth shut. "I found her at a local fight. She's good."

"A local fight? She's from here?" I scoff. This little town in Wisconsin doesn't produce much talent. Out of the 21,000 people who live here, only one has made it big. The idea that this place could crank out not one, but two, professional fighters? There's not a chance. Jason picked this place for his gym because he needed a break from the fast life, not because it was overflowing with talent.

"What, you're the only one in this shit-hole town that can fight?" He rolls his eyes at me, putting my ego in place. "Like I said, she's good."

"Where was she training before?"

"A basement. She started with self-defense classes."

I grit my teeth and turn my attention back to her. Self-defense. That's sloppy work. That's fighting to survive, not fighting to win.

Shoulder to shoulder, we study her. The neon sign of raw talent hangs above her and the bag. Form wise, she's way off the mark, but the power is there. A little more meat on her bones, a little more training, and she could be something. Not my level, but something.

"I can work with that," I inform Jason. Leaving him behind, I head her way. Each station I pass is filled with quiet whispers. If I wasn't so shocked myself, I would be annoyed with them. In all reality, though, it's a rare event. Jason has never taken a girl at Elite Gym before.

The girl slams her fist into the bag for the last time, finishing her combination. She looks at it as it swings, an artist appreciating her masterpiece.

"How'd that feel?" She startles. Two wide blue eyes focus on my face, catching me off guard. I don't think I've ever seen eyes so damn bright. I offer her a smile but she doesn't accept it. Instead, I'm rewarded with hands on her hips and a raised voice.

"Why would you sneak up on someone like that?"

"Uh, sorry?" I keep smiling because I know Jason is watching. When I take a step forward to extend my calloused hand, she slinks back. With an awkward thump, I bring my hand back to my side.

"Okay, then. I'm Caden."

She surveys the gym for a moment before allowing her eyes to meet mine again.

"Aubrey." She crosses her arms over her chest like the offering of her name suddenly took away her protection. *What the hell did I ever do to her?* I shake off the annoyance and try to remind myself that she's probably just uncomfortable.

"Would you like a tour, Bree?" As if she had already dismissed me, her focus is back on the bag. Clearly, I'm just background noise.

"No thank you." She lands a right hook into the bag and smirks. "And I would appreciate it if you called me *Aubrey*."

Shocked, I attempt to think of something sarcastic to say to her. Something to make her as uncomfortable as I feel in the moment, but I come up blank. Instead, I lock my jaw and head to Jason's office. There's something off about her, and I don't like it.

I interrupt Jason on the phone with three sharp knocks to his already open door. With a grunt of disapproval, he finishes his conversation. Once the phone is settled back in its cradle, he beckons me forward.

He stands, probably preparing himself for yet another complaint about the new girl in the all-boys gym. I haven't felt this nervous in his presence since I quit fighting. There's just something I've always hated about disappointing him.

"I don't mean to disrespect-" I stop when I feel the heat of someone behind me. Shifting to the side, I let Aubrey walk past me and into the center of the office. Gracefully, like she has no idea I was obviously about to complain about her, she approaches Jason's desk. I watch as she hands him a stack of papers with a smile.

"I'm in." The two words make Jason's entire face light up.

"5 a.m. practice. Don't be late." Knowing her attitude, I wait for her to object. Proving me wrong, she simply nods and leaves the room. When she's gone, Jason brings his attention back to me.

"I don't like her," I say, ripping it off like a band-aid. He creases his eyebrows, trying to understand the problem.

"She's talented Caden. You haven't even seen her fight."

"That's not what I'm questioning. I'm not okay with her, like, as a person." There's a sudden seriousness that grows in his eyes.

"Maybe there's more to the story." The phone starts ringing again, cutting the meeting short. "You'll figure it out."

"How am I going to do that?" Jason hands me the stack of papers he's holding. I survey them, a dull ache beginning to form between my eyebrows. It's her contract to train at the gym. To train under *me*, specifically. I lock eyes with him, ready to protest, but he answers the phone instead.

"Elite Gym, Jason speaking." I start to back out of the room but I'm not fast enough. Jason places the phone against his chest, blocking the sound, and says in his best attempt at an authoritative tone, "Caden. 5 a.m. tomorrow."

I sling my bag over my shoulder and storm out of the gym. Not before flipping him the bird, though.

He's been creative with punishments for me quitting. In the last few months, I've scrubbed toilets, mopped the sidewalk *during a rainstorm,* trained acne faced kids who only show up because mommy and daddy said so, and even broke up with a girl for him.

This one takes the cake, because this girl will be the death of me. I can already tell.

CHAPTER TWO
Caden

For the third time this morning, I try to wipe the sleep from my eyes. The last time I was at the gym this early, there was snow on the ground. Sleeping in was one of the only good things to happen since I quit.

I shake my head to clear all the negative thoughts that have been piling up over the last twenty hours. Jason isn't going to let me out of this easily, so I might as well embrace the situation.

Lights are on inside, meaning Aubrey's already in there. If I wasn't so crabby and exhausted, I would be impressed with her initiative, but I could be doing a million things right now. Like sleeping, or slamming my head against the wall, both of which would be more enjoyable.

She's in the back corner again, pounding harsh combinations into the leather bag. I cross my arms and watch her carefully. Each movement is loose, but steady. A controlled chaos. Her shoulders bunch as she speeds up, one side of her sweatshirt sliding down her arm. Each punch lands a little more off than the last. Finally, one slides right off and sends her flying forward. She shouts into the emptiness. No words. Just a guttural sound of anger and frustration.

After a moment of hanging her head, she turns to where I'm now standing. I hadn't realized it, but I'm closer to her now. At some point, I had begun to gravitate to her. Her reaction to my presence isn't what I expect. She smiles at me.

"Good morning."

I paste a smile on my lips, trying to embrace the new attitude. "Good morning. Ready to get started?"

"Are you a trainer?"

"Technically, no." I laugh but she doesn't join in. "Rest assured, I know what I'm doing."

"Caden Larson. 22 years old. 145 pounds, 5 feet 9 inches. You were ranked number one in the country but quit. Just a few months ago. It was the night before signing a major contract."

I raise my eyebrows. "Congratulations. You know how to use Google."

"Rob, the guy training me before, mentioned you when he convinced me to come here. I figured I'd do some research."

"Aww, you came here for me? I'm so flattered."

She crosses her arms over her chest. The movement sends her sweatshirt sleeve further down her arm, revealing a purple sports bra and a few stray freckles. I force my eyes to focus. It's easy once she starts talking again, each word forced through gritted teeth. "I did not come here *for* you. I came here because Rob asked me to give it a chance. That's the only reason I don't walk out right now."

I don't care how the gym air reeks of dirty ball sack, I take in the deepest breath I can through my nose to remain calm. Not only does she have a terrible attitude, but now I find out she doesn't even want to be here? This once in a lifetime opportunity, something most people work for since they're old enough to flip through the channels and discover fighting, and she's only here because some old dude asked nicely?

"Walk out if you want to, sweetheart. I'd much rather be sleeping right now."

"Don't call me sweetheart, you stupid, misogynistic, jerk."

I let out a low whistle and cross my arms. "Let's just get this over with. We're wasting time."

She zips up her sweatshirt so the sleeves are back where they need to be. The optimist in me believes this means she's ready to get started.

"I know that you know what you're doing, but I'd prefer to be trained by an actual trainer. Just, please?"

"It's better than some basement. Beggars can't be choosers."

Her demeanor changes from fake friendly to pure anger again. "You don't know anything about Rob's, so shut up."

"You're right. We should just workout." I storm over to my bag and grab the packet I prepared for her. With contempt, I place it in the open air between us and let go.

While she scrambles to grab it, I begin listing what she will find inside, "This is your new life. Use that great memory of yours to study up. I want you to buy what's on that list, to follow that meal plan, and to start lifting weights. If we don't lift weights in our session of the day, you need to get your ass to a gym and lift them at some point later. There's a list of pain relievers that are allowed by Jason's standards. It's a short one. You'll have weigh-ins every Monday."

I revel in the look on her face. Blue eyes stunned wide, white teeth clamped on her bottom lip, and worry etched across her forehead. If she had a better attitude, I'd feel bad for how overwhelmed she must feel.

"You got all that?" She obviously doesn't, it's a lot to process, but I enjoy rubbing the shock in. Staying true to herself, she lifts her chin and gives me her best smile.

"Of course."

"Great. Let's get started, then." I step towards one of the training stations. She doesn't follow. Instead, she speaks.

"You could have gone all the way you know." I cross my arms and settle my gaze on her. Hopefully it's as cold and hard as I want it to be.

"So I've been told." The glaring doesn't get her to back away, or apologize. She's stubborn, I'll give her that. "Those people don't know shit."

"They're experts. I think they know a lot," she says, fixing her glare on me. "Why did you quit?"

The question scrapes my bones and I snap. "Why did you?"

Her look of confusion irritates me. "I haven't quit. I'm here, aren't I?"

"Aubrey Pierce. 20 years old. 129 pounds, 5 feet 6 inches. No national ranking. No official championship title. 4.0 GPA, 31 ACT score, honor roll, lettered in nine sports, and Student Council President. Was planning on attending Brown, on scholarship."

She shifts uncomfortably, her light blue eyes cloudy now. I push her one step further by continuing. "Well, that used to be you at least. Until December of your senior year."

"People change." Her voice is rubbed raw with sadness.

"Why did you?" I watch her squirm, hands fiddling with the packet of papers. When she clearly isn't going to answer, I turn and gesture to the equipment. "I guess we all have our secrets, don't we, Aubrey?"

CHAPTER THREE
Aubrey

"Bree, dinner's ready." Myla's voice vibrates through our small apartment. I stare up at the ceiling of my room, willing my body to move. Ice packs weigh me down and my head is pulsing. Every inch of my body feels as if I fought ten rounds instead of an easy, two-hour workout.

Slowly, I sit up and push the ice packs away as I swing my legs to the side of the bed. I groan, partially in pain and partially in anger. There's no way the work out with Caden was this hard.

"Bree! Dinner!" The screaming increases my headache from a level six to an eight. I must remind myself half a dozen times how much I like her as I limp down the hallway and into the kitchen.

Myla offers me a sympathetic smile when I appear. As usual, I ignore the action. Pity parties aren't my thing. I start to pile large amounts of food onto my plate in silence. I think she gets the hint when she apologizes. "Sorry, too loud?"

"A bit." I force a smile. She's the best friend I've ever had, but she's all energy and no calm. There's no one in the world I love more than her, but it's been hard dealing with her fire now that mine's burnt out.

"How was your first day at the gym?"

"It was great." She just stares at me with an eyebrow raised. I roll my eyes. "Okay, it was terrible."

"Why?"

"I'm stuck with this trainer who's a total crab. And I'm super sore which pisses me off. He barely worked me." The force of my rant takes the wind out of me. "Shrug."

"Sigh." She pushes the food around on her plate. "That sucks."

"How was *your* day?" I shift in my seat to give her my full attention.

"Oh, it was fine." She waves her hand in the air, and I almost snort at how obvious she is.

"What happened?"

"Well, if you must know." She puts her fork down and turns to look at me. Her smile is stretched full across her face and her cheeks are flushed. "I think I met the love of my life today."

Oh, here we go. "Is that so? Where?"

"At the gas station."

"Ah, a very romantic place."

"Hey, now! You met—" she stops, her eyes searching mine for forgiveness.

"You're fine. Tell me all about him." Twirling spaghetti around my fork, I prepare for what I'm sure is going to be too much detail about a man that will mean nothing in less than a month. Myla resists being tied down. She claims it's in her blood.

"Are you sure?"

"Yes. I want to hear about the sexy gas man." She giggles and puts her hands in the air like she's about to paint the story instead of tell it.

"Okay. So, I was pumping gas and he pulled up behind me, and he said—" my calf starts to cramp and I stop listening to her. I reach down and rub the muscle, instantly angry again. Caden is a total asshole, and I'm upset that not only did he get to me emotionally, but he got to me physically too. The speed talking finally stops, settling us in a blissful silence. She's staring longingly at her plate now, like she can see him in the chunks of tomato.

I'm jealous of her. As much as I know this relationship, if you could call it that, won't last, at least she's feeling something. At least she isn't numb. The thought makes me want to punch something, preferably Caden, but I'm not picky.

CHAPTER FOUR
Aubrey

Long fingers caress my neck, slowly beginning to tighten. Tears streak my cheeks as my airway closes off. I open my mouth, a fish still in water whose habitat is betraying her. Choked sobs escape me while I frantically claw his face.

"Don't fight me, Bree. Fucking relax."

I don't want him to touch me. I don't want to be here. I kick at empty air and hear him chuckle. My vision blurs as the unforgiving darkness creeps in.

"Aubrey! Aubrey, wake up!" Myla is standing beside the bed, close enough to get my attention but far enough away in case I swing at her. I don't, this time snapping out of the nightmare fast enough to figure out where I am.

I sit up and touch my throat, hating that the skin still feels bruised. With a sad smile, Myla sits beside me.

"I'm fine," I assure her, taking my hand away from my throat to wave her off. She doesn't look convinced so I repeat myself, "I'm fine. Totally fine. Just a stupid dream."

"That's the third this week." She pauses. Thinks. "They're getting worse, Bree."

"I know." The usual defense mechanisms begin, my body folding into itself without instruction. With three, long breaths I try to nip the anxiety attack in the bud, but the familiar fire starts to crawl along my chest anyway. There's no escaping it. Sooner or later he'll be out of prison and back in this town. Back in my life. I can just feel it. I can feel my control, my strength, slipping all over again.

"Are you sure we shouldn't go away for school? I know we already have a year in here, but I'm sure a lot of credits would transfer. Is this really where you want to be?"

"He doesn't get to take my hometown from me." Even as I say the words, I know they aren't true. He already took it away, a long time ago. The optimist in me just can't let it go, believing that maybe, one day, I'll feel safe here again.

"I swear, Myla. I'm going to be fine. He's not going to get out anytime soon. Plus, there's no way I'm walking away from Elite now. That gym is amazing. I could actually become a real fighter there."

She smiles at me and I'm not sure if it's because the words comforted her, or because she pities me for saying them. I'm too tired to interpret.

"I can stay in here tonight," she offers.

"Oh, that's not necessary." Despite my saying this, I push the blankets back for her. She crawls under them and squirms until our arms are pressed against each other. I stare up at the spot where I know the ceiling must be. I'm exhausted, but afraid. I don't want to see him again. I don't want to hear his voice anymore tonight.

"Bree?"

"Yeah?" I look over in her direction and see that she's staring up at the ceiling too. Whatever she wanted to say never comes, silence hanging in the air long enough for my body to finally relax.

Just as the grogginess is seeping in, she speaks again, "Bree?"

"Yes?"

"Maybe you should tell someone." The shaking hope of her voice breaks me. Every few months, she does this. She brings us full circle, reminding me of all the reasons why I shouldn't remain quiet. The system never works like it should, and he'll be out sooner than later. Maybe it would add time to his sentence. Maybe it will keep me safe. Maybe it will stop him from doing it to the next girl who recklessly falls in love with him. Maybe it will give me peace of mind.

What she doesn't know is that all those reasons aren't reasons. She never got to know him well, but I did, and letting that secret slip would never keep me safe, and peace of mind? I don't think that will ever be in the cards for me. Even behind bars, he haunts me.

"I did, Myla." I let myself sink further down into the blankets, praying she will let it go. "I told you."

I feel her breathing hitch beneath the weight of that, before returning to normal.

"Goodnight, Bree."

"Night, My."

CHAPTER FIVE
Aubrey

To my surprise, the gym lights are already on as I pull into the parking lot. I double check the clock in case I was wrong when I snuck out of bed after nightmare number two, but I was right.

It's just now turning four. No one should be here right now, including me.

I grab my bag from the passenger seat and head off to investigate. By peeking through the small window on the front door, I see that my luck is still terrible. Caden is inside, punching a Bobby at station five. Each movement is crisp, accurately hitting key spots with minimal effort. Embarrassing as it is, I'm entranced.

Many people have talked about the famous Caden Larson, it's not often a kid from a small town like this makes it big. Usually, the Elite Gym is full of guys from around the country, biding their time in this shit-hole town until the big leagues call them up.

Rumors aside, I've done plenty of Googling on my own, and I know he's good. Or, more accurately, *was* good. Yet, seeing him in action changes things. He's not just talented, he's proficient. Brilliant. Picasso with a mannequin.

I continue watching from the comfort of being hidden, trying to absorb every little movement and technique. During this further inspection, I realize he's shirtless. That's how I know I'm losing my touch. He's gorgeous, and I'm just now noticing his lack of clothing? Myla would be devastatingly disappointed.

After his combination is finished I decide to stop being creepy and go inside. Caden jumps at the sound of the door, looking at me, then the clock. "Why are you here?" His tone is defensive and I already forget how great I thought he was just a moment ago.

"I could ask you the same thing, hey?" I stand in front of him with my hands on my hips. The view is much better from here, just inches away, and his attention is on wiping down his Bobby. Allowing myself a few seconds of curiosity, I let my eyes wander over his dips and curves.

If you asked someone to draw the perfect example of what a fighter should look like, they would draw Caden. He hovers over the Bobby, every muscle rippling with the movements involved in cleaning.

As if he isn't cut enough, he has tattoos that make his muscles even more prominent. One of these is a tribal print, the stark black working its way across his pec, over his shoulder, and down just above his elbow. When I follow the tattoo back up, I see that he's staring back at me now, bright blue eyes full of mocking humor. I snap out of the fan-girl trance, reminding myself that I hate him, and ask, "So, why are you here?"

"Once I'm done training you in the mornings, I have to go to work. This is my only chance to work out myself." I try to act disinterested in his explanation as I push past him and make my way to the weight bench. The stupid, unnecessarily long packet he gave me says we're starting with this today.

"Where do you work?"

"I'm a cop." I duck my chin into my chest, hoping to hide the look of horror I know just flashed across my face. It makes perfect sense that Caden, the guy I hate, works as something I have such a bad history with.

I force myself to recover, saying, "I thought you worked here." He grabs a crumpled piece of cloth and starts wiping the sweat off his chest. In my own best interest, I force myself to look away.

"I did. I was paid to fight. Now I just help Jason out, kind of as a favor."

"Favor for what?" I bring my eyes to his but regret it instantly. Those bright blue eyes that were laughing at me earlier are now dark and cold. He doesn't appreciate the questions.

"Breaking my contract."

"Right, that." I itch to ask him more, but think better of it. He has just as much ammunition as me, and I'm not in the mood to fight like we did yesterday. Unfortunately, he doesn't seem to have the same plan as me.

"Your turn to answer. Why are you here an hour early?"

"Oh, right." I climb onto the weight bench, half hoping that the movement will prompt him to go away and let me workout on my own. It doesn't. "I couldn't sleep."

It's not a lie, but it's not all together the truth either. He studies me for a moment. "You should have been exhausted. Did I not work you hard enough, yesterday?"

"No, I was tired." I ball the cuffs of my sweatshirt into my hands and squeeze. "I'm just not a great sleeper. Not a big deal."

"Is a big deal, as a fighter. Rest is huge." The tone of his voice reminds me of my mother, back when she used to lecture me on the importance of perfection. That was before she gave up on me, of course. "There's a supplement you can take, all natural, to help you sleep. I'll grab a sample from the office later. I want you to try it, okay?"

"Okay." I let go of my sweatshirt sleeves, thankful that the solution, at least for him, was so simple. Who knows, since I'm trying to be optimistic and all, maybe it *will* help me sleep.

I get myself comfortable beneath the bar and lift my hands to it. A shadow falls over me as Caden moves into position to spot me. "Oh, I don't need a spotter."

"What, you're too cool to follow the rules?" He rolls his eyes at me but moves away. Proud of myself for the tiny win, I begin to lift the bar. "Slow down there, little lady. I'm just adding more weight. You can do better than this."

There he goes with the whole being an asshole thing again. *Little lady? Really?* If he hadn't made that comment, maybe I would argue that I really can't do more weight than what I put on. Perhaps that was his plan, to piss me off so I push harder and prove myself. Whatever his intentions, I'm sure as hell going to lift whatever he puts on that bar now.

"Try that. See how ya do." He smirks down at me, hands hovering a few inches above the bar as a reminder that he believes I'll fail. Gritting my teeth, I lift the bar off the hooks and begin my reps. If he's impressed with the ease at which I do it, it doesn't show. He remains stone faced during the ten reps, and frowns when I settle the bar back on the hooks.

I snap at his stupid frown, asking "What? Disappointed that I did it?"

"Nope." He turns his frown into a smirk. "Disappointed you stopped at ten. I would have preferred fifteen."

With a huff, I grab the bar and take it off the hook. I push the bar fifteen times, refusing to show any signs that my chest feels like it's about to rip apart. When I put the bar back, I glare up at his smug face and spit out, "If you have expectations, then tell me beforehand. I don't appreciate when men set me up to fail just so they can call me little fucking lady."

His mouth opens, the smirk frozen between shock and satisfaction. Then he gives me a genuine smile. "I think I'm going to like you, Aubrey."

CHAPTER SIX
Caden

A plate covered in tin-foil is waiting for me on the counter when I get home from my shift. Upon further inspection, I see that it's three-cheese lasagna. I throw away the foil and slide the plate into the microwave, swallowing the guilt I feel from eating yet another cold dinner.

While the slice of Italian heaven gets nuked, I fill a glass of milk and place it on the table next to my phone. For the last thirty seconds, I lean against the wall and close my eyes, trying to get a little rest.

The microwave beeps way too soon. When I reopen my eyes I'm even more exhausted than before. Maybe I should take my own advice and take some supplements so I can sleep.

Just as I take the plate out of the microwave and sit down to eat, Cassie dances her way into the kitchen. It never ceases to amaze me how much grace she has. How much energy and excitement. It breaks my heart that she had to quit dance last week. Dancing was her dream. She was going to be a ballerina. No four-year-old should be told no when it comes to their dreams. I grip the table to get my anger under control, then give her the warmest smile I can find.

"Hey Cass, how was your day?" She smiles as she skips over to the fridge.

"Great! I got to go to the park."

"Oh, Caitlin took you to the park today?" Cassie stays silent as she opens the fridge. As if she was summoned, Caitlin sulks her way in and stands behind her younger sister, scowling as she stares over Cassie's shoulder.

"There's nothing to drink," Caitlin states matter-of-factly. I sigh, knowing where this is going to end up. Every day comes a new argument.

"There's tap water, and there's a jug of milk right in front of your face." Cassie ducks under Caitlin's arm and whispers that she's not thirsty. She's talented at sensing when a fight is brewing. I wait until she's out of earshot before turning on Caitlin.

"Did you take her to the park today?" Her shoulders lift and fall as she sighs and shrugs at the same time.

"She's four years old." Since that's not really an answer, I wait to hear more. She continues to stare into the fridge, despite the beeping noise it's now making from being open too long. "No, I did not take her to the fricken park."

The curse word is mild compared to some that have slipped recently, so I let it slide. With a calming breath, I keep my voice nice and low and say, "The park is too far away. I told you she can't go alone."

Despite the calm I'm trying to maintain, she explodes. "I'm sick of watching her all the time! I'm not her fricken parent."

"Language, Caitlin!" I breathe before continuing. "Come on, you know money is tight since I didn't sign that contract. I can't afford daycare."

"If mom was here-" I stand up and she falls silent. Tears slide down her cheeks but I can't tell if they're from anger or sadness, since both make her cry. Slowly, as if it's taking a whole lot of effort, she closes the fridge door and speaks, "The milk is sour. And you're welcome, ya know, for the lasagna."

I deflate. Why does it feel like no matter what, I always lose? "Caitlin. I'm trying."

"Try harder." She walks out of the room, her footsteps growing heavy as she makes her way down the hall. With a tight chest and one stray tear of my own, I look around the house. My parents' house. The usual grief begins clawing up my throat, but I swallow it down. There's a time and a place for it to come thrashing it's head. Here, with the girls home, is not it.

I take a swig of my milk, but end up coughing it back up. Right, spoiled milk. Already forgot.

With shaking hands, I pour the milk down the sink and grab the carton from the fridge to do the same. Once all traces of the chunky dairy product are gone, I sit back down to eat my lasagna. It takes effort to cut a piece off, because all I can picture is Caitlin, sixteen-years-old, with the weight of the world on her tiny shoulders, pouring herself over mom's recipes to make this for us. I force myself to eat, not wanting to waste her hard work, but my own hatred for myself masks the taste of it.

Once my plate is clear, I look up at the ceiling and whisper, to no one in particular, "I'm trying."

CHAPTER SEVEN
Caden

The next few days are long and mundane as I settle into my new routine. I show up at the gym, train Aubrey, and try not to curse or throw anything. Then I shrug on my uniform, show up to work, and try not to hate all the lowlifes I'm forced to deal with. After all that lovely shit, I come home and the girls ignore me. Well, Caitlin ignores me. Cassie just avoids me. After that, I try to get some sleep, try being the most important word.

Repeat.

On Thursday, something slightly more exciting happens. The chief ducks his head into the breakroom after lunch and asks me to come into his office.

"Yes, Sir." I stand up and straighten my uniform, preparing for what I'm sure is going to be a scolding about how terrible I am at filling out reports. He walks fast, leaving me to feel like an idiot as I try to keep up.

When we enter his office, I'm surprised to see I'm not the only one joining him. There's a guy standing in front of the oak desk, staring out the window. He's my age, give or take a year, but the look in his eyes is hardened. When he turns to look at us, that look in his eyes intensifies into pure hatred. It's clear that he's done time.

"Caden. I want you to meet our new informant." The guy crosses his arms over his chest, revealing two full tattoo sleeves. Since he's obviously not going to introduce himself, I look at the chief for more information. "I'll have his file put on your desk first thing."

"Wait." I glance at the man, then the chief, in confusion. The last thing I want to do is show any weakness in front of this guy, but I must ask, "He's mine?"

"Yes, you'll be overseeing his probation as well as meeting with him on a regular basis, and you're going to be the head of the operation."

I'm stunned. I can't think of any words right now. The chief glances up from his desk. "You put in for a promotion, didn't you?"

"Yes, I did." It was a shot in the dark. My degree was a bullshit one from a crap college that offered online courses. I never thought I'd need it, since fighting was going to be my career. Still, a degree is a degree, and with it I technically met all the requirements. I just never believed I'd get it.

"You'll take a break from patrol. If this case goes well, we'll make the position permanent. Is that a problem, Officer Larson?"

"No, not at all." The guy looks like he could care less about any of this. He's itching at his tattoo sleeve absentmindedly, back to staring out the window.

"Perfect. Jameson, this is Officer Larson. You'll be working with him, as well as an undercover agent coming in from a different county." I offer my hand to the guy, not because I care to show him respect, but because the chief is watching me. He takes it, shaking it twice, a little too hard.

"It's nice to meet you," he says through gritted teeth. It's clear he doesn't want to be an informant. None of them ever do.

"Same goes to you." I take away my hand, fighting the urge to wipe it on my pants. He's a clean guy, I'm just overreacting. It's not like being a piece of shit is contagious.

Chief waves us toward the door. "You're dismissed then. You can take Jameson to your desk."

"Alright." I turn around and head out of the office, pleased with the fact that Jameson follows. When we reach my desk, I pick up the promised file and begin scanning it. While I read, he waits, not so patiently.

It takes me less than a minute to decide that he's a shitty person. Possession of an illegal narcotic, heroin to be exact, with the intent to sell. About nine grand in his apartment, waiting to be laundered. Drugs in his system at the time of arrest. Possession of an illegally obtained weapon. Blood all over his clothes from an altercation that was never identified.

This guy's lucky he only got five to ten years. He's damn lucky he got this deal only a year into it.

When I glance up from the file I see him looking at the pictures of Caitlin and Cassie. The look of curiosity on his face makes me shiver. I shouldn't have those up in here. *How did I not see that before?* He points to them as if he knows what I'm thinking. "Are they yours?"

"Kind of." It's none of his damn business. Some people say that you should form a mild relationship with your informant, but I'm not that guy. "So, since you're getting out early because of a deal there's a few rules you need to follow."

He scoffs. "Just a few?"

"Okay, a lot of rules." If I wasn't in such a great mood from the news of the promotion, I would tell him exactly what I think about his attitude. Who complains about following rules when they're getting a second chance? This is his break, whether he likes it or not.

"I'll give you a full list, but obviously you need to stay away from illegal activity because of your probation. As for drinking, you-"

"I won't be doing that." I almost snort at how unrealistic that seems, but then I look at him. There's no humor in his eyes, leaving them a dead green. He scratches his stubble, annoyed that I'm smiling at him right now, and I believe him. Well, I believe that he believes it.

"Alright." Whatever floats his boat. If he believes he'll magically become a shiny new person, good for him. Me, on the other hand? I believe pieces of shits don't change

CHAPTER EIGHT
Aubrey

While most sane people are sleeping, I drag myself to the gym as the sun rises. I'm exhausted after spending the night trapped in nightmares. The supplement Caden gave me worked, but I now know that I'd prefer to be awake. It's better when I can wake up and escape, even if it means being exhausted the next day.

Right off the bat, I can tell he's in a mood. He doesn't even glance at me when I walk up to the station he's working at. Instead, he continues fiddling with the machine in front of him.

"Good morning," I finally say after another minute of being ignored.

"Morning." Still, his focus is on the machine. There can't even be anything for him to mess with anymore. It's one lever, a simple lift the seat up or down.

"Should I get started, or?"

"Yeah." He finally looks at me, eyes squinting like I'm blurry. "Sorry, my mind is all over the place today. Lots going on at work."

I try not to feel hopeful that he's offering up information about himself. Maybe he's starting to warm up to me. Maybe I can try to warm up to him, since we're obviously going to be spend a lot of time together.

"It's not a problem. Where do you want me?"

"Uh, hop on a treadmill, just to warm up. Then we can start doing stations."

"Aye aye, Captain." I honestly don't mean the comment to come off sarcastic, but he shoots me a glare which means he takes it that way. Just like that, the possibility of warmth is ruined.

As I go through my mile warmup, other members begin to trickle in. Guys smile at each other, shouting things back and forth as they set up for their workouts. I can't help but feel a pang of loneliness. The only person I really know here can't stand me.

As if to rub it in, Caden leaves the machine he's been mysteriously focused on, and walks over to a guy a few years older than me. He adjusts his form, steps back and watches him for a minute. A smile splits his face and he gives the guy a thumb up. I don't think he's ever done that, smiling while training me. At least not a real one. Training me doesn't bring him any sort of joy, and I was fine with that when I thought he was just an asshole in general, but now I see it's me that's the issue.

Still not looking at me, Caden joins a conversation with two guys next to the station we're supposed to be starting at. I head over there, wiping my face with a towel. Rob's basement didn't have stations, so I have no idea what to do at most of them, including this one. Trying not to look too awkward, I stand and wait for him to come over and help. He doesn't.

They're talking about a party. It's apparently someone's birthday, and since the gym is closed on Sundays, they're throwing a huge bash. I try to remember the last time I was at a party. It had to have been at least a year ago, probably longer. The last one I can fully remember ended with me dragging an unconscious Elliot to the car, with the help of one of the other girlfriends.

Eventually, after twenty minutes of my morning is wasted, Caden makes his way to me and explains the station. In between each round and each new station, he laughs and talks with the other guys in the gym, leaving me as an afterthought.

Jason arrives at the gym just as I finish at my last station. I wipe the equipment off and rush over to his office before he can close the door. His head snaps up at the sound of my knock, but he doesn't look too bothered by me.

"I was just thinking about you, Aubrey." His smile is warm, but cautious. "I hope you're settling in okay."

I glance out the large window that takes up half of his office wall. There's a ring in the center of the gym, and it was empty just a minute ago. Now, there are two people fighting in it, one of them looking a lot like Caden.

"I like it here." It's not a lie. It's not the truth either. I miss Rob's basement, with its warm lighting and Classic rock. I miss Rob. My life had been a mess when he found me and showed me how to fight. If it wasn't for him, I probably wouldn't be here anymore. Then again, if it wasn't for him, I would have escaped the burden of having to interact with Caden Larson.

"It's just-" I stop, looking out the window again. It *is* Caden fighting in the ring, I recognize his bright blue tap out shorts. What a total asshole. He makes me do stations but hops in the ring first chance he gets to help someone else out?

"Different?" Jason asks, attempting to fill in the blank for me.

"Yeah. It's just different." I yank my attention away from the window and back to him, but it's too late. Jason glances out over to see what I was looking at, eyes lighting up like he's in on a joke. *He probably is.*

"But it's a good different, I hope?" I don't answer, and instead we both watch Caden for a minute. Then Jason clears his throat and asks, "How is your training going?"

"It's pretty good. I want to fight, though." We both watch as the boys in the ring push against each other. There's no punching or kicking, just pushing. It's a strange exercise, something I have never done before. It looks exhausting, but in a good way. I'd give anything to be doing something like that, or to be doing anything, other than conditioning.

"Caden doesn't fight, Aubrey." I shift my gaze to Jason. The world tilts, reshaping into something I should recognize, but can't.

"What do you mean, he doesn't fight?"

"He quit, a year ago." I knew this. My google search, though not extensive, revealed this. That doesn't mean he doesn't fight though. That just means he doesn't do it competitively, right? I can feel a headache starting to form.

"You're telling me he doesn't fight? Like, at all? Not even here, with the other guys?"

I glance out the window again. He's in the ring, that's true, but he's not fighting. It's just an exercise.

Have I seen him fight? Now that I think about it, I haven't. The only punches he's thrown have been at a Bobby or a bag.

"You're correct. I'm surprised he's even in the ring right now."

"Let me get this straight. You gave me a trainer who refuses to fight?" Jason nods, a mysterious smile playing on his lips. There he goes again with that secret I'm not in on. "That doesn't make any sense."

"Do you need something today, Aubrey?" The air in the office shifts, him not liking the way I questioned his decisions. When I don't answer him, he stands up to usher me out.

"Because I have a bunch of paper work that needs to be filled out," he informs me, a slight annoyance in his voice.

"Yeah." I try to remember why I came in here, my thoughts now feeling sticky. "I was hoping you would allow me to work out tomorrow morning. I know there's no training on Sundays, but I wouldn't need Caden. There's just a lot I need to work on, and I could really use the extra time."

"No."

"But-"

"No." I open my mouth to protest again but think better of it, since I already made him crabby by questioning him once.

Jason brings me to the door, dropping me off at the exit like a child. "Aubrey, go out tonight. Let off some steam. There's a party, and everyone from the gym will be there. You should go."

"I wasn't invited."

"I'm sure you will be." We stare each other down for a moment. There's a clear implication that this isn't a request.

"I don't drink." He continues to stare at me, his eyes dull and tired. This was an obvious statement, since I'm both underage and under contract.

"I really think you should go." The phone rings, and he takes the opportunity to turn his back on me and walk away.

Feeling like I was just scolded, I sulk out of the office. When I round the corner, I run face first into a sweaty chest. Caden places his hands on my upper arms to brace me as I stumble back. It's so random, so unplanned, that I snap back for a moment. Equipment and safety are no longer surrounding me, and I'm suddenly back in that apartment, Elliot pushing me against the wall.

"Don't touch me!" My own voice takes me away from the moment, but not before I shove him.

Caden takes a step back and waves his hands in the air. "Chill the fuck out, I saved you from falling on your ass."

He thinks I'm being a bitch, which is better than him knowing what just happened to me. The bubbling in my chest won't slow down, creating an obstacle for me to breathe. With each inhale, my body lies to me, saying I'm not getting the oxygen I know I am. If he notices, he doesn't care.

"You know, Aubrey, there's a party tonight. You should come, since you're so much fun and everything. I bet everyone would just be so happy to see you there." His sarcasm pisses me off, but the anger does good things to me. It takes my mind off the fact that I'm drowning in air. The fire replaces the bubbles, and I let it save me.

Just as I'm about to tell him where he can stick his stupid party invitation, Jason interrupts, "She was just telling me how she's so excited to go."

"I doubt that." Caden says once Jason is out of ear shot. He chuckles, and I want more than anything to ask him what this joke is that everybody is in on.

"What's so funny, asshole?"

"Oh, nothing. Party starts at 9. Bring your gloves." He winks at me and walks away. I stand there confused and pissed off. Bring my gloves? Whatever this ongoing joke is, whatever has everyone besides me so fricken happy, I'm not appreciating it.

CHAPTER NINE
Aubrey

"So, I, um. I kind of made plans tonight." Myla doesn't look at me as she says this, staring instead at her empty plate. I'm pretty sure she could sense my mood from the moment I walked in today. Normally, I would feel guilty, but I'm still too infuriated to care.

"With gas station guy?" It bothers her that I don't call him by his name, but I honestly don't remember it. Not that I tried.

"Yes. With *Jesse*."

"Great." Knowing I need to say something, anything, to make the conversation less awkward, I feign interest and ask, "What are you guys going to do?"

It's a dangerous question. She could answer simply, or she could gush. Thankfully, she chooses the first. "Just seeing a movie, maybe bring him back here after." She shifts in her seat. "If I do, I'll keep it down."

"Myla, you're fine. It's why we got our own place after graduation, remember?"

"Yes. Well, that and the fact that I don't have a family and your parents are nauseating." I choke on my chicken and she laughs. "Sorry, too much?"

"Honestly? Not enough. You know, the one thing that was good about dating Elliot was the look on my parents faces when he walked in." Her smile slips before she can catch it.

It hurts that there's a section of my life that's awkward to bring up. That's blackened by his presence. Thankfully, Myla's skilled at handling these situations, always knowing how to lighten my darkness.

"I wish I could have been there to see that. Your mother was probably so fantastically pissed. Oh my god, and when she saw his tattoos? Her face must have been priceless." She lets out a laugh, and I let myself join in. The air feels better again.

I take a sip of water and decide to rip the band-aide off. "Anyway, I have plans too. There's a party I'm going to check out."

"Oh." She puts her fork down and smiles up at me. The look she gives me is the same look I used to get from my mother, stuffed full of expectation. I shudder.

"It's nothing. Seriously. I'm pretty much going just to piss off Caden."

"Caden?"

"Yeah, the douche who's been training me. He invited me as a joke so now I have to go." I stab at my asparagus, imagining it's Caden's face. "I'm probably going to have to bond with people."

"Oh. I'm so proud of you, honey." Her voice is extra high and airy. I laugh at her great impression of my mother.

"Screw you." I push at her face and explain myself. "It's just some people from the gym. It was kind of implied that it's mandatory, anyway."

"Ooh, some people from the gym." She beams. "The all *boy* gym."

"Yes, Myla. There will be boys there. But I doubt it's exclusively male." At least I hope that's the case. It would be awkward to be the only girl at the party.

"Well, either way, boys are good. We like boys, remember?"

"I don't have the time or energy for a relationship right now. I just started training."

"Yeah, I know." She stands up and starts clearing the table. By the amused look on her face, it's clear she doesn't believe a word.

I excuse myself, "I'm gonna take a shower and get ready."

"Alright. It's already pretty late so I might be gone by the time you get out." She glances at the clock, then back at me with a concerned look. "Call me if you need anything tonight."

"I'll be fine, My." Sadly, I'm already doubting if this will be true. I haven't been to a party since Elliot.

Dating a drug dealer was wild. It's been a nice change, just sitting around reading books, or training. I can't even remember the last time I washed puke out of my hair or screamed my lungs out at two in the morning. Not that I plan on letting tonight's party end either of those two ways.

As I strip down, I imagine that I'm shrugging out of all those memories, leaving them on the floor to crumple. While waiting for the water to warm up, I study myself in the mirror. Caden is probably right about the whole needing to gain weight thing. All the stress these past two years really scraped it off me. What used to be a healthy amount of fat and muscle is now angles and bones. Elliot liked me this way, tiny and easy to throw around. Breakable.

There I go, again. I was supposed to leave him on the floor with the clothes. Angry at myself, I climb into the shower with the hope that the burning hot water will chase him away.

Despite my best efforts, I can't escape my own mind. I even shiver when my fingers touch the base of my throat, the skin there imagining his calluses where they aren't.

Jesus, Bree. Get it together.

I give up on the hope of letting him go. It's been a year since he laid hands on me, and I'm still scrubbed raw. It feels like every word in my vocabulary is tangled with him somehow. Every thought, or memory, is attached to his ghost. I am officially haunted.

CHAPTER TEN
Caden

"Girls! Dinner's ready!" I turn the stove off and make sure none of the hot pans are sticking out for anyone to bump. Cassie's tiny bare feet slap against the hardwood floor as she dances down the hall. She nearly runs me over when she comes around the corner, arms flapping through the air. "Woah, slow down there, killer."

She smiles up at me, her cheeks flushed. Still moving to imagined music, she slides into her usual seat. I scoop two spoonfuls of macaroni on her plate, right next to a hot dog with a perfect squiggly line of ketchup on it. It's no three-cheese lasagna, but it's at least warm and served to all three of us at the same time.

Caitlin slumps down into her own chair, hair curled and face covered with a little too much make-up.

"What are you all dolled up for?" She stares at me, waiting for the punch-line. Wracking my brain for any available information doesn't get me anywhere. Whatever she has planned, I completely forgot about it.

"I have a birthday party. Remember?" I glance up at the calendar on the wall. Sure enough, there's the big red circle marking the date. *Shit.*

"I needed you to watch Cassie." Uncomfortable silence fills the room. The youngest at the table slinks down in her seat, trying to disappear. It's not fair that we always fight over who's responsible for her, both of us trying to prove whose life is more important than the other. I can't imagine the way we make Cassie feel, like she's a burden we both forget to remember.

I check myself, pasting a smile and deciding from now on this won't be an argument. Her plans are much more important than my plans, it's part of the whole parenting thing, and from now on I'll make the whole taking care of Cassie situation run smoother.

"That's okay. You should go and have fun. Cassie will just get to come on an adventure tonight." At this new development, Cassie sits up in her chair and smiles.

Caitlin doesn't say anything, not even a thank you, but I tell myself to let it go. In her defense, it's me who messed up this time.

I scoop macaroni and cheese onto her plate, right next to a hot dog, and she pushes it away after announcing that she's a vegetarian. Defeat grows thick in my gut.

"Since when?"

"Today." I turn around and place the pot back down on the stove. I can feel tears pricking the corners of my eyes and I try to breathe through it. Placing both hands on the counter, I focus on looking out the window so my mind will stop racing. A neighbor is jogging down the sidewalk aside a large golden retriever on a leash. So normal. Easy. I jam my fingers into my eyes and rub any sign of weakness out of them.

Both girls watch me as I pull out the bread and the peanut butter. I grab a butter knife and make a simple sandwich before walking it over and swapping it with the hot dog on Caitlin's plate. I force a smile, hoping it's warm. "I'll make sure to buy some different stuff for you tomorrow, then. I'm sorry."

In response, Caitlin stares down at the plate. The tension in the room is thick as we all wait to see what happens next. A car outside beeps its horn and she jumps up.

"That's my ride." She starts retreating, slipping into a pair of shoes as she goes.

"You didn't eat!" This doesn't seem to matter to her as she continues her escape. I've known her for sixteen years. She won't stop.

"At least grab your coat!" I yell, half standing to make sure she grabs it. Thankfully, she listens. I slump back down in my seat and grab the edge of the table, staring down at her full plate of food. Cassie's small fingers slide over my white knuckles and squeeze.

"What's a vegetarian? Can I be one?"

CHAPTER ELEVEN
Aubrey

Music is pounding through the house when I arrive. With sweaty palms, I smooth down the fabric of my top. Myla had put out an outfit for me on my bed, a simple pair of jeans and a flowy tank-top. Most of the time I would roll my eyes at her treating me like a child, but in this case I think it was for the best. This outfit is way better than what I was planning on wearing- my usual baggy zip-up hoodie that has a hole in the cuff. She knows me way too well.

Weaving through the crowded house, I start to realize that I don't recognize a single person. This probably should have been expected, since I've never even met the guy whose birthday it is, but I figured there'd be a lot of people from the gym. So far, that's not the case.

At least there are girls here, although one of them is far too young. A little girl with blond pigtails pushes past me, running towards the kitchen and giggling. I look around in shock, trying to find her parents. *Who the hell would bring a kid to a party?* I follow the girl, honestly worried for her safety, only to find her climbing onto a counter behind Caden and another guy.

Caden looks different outside of the gym. Friendlier. His usual cut-off and baggy shorts are replaced with cargo shorts and a red and blue faded flannel, the buttons undone so I can see the plain white shirt beneath it. The cuffs are rolled up just below his elbow, hiding his tattoos. Now that he's not soaked in sweat, his hair has shape. It's long enough for the ends that aren't pushed back to curl onto his forehead, giving the messy impression that he just rolled out of bed. He looks scruffy and sexy and all of this makes me hate him ten time more.

The kitchen table is pushed to the side, making room for two guys fighting each other. People all around scream and cheer as they pound away. They're awful fighters, their punches barely making an impact. The little girl shouts and waves her arms as Caden takes a swig of beer.

I scan the crowd, hoping to see someone else, anyone else, but I still don't recognize anyone. Biting the bullet, I move toward Caden in the hopes that he won't be a total asshole tonight.

He nods at me to acknowledge my presence and takes another sip from his bottle.

"I thought we weren't allowed to drink?" I tease.

"I'm not under contract. Plus, I'm 22." One of his eyebrows is cocked at me while he smiles. I'm not sure if it's because we are out of the gym, or because he's drinking, but he seems happier. Even relaxed. "You, on the other hand, need to be on your best behavior."

"You're not the boss of me outside of the gym."

"Thank God. You're not easy to be the boss of. I need the break." I wait to see if he's teasing or really being rude. The stone-faced look he's giving me cracks, revealing a devilish grin.

"You could channel my mother and just give up." I give him the same stone-face he gave me, but I don't last as long. After a second, we're both smiling wide.

"Hit him harder!" I jump when the little girl behind us screams at the top of her lungs. Her tiny fist is in the air as she cheers, and I can't decide if she's scary or adorable. Maybe both.

"Who thought it'd be a good idea to bring a kid here?" I whisper to him, judgment clear in my voice. Caden's face contorts in pain.

"Actually, I did." Before I can react, he grabs the little girl and storms out of the room. I lean against the counter and try to process that information. There's no way she's his, but I can't see parents being okay with a babysitter bringing their child to someplace like this.

Just my luck that I would say something offensive right as we were starting to get along. I shake my head and decide to go after him, hoping I can stop him from hating me more than he already does.

I find him outside on a wooden bench, discussing animal rights with the little girl on his lap. As they talk, his fingers softly rework her hair-ties so the pigtails are straight. For the first time around him, I find it hard not to smile.

"Sorry to interrupt." Caden's back straightens at the sound of my voice. The little girl turns around to smile up at me, a chubby hand waving hello in the air. I wave back, ignoring Caden's grumpy face.

"Cass, why don't you go practice your cartwheels in the grass? Right there, where I can see you." She bolts across the lawn, obviously desperate to get her energy out. I watch her until she's far enough away, then turn my attention back to Caden.

"This seat taken?" The question is a formality, so I sit down before he can answer. He turns his attention away from Cassie long enough to give me a side glance.

"Is now."

"I just wanted to apologize. I have a really big mouth." He leans back on the bench and crosses his arms. Giving into temptation, I look over at him. His eyes are focused on the sky, but he knows that I'm looking at him because his face isn't relaxed. Since the cat is already out of the bag, I let myself stare for a moment longer. He looks tired. No, not tired. Exhausted.

Guilt eats away at my hate for him. "I really am sorry, Caden. I've been a bitch, like, since moment one."

"Don't worry about it." Something good happens in the house because everyone cheers loudly. We both glance over our shoulders, like the brown siding can give us a clue to what's going on inside. Once the noise quiets down to the usual loud music, he looks back at me and smiles. "Trust me, you're not as bad as my sister."

"Is she your sister?" He doesn't have to look to know I'm pointing at the little girl rolling around in the grass.

"One of them. I've got two."

"Got stuck babysitting tonight?" His body language changes, the relaxed exterior dissolving into something restless. He focuses his attention on the ground, kicking the dirt in front of us with the toe of his shoe.

"Something like that." His face fills with darkness. For whatever reason, I think of Elliot. Of that darkness that used to hide beneath the surface. Is Caden the same way? Full of secrets and demons, just waiting to come out and play? I don't think he'd be the type. Then again, I didn't think that about Elliot either, and look where that got me.

I watch Cassie, hoping for a distraction from my thoughts. Instead, I start thinking about how sweet and innocent she seems to be. How easily she might lose it, falling into the same trap I did. When I look back at Caden he's watching her too. I wonder if he's worrying about that sort of thing as well. Probably not, because he's smiling.

"You're somethin' else Caden Larson." I'm not sure what makes me say this. Something in that smile most likely. He looks over at me and his eyes travel along my face. In an unexpected turn of events, the attention doesn't make me uncomfortable. Instead, I find myself liking the way he looks at me.

"What's your story Aubrey?" The question catches me off guard. My response is cliché, but effective.

"You first." He laughs, and I can't help but feel disappointed. I wouldn't mind hearing about his life. Then again, I'm not willing to share my own information, so it's not fair for me to hope he'd share his.

Oh God, what would Caden thinks of my relationship with Elliot? As a cop, he'd hate it. He would hear about how I used to clean blood off Elliot's clothes, blood that wasn't Elliot's. He would hear about how I used to help him count his money after a big deal, wrapping each stack with a paper band. He would hear about how often I listened in on plans, watched illegal activities, and drove the getaway car. He would consider me on the same level as Elliot, nothing but a piece of shit criminal.

As a person, I wonder if it would be different. Yeah, he has that darkness inside him, but not everyone gives into their demons. Some people, proof being in the form of Myla, can have demons and darkness and still be inherently *good*.

"You should get in there and network. I gotta get this one to bed." He stands up, careful not to brush me as he passes. "See ya Monday."

Cassie sees him coming from her spot across the lawn. Little legs pump fast as she flies into his open arms. He picks her up and swings her around before settling her small body against his chest.

Her face nestles into the crook of his neck, feet swinging with every step he takes. I can't help but notice that he carries her like a father. Like at any moment, his strength will be tested. At any moment, she could be taken away.

CHAPTER TWELVE
Caden

I'm not entirely dreading training Aubrey this morning. Not that I missed her or anything, because a full day without seeing her was quite nice. Yet, she'll be the first person in the last twenty-four hours to like me. Well, to at least not *hate* me.

Cassie is pouting because I signed her up to start Kindergarten. Caitlin's upset because I told her she can't stay out past her curfew Friday night for a back to school bonfire. Jason's back on the 'Get Caden to Fight Again' campaign trail. My boss at work isn't impressed with the fact that I forgot to file some paperwork for our new informant. Oh, and that lovely informant? He probably hates me most of all for the piss tests I 'randomly' ask him to do every single day.

I run a mile on the treadmill to get my head straight. The release of energy is a relief after not working out yesterday. I know I'm allowed to come here even though no one else can, but I try to spend as much time as I can with the girls on Sundays. Not that either of them were interested in my presence, both remaining holed up in their rooms all day.

With my mind speeding through my never-ending list of things to do, I don't notice Aubrey walk in. I nearly fall off the treadmill when I catch sight of her.

"Jesus." I try to breathe, the track automatically slowing down since my chest string ripped off. She looks up at me and offers an apologetic smile.

"Did I scare you?"

"No." I put my hands on my hips and try to act cool. She doesn't buy it and snorts. It's a cute sound. *Woah, where'd that come from?* "Okay, maybe yes. I was a little out of it."

"Don't worry about it. I get like that when I work out by myself."

"Yeah. I've witnessed." I remember the first day I met her, when she was punching the bag in the back. Her concentration was insane.

Once her water bottle is full, she sits down on a mat and begins stretching. Since you can never stretch too much, I sit down on the mat facing hers and do the same. The silence between us is perfect, and that's how I should know it won't last.

She speaks first, eyes on her knees as she stretches forward. "So, Jason said you don't fight."

"Yup."

"Do you really think you can train me to fight without ever actually fighting with me?" She rests her chin on her knees and glances up at me. Damn, she's flexible. That'll work in our favor when she gets in the ring.

"Jason seems to think so." It's hard to focus. With her bent like that, the swoop of her tank-top is showing just how strained her breasts are against her sports bra. She huffs, but her eyes are closed, so I assume it's because of the comment and not because I was checking out her chest. "Do you have a problem with me training you?"

"Yes." Her honesty surprises me. Jason already told me she came to him but I didn't expect her to come to me, too. Maybe she has more fight in her than I thought.

"Well, you can put in a request for a different trainer." It's true. Jason really wants us to work together, for whatever messed up mind-game reason, but she has the right to pick a different trainer. Although, I have a feeling Jason would remind her she also has a right to go to a different gym.

She must think the same. "Shrug."

I wait but she doesn't shrug. This girl continues to get weirder. "Well, then it looks like we're stuck together."

"Looks like." She stands up, balancing on one leg to stretch out her quad. Silence wraps around us for a while, this time thick and uncomfortable. It takes her until she's done with both legs before getting the nerve to ask the next question.

"Do you think you'll ever fight again?"

"No." The sudden flash of anger within me drives me up and forward. I head to the first station, adjusting the Bobby so it's facing the direction I want it to be. She doesn't get the hint, or doesn't care about the hint, and keeps pushing.

"How can you say that? You were amazing, and you loved it."

"You don't know anything about me." I say this low enough for just her to hear. There's no reason to start an argument now that the gym is filling with other people.

"How the hell do you expect me to get anywhere if you can't teach me to fight?"

"You know how to fight." I grab her by the shoulders and place her in front of the Bobby. Every muscle in her body goes rigid. Then they kick into overdrive, creating visible tremors. "Are you cold? Where's your sweatshirt?"

Now that I'm thinking about it, she's wearing something other than her ratty, black sweatshirt for the first time since I've met her. She's not looking at me, her eyes focused on something far away. I turn to see what it is, but all that's there is the gray brick wall. "Aubrey?"

"Yes." The word comes out in a breath. Bright blue eyes blink once, then focus on me. Like nothing happened, she smiles. "Sorry, I zoned out."

That's one way to describe it. Not sure if it's the route I would go. "Do you need a sweatshirt?"

"No. I left it in the car on purpose. It's getting in the way of some of the exercises you taught me."

"Okay." I scratch the stubble on my chin as I mull over what to do. If I call her out on acting weird just now, I might pop the delicate bubble we have going. Then again, if I don't call her out, it could affect our future relationship. As a trainer and fighter, of course.

"What just happened? You were shaking."

"Yeah, sorry. I don't feel well. Didn't get much sleep, is all."

She's lying through her teeth. "Those supplements aren't working?"

"I forgot to take it last night." It's another lie. Each one scrapes against my skin. How does she expect me to help when she's not committed? When she's lying?

"We won't train today, then. Go home. Get some rest."

"No, really. I'm fine."

"You're not." I grab her bag from beside the water jug and hand it to her. The shock on her face almost makes me regret cutting our workout short, but I'm not in the mood to deal with her.

"Is this because I questioned you training me?"

"No. I couldn't care less what you think about that. You don't want me to train you? You march your ass into Jason's office and tell him." I offer her the bag but her arms are crossed over her chest and she doesn't seem ready to change that.

Our best fighter comes up to the water jug, cautious eyes taking in our encounter. "Hey, man. You coming to the fights this weekend?"

I turn my back on Aubrey and give him my full attention. Trevor is a great fighter, and, more importantly, he has a good attitude. Unlike most of the assholes that breeze through here on the way to the top, he's humble, respectful, and always eager to learn. Jason and I will be sad to see him leave, but his time is coming.

"Probably not, Trev. I've got work." I don't. Now that I'm off patrol, I'm working normal hours. Work is just so much easier to say than the long-winded explanation of my home life.

"Ah, that sucks. Don't worry. I can give you the highlights right now. I'll take home the cup." He winks at me, and I realize the ease of the moment. This feels great. I trained Trevor for three weeks, back when he first showed up. Working with him felt natural. In fact, almost every guy I've trained, besides the one or two complete assholes that didn't last long, have felt that way. Aubrey is wrong. I am a good trainer. I'm just not good *with* her. We don't work.

"Well," Trevor finishes filling his water bottle and shrugs, "I hope to see you there, but if you can't, then stay safe on the streets."

"Thanks. Good luck, my man." I pat him on the shoulder before turning back to Aubrey. If it's possible, she looks even more pissed now.

"What now?" I ask with the calmest voice I can find.

"We were in the middle of a conversation."

"No, I was in the middle of trying to get you out of my hair, and you were in the middle of acting like a spoiled brat."

"Yup, you're right. That's totally accurate." She yanks the bag out of my hand and slings it over her shoulder. "I guess I'll see you tomorrow."

"Guess so. Let me know if you want to switch trainers. I'd be more than happy to get you off my plate."

"Sorry, pal. You're stuck with me." She gives me a smug smile and I return it.

"Can't wait."

"Me either." She pauses, her body ready to storm off but her mind obviously kicking up a different plan. All the anger in her settles for a moment. "Shit, I start school next week. Will that be a problem?"

The strangest thing happens. Even though we were just yelling at each other a minute ago, I want nothing more than to hug her. I bite my cheek to punish myself for the ridiculous impulse. "I don't know. Will we need to move our morning workouts?"

"No." She looks up at the ceiling like her calendar is taped there, then frowns. "Oh, wait. I do have an eight a.m. on Wednesdays. I'd say I could come extra early but by the time I shower and drive, we'd have to be done here by seven."

"Oh. Okay." I try to picture my schedule now that the girls are going back to school. That would mean not seeing them all day, then being gone most of the night. Caitlin already hates the fact that she'll need to get Cassie to and from school. Although, in my defense, Caitlin hates most facts nowadays. "I can try and do Wednesday nights."

"Do you work those nights?" She seems genuinely curious but I hate her for asking. I hate that she'll eventually find out about my situation. Not the whole thing, only Jason knows the whole thing, but even a part of it. I don't want her to have that over me.

I dodge her question. "I'll get back to you as soon as I figure it out."

"Okay." She smiles at me, and it's warm and kind of nice to look at. All my thoughts about her from just a few minutes ago dissipate.

Jason shouts something at a guy messing around on the weight bench and her attention snaps in that direction. I take the opportunity to look at her, like really look at her. It's the first time I've seen her as anything other than a pain in my ass. An obligation.

Her brown hair is pulled back into some sort of braid, starting at the top of her head and coming straight down to a point. The way it's arranged shows off the little blonde pieces that streak through it. The tank-top shows off her tanned skin, covered in thousands of freckles. Just like the sweatshirt, it hangs from her body, revealing how skinny she is. I make a mental note to check back with her on how the meal plan is going. Then I get distracted again, this time by her eyes. She's looking past me, bright blue eyes framed by eyelashes that make her eyelids disappear. There's something so simply beautiful about her.

"Hey, Aubrey?"

Her eyes come back to focus on me, the slightest smile playing across her lips. "Yeah?"

"I'm sorry for being an ass. Get some rest, okay?"

The kindness catches her off guard. She adjusts the bag on her shoulder and nods. "Me too. I'll see you."

Why do those final three words make me feel so much better?

CHAPTER THIRTEEN
Caden

This goddamn asshole is going to be the death of me. First, he argued with the written directive. Then, he argued that he should be getting paid for doing, in his words, *my job.* Paid. Like he didn't get out of prison years before he was supposed to or anything? Now, he wants to know if he can carry a weapon? *Jesus Christ.*

"No."

"But,"

"Nope." I readjust myself in my chair and glance at the clock. This shift needs to be over.

"You don't know the guys I'm running with, man." I can't help but laugh, like to the point where I end up snorting through my nose. Isn't that the point? If I knew the guys he was running with, why would we need him?

"You're their friend. They're not going to hurt you."

"Yeah, well." He crosses his arms and shrugs. Tattoos snake up his arms. There's one on his forearm that's brighter than the rest. I'm not sure if it's a special ink, or if it's just because it's newer. I want to know what it is, but it's mostly covered by the rolled-up sleeve of his dress shirt.

"You have my number, both work and personal, if you need help. And there's no reason they should want to hurt you unless you tip them off."

"They're curious why I got out early."

"We discussed the possibility of that." I tap my pen against my thigh. This is my first time on a big investigation and I don't want to mess it up. "What did you tell them?"

"That my dad got me a deal for good behavior." His dad owns an auto shop, the only one in town that isn't a chain. He belongs to a few boards, belongs to the city council, and is good friends with some of the right people. He's not who got this kid his deal but I wouldn't have been surprised if he had.

"That's believable. You have no idea how often that shit goes down."

"A cop admitting that the system is flawed? Interesting."

I don't acknowledge the comment. Almost every cop here would admit that. We go through hell to catch criminals and get rewarded with plea deals and defense attorney's that spend months poking holes. I catch sight of the chief coming around the corner and take the moment as a reminder to stay focused.

"Listen. You can't have a gun, okay? I can try and get you fake proof of your good behavior deal if they really want to push it. This investigation is important. We need you with us."

"I'm with you." He sits forward in his chair and looks straight at me. His eyes are bright green and clear. His hair is buzzed short, military style. His jeans fit, his dress shirt looks expensive, and he's clean.

It's quite a contrast to what I hear he looked like when he was first brought in a few months ago, high off his mind, covered in blood, and screaming something about a girl. It's all over his arrest file. He was demanding to see *her* but would never say who she was. According to the notes on the case, there was reason to believe it was her blood on him. If I wasn't afraid of stirring the pot, I'd ask.

He stands up abruptly. I follow suit, only because I don't want it to seem like he has the power. "Same time, next week? You'll get to meet your partner."

"I'll be here." He scratches at his arm, right over the brighter tattoo. " Isn't it a little sketchy that I'm coming by the station all the time?"

"You mean, for your friends?"

"Yeah." I watch him shift uncomfortably and wonder how he ever was the man his file says he was. Apparently, he was feared on the streets. There were rumors he did a lot worse than what he got caught for. He's either changed, which I don't believe happens, or he's the best actor around.

"It's a small town. Even if we meet somewhere else they'll know I'm a cop. Tell them it's part of your probation. We have probation officers here so they can't argue."

"Shit, yeah. Okay." He laughs a little. "I'm really bad at this."

I don't laugh at all. My reputation and future at this department, along with an investigation that's been going for three years, rides on this guy being good at this.

CHAPTER FOURTEEN
Aubrey

The rest of the week goes by in a blur, my attention caught between preparing for school, and training. I wouldn't necessarily say Caden and I are growing comfortable with each other, but we are making slight progress. I don't feel the need to be sarcastic all the time, which is something.

Our real test is tonight. Right now, in fact. Nine of our gym's fighters are competing in the next town over. Jason is requiring Caden and I to be there. As in drive there, together, and sit there, together. Training is one thing, but forty-five minutes in a truck and a three-hour event is asking a lot.

I've spent the better part of the drive listening to the dull sound of a children's cd, Caden too ensconced in his own thoughts to notice. He merges onto the freeway, clearing his throat. Desperate for music that doesn't involve learning about the alphabet or numbers, I get up the nerve to ask, "Can we listen to something else?"

He shifts his attention from the road down to the radio, his eyes lingering a dangerously long time, then gestures to the radio as if to say *go ahead*. I seize the opportunity and switch it to the local classic rock station. Something that almost never happens, happens. I catch the Bohemian Rhapsody just as it begins. The moment is too rare not to seize.

I don't think Caden is prepared for my incoming outburst. Softly, I sing the first set of lyrics, not that into it yet. Everyone knows it's the second set that deserves to be belted, as well as the rest of the song. Right on cue, I shift my weight and lean forward. "MAMA! JUST KILLED A MAN!"

I swear, Caden jumps a foot. I'm surprised he doesn't hit his damn head. The song continues and I try to sing along, but I'm laughing way too hard. He keeps looking between me and the road, shock stretched across his features. But he's smiling. A real smile, the kind that reaches his eyes. He even has dimples.

"You're so fucking weird." It's a compliment inside an insult. I have to look out the window to hide the smile it causes. He turns the music down a fraction and I wince.

"Did you seriously just turn down the Bohemian Rhapsody?" I turn on him, my smile gone. *How dare he?* Granted, it's the instrumental part, but still. There's a code.

"I'm sorry." He turns it back up immediately, a playful grin stretching his dimples further. It's hard to see in the dim light with the sun setting, but it looks like his dimples are layered. Each one is a wrinkle that takes a little more work to appear than the last.

I finish singing the song as loudly as I can, throwing my head around so my hair whips him a few times. The air drums even make an appearance, no shame existing in the moment that is Bohemian Rhapsody.

All of it is to annoy him, but when I slow down to a finish I see I've done the opposite. He's laughing, but not in a mean way. It's the kind of laugh that makes you feel floaty. The kind of laugh that bubbles out of you when you're purely enjoying yourself. Without meaning to, I find myself joining in.

I watch him rest a hand on the knob for the volume. He looks at me, cocking an eyebrow for permission. "Go ahead." I say with an eye roll. It's just a commercial but I enjoy being sassy. There's just something about keeping other people on their toes. Probably a control thing.

"That was something else."

"The Bohemian Rhapsody deserves to be sung."

"Yeah, but like that?"

Skepticism? When it comes to Queen?" I shake my head in disappointment. "What has this world come to?"

"It's fucked."

"Preach." There's plenty about this world that supports the argument. "It's Myla's favorite song. We sat on her bed in middle school and learned every word. We must have listened to it thirty times that day."

"Myla?"

"Yeah, she's my best friend."

"Gotcha." We pull into the overcrowded parking lot, finding a lucky spot near the front. "That's a good sign, eh?"

I smile when his accent peeks through. My generation has watered-down accents compared to their parents and grandparents, but they all show it from time to time. Usually it's something most of Elliot's group liked to hide. God forbid they sound like the people who live in this Podunk little area.

I've always liked it. My parents were both out of towners, my mom with a southern drawl and my dad with just a hint of Jersey. They only came here because they heard the area had a lack of good lawyers. The plan worked, and they made a fortune, but the accent never touched them. It only ever affected me, because of the teachers and the other students growing up. So, I sound like a Yooper instead of a rich kid, and I don't mind. Anything that separates me from them is great in my book.

I climb out of the truck and join him as we make our way towards the arena. Maybe we're more alike than I thought. Maybe it'll be an okay night.

CHAPTER FIFTEEN
Aubrey

The fourth fight of the event is my favorite. It's two brothers who have clearly been fighting since they learned how to walk. Their bodies are so in sync that it feels like the fight is scripted. I watch them float around the ring, ducking and swinging in a strange dance. It's beautiful. I tell Caden this, too entranced to be embarrassed. He doesn't make fun of me like I expect him to, instead just smiling like he understands.

It seems like the fight will never end, each of them knowing the other too well to lose. Then the taller brother makes a slight mistake, moving an inch too far to the left, and the shorter brother takes him down. Caden and I both jump up in excitement, as does the rest of the crowd. I'm so lost in the moment that I turn to him and do a happy dance. He laughs at me but it's friendly, not critical.

The next fight doesn't start for another five minutes. Blood and sweat needs to be cleaned from the ring. Caden asks if I want anything from the concession stand while we stand to stretch our legs. "I'll take some skittles, if they have any."

"Skittles. Got it." He heads over to the nearest kiosk. I watch him go before moving my attention to the sea of people around me. Most look exactly like the type of person to attend something like this, but a few don't. There's a woman to my right that looks just like my mother, in a conservative blue dress and a string of pearls. I wonder why she's here, and if she's enjoying herself. I don't think my own mother would ever come to something like this, even to see me.

"You're a pretty little thing." A husky guy with two arms full of tattoos and buzzed short hair approaches me. I try not to cringe as some beer sloshes out of his cup and onto my chucks.

"Thanks." My arms instinctively cross over my chest, burying myself in my sweater. If he came near me I could easily strike out, but that's only if my mind cooperates with my body.

He steps forward and the beer spills again. I want to ask him if he knows that his damn beer is almost empty from how much he's moving.

"What's a pretty little thing like you doing all alone, around people like this." He gestures to the crowd but he should be pointing to himself. He's probably the sleaziest person in the area.

I scramble for something to say but I can't concentrate. Somehow, his fingers have snaked their way to my wrist. The warmth of it sends shockwaves up my arm and down my spine, effectively paralyzing me.

Using his grip, he pulls me closer to him. His green eyes are bloodshot and glossed over. Until I saw them, I was holding it together, but those eyes were the final straw. I'm there again, standing with my back against a wall while Elliot screams.

I think I might vomit.

"Please get your hand off my girlfriend." The words are calm and controlled. Caden hovers a foot away, popcorn in one hand and a water bottle in the other. They must not have had skittles. Not that I care about the skittles. Right now, all I can care about is the fact that my toes feel numb and my mind won't stop churning memories.

"Your girlfriend looked lonely." This guy sure has a lot of nerve. If this was Elliot instead of Caden, he'd be lying on the floor bloody by now. Instead, Caden is standing there looking exactly like a cop. Calm. Collected. Pissed.

"She's not lonely. You can leave."

"I don't know man." His hand tightens on my wrist. He must be really drunk.

Caden takes a step forward. I watch as he slowly places the popcorn and water down on the empty seat behind us. People are starting to watch and whisper. When he straightens up, he seems bigger somehow.

If I wasn't struggling so hard to breathe, I'd find him attractive. Oh, what the hell. I *do* find him attractive. It's possibly the only reason I haven't passed out yet. He's keeping me grounded. His familiar blue eyes are keeping me here, because they're nothing like Elliot's. He's nothing like Elliot. I concentrate on that, feeling the tiniest bit of oxygen starting to filter back into my lungs.

"Take your hand off her. Now." I've never heard his voice so low. It sends a shiver up my spine. The guy lets go of me, laughing like it's no big deal. Both of his hands go up in a surrender, spilling the rest of his beer all over some guy in front of us. Now that guy is standing up, staring drunk guy down right next to Caden.

Finally, I find my voice. "I really don't think you're wanted here, pal." I'm proud of how steady I sound, despite the way the inside of my body is shaking. Caden glances over at me and I want to hug him for saving me. I also want to punch him for thinking I needed to be saved, even though I kind of did. It's not that I can't handle myself. It's that I wasn't myself.

"Fuck you. Tease." He spits at me but I stand my ground. I've been spit on before, and I've had those words yelled at me once or twice. If he's not touching me, I can handle it.

He glances down at his empty cup and grunts, just noticing it's empty. Without another word, he storms off towards the concession stand. I hope someone cuts him off.

Since my legs are a shaky, I sit back down in my seat. The next fight is about to start and the crowd around us bristles. It takes me a full minute to realize they're not whispering about drunk guy. They're whispering about Caden.

He picks up his food and water, then takes a seat next to me. Everyone continues to whisper. Caden keeps shifting in his seat, visibly uncomfortable from the attention. I hear someone say *Larson* and finally understand. They recognize him.

The next set of fighters start getting announced. Music fills the arena, pounding against the walls and high ceiling. The people around us remain focused on Caden. He rolls his shoulders once or twice, then cracks his neck. I've never seen him look so uncomfortable.

"No skittles, huh?" I yell over the music, trying to ease the mood. He leans back and digs in his pocket, handing me a king-sized pack.

"Sorry. Asshole made me forget about them." He looks down at me, the first set of his dimples showing. I missed those. I hadn't realized how much I liked them until they were gone.

"Thank you." I doubt he hears it over the announcer, who's yelling about one of Elite's fighters. We both stand up in unison and cheer for him. The guy looks nervous. Caden told me it's his first fight. I wonder if I'll look like that at my first one. The fights Rob set me up with had audiences of twenty, maybe thirty. This is a different level entirely.

The couple in front of us has their heads close together. The woman turns around and looks straight at Caden, not caring that he sees her. When she turns back around she nods. I watch as she leans over to the other couple they're with. Then all four of them glance back. I feel Caden shift against me. For now, he's still eating popcorn.

CHAPTER SIXTEEN
Caden

I'm two seconds away from punching one of them. Not the girls, of course, but the guys sitting with them are fair game. The blonde on the end, the one who doesn't have a guy with her, turns around and smiles at me. It's the third time she's looked at me since the fight started.

I ignore her, stuffing more popcorn in my mouth to keep from saying something to any of them. Aubrey is the only thing keeping me grounded. She's doing little movements as she watches the fight, like she's up there fighting herself. I concentrate on her, deciding that she might be just a little cute. The thought is dangerous. Especially considering the thoughts I had earlier, when I saw that guy messing with her.

Dangerous, once again. I can't believe I called her my girlfriend. I'm banking on the fact that it was the easiest thing to say. Hopefully, she doesn't read into it. Hopefully, she doesn't realize how easy I said it. Like it was natural. Like I would want such a thing. The last thing I need is to make shit more awkward right when we're starting to get along.

The first-round ends and the music starts playing again, filling the gap while coaches talk to their fighters. Jason is screaming something, pouring water on Brian's face. Poor kid's doing the best he can for a first time. Surprisingly, he's still steady on his feet.

The guy in front of us turns around. I finally look back, keeping my eyes cold and angry. He gulps but doesn't turn away. Instead, he leans forward and yells over the music. "Are you Caden Larson?"

His wife, or girlfriend, or whatever, turns around and holds up her phone. I can see an older picture of me pulled up on Google. They Googled me? Great. "Yup. That's me."

The girl's face splits into a giant grin. "I told you I recognized him." She flips her hair. "He thinks I don't know things because I'm a girl."

"Yeah." I throw some more popcorn in my mouth and chew obnoxiously. None of them seem phased.

"Why'd you quit man? I was so pumped to watch you fight. We had a party and everything. I had money on you."

"How much? I'll pay ya back." Sarcasm drips from my words but he just laughs.

"Nothing big time, man. Don't worry about it." *I'm not worried about it. Not even a little.* "Worry about getting back in the ring, man!"

If this guy says *man* one more time I will punch him.

"That won't be happening." The second round begins. None of them move their attention from me. In fact, more people are starting to stare. "Fight happening." I gesture in the direction of the ring.

The blonde girl leans forward. "Weren't you about to get into the UFC? Isn't that like a huge deal or something?" Her voice is squeaky, and judging from her deep brown roots her hair is fake.

"Pretty big. Yup."

"What the fuck, man? You just gave up." *Man.* That's my final straw.

I did not give up. None of these people know shit. I drop my popcorn, not caring as half of it spills, then I'm on my feet and ready to pounce. Finally, his smile slips.

"Caden." Aubrey reaches up, her cool fingers wrapping around my forearm. All the anger inside of me simmers. I look down at her and breathe. She looks scared, like the situation is getting out of control. Maybe it is. I'm more focused on the fact that the girl who hates being touched is willingly touching me.

"I'm sorry." I step back from the guy, the backs of my knees hitting the bench I was just sitting on.

With Aubrey still touching me, I start walking away. She follows, never taking her fingers away from my skin. When we reach the warm summer air I pull away, digging in my pocket for my keys. "If you want to stay, you can. Jason would drive you back."

I'm not sure why I'm so pissed off. All I know is it's taking everything in me not to run back in there and find that guy. Show him just how good of a fighter I am. The only thing stopping me is Aubrey, just inches away, biting her bottom lip. Am I making her do that? Is she nervous?

"I'm going wherever you're going." She finally says. *God, why do I hope that's true?*

CHAPTER SEVENTEEN
Caden

She falls asleep on the ride home, during the commercial break between Stairway to Heaven and Come Together. I wonder if it's against her supposed code to change the station once she's asleep. Not that I mind her music, but I could use some country.

I endure for two more songs before making the move, turning the volume down just in case. One of my favorite songs is halfway through. I sing along under my breath, tapping the steering wheel with my fingers. Aubrey shifts beside me, drawing my attention away from the dark road.

She was leaning earlier, using her own left shoulder as a pillow. Now she's falling. I watch as her body lands softly on the middle seat, soft curls settling over my thigh.

The song changes, this one soft and slows. I realize the lyrics are practically describing us right now. A beautiful girl in my beat-up truck. It's nice.

Caden. Stop.

I force my thoughts to drift elsewhere. Jason's been hounding me to fight again. Nothing big time, just local like tonight. Even if I wanted to, I know I can't. There's the girls to think about, and my emerging career. I'm not the same person I was last year. I'll never be *him* again.

It's kind of ironic. Jason wants me to fight like crazy, and I refuse, yet Aubrey is practically begging for it and he says no. Well, he hasn't told her no yet. She hasn't been training long enough to really ask. But it's coming and she's going to be pissed. I only hope she trusts him. Jason can be a presumptuous asshole, but he knows what he's doing.

Something hits my leg and I jump, tapping the gas a little too hard. Thankfully, the roads are empty. I glance down to find that Aubrey has shifted again, her entire head and neck now on my lap. The sleeve of her cable-knit sweater brushes against thigh and I shiver.

She's moving in her sleep, her heart-shaped face twisted with emotion. A particularly violent tremor goes through her. When her body final stills, I look down to find her hand is on my shorts. All five of her fingers cling to the fabric as she lets out the tiniest whimper.

Is she having a nightmare?

I focus back on the road, trying not to notice the way she continues to cling to my shorts. After another twitch, my body reacts on instinct. I place my right hand over hers, the rest of that arm falling across her back and shoulder, and hold her still.

I wait for her to freak out. To sit up and scream at me about touching her. None of that happens though. My country music keeps playing. The road remains empty. And Aubrey? Aubrey doesn't move for the rest of the drive.

CHAPTER EIGHTEEN
Aubrey

I'm late Saturday morning. It's 5:37 by the time I rush into the gym, strands of hair falling out of my pony and a wrinkled tank top hanging off my shoulder. I start to prepare myself for the lecture I'm about to get and try to think of a good excuse.

Maybe I should just tell him that I finally didn't have a nightmare last night. That I got home and crawled into bed, for once feeling at peace. It's been 33 days since that's happened. 33 days of no real rest. I'm surprised I got out of that bed at all today. I wanted to take advantage of every minute of peaceful sleep I could.

"I'm here. I'm here. I'm sor-" I stop short, letting my bag fall to the floor. The gym is completely empty. I'm late by a half-hour, and he left. I scramble for my phone and check it. No messages. No missed calls. He didn't even care to track me down? He didn't even stay around to workout himself?

I let out an exasperated sigh and look around the gym. Maybe this isn't so bad. It could be relaxing to have the place to myself. The possibilities are endless.

The door opens and shuts behind me while I'm rifling through my duffel bag. I stand and turn to say something to him about being late, only to realize it's not Caden. It's Jason. He stops short and stares at me for a few seconds before glancing around the gym.

"Why are you here?"

"Uh, I train here?" I look around as if there's some proof I could point to, but I haven't left my mark on this gym yet.

"Yeah, I know that." He checks his clipboard and looks up at me, eyebrows pulled in tight above his nose. "It's the twenty-sixth."

"Yes." I'm unbelievably confused. Is the gym closed on the twenty-sixth? What's so special about the twenty-sixth of August?

"Caden doesn't work today."

"Like, every month on the twenty-sixth? Or today, specifically?"

"Every month."

"That's odd." Apparently, he doesn't think so, because he just stares at me with a dead expression. We remain in our stand-off, neither of us sure what to do. If

I go home, this means I've missed two sessions in one week. That's not the kind of fighter I want to be.

"Do you mind if I stay and do my own thing, at least? I don't want to miss a workout."

He glances at his clipboard again, then scratches his head. "I can train you today, if you want?"

God, what would I give to be trained by someone who fights? Would he let me spar with him? Not caring that I look like a kid on Christmas, I smile and nod.

"Yes. Please." I glance over at the ring, giving a not so subtle hint that I'd prefer to be in it. This makes him laugh.

"Itching for a fight, are we?"

"You have no idea." I widen my smile, hoping he doesn't turn me down. He drops the clipboard on the table beside the water jug and winks at me. Seeing him this carefree and up-close throws me off. Usually, he's walking around with a scowl and clipboard, yelling at people and giving stern lessons. When he lets his guard down, it's like ten years come off him.

He's young. How did I never notice how young he is? I blush when he notices me looking.

"What?" He kicks my bag towards me. "Grab your gloves."

"Nothing. Just, um, nothing." I squat down and dig my gloves out of my bag.

I strap one of my gloves on and wiggle my fingers to make sure it's snug. Then I start on the other. It feels amazing to have them on again. Caden has been working a lot on my form, as well as building muscle. It's been too long since I've suited up and punched something.

Jason walks towards the ring and I follow, pausing so he can throw his dress shirt in his office and grab his own gloves. His undershirt is a soft gray and clings to his body. Despite him not being an active fighter, he's still ripped. He catches me looking again, and I hate that he probably thinks I'm checking him out. It's not that at all. It's the age thing. I'm thrown off by how young he is.

When we reach the ring, I blurt it out, "How old are you?"

He laughs. "What, you didn't Google me like Caden?"

I bite the inside of my cheek. "He told you about that?"

"Yeah. Don't worry, it wasn't tattling. He found it cute."

"Cute?" I practically squeak. Oh, great. Not only am I the only girl here, but now I sound like a total school girl. Thankfully, he doesn't seem to have noticed.

"Don't worry about it. Him telling me, I mean. Caden and I are close. He's like my little brother."

"Little brother." I nod and smile at him. "Back to your age again."

He sighs dramatically and enters the ring. "I'm twenty-three."

"Oh, wow." I glance around at the place before following him. "You're young."

"Is that your polite way of asking how the hell I own this place?"

"No." I hop up and down to warm up. "Okay, maybe."

He smiles. He's very easy going compared to Caden's usual grumpy mood. "I used to fight."

"Well, obviously." He looks at me like I'm missing something and I stop moving around. I'm not sure what he's getting at, and he finds this amusing. Suddenly, I'm back to feeling like I did last week, when everyone was in on the joke but me.

"What are you smiling at?"

"I just forget sometimes how disconnected you are. Most fighters spend years studying other fighters and training like them. They take every opportunity to watch fights and meet fighters. I just forget that you didn't start that way."

"Is that a bad thing?"

"Usually, I'd say yes. But your raw talent is incredible and I don't know what drives you but whatever it is, it is much better than experience. Experience you can gain, but talent is something you have or don't." He fixes his gloves. "Caden's jealous of it, you know?"

"Caden? He's one of the best fighters in the country." I pause. "Well, was."

"Yeah but there's something in you. Something that I think reminds him of himself. It reminds me of him at least. Him, before. You've got a fire that he used to have."

"He doesn't have it anymore?"

"No. Caden lost his fire a long time ago." If only Jason knew that I did too. That I'm nothing but embers floating in the night sky, getting little bursts of oxygen from things like fighting and Myla. Is that how Caden feels? Just waiting for the moment when he finally burns out?

Jason cracks his neck and moves closer to me. "Anyway, I fought professionally. In the UFC."

"Oh. Wow." Now I feel like a total idiot. How did I not know this about the owner of my gym? I've been so wrapped up with all the Caden drama that I haven't taken the time to learn anything. Did he mention his experience when he found me? I don't remember it. Although, in my defense, I had just finished a fight and my ears were still ringing.

Maybe he told Rob and it got lost in translation. Or maybe everyone expected me to just know. I make a mental note to watch more fights, even though school is about to start and I'll barely have time.

To get my attention, Jason taps me on the shoulder. I smile at him apologetically and he taps me again. It's playful, but it gets my heart rate up. I haven't fought anyone in a long time and the only man I've ever fought was Rob. Jason is a lot more intimidating than a retired marine with too much time on his hands. His punches probably feel like Elliot's.

Just as I feel panic welling up in my chest, I remember where I am. I tell my anxiety to shove it, because he isn't Elliot, this isn't dangerous, and I'll be damned if it ruins my one-one-one training with the damn owner of my gym.

Jason travels around the ring on his toes, warming up as he speaks. "I bought this place after I won a title. It came with so much money and, honestly, all I cared about was the belt. I didn't want a crazy house or car or anything like that. I thought it'd be nice to have my own gym with my own rules." He taps me again. "Good thing I bought it too. I blew out my knee a few months later. It didn't have to be career ending but I was kind of ready for it to be. I'm not as fast as I used to be. Plus, I love just running the gym. Messing around with kids like yourself."

He taps me again.

"You can't call us kids. You're only twenty-three."

"Yeah, yeah." I roll my eyes up at the ceiling and he taps me again. It catches me off guard and I swing at him, just missing his jaw.

He hops up and down, making the same sound that kids make when someone gets called to the principal's office. "There you go. Hit me."

Rolling my eyes, I swing again. It's weaker this time around, giving him all the time in the world to dodge it. He pouts playfully and shakes his head. "Hit me, Aubrey." I swing again. Then again. Nothing. He stops moving and looks at me. "Hit me."

I swing again and it's the same. How can I be this rusty? I feel myself getting frustrated, cheeks burning bright red. What if he realizes I'm not what he thought I was? What if he and Caden get together and decide I'm not cut out for this?

I try to tap into my energy, channeling every ounce of this so called talent everyone keeps bring up. Before I can get myself together, he hits me again, this time right against my cheek. It's playful, not even hurting, but my body shifts into survival mode anyway. I turn on him, slamming my fist into his nose. It's not enough to make him bleed, but he does go reeling backwards.

"Oh my god. I'm sorry." Here he was being playful and I had to go crazy. I rush towards him, but he's already steady on his feet and smiling.

"No. It's good. What were you feeling when I hit you? Why'd you snap?" I shake my head, keeping the answer to myself. Honestly, I got caught off guard. I wasn't in the right place in my head, my focus on too many things. My body must have thought he was Elliot.

"I don't know."

"Come on. You were angry." No. I was scared. Was I angry? I don't think so. He watches me for a minute, like he thinks I'll tell him. When he realizes that I won't he sighs, hands on his hips. "Best advice? The anger is good but you can't fight angry. You need to take that anger and redirect it. When anger leads to motivation, it's good. When anger leads you to start swinging, you'll lose. You'll lose every time."

"I've won plenty of fights."

"Have you?" He lifts his hands in the air like he's not sure.

"What if it wasn't anger?" I'm not sure what makes me say it. Maybe I don't like the way he's looking at me, all smug and knowing. He doesn't know me. He doesn't know a thing about me.

"If it wasn't anger, what was it?"

"Maybe it was fear." I want to punch myself as the words tumble out of my mouth. I've said too much. He stares at me for a moment. Something in his face softens, confusion rippling through his smile.

"Maybe it was."

"What? No wise words about fear?" He smiles. Then he squares up in front of me and raises his fists.

"Hit me Aubrey."

"Hit me Aubrey."

"Stop it." *I try to move out of his way but he's got me pinned to the wall, a hand on each side of my face. His stomach presses against mine and I want to throw up. I want to scream. I want to kiss him.*

"Hit me. Come on."

"I don't want to hit you." *My voice is barely a whisper, weakened by his sinister laugh.*

"Come on. I know what you've been up to. I know where you've been the last couple of weeks."

The roaring lion of anxiety caves my chest in, sending all available oxygen straight out of me. He can't know. It's not possible. Rob and I have made sure to cover every track. Every angle.

Even so, I believe him. My mind tries to weave a web of words that will calm him down. I have, maybe, ten seconds before he starts hitting me. "Elliot."

"Self-defense classes? That's fucking hilarious." *He laughs again, and I wince at the sound. I think I might be crying but my body is too numb for me to know for sure.*

"I just thought it'd be good. I mean, in case you get into a fight or something. I could-"

"In case I get into a fight? With who, Aubrey? With you?" *He pushes away from the wall and looks up at the ceiling. Does he think someone is pulling a prank on him? Or maybe the prank is on me. Some cruel joke my parents came up with to teach me a lesson about tattooed boys who promise you the world. I look up at the ceiling but before I can check for the hidden cameras myself, his hand is around my throat.*

"Elliot. Please." He was in a good mood today. He got a new sale. A big one. Enough to pay next month's rent and take us on a little vacation. Then he got a phone call after dinner and everything shifted. The world beneath my feet moved and I was too busy washing dishes to notice.

"I had Kyle follow you. He's been begging to get in with the group and I figured I'd torture him a little. I thought he'd come back with news about dance practice and hair salons. I thought, maybe, he'd catch you flirting like a little slut with some stupid high school boy." He squeezes my neck and licks his lips. "I never fucking thought, Aubrey. I never thought you'd be in some basement learning how to fight."

"Elliot." His name is barely audible but he understands. He relaxes his fingers and composes himself.

It doesn't last. Something else must come to mind because a new wave of anger floods through him, and his fingers tighten once more.

"Did you think you'd be able to leave me? Huh? Learn how to punch and all of a sudden you're free?" I try to speak but I don't have enough oxygen. I just shake my head. It doesn't seem like he notices. Or cares. "You'll never be free, Aubrey. You're mine."

"I know." The words are choked and raw. He relaxes his fingers again, lifting them to my face. I force myself to hold still, knowing the slightest twitch could set him off. He runs the tip of his thumb along my cheekbone, then my jaw. He lifts my chin and kisses me. I melt into it and hate myself. When he decides we've kissed enough, he pulls away and rests his forehead against mine.

"You can't leave me, Bree." I feel my body relax. I'm Bree now, not Aubrey. It's a good sign.

I put on my best smile and cautiously reach my hand up, waiting for permission. There's a slight hesitation, but then he rests his cheek in my palm, letting me cup his face. I search for the right words, because we're so close. I'm so close to getting out of this, if I could just say the right thing, pass the test, we could be okay again.

"I won't leave you. Never." My chest constricts with the honesty of it, because I won't leave him. Partly because I am afraid to, but there's also that small part of me that's still in love with him. The part that remembers the way his laugh can consume me. The way he kisses the crook of my neck just to hear me giggle. The way he holds me when we're around his friends, like I'm something he's not willing to lose. Loving Elliot is the unhealthiest thing I've ever indulged in. My own form of addiction.

His mood shifts again, so fast I don't notice it. I'm still cupping his face when his fist comes through the air. He lands it across my cheekbone and I see white for a moment. It doesn't hurt as bad as it used to. I'm not sure if that's from my experience with Rob, or if I'm just becoming numb to it all.

"You're a liar." He's screaming now, and crying. The veins in his neck and forehead pop out. For whatever reason, in the middle of this chaos, I take the time to notice that they're pulsing. His hand returning to my throat reminds me to pay attention. "You wouldn't have gone there if you didn't want to leave me!"

"I didn't. I don't want to leave you, I just."

"You just what?"

"I just want to stop you from hurting me." The words come out in a shout, and I freeze. I wish I could suck them back in and swallow them whole, even if it meant that they would burst inside me. Even if it meant I would explode.

His eyes turn cold and I slump against the wall. His eyes were the only thing left with my Elliot in them. This entire time, they've still been warm. It's always his eyes that give him away.

He's gone now. As if to prove it, he hits me again.

"How's that class going?" He wails on me as he laughs, then grabs my hair and pulls me away from the wall so he can slam me back into it. Warmth floods the back of my head, running down my neck. "Feel safe, yet? You're doing a bang-up job of stopping me."

He keeps laughing, the sound a cruel echo of the same laugh I love him for. One time isn't enough for him, so he repeats the action of slamming me into the wall. He must be going easy on me because there's no drywall falling around us.

"Sorry. I'm sorry."

He shoves away from me and shakes his head. Then he starts smiling. It's a foreign smile. One I've only come across once or twice, when he's high off his mind and thinks of something crazy. "Let's play a game, Aubrey."

"No." I shake my head and try to inch away. The bathroom is only a few feet to my right. He's not distracted enough though, and he notices.

"Don't fucking move!" He screams, his hand just inches from my face as he points at me. I try to seep into the wall but it's still solid. Funny. My whole world feels like mush. "Hit me Aubrey."

"What?" We're back to this again? I'm not going to hit him. It'd be suicidal.

"Hit me. Come on. Maybe it'd be good for us, hey? Maybe we'll be the kind of couple that just beats on each other."

"No." He scoffs like it's hilarious that I think I have a choice. That I feel as if I can turn him down. His face comes right in front of mine and hovers.

"I swear to God, Aubrey. I will put a gun to your fucking head. Hit me."

I don't have to think about it. He's threatened one person that I know of before with his gun. One person. He turned up dead less than a month later. He's never threatened to kill me. He's never told me where his gun is, or if it's even in his apartment. I've just assumed.

Fear rushes through my veins. He's never been this bad before. He's never wanted to kill me.

"Hit me Aubrey." I push at him and he stumbles back. It's fake, I know this. He's playing the game, so I guess I should too. With my mind numb from the anxiety, and my head *throbbing from the two wall slams, I try to think of everything Rob's taught. Nothing comes to me. We've only been together a few weeks. None of it is in my muscle memory. None of it is easy yet.*

I put my hands up, because it's the obvious move. I've always done it, even before I learned to. It's instinct.

I swing at him and he ducks. I swing again and he lets it land against his jaw. It makes him laugh, like it tickled. I grit my teeth and come closer. His mouth is wide open in a smile and his eyes are closed. I brace myself for how bad it will hurt and punch him right in the mouth, catching the bottom of his nose and his lip.

He stands there for a second, bringing a hand up to wipe at the blood. Then his eyes focus on me. In this moment, I know exactly how an animal must feel like when a Lion catches them in the open. Fear course through my veins, pumping me full of enough adrenaline to numb whatever will come next. All that runs through my head is a mantra: I'm not ready to die.

"You fucking bitch."

He advances towards me and I panic. I kick out at him but he catches my ankle, throwing me off balance. I fall on my back and hit my head, my neck cracking as it bounces off the hardwood. He crawls on top of me, weighing me down. I wait for it to happen. For him to choke me again, and not loosen his grip. For him to pull his gun out. At the very least, for him to hit me. Instead, I'm rewarded with a kiss. Then another. A third.

He pulls away and his bright green eyes are back. "Bree." His voice is the softest whisper, scraped bare from all the screaming. I shiver at the sound of him. My Elliot is back. I reach up and start unbuttoning his flannel. He starts on my jeans.

Before I know it, we're ripping at each other's clothes. Then we're naked, and he's hovering over me, and I'm not scared anymore. This is my place. I remember now. "You'll never leave me, Bree. You can't leave me."

I ball my hand ups and close my eyes. He's moving too hard. Too fast. "I won't ever leave you."

CHAPTER NINETEEN
Caden

The sun glistens off the black stone, making my eyes water. Well, to be fair, my eyes are also watering because I'm crying like a fucking baby.

Cassie is busy placing flowers at the base of the headstone, her lips in a soft smile. The tulle of her pink dress comes up as she finishes with a little twirl in the wind. I can't help but smile at her. Dad would love that she still dances, even though he's not home at night to put her toes on his and waltz around the kitchen.

Caitlin crosses her arms over her chest and looks away from the scene. I watch her as she tries to pull herself together, chest stuck in a rapid rise and fall. Everything about her is broken. She looks exhausted, and far too skinny. I rub at my eyes, feeling a headache starting to form. How the hell do you get a vegetarian to gain weight? I'll have to Google it.

"You girls ready to go?" They both nod, one much happier than the other. I scoop Cassie up in my arms and let her settle her cheek against my shoulder. A dandelion is still clutched in her hand, yellow dust staining my shirt.

Caitlin doesn't move when I pass her. I turn around to ask her to come, trying to keep the desperation out of my voice, but stop when I see that she's not being defiant. She's approaching the headstone.

It's slow motion and hard to watch, but she's doing it. I feel my breath catch in my throat as she slowly reaches her hand out and touches the stone. It's the first time since our dad died that she's acknowledged it. We've come here together eleven times now. Eleven times, always on the twenty-sixth. Why was today different? I search for any possible reason, wanting to repeat it next month. All I can think is that I made pancakes.

She whispers something I can't hear, shoulders shaking around her ducked head. After a few more seconds, she stands up. It's my moment to be the big brother. To come up with the perfect thing to say that will make her feel better. Something poetic, maybe. At the very least, something at all.

She doesn't give me the chance, shoving right past me, arms crossed and face empty. I want to reach out to her but I know she'll just pull away from me, and I'm barely holding it together myself.

"Wait!" Cassie screams, her body writhing in my arms. "Aren't we going to say goodbye to Momma too?" Caitlin looks back at me, her fingers already wrapped around the car door's handle. I start crying again. *Jesus, Caden, get yourself together.*

I cling to Cassie and try to stop my hands from shaking. No words come to me as an explanation. My mind has abandoned me.

"Mom isn't here Cass. She's in a different graveyard." Caitlin steps forward and takes Cassie from me. I watch helplessly while she gets her strapped in and closes the door.

Once the little one is out of ear shot, the words begin to pour out, "I'm sorry, I froze. It's just-" She puts a hand on my shoulder and squeezes it. The act, though simple, catches me completely off guard.

"It's only been a few months. It's harder. I get it. But, eventually, she's going to want to see her." It's the most compassion Caitlin has showed me in months. With guilt crushing my lungs, I walk to the driver's side of the car and yank the door open.

How the hell am I going to do this? I'm messing everything up. I don't know how to take care of them. A year ago, I barely knew how to take care of myself.

Anger bubbles up inside me but I choke it down. There's no time for that. Anger, here, in this moment, would be selfish.

"Caden, can we go see Momma today?" Cassie asks this before I can even start the car. I hold tight to the steering wheel and watch as my knuckles turn bright white. If I don't punch something, soon, I will surely explode.

"Maybe a different day, okay?"

CHAPTER TWENTY
Aubrey

I'm just finishing up at the water jug when the gym door bursts open, slamming back against the concrete wall. The noise makes me jump, but I breathe through the ache in my bones. The usual assessment runs through my mind, relaxing me as I repeat it: *I'm safe. He's not here.*

I look at the door, just to be extra sure, and find a very disheveled Caden.

"Well, look who decided to show up!" I joke, in a great mood after my session with Jason. Even though I got caught up in a memory and went crazy during our fight. Embarrassing as it was, it helped. I didn't tell him what I was thinking or anything, but he still gave me great advice about control and form.

Plus, it felt amazing to be fighting.

Caden drops his bag next to mine without even glancing at me. I start to repeat myself, thinking he didn't hear me, but stop when I see where he's headed. The other fighters in the room move out of his way as he storms towards the ring in the center of the gym. The energy coming off him is dangerous.

"Who wants to fight me?" The guys in the gym stare at him, frozen in either shock or fear. "Come on! Someone get the fuck in this ring!"

His hands are bare, and his clothes aren't meant for fighting. He's in a dress shirt and cargo shorts, but he just shoves his sleeves up and pops a few buttons loose.

Bouncing up and down in the same warmup that Jason did earlier, he yells out for someone to join him. While he waits, he cracks his neck and shakes out his hands.

I've never seen him fight, but it's looking like I'm about to. I take a few steps closer and see that his entire body is shaking, and tears are running down his face.

"Come on, you pussies!" He shouts at the rude tourists standing outside his zoo exhibit. He grabs a training block and chucks it, letting it crash against a weight bench just outside the ring. The guys start backing off, but I stay frozen in place. *Should I do something?*

"Fucking fight me!" He screams this while turning in a circle, eyes scanning for a victim.

Jason comes out of his office and starts running towards the ring. "No one fights him!" I move out of his way as he drops the papers in his hands and climbs into the ring, not even using the door.

"Fuck you, Jason!" Caden steps towards him but Jason is still looking at all of us.

"Go back to what you're doing. Nothing to see here." Everyone listens immediately, just a few of them glancing over their shoulders at the scene. I'm glued to the spot though, shocked at what I'm seeing. Caden and I have had our disagreements, and he's even raised his voice once or twice, but this is something else entirely. This is violent, like he opened himself up and let all those demons destroy him.

What the hell happened?

I gasp when he throws a fast punch at Jason, catching him right in the nose. Jason's poor nose today. The older of the two grabs the hem of his shirt and wipes at the blood running down his chin. Then he puts his hands up, giving into the fact that they're going to fight.

I try to look away but it's the most interesting train crash I've ever seen.

Jason ducks as Caden throws another punch, but Caden's knee catches him right in the face. His arm wraps around Jason now that he's hunched over, and his right fist starts slamming into his side. Jason gets out of the hold with ease and pushes him off.

Caden doesn't let up. He advances again, and his fists start to fly. Jason catches one of his wrists and twists it, pulling his body down and forward. Caden's face collides with Jason's chest and he melts. His sobs fill the stunned silent gym.

I back away slowly, shaking my head. Jason is speaking fast into Caden's ear, the words muffled by the echoing grief of the man in his arms. This is bad. I don't even know what this is, but I know it's bad. I grab my bag and look over my shoulder one last time.

All I can hear is Caden, just before our first session. *I guess we all have our secrets, don't we Aubrey?*

CHAPTER TWENTY-ONE
Caden

Jason drags me by the collar to his office. I'm drained after that breakdown, my bones feeling heavy in my skin, so I just stumble along.

What a stupid thing to do. If this was any other gym, I would be banned for pulling a stunt like that. Jason always talks about anger. It's one of the only things he pounds into his fighters' heads. *Don't fight angry.* He must be so fucking disappointed in me.

I pick at the dried blood on my knuckles while he closes the door and pulls the shades shut. Little flakes of it fall to his floor and I make a mental note to offer to clean later.

He rests against the edge of his desk, kicking his legs out in front of himself. When we came in, he dumped me in the chair in the corner, so that's where I stay. It helps anyway, giving me a little space to breathe.

He continues glaring at me for a while before finally taking a deep breath. His words come out slow and calm, which makes them scarier. "What the fuck was that?"

"It's the twenty-sixth." It should be enough. If he wants more, I can't give it to him. There's nothing left.

"I know." He ducks his head. It makes me feel like he's trying to see me from a new angle. Like he's trying to weave his way into my head. "What happened?"

"Cassie," I try to speak but my throat is closing. With shaking fingers, I wipe a hand down my face and try to reset myself. Is this room smaller? Did he switch offices maybe? It seems really fucking small in here. "Cassie asked to see her. To see mom. Well, her grave."

"Shit." I don't bother to look up at him. I've known him long enough to know his facial expression right now.

"It's just, she's been through so fucking much. They both have." I start to break down again, thick sobs bubbling out of my mouth. *Jesus Christ.*

"I know." Jason doesn't come over to me, letting my emotions run their course. I get them under control remarkably fast, though it has less to do with strength and more to do with the fact that my tear ducts are running out.

When the room return to silence, he speaks again, "You had to have known she would ask eventually, Caden."

"I guess." I dig my hands in my hair and yank, not caring that the movement will make the sweaty stands go crazy. "It just came out of nowhere, and it reminded me of how shitty I am. How shitty I'm doing. I'm fucking it all up, Jase."

"No. You're not." When I don't answer him, he throws a rubber band ball at me. It lands on my chest and bounces onto the floor.

"Fuck you." I say quietly, even though I can feel a smile pulling at my lips. There's so much I want to say, but he would listen, and he doesn't deserve to carry any more of my shit around. He must sense that I need a change of conversation, because he switches topics.

"I trained Aubrey this morning." *Shit.* Just another thing I fucked up.

"I forgot to tell her."

"You forgot, or you didn't wanna have to explain?" It's something I ponder for a moment. I did mean to tell her last night, but I kept getting distracted. *She* was distracting.

He doesn't wait for me to answer. Instead, he changes the subject again. "She said something today, while we were fighting."

"You guys fought?"

"Yeah. She's good. Messy, but good." I believe it.

"She deserves better, Jason." I can see he's about to argue so I lift my hand to stop him. "I'm serious. She needs someone who will fight with her. Who can teach her."

"No. She's got the drive and the talent to be in the ring. What she lacks is the basics. That's the stuff you teach with training exercises."

I hate that he makes sense. It would be such a relief to shrug out of the responsibility that is Aubrey. The mind games and little arguments are grating.

On top of that, I don't like how I'm starting to feel comfortable with her. The last thing I need is another distraction from the girls. The last thing I need is another person to lose.

I return to an earlier subject. "So, what did she say?"

"Huh?"

"You said she said something, when you were fighting."

"Oh. Right. Well, we were talking about anger." Ashamed, I sulk further down in my seat. He was probably giving her the same speech I get all the time. The one I went against this morning by freaking out.

He explains himself further, "I asked her why she was angry and she said something that I can't shake."

"What'd she say?"

"Well, I was talking about how she needs to get a grip on her anger, and she said maybe it's fear. And something in her eyes made me think that maybe it is. I mean, she's still got a hell of a lot of anger. Like enough to match yours, even. But once I started watching her- the fear's there. It's right there. I got her to let loose and come at me and I could tell she wasn't even with me anymore. She just transformed. She was hitting me and responding to me but she was somewhere else. It was like whatever she was feeling consumed her."

I huff at the irony of what he's saying. It sounds familiar, in fact, it sounds a lot like me.

"It's dangerous to fight like that," I say, just repeating what he's always drilling into my own brain.

"You would know." He crosses his arms and looks at me. His gaze is meaningful, but I'm too tired to care about it right now.

"What do you want me to do?" It's a plea. I want him to take my life in his hands and fix it. Give me a solution, literally any solution, and maybe I could find some hope.

He either doesn't get that I'm referring to my life in general, or he doesn't want to acknowledge it, because he turns the focus back to Aubrey.

"I don't know. Just watch her, alright?" He pushes off his desk and begins pacing. "There's something about her. I don't like the idea of one of my fighter's being scared. Anger is one thing, but fear is a whole different ballgame."

"I can do that."

"She shouldn't fight anymore either. I don't like wherever she went when she started swinging. I'll spread the word around but she'll probably be asking you soon to sign her up for one. It's not a good idea yet."

"Great. Just another reason for her to despise me." Jason looks up at me with concern but I wave it off. I can handle Aubrey. Whatever the thing is that we have, it's manageable.

I stand up and head towards the door. Caitlin is home with Cassie, and it's not fair to her that she's stuck babysitting on her last weekend before school. When I reach for the handle, Jason puts a hand on my shoulder to stop me.

"I'll come over tonight, after I close up."

"You don't have to."

"I've been there the last eleven times. I'll be there tonight." I don't argue. Instead, I do something that would probably embarrass the hell out of me if it was with anyone else. I grab him by the shoulders and pull him into a tight hug.

He hugs me back and speaks softly, as if others are around. "You're doing good, Caden. I'm so damn proud."

CHAPTER TWENTY-TWO
Aubrey

Myla rushes into my room, out of breath and shirtless. "I have nothing to wear!" She screeches at me.

"Go ahead. Look through my closet." She's already looking, passing the blue, purple, and pink sections to get to the red. The top she picks out is a new one, tying behind the beck and billowing out in a baby doll style. She throws it on and fluffs her hair.

"How do I look?"

"Great." I say it out of obligation, but I also mean it. Her dark blue jeans are skin tight and hug her hips. The tank top puffs out just enough. Myla, as usual, pulls off that look of being sexy in an easy way.

She slumps down on the bed and flips her hair over her shoulder. It's how I know I have a lecture coming. Anything important or controversial she needs to say is always started with a hair flip.

"Is this, um, what you're doing tonight?"

"No."

"Oh. Are you going to another party?"

"Well, no. I'm staying in." I point to my laptop, which has my email open as well as a tab of local fights coming up. "I'm just not doing *this* all night."

"What are you doing, then?"

"Um," I pick at the corner of my sweater. "I'm going to organize my school supplies and maybe read a chapter or two in my books. Get a head start."

I groan. "Oh, and call my mother."

She sticks her tongue out, fake gagging. We both know how that lovely once a week obligation will go. Especially if I finally get the courage to tell her I'm not enrolled as the major she wants me to pursue. It's bad enough I didn't go to an Ivy League, but to not want to be a lawyer? She'll die.

"Well. There's a bottle of wine in the fridge for when you need to recover from that conversation." She frowns. "Do something fun, okay? Even if it's just something on Netflix."

"Yes, mother."

"Oh, ew. Am I really that bad?" I laugh and grab her hand.

"Not at all. You're fine." She squeezes me, then stands up to leave. Watching herself in the mirror, she does a little shimmy and smiles. When she's done, she turns to me and puts her hands out as if to display herself. I give her a thumb up. "Looking sexy."

She winks at me before skipping out of the room. I settle into the mattress and finish reading my emails. Once I'm done I look at the amateur fight page. There's no fights coming to town in the next week or two so I close that tab and move on. I wonder if I should google specific fighters but decide against it. There's a huge pay per view fight next weekend that I'll catch. I can study that.

My fingers hover over the keyboard for a moment. I've Googled Caden already, but I was looking for his fighting career. Highlights, titles, and training. I wasn't look for anything personal.

I shouldn't now, either. Whatever he has going on should be respected. I know if my shit was on Google, I wouldn't want him poking around. To avoid the temptation, I close my laptop and move on to my next task.

It's already eight and my parents don't stay up much later than nine or ten. I dial the familiar number and hope they aren't home. Just like every other time, I'm disappointed.

"Aubrey. Hello, my dear."

"Hi, mom." I lay out on my stomach across the bed and try to get comfortable. These tend to go on for a while.

"How are you? Your father and I were worried when you didn't call yesterday."

"I know, I'm a little late." I pick at my bedding. "I've been really busy training and it slipped my mind, honestly."

It's not honest at all. These calls never slip my mind, I just put them off.

"Well, how nice to hear that we're always on your mind." Her tone is clipped and sarcastic. I can't help but roll my eyes and hope she can't sense it. She never calls me either so, really, who cares less here?

"I'm sorry mother." I grit my teeth and try to think of something to say before the conversation can spiral. "School starts Monday."

"Yes, I know. I do pay your tuition, remember?"

"How could I forget." I want to push my face into the bedspread and scream. I refrain from such actions merely out of respect for my own life. If I provoke her, I'll be miserable until I beg for forgiveness. I've learned this from experience.

I had to apologize to her while lying in a hospital bed the night Elliot got arrested. Stitches and concussion aside, she demanded both a 'you told me so' and a sincere apology. She crossed her arms, and waited. She never even asked what happened. She didn't care.

"Do you have any political science or ethics classes this semester?" I bite the inside of my cheek. I have both sociology and introduction to political science, but I'm taking them for the wrong reasons. I don't want to get caught in a lie so I tread lightly and tell her my schedule.

"Oh, honey. You'll love learning about policy and different supreme court decisions. Introduction to political science was one of my favorite classes." From here, she starts going on about her own path and how I should follow if I'm smart. She says something about my father. Something about their old law firm. Connections. How I'm lucky. How I'm blessed. I shiver at the usage of the word but for the rest of it I just keep agreeing.

When I look at the clock again I smile. Her selfish, one-sided conversation, took up fifteen minutes of our time. Just as I decide to tell her that I need to go, she brings up the one thing I was hoping to avoid.

"You know, when I logged into my portal to pay your tuition I noticed something."

"Oh?"

"Your major is undeclared." Yes, because if I declare it I either have to choose hers or mine, and I'm not ready to do that yet.

"I technically don't have to declare until Junior year. It's just General Eds right now."

"Well, yes I know. That rule is for slackers, Aubrey. Are you a slacker?"

With the calmest voice I can find, I answer, "No, mother. I'm not a slacker."

"Then declare your major. You don't want to look undecided, right?"

"Right." I scramble for something to say. "Well, I'm torn between a political science major and an English major. I've done some research and sometimes English majors excel in law school because of all the reading."

"You should really stick to the prelaw track, dear. I think you should make an appointment with your advisors. They'll probably tell you the same thing."

"Okay." I bite the inside of my cheek. God, I can't stand her.

"The only reason some people do other majors is because they aren't confident about law school. You don't have that problem."

"Okay."

"You really should declare, Aubrey. I don't want your professors to think you're not committed."

"Okay."

"And another thing." Oh, here we go. "You shouldn't let that silly gym get in the way of school. If you went a whole day without remembering to call me, I

69

can't imagine what will happen to your schoolwork. I will not accept bad grades, understood?"

The words *silly gym* echo in my brain. "Okay."

"When you got involved with that boy, you lost everything. You lost your spot on the dance team, your grades slipped, and you barely got into Brown."

"I actually quit the dance team." She just keeps going, as if she can't hear me.

"You aren't even going to Brown, either. You did all of that work growing up and you're staying *there*." Yes. *I* did the work.

"It's a good school, mother. You just don't see that because, God forbid, it's not Ivy League. And I worked my ass off to get into Brown, yes, but that makes it *my* decision on if I should go to it. You can't control everything just because you and dad have a fat bank account." *Shit.* That was not how I should have responded.

"Well, young lady, if you feel like that then you can figure out a way to pay for your own tuition at that silly little school." She scoffs like it's the craziest thing she's ever heard. I grit my teeth.

"Fine. I will." I go to hang up but I decide that I'm not done. I might as well say it all, now that she's withdrawn her money. "And for your information, Mother. I started dating Elliot because I knew it would push your buttons. You put me in this tiny box all my life and he took a sledgehammer to the walls."

"Look where that got him." She doesn't say it but I hear it in her tone. *Look where that got you.*

CHAPTER TWENTY-THREE
Caden

Jason comes over for dinner. I make steak and potatoes, and Caitlin is so focused on him that she doesn't even complain.

"Thought you were a vegetarian?" I tease her as she loads her steak with some sautéed mushrooms. She pauses, as if she didn't even notice the meat on her plate, then sighs.

"It depends. What are my other options here?" I wrack my brain. I haven't gone to the grocery store in a while.

"Probably a peanut butter sandwich. Maybe some ramen noodles." She laughs. It's an amazing sound. I don't think I've heard it in months.

"I give up. I'd rather eat meat and feel guilty than eat one more peanut butter sandwich." She continues scooping, then takes a seat at the table right next to Jason. He smiles at her and I can almost see her swoon. I bite the inside of my cheek to avoid making fun of her.

We all start eating in a comfortable silence. I wash my food down with half a bottle of beer and try to relax. It's been a long day but both the girls seem to be fine. Especially Caitlin, which is a nice break from the usual.

"Did you ever get ahold of Aubrey?" Jason peaks at me over his bottle. I shake my head and look away.

"Ooo, who's Aubrey?" Caitlin shuffles in her seat like something incredibly interesting just happened.

"No one." Her grin is incredible. I can't imagine why she's in such a good mood, all things considered, but I'll take it. "She's just the girl I'm training at the gym."

"I thought the gym was an all-boy gym," Caitlin asks Jason instead of me, taking the open opportunity to speak to him.

"That was never official. I just don't recruit, well besides her, and it was only ever guys that came to me."

"And you're training her? Like, specifically you?" She's scandalized, and I stick my tongue out at her.

"Yes. It's just because I'm not fighting. I have more time on my hands."

"She's not good enough for Jason?" She turns her attention back to him. "Don't you always train the really good people? You're who trained Caden."

"She's plenty good enough for me." Jason takes a swig from his beer. "Her and Caden just have a nice symmetry."

He winks at me. Trying to use our best-friend telepathy, I flip him off in my mind. From his smirk, I'm assuming he gets the gist of what I'm feeling.

"I want to meet her!" Caitlin exclaims, her fork clattering against the plate. Cassie sits up straight and nods.

"Me too! Me too!"

"Maybe one day." I feel like a broken record, always promising things that I don't know will happen.

Jason sits forward and smiles at me. "Actually, I was thinking about something today."

"Oh, I bet." I finish off my beer and stand up, heading to the fridge to grab another. "Is it something that will give me a headache?"

"Probably." This makes Caitlin giggle. Despite my best efforts, that gets me to smile. "I think it'd be good for Aubrey to see some fights and learn a little about the bigwigs."

"I'm not giving her a slideshow presentation too." He gives me a warning look.

"Don't be dramatic. I was actually thinking that we should invite her next weekend."

"Invite her to what?" I try to search for something that's coming up. No parties. No local fights. Oh, wait. "You mean the pay per view fight?"

"Yeah. I thought it'd be a good idea. She could learn a few things, and we could all get to know each other better."

"Why?" I can't help but feel defensive. We watch the pay per view's here, so that the girls can sleep in their own rooms. I don't want Aubrey here. That'd be confusing, especially for Cassie, and Aubrey would ask questions. Questions I don't want to answer. "Why do we all need to get to know each other?"

Jason lets out a low whistle and I realize how awkward I've made the conversation. Caitlin is pushing her steak around again instead of eating it.

"It was just an idea, man. Forget about it." I want to go back to before. When everyone was laughing. When Caitlin smiled.

"No. She can come over. I'll invite her tomorrow." Both Caitlin and Cassie perk up and Jason smirks. I try to frown at them but can't. Maybe it wouldn't be so bad to let Aubrey in. I mean, I'm exhausted enough as it is. Letting a few walls down would be a relief.

CHAPTER TWENTY-FOUR
Aubrey

I wake up Sunday morning with a raging headache. Even though I had the opportunity to sleep in, I struggled with the sleeping part. I'm exhausted. All I want to do is crawl back under my covers and sleep.

Instead, I push myself out of bed and make my way to the kitchen. Myla's heels are lying on the welcome mat, right next to a pair of men's dress shoes. I cringe, feeling self-conscious in my tiny silk pajamas.

I start the coffee pot and scurry back to my bedroom, searching for something with a little more material. In the process, I find my phone lit up with a missed call from Caden. I dial him back, walking over to the door of my closet to double check the day on my paper calendar. It's definitely Sunday, so I didn't miss a workout.

"Hello?"

"Hey." My voice cracks from not being used yet today. I clear it and try again. "Hey. You called?"

"Yeah. I know we aren't supposed to work out today but I kind of need to get some energy out. Want to do something outside of the gym?"

I stare at the calendar. More specifically, I stare at the little 26 in the corner next to today's box. He was so broken. "I think that'd be fun."

"Great. Get your workout stuff on. I'll pick you up in a half hour." He pauses. "I'm not a stalker for knowing where you live, I promise. I just have your application here."

He sounds nervous. I don't know why that makes me smile.

"Okay."

"Okay." He coughs. "Okay. See you soon."

At least this solves my dilemma of what to wear. It might even solve the dilemma of having to deal with gas station guy, if he doesn't wake up in the next thirty minutes.

After pulling on shorts and a baggy shirt, I head back for my coffee. I only fill half a mug, not wanting too much caffeine in my system before working out. My heart already feels like it's trying to beat out of my chest when I do cardio, and, lately, when I'm around Caden. There's no reason to give it a better chance.

Caden texts me five minutes early, letting me know he's outside. I grab my phone and water bottle, kicking the dress shoes away to open the door. I don't necessarily feel bad. Okay, I don't feel bad at all. *Stupid gas station guy.*

Country music is spilling out of the open windows of his truck. I fight the disgusted shudder that's trying to work its way through me. His vehicle, his music. *But why does it have to be country?*

"Morning." He turns the music down, giving me a smile.

"Morning." I give him a little wave before heading around the cab to my side. Heat seems to radiate from the big red door, making the hot summer air feel unbearable. The inside is even worse. He isn't using his air conditioning.

"It's hot in here."

"Yeah, sorry. I like fresh air better." He grins over at me, both layers of dimples showing. I'm pretty sure I was annoyed a second ago, but I can't remember why.

"So, where are we headed?" He pulls through the parking lot and onto the road, picking up speed. The fresh air *is* nice.

"I thought we could hike the Mount." It's a twenty-minute drive outside of town but I don't care. The view from the top is always worth it.

"That sounds great." I stare out the window, letting my hand linger in the air. If I closed my eyes, I could be on a motorcycle, open air pushing my hair back and cooling my face from the sun. Elliot never made me wear a helmet. I think he liked that it was still him putting me in danger. His life was always in my hands. *Dammit, Aubrey. Stop.*

"You can change the station if you want." His smile is warm. I tell him it's okay, even though some guy is literally singing about fishing. Who likes songs about fishing? Maybe I'm not as good of a Yooper as I thought.

He turns down the music and speaks again, "I'm sorry about yesterday."

"Don't worry about it." I look over at him. "Seriously, it felt good to work with Jason a little anyway."

"You should be working with him all the time." His voice is low. "He can do better for you."

"What happened to Mr. I-know-what-I'm-doing?" I think back to our first workout. He was so cocky. So annoyed that I was questioning him.

"I thought he did." He shrugs like this isn't a major thing for someone to admit.

"Well, I don't want Jason." I look back out the window. "I don't care that you don't fight."

Is that true? He has been helping me, even if we haven't been fighting. There's more to being a fighter than just the fight itself. When I'm ready, I'm sure Jason can help, but for now I really like working with Caden. I really like Caden.

"Listen," he glances at the radio like he's regretting turning it down.

"Jason doesn't really want you fighting right now."

"Me? Why?"

"He just wants you focused on the basics." I can tell that's not the only reason. My feelings are hurt at the idea that I'm not good enough to get in a ring yet, but I won't show that.

"Shrug. Not a big deal."

"What is that?"

"What?" I look away from the trees we're passing, focusing back on his face. He isn't smiling anymore, his eyebrows crinkled in confusion. "What is what?"

"Shrug? Or sometimes you'll say, sigh. But you won't shrug or sigh."

"Oh."

"It's an inside joke with Myla. We used to write notes to each other in school since the building didn't get cell phone reception. We started putting those in parenthesis so we didn't have to write out an explanation on how we're feeling. It's a lot easier to go (sigh), (shrug), (eye roll), etc. than have to write out 'this makes me really mad or annoyed. After a while it kind of just caught on, even in actual conversation."

My long explanation makes him laugh. "You guys sound weird."

"We are." I smile over at him. "Shrug."

His laugh echoes in the car before escaping through the open windows. It's a great sound. Better than the damn music that was assaulting my ears earlier.

When he catches his breath, he glances over at me, one hand slung lazily over the steering wheel. His other is resting on the space between us. Is it an invitation? *Woah. Where did that thought come from?*

"You make me laugh." He says simply.

I stay focused on his hand.

"Is that a good thing?"

"Very." He looks back at the road. "I don't laugh much anymore."

"I've noticed. You're a very grumpy person." He pouts but doesn't look away from the road. My eyes drift back to his hand. Still there. Maybe it's just comfortable.

"My sister claims the same thing. Sometimes she calls me grumpy cat." He shakes his head and smiles, like he's thinking of a fond memory. "I think it's a teenage girl thing."

"It is." I assure him. "Do you guys get along?"

"We survive." The words seem to have a double meaning. His smile is gone so I don't push him on it. For once, I don't want to annoy or piss him off. "You have any siblings?"

"God, no. One was enough for my parents." I glance back out the window, holding my own hand so I won't grab his. "They should have never procreated in the first place."

"Then you wouldn't be here."

"True." I squeeze my hands together so I don't reach for his.

This conversation is way too depressing. I search for something, anything, to say. We pass a sign advertising for ice cream.

"Have you ever been there?"

"Where?" He looks at where I'm pointing. "Oh, yeah. They have amazing flurries."

"Maybe we can stop there later."

"Yeah. You'll be hungry once I'm done with you." He glances over at me, something burning in his blue eyes. I feel it all the way down to my toes. I'm hungry now, just not for ice cream.

CHAPTER TWENTY-FIVE
Caden

We're both drenched in sweat by the time we reach the top of the Mount. It's empty, both up on the wooden viewing station and down on the grassy clearing. Aubrey walks straight to the wooden railing, leaning her body over it to look down. Lake Superior is laid out before us.

"It's beautiful." She whispers. We haven't talked since the hike began, both too focused on not tripping or running out of breath. I missed her voice.

"It is." I scan the water. "If we were closer, I'd jump in right now."

With it being a few days into September, I know the water is probably freezing. It doesn't matter. My skin is overheating, the temperature being unusually hot today. I must be out of shape too because that climb kicked my ass.

I peel my attention away from the water to find Aubrey staring at me. Her eyes are as clear as the lake. "Follow me."

Before I can process what she's asking, she's on the move. I watch her climb over the railing, nearly giving me a heart attack, before glancing back at me. "Are you coming with me or not?"

Yes. Anywhere.

I climb over the same spot she did, joining her beneath the leaves of a tree. We take a few steps until the line of trees gets thicker. I think we're climbing down. It feels steep, and there's no path.

She starts talking after a minute of silence. "I found this a year ago. Last summer."

"Where does it lead?" She pauses, her foot halfway through navigating a root, and smiles back at me. That smile is full of mischief.

"You'll see."

"Are you going to murder me?"

She laughs, still moving forward. "Don't be so dramatic."

"Are you going to take advantage of me?"

"If you're lucky." I feel a light start to radiate inside my chest. This feels good; talking and joking with her. Acting my age.

It takes a while before we finally break out into open air. Two turns, one to the right and one to the left, and we're there. I know we have to be, because there's nothing but water in front of us. We stand on a set of black rocks jutting over the lake.

"Holy shit." I start walking forward, peaking over the edge. I half expect her to push me but she doesn't. Instead, she stands back and watches from afar. Something in the way she looks at the water is personal.

I give her time, investigating the area. You can't see the viewing area on the Mount from here, which makes sense. I don't recall seeing these rocks when we were up there either. It feels like we discovered Narnia.

She finally speaks. "You want to swim?"

"Here?" I glance over the side again. It's not too far down.

"There's a little patch of beach if you climb down there." She points to a spot that's covered by trees. Must be another secret path. How much time has she spent here?

"What? You afraid of jumping off the rocks?" I lift my eyebrow, daring her. She peels her shirt off, not even looking at me. Her blue eyes are focused on the water.

I follow suit, taking my own shirt off before stepping out of my shorts. At least I didn't bring my phone or wallet. If anyone possibly finds this place, they can have my twenty-dollar outfit from Target.

Out of respect, I keep my eyes on the water when she's finished. Even so, I can see all the bare skin in my peripheral vision. It's distracting.

She jumps first. No warning. No explanation. I watch her flip through the air, yelling at the top of her lungs. Jason is wrong. This girl has no fear. She's all control and it's intoxicating.

I jump over the edge. Nothing fancy. No noise. I break through the surface with a sickening sound, but it doesn't hurt.

The water feels amazing. I push up to the open air, taking in oxygen with a smile.

She's a few feet away, dark hair floating along the top of the water. She's looking up at the sky, smiling.

She catches me staring, a blush creeping up her wet cheeks. "What?"

"Nothing."

She smiles. "How did it feel?"

"Amazing." I swim closer to her so I don't have to yell. "You scared me for a second."

I'm joking, but her smile disappears. She looks over the surface of the water, out to the horizon. "There's nothing scary here." Her words morph into something else once they hit the open air. Nothing scary *here*. Meaning, scary exists somewhere else. She knows this for a fact. You can tell by the clarity in her voice.

"You're right. This place is perfect." I hover just a foot away. We're so close I can see the blue in her lips. She's shivering. "How'd you find it?"

"I was running." Her voice is as soft as the tiny waves moving us towards shore.

"Like, for a workout?" That's a dangerous adventure. What kind of person goes for a run on the side of a cliff? Especially with no path?

"No. Not like that." She doesn't elaborate and I don't need her to. She was running from something. Someone, maybe. There's that fear Jason was talking about. I feel my anger start to swirl in the pit of my stomach. It warms me, the cool water not having any effect anymore. I'm shaking for a new reason.

"Did you get away?" It's too personal, I know this, but I have to ask. I need to know.

She stares up at the sky again. I can't read her expression. It's not a smile, but it's not a frown either. It's empty.

"No." She says after a long pause. "I guess I never really did."

CHAPTER TWENTY-SIX
Aubrey

Caden drops me off after we grab ice cream. The rest of the day was full of conversation, all of it avoiding heavy subjects. He talked about the police academy, his job, and even told a funny story from when he was on the road for a fight.

I tell him about Myla, about school, and even offer up a story about my first concert. I substitute Myla's warm presence for Elliot's hand on my wrist, holding me steady as I dance. The tickets were an apology present, for the broken picture frames and dishes scattered around his apartment.

The story was better with Myla.

Caden even made me laugh a few times. Made me do some other things too, like blush and think of how good of a kisser he probably is. It's bound to happen when you swim almost naked with a guy as attractive as Caden Larson.

Half his appeal is how easy I can talk with him. How much I trust him. It's also everything that turns me off. Those are dangerous things. Things I promised I'd never do again.

Myla is waiting for me when I get home. She arches an eyebrow, scandalized. "And where have you been?"

"I went to the Mount." I feel my wet hair soaking through my dry top. I can sense her studying it.

"Your hair is wet."

"I wanted to cool off after the hike."

"Your shirt dried awful fast."

"I took it off."

"Mhhm." The noise is low and drawn out. That damn eyebrow is still arched.

"How was gas station guy?" I plug my phone into the charger beside her. She watches my every move.

"*Jesse* was fine."

"Just fine, eh?"

"Don't go changing the subject." She waves a finger at me. "Who were you with?"

I contemplate lying to her, but what's the point? It's not like I was doing anything wrong. "Caden."

I turn my back to her, focusing my attention on my phone. I need to check my emails before school starts tomorrow, in case any of my professors sent one out. Her response takes longer than I thought it would. When I eventually glance back at her, she's staring down at the carpet.

"What?"

"Bree."

"No, don't Bree me. What's wrong?"

"Don't be self-destructive. Please." She eyes me, probably waiting for me to snap at her. I roll my eyes and focus back on scrolling through my emails, deleting the junk one at a time.

"I'm not. It was a workout since the gym is closed."

"If you get involved with a trainer, you could get in serious trouble. I mean, what's the policy on that?"

"I don't know. It doesn't matter. It was just a workout."

"Okay." She sighs dramatically. "I just think it's strange that you went skinny dipping with a workout buddy."

"Myla." It's a warning. I was in a great mood until she started on my ass. "We didn't skinny dip, I had my sports bra and underwear on. Which is more than a bikini. It was just a workout."

She stays quiet for a long time. I get through all the advertisements and coupons, finding a new email from the University itself. *That's strange.*

I open it, expecting some newsletter welcoming the new students. The first sentence is interrupted when Myla speaks again.

"Did you bring him to the rocks?"

"Yes." I stare at the University logo on the top of the email. My skin is starting to crawl from this conversation. For once I had a good day, out in the open with someone I might be starting to trust, and she's ruining it. She's making me feel guilty about it.

"Did you tell him?"

"Tell him what?" The screen of my phone goes black. "Tell him that my ex brought me up there to kill me once? That I ran until I couldn't breathe? That I found that place and stayed there until morning, even though I could hear him calling for me all night? Or how about the fact that I found my way back to the road, borrowed a phone, called you, and then went back to him two days later?"

"Bree."

"Just stop." I unplug my phone and bring it with me to my room, making sure to slam my door. Not that my parents were ever around to hear the door being slammed.

I know Myla will come in here eventually. She'll give me time to cool off before knocking with her tail between her legs. With a huff, I throw myself on my bed and plug my phone back in. When it lights up again, I finally read the email. It's from the finance department. My tuition isn't paid.

CHAPTER TWENTY-SEVEN
Caden

Jason invites me out for a beer to watch the Packer game later. Cassie is already worn out from a full day of playing outside while Caitlin tanned. She's passed out in her bed, still in her princess dress. Caitlin is busy picking out what she's going to wear for her first day of school. The floor of her room is unrecognizable, covered in different multi-colored fabric.

She doesn't even look at me when I ask if she can hold down the fort for an hour or two. She waves me off, too busy holding up a sweater to her image in the mirror. "Does this make me look too pale?"

"No. It looks great." I give her a thumb up even though she's not looking at me. She probably doesn't care about my opinion. "Cassie is already sleeping, but if she wakes up will you get her in some pj's?"

"Yeah." She glances over at me. "Do you have a date?"

"No. I'm gonna go watch the game down at Grub's. With Jason," I clarify. If only she knew who I went out with earlier when I said I was going for a workout. She'd die.

"Alright. I'll be here. Drinking vodka and sleeping with the neighbor." I laugh, shaking my head. Our neighbor is a seventy-year-old man who still thinks he's in the marines. Plus, I'm pretty sure Caitlin doesn't drink. That might be naïve of me, but a man can hope.

The bar is full when we get there. Grub's, the owner, usually offers free shots whenever the team scores, and it's supposed to be a blowout. I find Jason at a high-top table near the back, right next to a flat screen showing the team warming up.

"Prime spot." I tell him over the voices of the game announcers. Most bars would have music playing over the game. Most bars would have more than one game on. Not Grub's. Every monitor is turned to the exact same thing, the speakers broadcasting it for the few unlucky guys who can't get a good enough view.

My dad showed me this place. He used to sit me up on the bar and tell the bartender I wanted a beer, and I would giggle and clarify that I wanted a root beer. Then we would sit and watch the games, cheering and booing along with the rest of the crowd. Around here, it's not strange to see a kid in a bar. Especially on Sunday's when a game is playing.

"I snagged it almost an hour ago." He takes a long pull from his bottle. "It's been a shitty day."

"What happened?"

"Just negotiating contracts, talking to agencies. If someone would have told me all the paperwork and bullshit that goes into owning a gym like mine, I would have reconsidered."

"No, you wouldn't have. You love it."

"Yeah, well. Maybe I'm a masochist."

"Maybe." I wave the waitress down and order myself the same thing he's drinking. Her eyes linger a little too long on my face before she walks away. Jason watches her, smiling like a total idiot. I can see where he's coming from. She's a stacked blonde with a football jersey on and very short jean shorts. I would have been plenty happy with that just a few months ago. Now, I can't help but compare her to Aubrey. The thought is concerning.

"They want you, ya know?" Jason concentrates on the label of his beer, tracing the outline with his finger. He doesn't look at me.

"Who wants me?"

"Everyone."

"Well, that sucks for them I suppose."

"Yeah, I suppose." He drinks his beer. The waitress brings me mine, leaning on the table with her elbows once it's on the coaster. I offer her a smile. She stays where she is, breasts pushed up against the table. Jason watches me instead of her.

"Can I get you anything else?"

"No, I think we're good." I nod at Jason, begging for him to say something. At the very least, to draw her attention to the other attractive male at the table. She stays focused on me.

"You sure? I mean, *anything.*" Oh, God. What's her attraction to me, anyway? There's at least thirty guys in this place.

"I'm good."

"Alright. Well, let me know if you change your mind Caden." She winks at me, bouncing away toward a table across the room. I roll my eyes at Jason.

"Wonder how she knew my name."

"Gee, I don't know. Maybe because you're kind of famous. Especially around here."

"I'm not that guy anymore."

"She doesn't know that." He pauses. Drinks. "Everyone thinks you're just taking some time off. Because of your dad."

"They'll believe me eventually." He makes a noise, something between a grunt and a laugh. I raise an eyebrow at him. "You'll believe me eventually."

"Yeah. Maybe." We continue drinking, neither of us speaking. A different waitress brings us our second round. I wonder if I hurt little miss jersey's feelings. I didn't mean to.

I search for her, finding her behind the bar making drinks. She catches me looking and smiles. Maybe I could be with her. Maybe it'd feel good, doing something I used to.

"Caden."

"What?"

"When are you getting back in the ring, man?" My attention drags from her to him. All thoughts of sleeping with that girl fade away, a numb feeling replacing them. I drink my beer, hoping the cold will chase it away.

He tries again. "Just hear me out man. I know what you went through. Out of everyone, I know the best. But you can't hide from all of that. You would feel better if-"

"I said no. Never again." I finish my beer and push away from the table. "I'll get us some more."

The girl perks up when she sees me.

"What can I get you, sexy?" I drag my eyes up and down her body. Slow and steady.

"I could use something a little stronger."

"Hmm," she hums under her breath, a smile pulling at her lips. "I can help with that."

"Yeah?"

"Vodka, whiskey, or me?" She whispers, leaning over the bar so only I can hear. I duck my head down, staring at the scratched wood. This is the very spot my father used to sit me. When I lift my head again, I make sure my dimples are out. I have to dig down to find them, pulling a memory of today from the archives. Aubrey, staring up at the sky. Smiling.

"You."

"Hmm." She pushes away, whispers something in the other bartender's ear. When she comes around the corner I follow her.

We walk past Jason, who lifts a beer to me. I can't help but notice that, despite the cheers, he's not smiling. In fact, he looks concerned. The girl leads me back to a giant pantry full of case after case of beer and liquor. "Well, here I am."

She closes the door behind us and locks it. With two steps, she's against me, the number twelve pressing into my stomach. She's a full head shorter than me. I have to lean down to kiss her.

The moment my lips are around hers, I know it's wrong. This isn't what I need. This isn't what I want.
I pull away and turn around, staring at the wall of microbrews.

"What's wrong?" Her hand rests on my shoulder. I close my eyes, wishing I was somewhere else. The Mount again, maybe. With Aubrey.

"I'm sorry. My heads just a mess."

"I can help."

"No, you can't." I turn to look at her, trying to fix the situation as I break it.

"I'm really sorry, um?"

"Kelsey." She folds her arms in defense.

"I'm sorry. I'm really sorry, Kelsey. You're great. I just can't."

I push past her, unlocking the door. "Do you have a girlfriend?"

"Yes." I don't know why I say it. This is the second time this weekend I've lied about this. I'm starting to feel confused myself.

Kelsey doesn't say anything. I take it as my cue to head out the door, back to Jason. He's sitting there, staring at the game. There's two glasses in front of him, both filled with a golden liquid. I slam the first one, only registering that it's whiskey once it's down my throat. The burn in my gut feels incredible.

CHAPTER TWENTY-EIGHT
Aubrey

I'm shaking with rage as I show up to the gym. It's an hour early, and Caden is still working out on his own. I storm through the doors and smile at him. He's paused through a set of shoulder presses, eyebrows raised in surprise.

"What's up?"

"Nothing." I wave my hand in the air. "Just do your thing. I need some time."

His eyes follow me all the way through the gym until I reach the treadmill. The air conditioning must not have kicked in yet, because the air is stuffy. I shrug my sweatshirt off and throw it on the floor next to my bag.

I push out a mile on the treadmill, loving the way the fire burns in my lungs, but it's not enough. My mother's words keep ringing in my ears. I wish I could stop them, or at least turn the volume down.

I skip the gloves and head for a Bobby, wanting to feel my knuckles colliding with something. As I start to pound my fists into it I fill with even more anger.

I hate that she was right about Elliot. I hate that she has any power over me. I hate that she followed through with not paying my tuition. I hate that, even when lying in a hospital bed, all she cared about was being better than me. I hate that I shut my own emotions off to avoid conflict with the woman who's supposed to take care of me. I hate that my father goes along with all of it, kissing her ass the entire time.

I hate Elliot too. I hate him most of all. I hate that I met him. That I fell in love with him. That he decided to love me back. That he did drugs. That he sold drugs. That he always got so angry. I hate that-

"Woah. Calm down." I come back to the present, my arms still swinging. I'm not hitting a mannequin anymore. Now, I'm hitting Caden.

He grabs my wrists and holds them to his chest, his face hovering inches away from mine. Panic shakes me to the core as he holds me there. Every breath is hard as I keep fighting for air, pushing at him. His grip tightens.

"No. Stop. Stop." I try to pull my hands away from his, bending my knees to get more space. To escape. It doesn't work, he keeps holding me, so I screw my eyes shut and focus every ounce of energy on not passing out. "Please. No."

"Hey. Breathe." He loosens his grip, assuming I won't hit him anymore. "Jesus. Are you okay?"

It takes me a long time, but I finally get enough oxygen to speak. "I'm fine."

"That was, something."

"I know. Sorry."

"Your concentration is insane." He laughs but it's forced. I just showed him something he wasn't supposed to see and we both know it. "Are you okay?"

"Yeah." He glances down at my hand, sucking in a breath. I follow his gaze and wince. My knuckles are covered in blood, little flecks of skin stuck to the liquid. I'm too numb to feel it right now but I know from experience it's going to kill later. Great.

I try to explain myself. "I was just getting some pent-up energy out. I got a little carried away, I guess."

"More like pent up anger." He puts a hand on my shoulder and I flinch away. If it bothers him, he doesn't show it. "I'm not judging. I've had the anger thing down for a while."

"Gee. Let's hold hands and talk about it." I push past him and head to the water jug. He follows me.

"Alright. Let's not talk at all." He sighs. "I'm going to get something for your hand, then we can do some cardio."

"I hate cardio." Embarrassing as it is, I'm full on pouting. This day is terrible.

"Yeah, well you aren't hitting anything with that hand today so looks like you screwed yourself."

"How about you screw yourself instead."

"Just for that I'm going to make you wash those knuckles with hydrogen peroxide." He raises an eyebrow. "We're still talking, by the way."

"I know." I finish my drink and throw the empty cup in the bin. "I'm sorry. I had one hell of a night last night."

"What happened, if you don't mind me asking?" He starts walking towards the first aid kit. I know if I stay here he'll probably drop the topic. I wonder if I can ask about the twenty-sixth if I tell him something. Maybe it'd feel good to share a little of my stress.

I follow him, treading slowly.

"I had a huge fight with Myla." He remains silent, rifling through the bandages. I lightly tap the toe of my shoe against the wall. The silence is unbearable. "Plus, I'm fighting with my mother. She pretty much said that my dreams of being a fighter are silly, and that she's not going to pay for my college if I don't want to listen to her. I thought she was just being dramatic but she apparently meant it. I got an email from the finance people and my tuition isn't paid."

All the words feel good coming off my chest. Too good. I keep going. "She hates me. I mean, she used to love me. I was the perfect little daughter until-" I freeze and look up at him. His hand is on a bottle of peroxide, but his full attention is on me. Blue eyes wash over my face, taking in every inch.

"Until what?"

"I just made a few mistakes."

"In December?" I forgot that he has my file, feeling exposed all over again.

"I started the mistakes before December. That's just when it all caught up with me." He takes my hand carefully, probably afraid that I'll hit him again. His touch makes me uncomfortable, but it's better than feeling numb.

"What were the mistakes?" He holds my hand over the garbage, pouring a small amount of liquid over my cuts. The dips in my knuckles start to bubble. I focus on the pain, forgetting to answer him. After a moment, he speaks again.

"Listen, you don't have to tell me." He dabs at my knuckles with a cotton ball. "It sucks about your mom."

"Yeah, well. Parents, right?" I try to laugh it off, but he doesn't smile.

"Don't you live with them?"

"No. I have an apartment with Myla." He adds a little more peroxide. Thankfully, this time it doesn't sting as much. "I moved in with her before graduation."

"In December?" He's starting to figure it all out, which isn't good.

"Yes. A week before Christmas." I study the way he slowly wraps my hand, making sure the pressure is just right.

"How'd you afford that? Rob a bank or something?" *Or something.* I try to think of what to say. For a while, I worked, but when I started training for real I decided to quit. That job barely got me enough money for groceries, anyway. I have money from somewhere else.

When Elliot got arrested, it took them four hours to get a search warrant. I got out of the hospital in three. With my head spinning, I grabbed four thousand dollars from his dresser and a wad of hundreds from the safe. I left his gun, the cocaine, the heroine, and the rest of the money. I made sure there was enough to get him in trouble. Enough to get him away from me.

"It's a small place, and I had some money saved up."

"So your parents pay for your college even though you bailed when you turned eighteen?" He starts packing up the aid kit, letting me take my hand back.

"Yeah. Well, they were going to at least." I wonder what he must think of all this. Of my crazy, messed up life. His parents are probably perfect and caring. The worst thing he needs to worry about is babysitting on a Saturday night.

"Your parents sound intense."

"They're all about appearances. No one ever knew I moved out early, besides Myla, who didn't care. I didn't have many friends back then. A lot of the girls I thought were my friends ended up turning their backs on me after I got, well, made my mistakes." I avoid eye contact with him. "Anyway, they're retired so they moved down south in June and played it off like it was all a part of the plan. They weren't impressed when I decided to stay here for school but a daughter in college is better than nothing, so they offered to pay."

"What about all the mistakes you made? They didn't care about any of that?"

"Oh trust me, they cared." I think back to my mother's face in that hospital. I was so ready to tell her. To beg her for help. Then she turned her cold eyes on me and immediately started scolding. "It's complicated."

"Sorry. I didn't mean to pry."

"Don't worry about it." I wave him off, my hand throbbing.

"Listen. Do you have any plans next weekend? Saturday night?"

"Oh, no. I'm not going to another party." This gets him to laugh and I decide I want to hear that more often. I like the sound of it.

While I'm on a roll, I kind of like his eyes too. And his smile. And the way he- *stop it, Aubrey.*

I push the thoughts out immediately. He's my trainer and he's annoying. And I'm not ready for that. I don't think I'll ever be.

"It's not a party. There's a pay per view fight that night. Jason and I are buying it at my place and we figured you'd like to come."

"Oh." I'm pretty sure it was fully Jason's idea, but it still makes me blush a little. Geez. I confide in the guy about my mother and suddenly I'm in love? *Gross.* That's not me. I'm way too emotional today. "That sounds great."

"Great." He looks shocked that I actually said yes. "Alright, now. Enough distractions. Let's get this cardio over with."

CHAPTER TWENTY-NINE
Aubrey

Myla comes home to find me lying in the middle of the living room floor, dying. "Well, I'd ask you how your day went but I'm assuming not good."

Just in case she's not certain, I inform her that I am dying.

"You're not dying."

"Dead. Gone. Goodbye." I look up at her. "Play Stairway to Heaven at my funeral and put a harry potter quote on my tombstone."

"Sure thing. Can I keep this top, then?" She pulls at her blouse, which I realize is mine. I look away and close my eyes. The room is starting to spin.

"You go right ahead. Take the whole closet." She makes a noise of acknowledgment as she walks past me. I'm too exhausted to open my eyes but it sounds like she's heading towards the bathroom. I go to tell her that I was just about to head to the shower but realize it would be a lie. I was headed there an hour ago when I found this very comfortable spot.

An entire day goes by while she showers and gets dressed. Okay, not a day. Probably a half-hour, but I'm dying and it's taking too long.

When she finally emerges, she's dressed in sweatpants and an oversized dance shirt. She smiles when she sees me looking at her.

"Oh look. Still alive."

I stick my tongue out at her. "You look comfy."

"Yeah. I figured I could just stay in with you tonight."

"Oh, no." I take every ounce of strength left in me and push myself up to a sitting position. I'm not sure if I have the energy for this but I will try my best. "Gas station guy sucks?"

"He does." I know it's over because she doesn't correct me on his name. She sits on the floor in front of me, her legs crossing to form a pretzel.

"But you spent the night?"

"Well, yes. He didn't suck the other night because we were wasted. The only reason he stayed here was because he started to pass out in the cab and the guy wouldn't drive him anywhere else. Then yesterday, he didn't suck at the movie because he couldn't talk. And he didn't suck at the club because the music was so loud. And he didn't suck in bed, because I haven't been laid in a month and he sort of knew what he was doing." I push that mental image out of my head and force myself up to my feet. I need water.

"So, what happened?"

"Siiigggh." The word is long and drawn out, like a dramatic sigh would be. I grab both of us some water and head back to our spot on the floor.

"He turned out to be atrocious. I mean, seriously, he was terrible." She chugs half her water before continuing. "He had this thing about calling me sweet bottom. Like, seriously, sweet bottom? And he was so clingy. Oh, and he wanted to know everything about me. I felt like I was trapped in a sappy romance novel. Like, what's my biggest fear? Really? Oh, and then he asked me if I would make him breakfast. He claims it's what woman do for their men." She shakes her head and huffs.

"Wow. Sounds like a doozy."

"Yup." The bottle in her hand crinkles as she begins squeezing it. "I think I need to take your approach and just swear off men."

"Hey, it's treating me well." If only she knew what I was up to. The thoughts I've been having about a certain trainer. I look at her, trying to hide my guilt. Her hair is wet and dripping onto her shirt, and her sweatpants have a hole in the knee.

I love her the most when she's like this, all comfortable and easy. It's the way I met her, at our first dance practice. It's the way she always was at our sleepovers, or when I would wake her up at four in the morning by climbing in her window. She's been my best friend for so long, I can't imagine not having her around. She's more stable than my family.

Shit. My family. "I spoke to my mother the other night."

She must be able to tell from my face that it went bad. "How bad?"

"On a scale of one to ten? The newest Justin Bieber song." Her eyes widen. "That's bad."

"She told me she won't pay for my college anymore."

"What?" She sits up straight. I'm not sure why she's surprised at all. If anyone, other than me, knows how shitty my mother is, it's Myla.

"Sure enough, I checked and I'm on my own. I only have two weeks to pay for it."

"Do you, um." She pauses and gives me a somewhat nervous smile. "Never mind."

"No, what?"

"It's nothing. None of my business."

"Myla." I feel like I'm scolding a child.

"I was just going to ask if you still have money left over. To pay for the semester."

"Not really. I've got enough for a few months of rent, and that's more important than school."

"You should have taken all of it." I hear the anger flare in her voice.

"The money was part of his conviction. It helped prove he was dealing."

"I know." She huffs and finishes her water bottle. Then her eyes light up with an idea. "I could get you a job with me if you want? The manager loves me, and we're hiring."

"Yeah, maybe." I couldn't think of anything worse than working in an upscale boutique. Working with people like my mother. Well, I could think of a few, but they all involve severe injuries or being in a room with my parents. "I'll let you know if I can't figure anything else out. It would be hard to train, go to school, and work."

"Well I know our rent is cheap when we split it but tuition is a whole other issue hun." I inwardly groan when she calls me hun. It means that she's concerned and it takes a lot to get her concerned.

"I'll let you know, I promise." I stand up and groan. This shower better be worth the pain. "I'm hoping she's just trying to fake me out. If she doesn't cough up the money she has no control."

"God forbid Jessica Pierce loses control of anything." She finishes what she started by crushing her bottle into a jagged stick of plastic. "God, Bree. If I was you I would have thrown what happened with Elliot right in her face. I would have made her feel like total shit for not paying enough attention, for not being there for you."

"Myla." I rub at my eyes, trying to combat the ache emerging. It's not my favorite thing to think about. If we're all being honest with ourselves, my mother knows. My mother *knew*. Instead of caring, I think she saw it as a lesson. Her and Elliot are similar in that way.

"I'm sorry. It just pisses me off that you got stuck with parents like yours, plus Elliot. You deserve a break."

"I already got a break. I live with my best friend, I'm going to school for something that I think I'll love, and I'm training at one of the best gyms in the country."

"Still," she leans in, and it feels like she wants to hug me. I itch from the idea of being constricted into a hug. Even with Myla, that wouldn't be pleasant.

Thankfully she knows this already and doesn't go in for the kill. "I want you to be happy. You seem like you're going through the motions and you deserve better than that."

"I'll work on it."

"Try to find someone too."

"Myla." I feel my exhaustion setting in again.

"Never mind, I take it back." She slaps my knee playfully and hops up. "I'll find a movie on Netflix and make us some frozen pizza. Go shower. You smell like ball sack."

"Fine. Grab some wine too." I leave her behind to head towards the bathroom but I can feel her eyes on me the entire time. Will she ever accept the fact that I'll never be the same person again?

I start to doubt everything. Myla knows me better than anyone. Sometimes, she knows me better than I know myself. Maybe Elliot changed me into someone else, but I could change again. I could at least try.

CHAPTER THIRTY
Caden

The morning news gives me a pretty good indication of what kind of day I'm going to have. In the last week, there's been five Heroin overdoses. This morning marks the sixth. And the first death. *Shit.*

The chief meets me at the door of the station, probably on the same page as me today. He immediately starts walking to his office, speaking as he goes. I speed walk behind him to keep up, taking in everything he's saying and making mental notes of what I need to do.

"The investigation isn't going fast enough. None of the victims are talking, and obviously our OD from this morning isn't going to be saying anything. We need to know where they got their supply and who's in charge of all the distributors. I want to take this guy down, Larson."

"As do I, Sir."

"You need to call Jameson and get him in today. I need him to step it up which means I need you to step it up. That boy isn't delivering. He's given us one lead and it turned out to be nothing more than a guy selling his medicinal marijuana." He sighs. "Don't get me wrong, the more drugs off the street the better but we need to have priorities."

"Jameson claims that the guy was one of the biggest drug dealers he knew."

The chief scoffs and looks at me like he can't believe I believe that. I don't, I'm just stating a fact. "Tell him his ass will be back in prison if he doesn't buck up. The charges he got brought up on? The things we found in his apartment? He wasn't the top guy but he was high up, and he knows more than he's telling. He's on a clock here. We have people dying."

He pauses at my cubicle to drop me off like a child. The entire atmosphere of the station is different today. Everyone is moving in a quiet rush, the air thick with tension. The pressure is officially on.

I call Jameson, pleasantly surprised when he answers on the first try. Even more surprising, he says he'll be in right away, instead of the usual back and forth involved in dragging his ass here.

To pass the time, I check a few files and get some questions prepared. He shows up right on time but I'm less than impressed with his appearance. Instead of his usual nice jeans and dress shirt, he's wearing a pair of jeans with grease stained thighs and a plain white shirt that's so thin, you can see all his tattoos through it.

"You beckoned?" He looks angrier than usual. I wonder what he was up to and, since I'm supposed to be supervising him, I ask.

"Where were you?"

"At work?" He gestures to his jeans. "I'm helping out at my dad's auto shop."

"I didn't think you worked on Sundays. I apologize for interrupting."

"Don't worry about it. We aren't open on Sundays so I was just doing some extra work. He won't mind."

"He doesn't know you're here, though?" He's not supposed to tell anyone about his arrangement, not even family. Not until it's over.

"I told him I needed to come in for a piss test. He didn't argue it. My whole situation makes him uncomfortable."

"You getting arrested, or you getting out?"

"Getting arrested. He didn't expect me to go to fucking Harvard or anything but he expected a little more than getting arrested for dealing drugs and," he pauses, like he's not sure how much I know. I hide my smile. He must be afraid of spilling something that we didn't get him for yet. Must be stressful to be a criminal around so many cops.

"Well, glad you could come in. You see the news this morning?"

"No. I don't watch the news." He stops short. By the look on his face, I have a feeling he wants to say something. It takes him a second, his eyes looking anywhere but me, before he speaks again. "Was it about Lily dying last night?"

I force down any physical signs of excitement. "You knew Lily Johnston?"

"Kind of. She was a regular for me." He shrugs it off but I don't at all. This is good. This will get us somewhere. I pull out a chair for him and he sits down without being prompted.

"Alright. I need you to tell me everything you know about Lily."

He looks at me skeptically. "How far does that confidentiality run?"

"It's a fine line. You can't tell me if you're doing anything illegal right now, since the deal began. You shouldn't be doing drugs, dealing drugs, or in possession of a gun. Among other things. You can't tell me anything that would break your probation because I would have to report it."

"What about what happened before?"

"I know what happened before."

He pauses. It's clear that I don't know everything, which I figured. There were gaps in his case, gaps that he obviously wasn't going to fill until now. His immunity covers the gaps. "You don't know everything."

"Well, anything that happened during the time before your arrest is under your immunity agreement." I pause. I'm not sure if I need to say this but I figure it should be addressed. "There are some exceptions, one of them being murder. If you killed someone, yourself, we can get you for that."

"I never killed anyone." I study his face and try to decide if that's true. He doesn't seem like he's lying, but that could just be a skill of his. Then again, he was high up. He probably never needed to get his hands bloody. There were people for that.

"Well, then. Go ahead and tell me about Lily." I pull out a tape recorder from the drawer and he pales. "Don't worry. It's just for my own records."

He sighs and steadies himself. I prepare for what I'm about to hear and hope to God it doesn't make me hate him anymore. "I met her a few years ago. She was nineteen, I think, when she started hanging around the group. She dated," he pauses and looks at me. It's a name he's afraid to give. "She dated this guy in our group, one of the bigger dealers. We called him Jack."

"What would I call him?"

"I don't know."

"His name wasn't Jack?"

He laughs to himself, like he's thinking of a fond memory. "No, his name wasn't Jack."

"Why was he called Jack?"

"Because if you fucked with him or his boys, he'd jack you up."

"Interesting." I make a mental note about Jack. If someone as high up as Jameson didn't know his real name, he's probably one of the top guys. Either that, or Jameson doesn't want to snitch on this particular person.

"So, do you think he's who gave her the drugs she overdosed on?"

"No."

"That was quick. Why so sure?"

"He's dead." His face is void of emotion, as if he didn't know the guy at all. As if he could care less.

"Even when he died, you didn't know his name?" He scratches at the stubble on his jaw. "Didn't you go to his funeral? Or read the report in the paper?"

"No. He died in Chicago."

"That doesn't make a difference, there would still—"

"I don't think his body was ever found. I don't think he had family to look for him. We sure as hell weren't going to look for him. There's probably no record of him, but I'm telling you. He's dead." His nostrils flare as he tries to breathe through his unnecessary anger.

"Why wouldn't you guys look for him?"

"Because he was a dick who made a lot of enemies. I don't know if one of us offed him, or if one of his clients in Chicago did. I don't really care."

"How do you know he didn't just disappear?"

"Because, I do. You don't want me to tell you how." He looks up at me. Something in his eyes is unsettling and, without meaning to, I slightly cringe.

"Okay." I take his word for it. Either way, Jack seems to be a dead end. I cross him off in the mental note and move on. "So, did Lily hang out with anyone else?"

"Yeah. Once he died."

"Who?"

"Me." I didn't expect that. I sit back in my seat and wait for him to elaborate. "I'm the one who had to tell her he died. I went over to her place. She freaked out and started crying and I slept with her to relax her. She got attached."

Jesus Christ. I want a new job. "You slept with her?"

"Yeah." *Probably in return for free drugs.*

"Just that time, or?"

"No. It became a habit." He shrugs and looks up at me. His body language shifts from defensive to nonchalant. Unlike the Jack situation, this part of his life doesn't matter to him. "I wasn't her dealer at the time. We all kind of split up Jack's clients and she wasn't mine. We would do drugs together sometimes, but not often. I wasn't really doing them back then. But I wasn't dealing to her. I wasn't using her for sex and she wasn't using me for drugs."

He laughs. "Okay, I was using her for sex. But she wasn't using me for drugs."

"Fair enough." I fiddle with a pen on my desk. "What happened between you two? Did you date her until your arrest?" I get excited. Am I finally going to find out who the infamous girl is from the night he was brought in?

"God, no." He laughs. "I never really dated her at all. I slept with other girls, she slept with other guys, we just ended up together more often than not."

"When did that end?"

"I met someone." He pauses, and I know in an instant that *this* is the girl I've been waiting for.

"When was this?"

"March. Two and a half years ago."

"What was her name?" If I thought he was defensive with Jack, I hadn't seen anything yet. His jaw locks, green eyes full of anger and fixed on me. With a sharp rhythm, he bounces on the balls of his feet, sending his knees up off the chair.

"She wasn't in the life. She doesn't know anything or anyone. Leave her out of it."

"What was her name?"

"I haven't even seen her since I got out. I haven't spoken to her. I don't want her hurt, that's the last thing I want. You're not going near her."

"What was her name?"

"Jesus Christ, do I have to tell you?"

"No. You don't."

"Good."

I settle back in my seat and cross my arms. He continues staring at me. This is now a waiting game, and I've got more time than him. My shift just began. Finally, he glances up at the ceiling and sighs.

When he looks back at me, he's smiling. "You can have one name. Hers, or the guy who gave Lily the drugs."

I shift in my seat and lean forward. "How do I know you won't lie?"

"Because I have everything to lose." His response is instant. "I wouldn't lie about his name. Not if it means keeping her safe."

"Alright."

He begins talking, and I hide my smile by ducking my head. Now we're getting somewhere. Now I know just the spot to poke. His sweet spot. The girl.

CHAPTER THIRTY-ONE
Aubrey

I start my morning off with a protein shake and a pep talk in the mirror. Classes also begin today. I try not to be too stressed out, but my nerves are on fire. There's only a week left before I need to find the money to pay my tuition, and at this rate, the odds are not in my favor.

Even though I've interview at two different places, both haven't called me back. It's starting to look like I'll be taking that job with Myla after all, and even then, there's no way I'd make the money fast enough to get tuition covered.

Caden is stretching by the water jug when I walk in, pouting with my sweatshirt sagging from my body.

"Good morning." He says a little too loudly, taking my bag for me and putting it next to his. "I thought we could start with some warmups. We never do warmups. I mean, you run and stuff like that but I want to teach you some fighting warmups. Did Rob ever teach you some fighting warmups? They help a lot with-" He pauses, staring at me. I must look how I feel. He's rambling like he's high. Like he just got a hit and his world has transformed. I've heard rants like that. He's too happy. Why is he so happy? "What's wrong?"

I shake my head and put a hand up to indicate that I'm fine. "You just reminded me of someone, that's all."

"Why am I sensing that's a bad thing?" He steps forward and I instinctively take a step back. "What'd I say?"

"Nothing. Nothing." I start backtracking. *God, why am I such a freak?* Right when we start to get along. Right when he's finally being nice. "Just a lot of energy, is all."

"Oh, sorry." He kicks a shoe against the ground. "I had a good day yesterday. Like, a really good day. At work. I'm just in a great mood."

"What happened?"

"Just a major break in one of our investigations." He pauses like he wants to say more but can't. "It's confidential."

"Pretentious." I mean it as a joke and thankfully he takes it that way. We both laugh a little and the air feels light again. *Much better.* "I'm glad you're in a good mood."

"Me too." He smiles wide at me, but his eyebrows knit together after a second. "Any luck with your mom?"

"No. I haven't tried calling her."

He frowns. "You know. If you ever need help or anything. Or if you're, ya know, scared."

"Excuse me?" Just a moment ago, we were laughing. Now, I'm on high alert.

"Jason just mentioned that you were talking about what drives you last week. He was talking about anger but you brought up fear."

"That's none of your business." The words come out harder than I mean, but I don't apologize or try to take them back.

"Well, I'm your trainer. I kind of need to know what's going on in your head."

"No. You don't." I try to remain calm, not wanting to mess up the fragile relationship we've been building.

"Fine. Forget I fucking mentioned it." He takes a step forward and I whimper. Actually whimper. My heart is pounding in my chest, partially out of embarrassment, but mostly because for a moment he sounded just like Elliot.

He stops dead in his tracks and looks at me. "What just happened?"

"Nothing."

"Aubrey." He starts to put a hand out for me but he must realize it wouldn't be a good idea because it returns to his side. "Hey, did you think I was going to hurt you?"

"No. Of course not." He stares at me and I expect it to be angry or hard but it's not. Those blue eyes are full of concern and, fondness, maybe? It makes him look human.

I remind myself that he's nothing like Elliot. That there's no reason for me to be afraid of him.

"Aubrey." He looks conflicted. "I'm not the type of guy to pry. I'm going to train you the best I can no matter what. We don't have to get along and you don't have to tell me anything you don't want to tell me. But I meant what I said before. I'm here."

"Okay." I just want this conversation to be over. "Show me those warmups."

It takes him a moment to decide if he's really going to let it go, but he finally nods.

By the time we finish our session, I'm drenched in sweat and possibly even more exhausted than I was yesterday. When will my muscles get used to this? Hopefully soon.

Jason walks in as we're packing up. He greets both of us, swinging his clipboard like he's off on a mission. Caden takes a step forward, then stops and glances at me. For whatever reason, he looks guilty. When he turns his attention back to Jason, he calls out, "Hey, Jace. Can we talk?"

Jason pauses. "Yeah, come on in."

Caden avoids my stare, and I know deep down that it's about me. That I must have ruined something, or done something wrong. I probably freaked him out this morning, or any of the other times I've acted like a total psycho, and he's going to tell Jason that I'm not fit to train here.

The worst part is, that's not what bothers me the most. What bothers me the most, what makes my hands shake as I'm leaving the gym, is the idea that Caden doesn't like me. Not that he doesn't like me as a fighter, or as someone that belongs to their gym, but me as a person. Because, maybe, only maybe, I might like him.

CHAPTER THIRTY-TWO
Caden

Jason makes me wait a minute while he returns a call. I sit on my phone and scroll through my newsfeed, listening to him try and book one of our fighters at a larger event. He comes out on the winning side of the conversation and ends the call with a fist pumped into the air. I'm glad I'm catching him in a good mood.

"Alright," He focuses his attention on me, his smile nice and wide. "What did you need from me?"

"To talk a bit, if you've got time." He glances at his clipboard and I bite my tongue so I don't make fun of him. He's touchy about his clipboard. I think it makes him feel in charge, especially around a bunch of guys who are his age, if not older.

"I'm pretty much free for the rest of the morning. What do you need?" I can hear the hope in his voice. He thinks I'm picking up where we left off at the bar.

"I want to talk about Aubrey." I walk over to the window to check that she's gone. I don't know why I can't talk about her while she's in the building but it feels wrong.

"Shit." He sighs. The noise is full of disappointment. "You're falling for her, aren't you?"

Am I?

"No. Not at all, man. I'm just worried about her. I saw that fear that you were talking about today."

"What happened?" He's on alert now, sitting up in his seat with his eyebrows raised. "You didn't fight, did you?"

"No. Of course not. But I've seen that fear that you talked about a few times now. The other day I walked in on her warming up and she was so angry. I tried to stop her and calm her down but she freaked out, swinging at me and crying. I don't think she even knew that she was crying. And when I touched her she freaked out. She couldn't be touched or held down, she fully panicked. Then this morning, I don't know what happened but she got really freaked out again."

He takes a minute to think about this, and I use the time to ponder the fact that my absolute best friend thinks I'm falling for Aubrey. That's ridiculous. She drives me nuts. I mean she's beautiful. Don't get me wrong. She's gorgeous. And she's smart. And she can make me laugh pretty hard, which doesn't happen often nowadays. And when I'm with her, it's like the weight of the world disappears. And she-

"So, are you thinking what I'm thinking?" *Am I?* I mean, I like her, but I'm not falling for her. There's no way. "Caden?"

"What?"

"Do you think someone is hurting her?"

"Oh." I push all thoughts of liking Aubrey out of my mind and focus on this conversation. If she's getting hurt, I want to help. "I don't know. I have a theory but it's a little out there."

"Hit me with it."

"She has a really bad relationship with her mom. Like crazy bad. She only told me a little bit but she said that her mom hates her and she seems like she really thinks it. I guess she moved out first chance she got when she turned eighteen, but her mom still has control over her. Aubrey can't pay for college and her mom is holding it over her head. Threatening not to pay."

"You think her mom hurts her?"

"Maybe not anymore, but maybe when they lived together?"

"That's a little out there, Caden." He doesn't tell me I'm crazy or turn it down, which makes me feel better. Instead, he looks like he's picturing it. Trying to figure out the puzzle.

Then he sighs. "Either way, if she's acting like that we need to be on alert. You need to open yourself to her, even if you need to promise not to tell me. I don't have to know, just one of us does. Whether it's her mom or someone else, or something else, it needs to be addressed and handled. She can't fight like that."

I run my hands through my hair, tugging at the ends so they spike up in the front. It's a nervous habit that my mom used to hate.

"I know." I think of Aubrey, with her bright blue eyes void of emotion. With her breathing erratic and her entire body shaking. There's so much fear. "She can't live like that either."

CHAPTER THIRTY-THREE
Caden

"Caitlin! I said turn it down!" I take the broom I'm using to sweep the living room and bang it against the ceiling three times. I already have a headache from all the Aubrey in my head, and I don't need Taylor Swift adding to the mix.

"Can I have a snack?" Cassie asks, running into the room at full speed. I drop the broom and grab her around the waist right before her little feet go straight through my pile on the floor. She giggles as I lift her up and over it.

"Dinner is in the oven. You can wait fifteen minutes."

"I don't think so." She shakes her head, little blonde ponies swaying. "I'm starving."

"I don't think you are." I can't help but chuckle a little at how damn cute she is. I scooch her into a chair, careful not to step in the pile myself. "Stay here."

She sits patiently while I turn the corner and dig around in the closet, eyes lighting up when I return with crayons and her favorite coloring book. I hand them to her and go back to sweeping.

The music starts up again and I groan. At this rate, I'm going to learn all the damn lyrics. *Oh, who am I kidding? I already have.* I tap the ceiling again but give up when there's no response.

"Stay there, okay?" Cassie doesn't look up from her Cinderella picture, her tongue sticking out of the corner of her mouth while she concentrates. I storm up the stairs and stop at the second room on the right. With a deep breath, I knock three times. The music stops.

"What?" She yells just before yanking the door open. I take a deep breath and smile at her. There's no reason to fight right now.

"Dinner is almost ready. Why don't you wash up and come down?"

"Fine." She shuts the door before I can say anything else. I sigh and lean my forehead against the wood for a second. How did my parents do this? I'm exhausted.

When I come back downstairs, Cassie is still coloring in her book. I grab two hot pads and pull the chicken casserole out of the oven. Caitlin comes moping into the kitchen just as I'm setting it on the counter to cool, both hot pads beneath it.

"Can you set the table, please?" I don't have to ask a specific person. This is oddly one of Cassie's favorite chores. She's a little perfectionist with the plates and forks.

Caitlin gets up and grabs three glasses from the cabinet. I try not to get too excited that she's doing something helpful without being prompted.

"What do you want to drink, Cass?" Caitlin asks from the fridge. Cassie pauses, her fingers wrapped around three glass plates. She ponders the question like it's life or death.

"Chocolate milk, please." She nods like she's confirming this with herself, then goes back to setting the table. Caitlin glances at me.

"I'll take some ice water." I grab Cassie's chocolate milk and place it on the table for her, then sit down. Caitlin follows and hands me my glass.

Once they're both set, I go and grab the dish and put it on the center of the table. Caitlin goes for it first, scooping the casserole onto her plate, then I do the same for myself and Cassie. We all eat in silence for a few minutes.

I bring my fork through the rice on my plate and scoop some up, thinking of the best way to break the silence. "Did you have a good first day at school?"

"Oh, yeah. Totally. Junior year is just great." I stare at her. I'm not sure if she can tell that I'm really exhausted or if she just feels like being nicer today, but she apologizes. "Sorry. It went okay. I just took on a harder load than I thought this year."

"You'll do fine. You're smart." She shrugs her shoulders and nods. For some reason, I'm reminded of Aubrey's mom. It was her Senior year that she burnt out, but the mistakes started earlier. Did she push herself too hard? Did her mom push her too hard?

"I'll sign any permission slips, if you need to drop a class. Take art or something. Colleges like diversity." I feel like I'm speaking out of my ass but she beams at me.

"I'll think about it. Thanks." I feel like I've won the lottery. The feeling doesn't last long. I catch her pushing all the chicken to one side of the plate, eating the cheesy rice alone. *Oh, please not this again.*

"How was your day, Cass?" She already told me earlier but she's so excited that kindergarten turned out to be fun, I don't mind hearing it again.

"It was great. My teacher, Miss Lauren, is nice. She let us color and play with Legos and she reads to us." Caitlin smiles a genuine smile and I relax in my seat. She asks Cassie what book they read and I watch as they go back and forth about Dr. Seuss. Cassie giggles and that makes Caitlin laugh. The sound radiates through the whole house. I want so badly to be able to bottle it up and carry it with me.

Then it dawns on me. This is how my parents did it. This is how they kept going. These little moments. I have no doubt in my mind.

CHAPTER THIRTY-FOUR
Aubrey

The bathroom door shakes as he bangs on it. Each knock echoes inside me, rattling my bones. "Baby, open up. Baby. Come on." His voice is soft. It doesn't match the sound of his fists. I shiver and stay in the empty bathtub. This is where you're supposed to go when a tornado comes, right?

My entire body is shaking. I wrap my arms around my legs and try to calm down. My phone is in his bedroom but it wouldn't matter anyway. I have no one to call. I would never ask Myla to come here, especially when he's this upset, and my parents would probably laugh at me. They don't even know I snuck out of my window. They think I'm safe in my bed. I close my eyes and try not to cry. I wish I was safe in my bed.

"Open the door, Baby. Come on Bree." His tone makes it clear that this isn't a plea. It's a warning. "Bree."

I stand up slowly and wrap my sweater tight around myself. It's not as comforting as I hoped. He knocks again and I can visibly see the door shake. "I swear to God, Aubrey. I will break this fucking door down."

If he breaks that door down it will be worse. He will hurt me worse. I count to three and take a deep breath. With a hand that's shaking so hard I have to place it twice before it sticks, I turn the lock. The minute it clicks he pushes the door open and slams into me. He doesn't stop moving until I'm up against the wall, my head pressed against a canvas painting of a tree.

His hands travel along my body and I prepare. I take in as much oxygen as I can while trying to relax my muscles. It hurts less when I'm not tensed.

I'm so focused on all of this I don't notice that he's crying. I don't notice that he's not hurting me.

"Don't be mad at me, baby. Don't run." He rests his forehead against mine and breathes me in. He kisses me and I sink into him. He tastes like whiskey and sadness. It's a taste I've grown accustomed to.

He pulls away and rubs his nose against mine, chuckling. "God, I love you so fucking much."

"I love you too." I bring my hands up and tangle them in his hair. It's longer than usual and I should get him to cut it. I add this to my mental to do list, right behind LEAVE HIM. I usually don't go in a particular order.

"Don't hide from me again. Please." I'm not sure why but a surge of bravery rushes through me. Maybe it's the fact that he's being polite and gentle. Or maybe because he's so desperate to keep me.

"Don't hurt me again. Please." I peek up at him through my lashes and wait. The reaction is instant. His eyes melt into humanity just before they close. When they open again, he's broken. His knees buckle under the weight of it and he holds onto me.

"Let's make a deal." His voice is rough, scraped raw from all the yelling.

"Okay."

"I won't hurt you anymore. I won't lay a hand on you. But you have to promise to never leave me. To never run. No matter how bad it gets. No matter what you find out about me." If this was any other situation I would laugh. What more could I find out about him? He's abusive. He's an angry, jealous drunk and he's crazy when he does drugs. He deals to mean people who own guns, and he owns one himself. He's scary. Yet, I know for a fact, if I knew everything about him I would find him much scarier.

"Sounds like a deal."

He wraps his arms around my waist and lifts me up. I bring my legs around him and kiss him. Still carrying me, he stumbles to the room before dropping me on the bed-

"Shit!" I'm lying flat on the floor. My blankets are tangled around my legs and waist, and I'm drenched in sweat. I rest my head in my hands and try to breathe. That was a good night. That was a crazy night, consisting of cocaine and guns and broken glass across the floor, but it was amazing. He stopped hitting me after that, for a while.

My chest hurts and I hate myself. I can't get him out of my head and I hate it. What kind of person dreams of someone so terrible? It's been months. Why can't I get over this shit? Why did that stupid dream make me miss him a little? The good times, at least.

I'm fucked up.

Untangling myself, I search the floor and find a shirt to tug on. The door creaks when I open it and I hope Myla doesn't hear. I don't want to have to talk about this right now.

The fridge doesn't have any water left in it so I grab the half-empty bottle of moscato and head towards the couch.

There's nothing on the TV, other than infomercials and soap opera re-runs, so I curl up into a ball and settle on the weather channel. I watch the weekly forecast four times before turning the TV off and grabbing my phone, scrolling through the local news app. The fourth article makes me freeze.

Lily Johnston was found dead in her apartment after an overdose. No foul play suspected.

I read the article twice.

The wine bottle is now empty, and I think I might be crying. I'm not entirely sure and I don't care to check.

I can't stop staring at her picture. Her hair is curled perfectly and it's brown. Her eyes are clear and bright. She's in a sweater that comes up to her neck. I stare for a full minute, shocked at how different she looks.

This can't be the same girl with bleach blonde stringy hair and leather clothes who hung around Elliot's friend group all the time. The girl who dated James. Who dated all of them, even Elliot.

I wonder who sold her the drugs. I wonder if any of them care that she's dead. I wonder if Elliot knows.

I fall asleep, staring at the girl who used to be just like me. The girl I could have become.

CHAPTER THIRTY-FIVE
Aubrey

"Marry me." Half of his body is draped over mine, his chin resting on my stomach. One of his tattooed arms moves and his fingers start tracing circles on my bare skin. I watch him watch me and wonder if he's serious.

His eyes are bright and clear. He's sober, for six days now, and he's just promised me that he would never hurt me again. He promises me at least once a day. I'm starting to believe him.

"Yeah, right." I snort and smile at him. He doesn't smile back. "Oh, you can't be serious?" He doesn't say anything to this. He starts kissing my bare skin, dragging his lips against my stomach and along my ribs. I melt into him and almost forget his question.

"Bree?"

"Yeah?"

"Marry me." His voice is low and soft, like a familiar melody. A lullaby, maybe.

"I can't marry you." Something breaks inside him. I can feel him deflate against my body, so I try to soften the blow. "I'm too young to get married."

"You'll turn eighteen in two months."

"Yeah, but it's my Senior year of high school." It's a sore subject for him. He hates that I'm in school. We had a whirlwind summer but at least we were together almost every second. My mother would never imagine I would be involved in such trouble. She never questioned where I was or what I was doing, as long as I showed up to all my dance practices and competitions on time.

I always did. Sometimes with a few bruises. Once, where I was bawling. But I always showed and I always performed perfectly.

"Well, we can be engaged this year before we get married. I'll wait for you to graduate."

"What about Brown?" I wait for his face to fall like it always does when my future plans come up. It doesn't.

"I'll come with you."

"And do what?"

"Fuck if I know." He smiles up at me. "Community college. Find work somewhere. Stay in our place naked and waiting for you to come do very dirty things to me."

"Oh really?" I laugh. The conversation is making me feel a little giddy.

The idea of living with him in our own place is nice. As long as he doesn't throw any of our things in there. Or break down any of our doors. Or hurt me again. I try to assure myself that he would never hurt me again. He promised, and he's never done that before. He's always just walked away and expected me to stay.

He kisses the spot between my breasts and I can feel him smile against the skin. "Marry me."

"Elliot."

"Come on. Marry me." He props himself up on an elbow and looks into my eyes. All the playfulness has left them. "I'm so in love with you, Bree. I would follow you anywhere. I would do anything for you. I know I've hurt you and I've been really scary but I'm sober now and I'm going to stay that way, I swear. And if I leave with you for Brown then I can leave this whole lifestyle behind. All these fucking guys. I hate them, Bree. I hate this life. I just want to be with you and be happy."

"Elliot." My heart melts. To hear him say that he'll leave this life is too hard for me. It's everything I've wanted him to say to me. Everything I've needed.

"Marry me." I huff. It's everything I've wanted to hear but I still have faint bruises on my wrists. I still have scars across my heart. I don't know if I want to spend the rest of my life with him. I love him more than myself, and he loves me too.

Is that enough?

"You don't have a ring." He perks up.

"I can buy you a ring. Oh, baby. I'll buy you the nicest ring I can find." He practically beams at me. "I would take such good care of you. I could give you the fucking world."

"I know." God, I know. He could take baths in money if he wanted to. He could probably buy us a year's worth of rent for a nice apartment. He would buy me clothes, like he does now, and bring me to nice restaurants. Is that taking care of me though? I don't feel taken care of with him. But he's in a good mood and he's gentle and I don't want to ruin anything. "How about you ask me again when you get that ring?"

He smiles bright. "Sounds like a plan." He crawls on top of me and hovers there, his hands moving to touch every inch of me. "Now let me take care of you."

"Aubrey?"

"What?" I sit up straight and something crashes against the coffee table. I search for the source of the noise and find a broken wine bottle lying on the floor. Myla is standing over me looking concerned.

"Your alarm is going off. It woke me up." I'm surprised she's not more annoyed with me. Myla is the poster child for 'not a morning person'.

"I'm sorry. I must have fallen asleep out here." I start cleaning up the bigger pieces of glass and she brings in the broom.

"When did you come out here? We went to bed at the same time and you definitely went into your room."

"I couldn't sleep." I think about the dream I had last night, and the one this morning. A pang of sadness radiates within me. *I miss him.* God damnit, it's always worse when the dreams are good. It was the good moments that made me stay, and it's those moments that will forever haunt me.

"I'm sorry." She helps me finish cleaning the glass and sighs. "As much as I'd love to make you sit with me and talk about the big bad wolf, you're going to be late."

I glance at the clock and curse under my breath. I don't even have time for a shower. Myla watches me as I run around like a crazy person, throwing yoga pants and my zip-up hoodie over my sports bra. It takes me a full three minutes to track down my keys. It must be a record, though, because I leave the apartment at the same time I always do.

"Wait!" Myla tracks me down right before the stairwell, out of breath and holding my gym bag. I grab it from her and sling it over my shoulder.

"Shit. Thank you."

"No problem. Do you need your school stuff?"

"No, I'll have time to stop by here before class." She tucks a piece of hair behind her ear. I know she wants to say something. I don't have time to wait. "What?"

"Just the usual. I'm worried about you." She frowns. "When was the last time you went to group?"

"I dunno. A while ago."

"Maybe you should go. I would come with, keep you company on the drive." Back when I was falling apart every day, she dragged me to a group therapy session for victims and survivors of abuse. It was an hour away, so I couldn't complain about seeing people I knew, and it helped. I started going every week, until I felt like I could safely stop. I still feel like that. There's no reason for me to go back there.

"I'm fine." I picture Lily laughing. Smiling. Turning the music up too loud. Helping me cover up my bruises in a grungy bar's bathroom. Wiping my tears. Offering to take me home. She did my hair once. She let me borrow her lipstick. Now she's just dead. Gone. "I'm fine."

CHAPTER THIRTY-SIX
Caden

Aubrey's off her game. I knew the minute she walked in that something was wrong but I wasn't too worried until she started failing her stations and giving up instead of pushing through her pain. I have black punch mitts on, facing her with them at chest level. She's barely hitting me.

"Come on, Aubrey." I watch to see a difference in her but she doesn't sound like she even hears me. Her face is blank, blue eyes against dark circles void of humanity. She shouldn't be fighting like this. I pull the mitts away and let them hang by my side. She throws two more punches before registering it.

"What?" She shakes her head like she's coming out of a trance and looks at me. Her eyes are full of tears and it makes them look so incredibly blue. I could fall into eyes like that. Drown in them.

"Why don't we take a break?" I don't want to point out that she's crying, or that she was doing terribly. What if it makes her more upset?

"Yeah. Um, okay." She takes off her gloves and lets them fall to the floor, walking over to the water jug. I stare at the gloves for a few seconds, then follow her.

She drinks three little cups full of water before taking a seat on the padded bench. I wonder if I should say something. Surprisingly, I don't have to. It's her that speaks. "I didn't sleep last night."

"At all?" I look over at her. She's hunched over, her zip-up hoodie slouching off one her shoulder. Her face is in her small hands and I wonder if she's still crying. I can't hear it in her voice.

"A few hours but it wasn't restful." The words are muffled by her palms but I still hear them. I wonder if I should tell her that I understand, because I haven't slept peacefully since I found out two girls were suddenly mine, but I hate when people do that. It's patronizing. I don't understand just because I'm tired too. Everyone's shit is different.

"What was keeping you awake?"

"I had a bad dream." She looks up at me and her cheeks are damp. I wonder why the hell she's decided to confide in me, afraid that I'll mess up the opportunity.

"What about?"

"Same old shit." She lets out a long breath. Her chin is shaking. Does she want me to ask what she means, or did she forget that I don't know that she regularly has nightmares?

Before I can decide, she continues. "Someone I know died. A girl."

"In the dream?"

"In real life." This whole opening up to me thing is great, really, but I'm lost here. "She died Saturday, I think. Or maybe Sunday morning."

"Shit. I'm really sorry."

"It's okay. We weren't close." She bites her bottom lip. I watch her fiddle with a hole on her right cuff. There's a loose thread she's trying to yank out.

"It still sucks."

"Yeah." Her fingers pause on the thread and she looks up at me. There's something in her eyes, like a lightbulb just went off. "Yeah. It does." She sounds almost relieved. Maybe she thought she was crazy for being upset.

"How did you know her?"

"We, um. We ran in the same crowd." She goes back to the thread. "For a while, a few years ago. Our boyfriends were friends."

The word pings inside my chest. *Boyfriend*. Is that past or present? "We never hung out on our own but we were the only two girls around usually. We went through a few things together. She helped me when-"

She's not distracted. She stopped for a reason and I'm not going to push it. Her face goes back into her hands, the rest of her body curling in on itself. "When's the funeral?"

"Today." Her voice is just above a whisper. I pick at my nails. Why is this conversation bothering me? Why do I feel like I'm missing something important? "I can't go."

"Why? If it's our training, we can end early. Do you have class?"

"I do but I'd be done in time." She sighs. "I can't go, though."

"Why?" I feel like I'm pushing her too far but she keeps talking and it feels good to get inside her.

Shit, that's a bad mental imagine. Inside her *mind*, not inside *her*. I shake my head and pull myself together. What Jason said must be messing with me because there's no way I'd go there on my own. I can barely stand her.

"I just can't."

"And that's why you're upset?"

"Sort of." She pulls the ends of her sleeves into her palms and grips them tight. I watch as she brings her knees up and wraps her arms around herself. It looks like she's trying to hold herself together. I have a feeling she does this often. "There will be people at the funeral that I can't see."

"Can't, or don't want to?"

"A little of both." She huffs out a laugh, like she can't believe her life. So, she doesn't run with that crowd anymore. Does that mean she doesn't run with that boyfriend either? *God, why do I care?*

"Won't your boyfriend be going?" It's a stretch. I pray she takes the bait.

"No. He's in prison." She stares straight ahead, blue eyes still empty. "And he's not my boyfriend."

"Oh." Everything I thought about her flips over. Who the hell is he? What did he do? I want so badly to ask her a million questions but I'm a cop and I'm slightly jealous and I think it's best if I just stay quiet.

"You're judging me." She stands up and I grab her wrist without thinking. Her entire body tenses and it all pulls together. It was him, the boyfriend, that hurt her. Why the hell would I think it was her mom?

"I'm sorry." I let go of her, hands in the air to signal peace. She remains where she is, her back to me. Taking a chance, I stand up so my chest is only an inch or two away from her back. "I'm not judging you, okay? I swear. I just didn't expect it."

"This is stupid. I shouldn't be talking about this." She sounds like she's about to leave but I notice that she doesn't move.

"You're afraid of him."

"That's ridiculous. He's locked up."

"I didn't say that it isn't irrational. I said you're still afraid of him." I don't want to hurt her feelings or push her too far. At the same time, I need to know this. I need it like I need oxygen. I need to know that she is safe. "You are, aren't you? Still afraid?"

"Yeah." It's a breathy confession, as if she hadn't admitted it to herself until just now. Her shoulders lift from the relief. "I'm scared all the time." Her words crackle.

"Oh, Aubrey." I move forward so that my chest is against her back. She flinches but doesn't pull away. I put my arms out on each side of her and show her my hands so she knows what I'm doing.

Slowly, as if she's breakable, I wrap myself around her body and hold her. I expect her to freeze or yell at me. Instead, she melts and I hear a little sigh escape her. Then a sob. I hold her like her life depends on it. Every piece she lets fall is safe, held gently in my hands until she's ready to pick them back up again. I'll wait.

CHAPTER THIRTY-SEVEN
Caden

I'm furious. I should not be getting into my uniform and strapping on a gun. I should not have to deal with Jameson today. God, I hate that prick. I hate that I have to see him even more now that he gave all that information about Lily. About his group.

We're almost ready to introduce an undercover guy. It's a huge step and it takes a lot of coordination. I'm not in the right headspace for it.

After Aubrey pulled herself together, and pulled herself away from me, things got awkward. She thanked me without looking, then rushed out before I could catch her, taking advantage of the fact that some guys were coming in at the same time. It doesn't bother me that she left. I would have needed some space too after that. It bothers me that there's a guy out there somewhere that's hurt her. That still scares her.

Jameson picks up on my mood immediately. He's sitting in a conference room, where a few other people will be joining us today. It's our first investigation meeting that we're allowing him to sit in. He's finally earned it.

"What? You aren't gonna offer me coffee?" He complains.

"Nope." I nod over at the pot and clean mugs. "Help yourself."

"Wow. You're chipper today." He stands up and pours the coffee into a mug. There's no cream and sugar and I'm irritated before he even asks for some. "Where's the-"

"Don't know. Don't care." I set up my files and try to relax in my chair.

"Can I go find some?" I stare him down. He's back in his usual dress shirt and jeans. If he were just a few feet closer I'd be able to see that damn tattoo. The bright one on his forearm that I can't stop being curious about.

"You didn't get used to black coffee in *prison*?" I make sure to make the last word sound like it's disgusting. He frowns into his mug.

"I did. The exact reason why I want something to put in it. I promised I would never drink black coffee again."

"Promised who?"

"Myself."

"Well," I sit up and go to a cabinet in the corner. There's a box of Splenda packets as well as a canister of dry cream. I place them, a little too hard, on the table. "Can't have you breaking promises on us. We're kind of relying on your integrity here."

"Thanks." I watch him as he drowns his coffee. He looks up at me and lifts an eyebrow in question. "What's wrong?"

"Nothing." I can feel my blood start to boil again. I picture Aubrey and wonder if the guy she was with is anything like Jameson. *Bad idea.* Now I want to spill my energy out on him.

"Seriously, man. You drilled the importance of this meeting into my head a million times. I'm pretty sure you used the words 'be respectful' at least every sentence. Yet, here you are, in whatever this mood is."

"I'm not the ex con who should be cooperating."

"Touché." He sips his coffee and sits down in the seat next to me. I catch a glimpse of the tattoo on his left arm when he reaches his hand out for more cream. In the center of all the jumbled lines and script is a medium sized dreamcatcher. It looks like it's water colored and there's something in the middle of it. A compass as far as I can tell. I try to lean forward. There's words written inside it. I can't make them out. "What are you doing?"

I sit up straight and look away. Then I realize I probably seem like a total idiot. I have the control here. Why do I feel like I need to hide? "I was checking out your sleeve."

"Oh." He scratches at the dreamcatcher. "You like it?"

"It's different." I wonder if he'll let me look closer. Then I could read the words. "Can I take a look?"

"You want to get one, or what?"

"A tattoo?" It wouldn't be my first, but he doesn't have to know that. "I've been thinking about it."

"I can give you the name of my guy. Although, he might not like working on cops." He snorts like he just had a very funny image in his mind. Before I can question his sketchy tattoo guy he shifts in his seat and offers me his left arm. I lean forward and hone in on the dreamcatcher again. "The design is just some tribal stuff that I thought would look cool. Then there's some song lyrics and the quote that's on my mother's tombstone."

I listen and nod, noticing the bit about his mother. I already knew this information from his background check but it's different hearing it from him. I'm a little jealous, wishing I could talk about my parents like him instead of locking it all away.

"They're nice." I lean in further and I can finally read the words. I'm so excited I have to read them twice. Then I feel silly because, really, this tattoo is meaningless. To me at least. It was just something that's been bothering me so bad.

"I like the dreamcatcher." I say before I can think about it. He smirks and runs a finger over the words. *Her heart is my compass and suddenly I'm home.*

"Thanks. It's new." He shrugs. "Well, my newest one. I got it the month before lockup."

"I figured it was the first. The rest of the sleeve works around it perfectly." God, why am I even talking to him? Although, this conversation is helping me calm down. I've barely thought of Aubrey in the past few minutes. My chest doesn't hurt quite as much.

"Yeah. I think it's cool when sleeves work around something really big and important but I didn't have anything like that yet and I wanted to get started. I had my guy leave the space and when I finally decided what I wanted there, he was really good at making it look like it belonged."

"Nice." I wonder why he wouldn't work on a cop. I like his work, and I'm in need of a new tattoo. It's been too long since I've gotten a dose of ink therapy. "Where does this guy work?"

"The tattoo shop on main. He, um. You can't go to him." His words are rushed and I can't help but be amused. He backtracks quickly. "It's just, he works on all of us. My group. And it would look weird if you wanted to work with him. He'd probably ask how you heard of him and you can't say me and it'd just be weird. Plus, he would wig out if a cop came sniffing around. We all would."

"Why?"

"He, um." He wipes a hand down his face. I try not to smile. I'm pretty sure this guy never realized how corrupt all the people around him were until he started working with us.

"Let me guess. He works for drugs?"

"Sometimes." He itches the dreamcatcher. "He helps out a lot. He's as far into the group as he could be without being in the group."

"Interesting."

"He doesn't deal or anything like that. He's not important." I smile.

"Dude, I'm not going to go after the tattoo guy. We can do better than that." I glance at my file. "Are you ready to do this? Because after today, there's no backing out. You'll get officers killed if you do. You'll get yourself killed. This is dangerous and you can't freak."

"I'm ready." He stares down at the table. "I need to be here. I need to do this."

"Why?"

"It's personal."

"Well, if that personal reason falls through are you going to back out?"

"It won't fall through." He sounds confident but I'm still nervous. He can't mess this investigation up. It will make my life hell.

"Well, then. Let's just get this over with." As if I've summoned them, the chief comes in with three other officers and a lawyer. Jameson settles into his chair and takes another drink of coffee. I watch him for another second before standing up and introducing myself. I'm so not in the mood for any of this today.

CHAPTER THIRTY-EIGHT
Aubrey

Myla finds me on the couch in the same clothes from earlier. I'm shaking and I know my face must be a mess. Even my neck is wet from how many tears I've shed.

"Oh my god." She rushes towards me, her backpack falling off her shoulder to the ground. Shit, her backpack. I forgot to go to school today.

Great, second day and I'm already skipping. I make a mental note to write an email or something to my professors. Then I laugh. Who knows if I'll even have tuition anyway. My mother still hasn't called. Might as well drop out now.

The laughing bubbles into uncontrollable wheezing. She wraps her arms around me, and a new wave of tears sets in. I realize after a moment that she's hugging me, but I don't want to be touched so I pull away.

Why was it so easy to let Caden hold me?

"What happened, Bree?" She always gets angry when I cry, nose crinkled and eyebrows dipping toward her nose. It's like she takes it upon herself to make sure I'm happy. It's an incredible burden, especially in the past few years.

"I told someone."

"Told someone what?" Realization washes over her but she doubts herself. It's clear in the way she shakes her head. "Wait. No. About Elliot?"

"Kind of. Not really. Well, kind of." I start sobbing again and tell her everything. Even the stuff about Lily. She sits through the whole thing, nodding occasionally. I'm not even sure how much she could understand with how thick and shaky my voice is.

When I'm all done she grabs my hand. It's contact but not too much and I give her a squeeze to let her know.

"So, he doesn't *know* know. He just, knows."

"I guess." I let out another sob. "He's a cop. What if he tries to get involved? Or what if he tells Jason and Jason doesn't want me to fight for them anymore? Or what if he decides to not like me anymore?"

"Like you anymore? As in, he likes you?" She smiles a little and inches closer. "You care that he likes you?"

"No. I mean, maybe. No. I don't like him so who cares? Not me." I think of Caden, and how good it felt for him to hold me. And how he makes me laugh. I haven't laughed like that in a long time. I haven't felt safe in a long time, but with him I feel okay. Almost happy. *Almost.*

"Okay, we'll come back to that." She squeezes my hand again and tries to smile. "He's not going to do anything as a cop. From what you've told me about him, he doesn't seem like the type. Plus, you told him Elliot is locked up and you didn't tell him his name. There's no way he would get involved."

"Shrug." The words don't make me feel much better. I want to start over this morning and take them all back. He's going to look at me different now. I didn't even know I liked how he looked at me until this moment.

I'm labeled now, like a neon sign: *victim.*

"Not that it would be a bad thing for Elliot to get in trouble. The little prick deserves to-"

"Myla." I'm too exhausted to listen to her.

"He put you in the hospital. Even if we forget about everything else he did, all the months of manipulating you, controlling you, hurting you, it all adds up to the same conclusion. He put you in the fucking hospital."

"You can stop repeating it. I remember. I was there."

"You weren't though. I remember visiting you and you were so out of it. You wouldn't tell them anything. You just kept saying that you fell. You had a handprint across your face, black and blue with a cut near the heel of his palm. Everyone knew, your mother must have known, and still- nothing."

"Stop!" I scream and stand up, not knowing what to do with all this anger building up inside me. I don't want to talk about Elliot. I want to talk about Caden and how my life is ruined now. I want to talk about Lily and how I missed her funeral. I want to talk about school and how I'm probably going to either fail, or drop out from being broke.

I'm so exhausted. I'm too exhausted to explain anything right now. I just want to crawl into a corner and sleep.

There's a bowl of fruit on the counter. I stare at it for a few seconds. One of the bananas is bruised. "Myla?"

"Yeah?"

"I'm still afraid of him." My voice starts to shake again. I've never admitted this before. Even with Caden, I didn't have to say the actual words. It feels strange, but liberating.

Elliot scared the hell out of me. I loved him more than myself. It was necessary. If I had loved myself more than him, I would have never stayed. But loving someone like that is scary, especially when they hurt you.

"Oh, Bree." Her face melts into sadness and she wipes a tear from the corner of her eyes. "I know. I'm sorry."

throw myself into her arms and let her hold me. It feels nothing like Caden. My skin crawls and I feel panic pressing down on my chest. I don't feel safe, but I force myself to stay. She clings to me like she'll never get the chance again. She might not.

After a minute, she starts moving us. I feel her shift so that only one arm is around me. We end up in my room, her pulling back the comforter for me.

"You need to get some sleep. What classes did you miss today?"

"Sociology and math."

"Were they both big lectures?"

"Yeah. No attendance." I get into the bed and bury my face in my pillow. She sits on the edge of the bed and picks a few pieces of lint off it. "I'm sorry about Lily."

"Thanks."

"I wish I could have met her."

"I don't." I reach over and touch Myla's hand. She never met any of them except Elliot, and even that only happened a handful of times. Usually not on the best of terms. "I kept you from getting pulled into that life. I'm really glad none of them ever saw you or knew about you. Some of those guys would have eaten you alive."

"I can handle myself."

"Yeah. Well," *Does that mean that I couldn't handle myself?*

"I wish I could have been there with you. I wish I could know everything you went through." I try to swallow my guilt. I've told her little pieces but she doesn't know a lot of it. It's too hard to talk about now that it's over, and while it was happening I didn't want to tell her.

At first, I felt ashamed. Then I felt too scared. Myla would have cracked her knuckles, put her hair in a ponytail, and kicked some ass. She would have helped me leave him and helped me report him and she would have made everything better. At the time, sick as it was, it wasn't what I wanted.

"You don't want to know, My. There's no reason to know the details."

"Maybe it'd take some of the weight off you."

"Maybe." I toss away the idea. It won't happen. I don't think I could talk about that stuff if I tried, anyway. Maybe there is something I can tell her though. Something to take a little bit of weight off. "My?"

"Yeah?"

"I loved him. I still do a little. He could be so kind. So loving." I wipe a tear off my cheek and look up at her. She's completely still. "He asked me to marry him once. That's what I was dreaming about last night."

"I didn't know."

"I never said yes. I told him to ask me again after he bought a ring and we just never got around to it."

"When did he ask you?"

"September, after school started. We got into a huge fight because I overheard him talking on the phone to some guy about a dead body. It totally freaked me out and I panicked. I hid in the bathroom and he forced me to open the door and I thought he was going to hurt me but he didn't, and then he promised he would never hurt me again and we slept together and it was so gentle and sweet. He sobered up and then a few days later we were in bed, and he asked me to marry him." I pause to breathe. "Sorry. I didn't mean to dump all of that."

"Don't worry about it. Seriously." She gives me a tight smile. "I bet that felt really good."

"It did." I let out one of the laughs that only happen when you're really relieved.

She bites her lip. "September, huh?"

"Yeah. He kept the promise for a while. Stayed sober."

"Until October, right?"

"Yeah. Homecoming."

"I remember that night." It was the third time she ever saw him. It was a tradition for the dance team to all wear a football player's jersey. I explained this to him and he seemed okay with it. But I uploaded a photo of me and the player together after the game, and he saw it and called me. My phone was on silent because I was at the dance. He found me anyway.

Long story, gory and short, the night ended with a bloody nose and being locked in the apartment by myself while he went out and got high. He never came back that night. He never brought up marrying me again. He broke his promise and I think he knew I wanted to break mine.

After that, he elevated. Fights happened daily. He was always paranoid. Always worried. I spent most of my time in the apartment instead of out with him. Instead of at school. Instead of at dance or other after school activities. He had become my after school activity. More accurately, he had become my after school special.

I didn't have an eighteenth birthday party. Well, I did. It involved him and me getting drunk together and having sex. He didn't hit me that night. He didn't even yell.

I quit dance for him. Quit student council. I stopped worrying about homework when he threw my math book across the room and cracked the television because I wanted to study instead of grocery shop. I stopped working out with Rob.

I had given up. I had given him my life. I was just waiting for him to take it.

I'm not sure when I started speaking out loud but I'm out of breath and Myla is looking at me with wide eyes. "I didn't know it got that bad. I mean, I did obviously. You ended up in the fricken hospital. But, still."

"Don't feel bad. I became skilled at faking it."

"Yeah." She bites her cheek and I'm pretty sure she's trying to hide a smile. "I do have to say it was interesting when you threw that fit at practice and quit. I mean, you could have just privately spoken with coach."

"And miss the opportunity to call her a self-centered bitch who's hypocritical and doesn't know what she talks about? Nope. Not a chance. It was great."

"It really was. I wanted to start a slow clap but you were burning down and I wasn't prepared to join you."

"Shrug. It's understandable."

I lay back on the bed and burrow down in the comforter. "I think I need a nap."

"I think that's a good idea." She pulls the blanket up like she's tucking me in. Then she leans over and turns the lamp off so the only light is coming through the crack between the curtains.

I close my eyes and try to calm myself down. After a few minutes, I hear the bed creak. I try to stay still, wanting her to think I fell asleep so she can do whatever it is she needs to do. I'm so selfish, always falling apart and making her drop everything to fix me.

I wait until I think she's out of the room before shifting to a more comfortable position. Then I hear her small voice whisper, "It's okay that you miss him, Bree." The words are followed by the faint click of the bedroom door closing. I stare up at the ceiling, playing those words over and over until I finally drift off to sleep.

CHAPTER THIRTY-NINE
Caden

Jason has his office pimped out for Cassie. A Disney Princess movie is on his television in the corner. I've never seen anything other than sports highlights on there. He has his couch that's usually tucked away in the far corner pulled to the center, facing the movie. His desk is covered in coloring books, crayons, plastic dinosaurs, and a miniature tea set. A veggie tray is on the corner because I told him she can't have junk food after seven.

I don't even worry about her when I close the door behind myself. Jason is sitting at the end of the couch and she's lying with her feet poking into him and her head against the edge. She's coloring and singing along with the movie playing while Jason scrolls on his phone.

Aubrey isn't here yet so I warmup with the jump rope hanging on the wall. I try to focus on my rhythm but can't keep my mind in check. What's tonight going to be like? I hope that she doesn't act weird now that I know what happened. Well, I don't know what happened exactly, but I know something happened and I'm sure that's enough to freak her out.

"Lookin' good." I almost trip on the rope when she speaks.

"Shit." The rope falls into a puddle on the floor as I turn to look at her. She's in a pair of shorts and a baggy shirt. I try not to notice how long her legs are, or how sexy.

"Sorry. I didn't mean to scare you." She bites her lip but the smile she's trying to stop still peeks through.

"You're fine."

She glances up at the office where the light is on. "Jason's here?"

"Yeah." I kick the rope out of the way and stretch my arm across my chest. "He's babysitting Cassie."

"Your parents work a lot?" I switch the arm that I'm stretching and glance up at the office window. "I'm not judging. Both of my parents are lawyers. I pretty much raised myself."

"I'm sorry to hear that." I wonder if her parents know what happened to her. From what I know about her mother, I doubt it.

I hate that. She deserved to be safe. That was their job. She was so damn young. She's still so damn young. *Shit.* Now I want to hold her again.

"What do your parents do?"

"My parents, are. Well." I tug at my hair. She opened up to me and she deserves the same back.

I suppose I can try. "My parents are gone."

"Where?" She pulls her long brown hair into a loose ponytail. I fiddle with the strings on my shorts. Just as I'm about to lie to her, it must click. "Oh. I'm so sorry."

"Don't worry about it." Her blue eyes meet mine before glancing up at the window again. When they come back they're full of understanding.

"They're yours then? The girls?"

"All mine." I try to come up with the words to explain the whole situation but I haven't been able to talk to anyone about it other than Jason. She knows they're gone, and they both are, technically. For now, that's enough.

"Is it terrible for me to say that that makes me feel a little better? Like I'm not the only one who's way too young and dealing with way too much shit?"

I laugh and shake my head. She laughs too, and it's the most beautiful sound. I don't even think before I take step toward her. She doesn't step back and I take it as a very good sign. I don't push it either though. Instead, I play it off by grabbing her hand. All her knuckles except for the middle one are healed.

"Does it hurt?" I ask, sliding the pad of my thumb along the thin scab. She lets out a breath.

"Not at all." Something in the way she's standing shifts. Her body comes forward just an inch, but it's enough to raise the tension level from a three to an eleven. I know I should drop her hand; I'm about to cross a line.

"We should start our workout. It's a school night."

"Right. We should do that." She doesn't move. Neither do I. The air around us shifts. "Caden?"

"Yeah?"

"I'm a mess." She pulls her hand away from my touch and stares at the floor. I give her time to compose herself, hoping she's not done speaking. When she looks up at me again her eyes are glossed over. "I think I'm actually kind of messed up. Like, I'm really screwed up Caden. I just want you to know."

"Okay." She knows herself more than me and if she thinks she's messed up then I'll give her that. I can still love her, even if she's a little messy.

Shit. Why did I just think that? I barely know her. "Aubrey?"

"Yeah?" The word comes fast.

"I'm a mess too. I'm not making your shit invalid, I swear, but I'm just letting you know it doesn't matter to me."

"Oh." She wipes at her eyes and smiles. "Well. Okay."

"Okay."

"Where should we start, then?"

"You need to warmup. Here, you can use the jump rope." I squat down and grab the rope. She takes it from me and moves a few steps back so she has room. The rope goes over her head once to get into the right position. Then she looks up at me.

"Caden?" The breath in my throat catches. Did I ruin it already?

"Yeah?"

"You can call me Bree."

CHAPTER FORTY
Aubrey

"Myla!" I whisper, shaking her hard. She groans and swings an arm out. It catches me in the chest, but I just shake her again.

"Go away." Her teeth are gritted.

"Myla, wake up." Something in her must register how late it is, or how concerned I sound, because she bolts upright and looks around frantically.

"I'm awake. I'm okay. You're okay! Oh my God, Aubrey. What's wrong?" Her words tumble over each other and I laugh. Why do I feel so light right now?

"Myla, calm down. I'm fine." I sit down next to her and turn her side lamp on. She squints at me and groans.

"What time is it?"

"It's only midnight you freak." I point at her alarm clock as if to prove my point. She doesn't follow my gaze. Instead, she focuses her energy on glaring at me.

"I was sleeping."

"Really? Huh. I had no idea."

"Please let me sleep."

"Give me ten minutes and then you can."

"No." She throws herself back and pulls the blanket over her head. I wait for her to say she's joking but she doesn't.

"I think I'm falling for him." I don't think I've ever seen her move so fast. The blanket hits me in the face when she throws it off.

Her lips are spread in the widest of smiles. "Caden?"

"Yeah." I bury my face in my hands. I promised myself I would never do this again. This won't end well. He'll hurt me, I just know it.

"Tell me everything. Why do you feel like that? What happened? Oh my God." She grabs my hands and pulls them away from my face. I tell her about today and her smile never slips. When I'm done she leans forward and makes a little squeak. "You're letting him call you Bree."

"Yeah." I nod quickly. Something is churning in my stomach. I've never even had a problem with being called Bree. I just told him that because I was mad at the time. Still, it became our thing.

"I need to meet this man." She declares, her hand waving in the air to make it more dramatic. I'm not entirely sure if that's a good idea yet. I don't even know if I like Caden outside of the gym. What if he's a total asshole? What if he can't handle all my baggage? I mean, I know that he said he can but I come with a lot. I can barely be touched and what guy would like that? Then another thought comes to mind and I'm filled with dread.

"He's a cop."

"Yes. We've talked about that."

"Yeah, but he's not going to like me." I bury my face again.

"Why would him being a cop mean he doesn't like you? Sigh, Bree. I think he *already* likes you."

"Yeah, but I used to sit in the passenger seat of a drug dealer's car while he made runs. I used to let him spend his dirty money on me. I used to hang out at parties where he was getting high or dealing, or both."

"You never did drugs. You never dealt drugs. You never did anything bad besides picking Elliot as a boyfriend."

I look up at her and groan. "Well, yeah. But-"

"If you 'yeah, but' me one more time I will punch you." She points a finger at me and shakes her head. "Don't mess this up before it even begins. Give him a chance to decide what he can and can't handle."

I'm just about to say 'yeah, but' when I stop myself. "Shrug."

"You should ask him out."

"What? No."

"Come on. That whole idea of a girl having to wait for the guy to ask her out is archaic. You're an MMA fighter and you're way tougher than you used to be. You don't have to sit around and wait for him."

It sounds like a fairly good idea. If he says no then the whole ordeal is over, instead of me sitting around for days just wondering. If he says yes, well. I don't know how I'll feel if he says yes. We'll cross that bridge if it comes.

"I guess it doesn't hurt to ask." She beams at me and pats me on the knee.

"That's the spirit. What are you going to ask him to do?"

"Oh. Um." Shit. That's a good question. "Help?"

CHAPTER FORTY-ONE
Aubrey

My tongue feels heavy. I've been trying to get words out all morning but nothing seems to be functioning correctly. Caden is focusing today on conditioning. We spent the first ten minutes working with the slam ropes in the corner. Neither of us said more than, "Hold them steady" or "I need some water". Very romantic.

Then we moved on to the weight bench, working once again in awkward silence. I push myself a little too hard on my last set and he needs to grab the bar for me. Once it's back in its spot I sit up and wipe my face with my shirt.

When I look up at him, I realize I'm in way over my head. He's gorgeous. His hair is cut in a fade and the top is just long enough to touch his forehead. The little strands rest against a scar there. Almost as if he can sense that I'm looking, he runs a hand through his hair, making the front piece spike and stick together.

"Dinner." The word tumbles out of my mouth, my tongue sticky and dense. He drops his hand and looks at me, his right eyebrow lifted in question.

"Dinner?"

"Yeah." I want so badly to bury my face in my hands. This is going terribly. I'm a total mess. "Dinner. With me. I was wondering." *Yoda, I am.*

This is embarrassing. He thankfully doesn't make me boil in my own misery. With a smile, he nods. "Dinner with you sounds great."

"Oh." I can't even hide my surprise. I figured he'd make up an excuse or flat out say no. Our moment the other day was probably just out of pity. Maybe this is too. I feel myself deflate."

"What night were you thinking?"

"Maybe tomorrow night?" It's what Myla and I had agreed on. It's not too last minute but it's close enough where I won't have to wait all week long. It's also a weekend so it's not a school night. This works for both myself and his girls.

"Tomorrow night works." He looks as if he's trying to calculate something in his head. Is he trying to come up with an excuse? "There's actually a place I want to bring you. It's a little unorthodox though."

My stomach is starting to churn again and I feel like I might start giggling at any moment. *When did I turn into such a school girl?* "I'm okay with that."

"Great. I could pick you up?"

"Yeah." I have to fight not to roll my eyes. Myla will be all over him when he shows up. I have no doubt that she will cancel all plans just so she can meet him. "How about six?"

"Perfect." The way his lips look when he says this melts me. His blue eyes come to meet mine, sparkling with the same excitement.

It's official. I'm a goner.

CHAPTER FORTY-TWO
Caden

"Not that one."

"You've said that four times."

"Because the last four outfits have been terrible." Caitlin gets up off my bed and walks over to my closet. "Where are you bringing her, again?"

"The diner."

"What diner?" She pauses with her hand on a flannel and looks back at me. "Oh, god. You're bringing her to Karen's?"

"Yeah." I hope the information doesn't freak her out. Karen was my mother's best friend all throughout high school. We used to go to the diner for every special occasion. It's a thirty-minute drive but that never stopped us.

"You like her." She doesn't look at me but her voice is a little too steady, like it involves effort to keep it that way. "Like, you must *really* like her."

"If you don't want me to bring her there I understand. I didn't even think." Okay, I did a little. I was excited to share something special with her. What I didn't think about was the effect it would have on the girls.

"We haven't been there since mom."

"I know." I wait for her to say or do something. She's standing frozen, and I can't see her face. Finally, she speaks.

"She'll love it." She pulls a long sleeve Henley t-shirt from the closet. When she looks up at me she's smiling. "Karen always cranks her air so this will keep you warm. The gray will make your blue eyes pop."

"I don't care about my stupid eyes."

She sighs. "You should. They're your money makers." She grabs a pair of cargo shorts off the floor and throws them on the bed next to the shirt. "Now shower and get ready. You shouldn't be late."

"Are you sure you're okay watching Cassie?"

"Yeah. I have homework anyway." She shrugs but doesn't make eye contact with me. I think it makes her feel weird when we talk about our situation. Like it's easier to just forget.

"Okay. Make sure she's in bed by ten." She pauses at the door, her hand resting on the wood.

"You won't be home by ten?"

"Oh. I don't know." *God, this is awkward.* I haven't dated since before I got the girls, and I lived on my own then. I didn't have to run my plans by anyone. I didn't have to worry about bringing her home quietly or sneaking her out in the morning.

Shit. Am I going to have to do that? Surely not tonight. I'll worry about it a different time. "I can be home sooner if you want me to."

"No. It's just, weird." She bites her lip and the air feels heavy. Is she about to ask me not to go? I would do it for her but it'd be hard. Aubrey's the first person to make me feel anything since my parents. Even with Jason and the girls, it always feels like I'm dragging through the motions. Like it's all scripted by some cracked out screenwriter. I've felt empty for so damn long.

"I can stay home." It hurts to even say.

"No. Absolutely not. You deserve this." It's so out of character that I need to do a double take to make sure the words actually came from her. She looks just as surprised, her cheeks flushed with embarrassment. "Just drive safe."

The words are loaded. I promise her that I will.

CHAPTER FORTY-THREE
Caden

I'm crazy nervous, my stomach flipping worse than any time I've gotten in the ring. I check my phone three times to make sure I have the apartment number right, then stare the number four down for a while. It takes an embarrassing amount of time before I bring my fist to the door.

I knock three times and wait. A girl with bright auburn hair answers, out of breath and smiling. "Hi!"

"Hey." I glance over her shoulder at an empty living room. "I'm here for Aubrey. Bree." I sound like a total idiot.

"*Bree*," she emphasizes the nickname with a smile, "will be ready soon. I'm Myla."

"Hey." The famous Myla. I nervously scratch at my chin, just now realizing I should have shaved. This is possibly more important than meeting Aubrey's parents. Actually, I'm sure of that.

"It's nice to meet you," I say while offering her my hand. She smirks before taking it.

"Nice to meet you, too." She's still smiling, and I hope it's a good sign. "Do you want a drink or anything?"

"No. I'm good." She sizes me up and crosses her arms. The apartment is nice. I look around and take it all in. It's big and roomy. Their living room has a cream-colored couch with purple throw pillows, and a large television mounted on the wall. I can only see part of a hallway and a glimpse of the kitchen, through the opening over the breakfast bar. The appliances look new and possibly stainless. I imagined worse.

When my attention focuses back on Myla she's staring me down. I flinch away and try to give her a warm smile, finding her a bit unnerving. "You know about her past, yeah?" Her voice is a low whisper. It's not concerned or nice, it's threatening.

"A little, yes."

"I let him get to her. I helped her get ready for their first date, just like tonight. I won't make that same mistake again. I won't let you ruin her. So help me God, I will chop your-"

"Hey!" Aubrey turns the corner and smiles at us. She's in a soft pink sundress with a jean jacket over it. Her brown hair is loosely curled, falling over her shoulders and down her sides. It's longer than I thought it'd be.

She is so incredibly beautiful, it makes my chest ache.

"Hey. You look amazing." I'm jittery and breathless, which is ridiculous. I've dated before. Okay, I've *slept* with girls before. I suppose this is the first real date since, well, I can't remember.

"Thank you." She tugs on one of her curls and gives her friend a pointed look. Myla steps back, her nice smile returning from earlier. Smile or no smile, I still fear her.

"Well, you two have fun tonight." She walks up to Aubrey and gives her a tight hug. If I'm not mistaken, the low rumble coming from them means that Myla is whispering in Aubrey's ear. When they pull away, Aubrey puts a hand against her face, playfully pushing her away. In return, Myla sticks her tongue out at her.

"Are you ready?" Aubrey tugs on that same curl again and walks through the open door. I start to close the door behind myself and catch Myla watching me. With Aubrey already walking down the hall, I take a second to lean toward Myla and whisper. "She's safe."

Her shoulders deflate in relief, her lips forming two silent words. *Thank you.*

CHAPTER FORTY-FOUR
Aubrey

It's kind of adorable that he's nervous. He keeps tapping his fingers against the steering wheel and asking me if I'm too cold or if the music is too loud. We've been listening to the Frozen soundtrack but I think he's too nervous to notice. I feel bad pointing it out so I try not to ignore it. Instead, I focus on Myla's words from earlier. *Relax, Bree. Try and have a good time tonight.*

Easier said than done. My nerves are on fire and I can't get my hands to stop shaking. I end up tucking them under my legs to hide them. When he asks if I'm fine, for the third time, I decide to be honest. "Um, maybe we could listen to something else?"

"Oh. Wow. Yeah." His cheek flush red as he slams a finger into the button that switches it from the CD to the radio. A country station is on and he notices that I wince. "No country, either?"

"It's not terrible." He laughs. I'm obviously not as good of a liar as I thought.

"You can change the station. Just turn the knob." I almost laugh at the fact that I have to turn a knob. His truck is a little old school, but strangely well kept.

I fiddle with the knob until I hear the familiar chorus of a Pink Floyd song. I take the liberty to turn the music up a little and start drumming my shaking fingers against my thigh. It helps, especially when he looks over at me and smiles.

"I don't think I pictured you as the kind of person to like Classic Rock."

"No?" I look over at him and see that he's smiling. This is nice. Comfortable. I can do this. "Did you think I'd like some boy band or something?"

"No. I guess I didn't think anything." He shrugs. "Have you always been into this music?"

"Not really. No." I tuck my hands again. This conversation is going in the wrong direction.

"What changed?" Our first date hasn't even started and here's Elliot, already ruining things. Caden turns the volume down and I decide to give him the truth.

"My ex had a really big record collection. It was mostly classic rock and it grew on me." My skin itches. It's weird to call him my ex. He seems like so much more than that.

"Oh." He taps on the wheel. I try to clamp my mouth shut but now that we've started it's too hard to stop. Words start spilling out before I can filter them.

"I spent a lot of time alone in the apartment. I probably listened to every single record." I smooth down my dress. "I have my own now."

"Own collection?"

"Yeah. Not as big as his or anything, but it's mine."

"So it's better."

"It is." He looks over at me and gives me an understanding smile. I have no idea if he understands me at all but at least he's trying.

"Why were you there alone all the time?"

"He," I pause. What should I say? He had to sell drugs and he didn't like me coming with him? He liked to lock me up so he knew I couldn't run?

"Never mind. You don't have to tell me."

"Oh, it's fine." I like the honesty streak I'm on, so I keep going. If I'm really going to do this, let someone in, I'm going to do it all the way. "It's just, um. You're a cop."

"Yes. I am." He shifts in his seat and I can tell he's preparing for the conversation. Well, if he's prepared then we might as well have it. I reach over and turn the volume down to almost nothing. *Here we go.*

"He used to do some bad stuff. He didn't like me being around when he did it. I guess he wanted to protect me from getting caught doing what he was doing. I think he was worried about bringing me around the people he was around too." I think of his group of friends and cringe.

"He wanted to protect ya, huh?" He finds this funny but it's the wrong kind of funny. He's shaking his head and his hands grip the leather steering wheel, making his knuckles white. I know what he's thinking. We're both thinking it.

"He was the only one who was allowed to hurt me." I hear the ghost of his voice say it along with me. It gives me chills.

"That's bullshit. No one is allowed to hurt you." He gives me a side glance.

"At least, not anymore."

"Well, yeah." I trace my finger over one of the flowers by my knee. "He's in prison, so."

"For how long?"

"A few years, I think." He arches an eyebrow at me and for whatever reason I give him even more information. "He got arrested with his best friend, James."

"What were his charges? The ex, not the friend." I can sense the cop coming out in the conversation. It makes me nervous.

"I honestly don't know. He asked me to come to the trial but I pretty much told him hell no. I'll get out of school before he gets out of prison, and I'll be long gone."

I sigh. "I don't know his charges but it had to do with drugs, like dealing them. He had a gun too. And lots of money. Honestly, there's more but considering he only got a few years I have a feeling they didn't find out."

I probably shouldn't have said that. Is it illegal for me to know things about him and not come forward? I have a feeling it's a blurry line because Caden looks over at me and his eyes are uncomfortable. That's probably why he changes the subject.

"Well, maybe I can see your collection sometime."

"Yeah. That can definitely be arranged."

"Good." He turns the music up a little, enough where we aren't pressured to talk but not so much where we can't. It's a commercial now so I think of more conversation.

"So, where are we going?"

"It's a diner. It's a bit of a drive but we're almost there."

"Okay."

"The owner, her name is Karen, she used to be my mom's best friend." He taps a finger against the steering wheel. If I didn't know any better, I would think he's relaxed. I know him better. "She makes the best milkshakes. You'll love them."

"Awesome. I'm excited." I smile over at him even though he's not looking at me. I want him to feel comfortable talking about his life. Especially the hard stuff.

We take a right at a stop sign in the middle of nowhere. The road stretches endlessly and I watch for any sign of life. In two or three minutes, we come across a small building with all its lights on.

The diner is painted a pale blue, and the sign is neon pink. I feel like I'm trapped in an old fifties move. There's six cars in the parking lot. Who the hell would drive all this way to get diner food? Oh, right. Us.

"Where are we, anyway?" He laughs as he switches the engine off.

"I know it seems like the middle of nowhere but there's actually another town just a few minutes down the road. We just came from the wrong direction." I open my door and he does the same. The air is warm, with a nice breeze. It's a perfect night. I look up at the sky and see a thousand stars. I can't imagine how many there would be without the neon sign. Caden follows my gaze. "I've come out here a few times, since my parents. We haven't eaten here since then but sometimes I'll take a drive to clear my head. All roads seem to lead back to here."

"It's nice that you have a place like that."

"It is." He exhales and it's very loud in such an open space. "Anyway, you can see for miles out here at night. Karen closes at midnight, sometimes sooner if it's dead, and she turns all the lights off when she does. The sky is practically more light than darkness then."

"That sounds really nice." I look over at him. "That place I showed you, with the rocks. I used to do the same thing at night. Sometimes, I'd fall asleep and stay all night. It felt safe."

"I'm glad you had that."

"Me too." I kick the ground. How long have we been standing out here? We probably look strange to the people inside.

He looks over at me and I look at him. His eyes are almost as bright as that obnoxious sign. The look he's giving me is intense, full of something he can't say but I'd love to hear. It takes my breath away. "Let's get inside. I'm starved."

He moves forward and I walk behind him, letting him lead. The inside of the diner is exactly how I imagined. The floor is tiled, black and white, and the booths are different pastel colors. A waitress in a pale-yellow dress is wiping down the counter. She looks up at us as we walk in and smiles.

"Welcome to Karen's." Caden smiles and nods.

"Is Karen in?"

"She's in the back. Who's callin'?"

"Caden." He slips into a booth next to a window and gestures for me to sit across from him. The waitress pauses, like she's heard the name before, then disappears through a door. There's a pile of menus stacked against the wall and I grab one. Caden does the same but I have a feeling he has the thing memorized.

"Caden!" An older woman, probably in her mid-forties, comes around the corner. She looks out of place in here, with dark blue jeans and a flowy dress shirt. Like she's time traveled. I suppose we look the same. Caden slides out of the booth and goes to her like he's magnetized.

Despite the fact that she's shorter and much thinner, she seems to envelope him in her arms. They look comfortable together. When she finally pulls away from him, she rests her hands on his face. "It's been too long, Caden."

"I know." His voice comes out thick. "I'm sorry."

"Don't be sorry." She wipes at her eyes and gives him a smile. Then her gaze focuses on me and I feel a thousand pounds heavier. "Oh. I figured you'd be with the girls."

"No. This is my, um. My friend, Bree." His face scrunches up and I know he must be nervous.

"Bree. It's very nice to meet you." She comes forward, leaving Caden behind. Her arms swarm around me and pull me into a hug.

"Oh, she actually doesn't like being-"

I remove myself from her arms and give Caden a reassuring smile. "It's okay." Even as I say this, my chest is tightening.

Then Karen gives me a look that feels a loaded with pressure. Now that I think about it, this is the closest I'll get to meeting his parents.

"It's very nice to meet you, Bree." She looks over at Caden, then back at me. "First date?"

I laugh at the look on Caden's face and nod. "Well, then. The food is on the house."

"Karen." Caden warns. She gives him a dirty look.

"Oh, you hush. Sit down and enjoy your night." Caden listens to her, sliding back into the booth. I follow his lead and go back to the menu. There's way too many options here. He watches me read and I start to feel nervous.

"Any suggestions?"

"She makes a really good burger but I'm getting her loaded french toast."

"French toast? It's dinner."

He shakes his head in disappointment. "Live a little. Breakfast for dinner is the best kind of breakfast."

"Hmm," I pick at the menu. I don't even see loaded french toast, just french toast. Karen comes up to the table with a waitress pad and pen.

"What will it be?"

"Oh. I'm not sure if she's ready-"

"No. I'm ready. You go first." I close the menu and listen to him rattle off his order comfortably.

"Loaded french toast, chocolate milkshake, and a side of fries." I look at him.

"Fries?"

"Yeah. For the milkshake." I stare at him like he's completely insane.

Oh, what the hell.

"I'll do the same." I tell Karen. She smiles at me and writes it down. When she's gone, Caden starts staring at his hands. I wonder if this will be the kind of date where we talk easily, or sit in awkward silence. I'm really hoping it's the first.

CHAPTER FORTY-FIVE
Caden

We sit in silence for less than a minute. It doesn't have time to become awkward. She speaks first and we fall easily into a conversation about the gym. I tell her about meeting Jason after high school. We fought against each other for a while, being in the same weight class, and when I was looking for a new place to fight his gym seemed like the obvious choice.

"Why did you need a new place to fight?"

"The place I was at was very corrupt. You had to know a person to know a person to know a person to get anywhere. I hadn't been in the business long, I kind of came out of nowhere, and my coaches didn't think I deserved a spot in the higher levels. Jason believed different."

"You never got there, though."

"No. You're right, I didn't." I unwrap my utensils just to have something to focus on. "That's the contract I gave up last year."

"Because of your parents?"

"Am I that obvious?"

"No." She smiles at me and I feel at ease. "Don't feel bad. You figured out my stuff too."

"Not all of it." There's still a few mysteries when it comes to her. I know she was in a crappy relationship but I don't know how far it ever went, or if she ever got involved with the illegal shit he was doing. I'm not sure if I want to know.

"No. Not all of it." She follows my lead and unwraps her utensils as well. She must be nervous too. *Thank God.* "I'm not an idiot though. It's not like I have you all figured out." That's true. She doesn't know about my mom.

Karen shows up with our food and I'm relieved. Aubrey looks at her plate with wide eyes and I wonder if she knew what loaded french toast was. Probably not, at least not Karen's version. The french toast is crusted with crushed captain crunch cereal and topped with chocolate chips, warm chocolate sauce, powdered sugar, and whipped cream.

"Wow." Aubrey hasn't even picked up her fork yet. Or looked away from her plate. I can't help but smile at her expression. We thank Karen as she places our milkshakes in front of us, then she leaves us again.

"There's no way I'll eat all of this." Aubrey announces as she pokes at the whipped cream with her fork.

"I'll eat whatever you don't." I grab the syrup and add it to the top of my french toast. Her eyes get bigger.

"You need even more sugar?"

"French toast without syrup? You're kidding." She cautiously takes the syrup from me when I offer it to her. I proudly watch as she drizzles a little over the top of the two slices. She scrapes a few chocolate chips off the top and cuts a bite. I wait for her to tell me what she thinks. It's almost instant. "Holy shit." She says, her mouth full. I laugh and take a bite myself. Ah, just like I remembered.

"I know. It's good." She laughs and nods, taking another bite. I grab a fry and dip it in my shake before plopping it in my mouth. She does the same, giving me a proud smile. She looks so good like this, laughing and messing around. *Happy.*

"So, the girls," she says after a few minutes of stuffing our faces. I stop cutting the toast and look up at her. She's not looking at me.

"Yes?"

"They're officially yours?"

"Yup. I get to sign permission slips." It sounds silly but that was the moment I realized that I was really responsible for two girls. Caitlin had brought home her slip to try out for the volleyball team and I had just stared at her. Now, it doesn't even cross my mind that it's unusual.

"Very official." She jokes.

"Yeah. I wouldn't have taken them in, you know, but signing permission slips is really my calling. I didn't want to miss out on the opportunity."

"Oh, totally understandable." She dips another fry in the shake and I watch her eat it. As she chews, her freckles dance along her cheekbones. God, she's beautiful.

"No, seriously though. It wasn't really something I had to think about. They're my family. They had to spend two nights in a foster home while I got everything sorted out. Two nights was two too many. They were so scared and sad and they needed me." I hang my head. The government wasn't fond of giving them to a twenty-two-year-old who punched people for a living. Those two days were hell. I explain this to her and she sighs.

"So, is that why you quit?"

"Sort of." I don't want to tell her. I haven't told anyone. Jason only knows because he was there that night. Karen only knows because she helped me legally. I've never had to say the words. I've never had to admit it. "My dad is dead."

She pauses. "I know. I'm sorry."

"It's fine." I put my fork down and clamp my hands together under the table to hide that they are shaking. "My mom's not."

"Not dead?" Her eyebrows close in on each other. "I thought you said?" She doesn't finish because she doesn't have to. We were both there. We both know what I said.

"My dad died almost a year ago. A year ago. On the twenty-sixth, actually." I see something come across her face. Recognition maybe? Clarity?

"That's why you freaked out."

"Yeah." I keep holding my hands. The shaking is getting worse. "We went to my dad's gravestone, like we do every month. I mean, I go more often but I only make the girls do it once a month. Caitlin knows my mom is alive but it was kind of easier to tell Cassie that she was dead."

"Oh." She's quiet and I can't tell what she's thinking. I hate that.

"My mom was still alive when my dad died. He was alone when he got in the car accident. She still had custody, that's not when I got the girls. They were still hers and I was still fighting. I actually had a fight the day after my dad's funeral. That's the fight that Jason talks about when he talks about me fighting with my anger. I almost killed the guy that night." I let out a deep breath. This feels better than I thought it would. And she doesn't look disgusted yet.

"So, that's why you quit? Because you almost killed him?"

"No." *God dammit.* My hands won't stop. "About a month after my dad died, three weeks actually, my mom unraveled. She just went crazy. She would be completely depressed some days, not wanting to do anything. Caitlin was practically raising Cassie for a while there. She thought she had it under control so she would lie to me when I would call her to check in. I didn't even know any of it was happening.

"Then my mom started getting these manic episodes. It started out simple enough, according to Caitlin, but the night of my fight against Noll I got a phone call from the police department.

"Just an hour before getting into the ring, I found out that my mother tried killing herself by locking the garage door and keeping the car running. She had just gotten back from the grocery store. Cassie had fallen asleep in the backseat. She was so fucking out of it she didn't even remember Cassie was back there. They both would have died if Caitlin hadn't come home from school."

"Oh my god." She breathes out the words and her entire body seems to shiver. I look at my milkshake. It's melted now but that's okay, as long as she doesn't run. If she runs, I don't think I'll recover. I look down at my hands and they've finally stopped shaking. "Caden?"

"What?"

"I'm just, I'm so sorry."

"Thank you." I grab the milkshake and take a drink. She watches me as I do it and I hope I haven't ruined everything. The last thing I need is for my first date in over a year to be with a girl who pities me. Thankfully, when I look up at her she isn't looking at me like I'm sad or pathetic. She's smiling.

"Thank you for telling me."

"Thanks for listening." I shake my head. "You have no idea how good that felt."

"I can imagine." She steals my milkshake and takes a drink.

"Excuse me?" I cock an eyebrow at her but can't keep my angry face straight because she has a little chocolate mustache on her upper lip. I reach across the table without thinking and wipe it clean. The shiver that runs through her body is entirely too satisfying. I can think of a few other ways I'd like to make her shiver.

"Mine was all gone." She shrugs in explanation and I can't be mad. She can steal my milkshake anytime she wants. I would give her anything. *God, this is dangerous.* I'm too wrapped up in her. "So, you quit because you got custody of the girls?"

"Yup. I think my flight took off right as my fight should have started. I didn't want that life anymore. A UFC contract doesn't work when you're handed two girls and a house to take care of. Jason helped me out immediately. He was at the fight with me and flew home with me. I don't know how I would have gotten through all of that without him. He never once told me I should stay and fight, like every other person was. He understood and he supported me. He was a damn good friend up until then, but that's when he became a brother."

"Good." She reaches over and offers me her hand. I place one of my own in her palm and am relieved to see it's still not shaking. She squeezes it, closing her cool fingers around mine. "I'm glad you had him, too. From what I can tell he's a really great guy."

"He is." I squeeze her hand back. When was the last time I held a hand other than the girls'? I can't even remember. I should be holding my mother's but she doesn't want to see me. Doesn't want to see any of us, even Karen. I push the thoughts away. The doctor's promise she'll get better. "Are you still coming tomorrow night?"

"Yeah. Do I need to bring anything?"

"You can bring some chips or something to snack on. We'll order pizza too."

"Okay." She starts playing with my fingers, examining each one. I feel the tip of her thumb pass across a callus and I shift to hide the fact that something's stirring inside of me. "What time do you want me over? I know they don't start until later."

"You can come whenever. We'll probably get pizza for six or seven. You're more than welcome to come then."

"Perfect." I watch her lips form the word and decide that I will not end this night without kissing her. I change the subject, in dire need of a distraction.

"So, how's school?" She starts in on a rant about classes and homework. I listen to her every word, hooked. She tells me that her major isn't declared, because of her mother, but she's going for social work. This makes me smile. The social worker who helped me with my sisters was a saint. Aubrey would be just as good as her, if not better.

She tells me her parents are convinced she's going to go to law school, and she's entertaining the idea because it's easier. They apparently wouldn't understand why she wants to be a social worker.

"What do you want to do as a social worker?" I ask, finishing off my shake.

The smile she gives me is nervous. "I'd like to work with survivors of assault and abuse. Actually, I think it'd be cool to run a clinic for them with self-defense classes and stuff like that. As a group therapy kind of thing."

My throat closes for a moment. This girl is too damn good for what she's been dealt. "That's awesome. Jason would help with that, if you wanted." I grab her hand again. "So would I."

With bright red cheeks, she shifts the topic and asks about my career. I tell her that I didn't want to at first, it was just something secure with benefits for the girls. Now, my opinion has changed. I really like doing what I do. Not as much as fighting, but I'll never go back to that. She makes a face at that, but doesn't interrupt.

When I tell her that I feel close to a promotion, she does a shimmy in excitement. I want to tell her about the investigation but keep my mouth shut. It's not worth losing my job.

I turn the conversation back to her and she talks about the things she used to love. She used to dance, both ballet and competitive. Ballet was more of a hobby while competitive was a lifestyle. Cassie would just about die to talk to her about all of that, and I tell her so. That makes her smile again.

For a while, she talks about school and all the other things she was active in. She even talks about the ex. Just a simple, "he didn't like that we were different ages and I had to go to school. I quit everything to make him happy. He liked spending time with me."

I wish she would tell me who 'he' is, but then I'd be tempted to look him up in the system, and that's a fire able offense. He's not worth it. Not yet, at least, so I try not to ask questions about him. He liked spending time with her and made her quit all her favorite things, yet he would make her stay in his apartment alone all the time? Sounds like a controlling bastard. Anger bubbles in my gut, so I switch the topic to Myla. Her whole face lights up.

"I'm glad you got to meet her. I wouldn't have heard the end of it if she didn't get the chance to at least see you."

"Hopefully I passed the test." She throws her head back and laughs.

"You didn't." She says, breathless and wiping her eye with a free hand. I freeze. That's not good. Why is she laughing? She must see my reaction because she gets serious and shakes her head. "Not a bad thing. You're the first person I've dated since, well, and she's very protective. She's the only person, besides you now, who knows what happened. Not the gory details or anything but enough to understand. She's like a mom, a personal security guard, and the KGB all in one."

"Great."

"It is." She says it in a way that's comforting. "She'll be like that until she trusts you, but she also wants me to be happy. I think it's her number one goal in life, to show me that I can actually be happy again. So, if she approves of you you're not just the normal in. You are *in*."

No pressure. I try not to worry about it. I've never felt so serious about someone I've just met. I don't see her being happy as being a future problem for her. Like I've said, I'll give her anything. The world, if she lets me.

"She threatened my dick." I inform her.

She chokes on her laughter. "Yeah. Well, like I said. You're not in yet."

"Fingers crossed that it happens soon."

She looks at me and an odd expression comes over her face. Then her nose scrunches in the most adorable way. "I think you're good."

CHAPTER FORTY-SIX
Caden

The kiss starts out gentle, but when I try to pull away she follows. Before I know it, her hands are tangled in my short hair and I'm pushing her against the apartment door. I drown in her, not feeling like I need any air. It's a dangerous, intoxicating, feeling.

Proving that she's much stronger than me, she pulls away first. Her cheeks are flushed as she straightens my flannel.

"Sorry. I just haven't kissed anyone in a long time." She lets out a shaky breath and peeks up at me.

"It's fine. I haven't either." At least not like that.

"It feels good." She sounds guilty from the confession. I smile and rub my nose against hers, wanting more than anything to kiss her again.

"Yeah. It does."

She bites her lips, sending me over the edge. Without thinking, I dive back in. Then something shifts and we're falling. I end up in a squat, catching her just before she hits the ground.

Myla is staring at us with devil eyes. She's in flannel pajamas and her hair is a rat's nest on top of her head. She looks like she's been forcing herself to stay awake, and apparently this has caused a terrible mood.

"Sorry. I thought I heard something." She glares at me, then smiles sweetly at Aubrey. I can't even be upset. This night has been too amazing.

"Yeah. Sorry." Aubrey is breathless as she pushes her hair off her face. She turns to me and puts a hand on my chest. I want to bring her home with me. I don't want to be without her. I don't even care if we don't do anything, I just want to listen to her talk. I just want to lay beside her and breathe her in. I could do that for hours. "I had a really good night, Caden."

"You have no idea." The words are embarrassing but I'm so far out of my head right now I don't care. I don't even notice Myla glaring at me. All I can see is Aubrey, standing just a foot away. God, I need to kiss her again.

"I'll see you tomorrow." Her hand is still on my chest and she glances over her shoulder at her friend. I'm not sure what kind of face she makes but it gets Myla to walk away. Once we're alone, I wrap my arms around her waist and pull her in. Her lips find mine easily and I decide that I can get very used to this. It already feels like a habit.

This kiss stays gentle, and it's over way too fast. I let her go when she pulls away, knowing her issue with being confined. She smiles at me and gives a little wave, fading into the apartment as I stand at the door. "Good night, Caden."

"Good night, Bree." I stand there and watch her disappear, the close the door. When it clicks shut I sag, putting my hands against the wall to steady myself.

Fuck. That girl has me in way over my head. I'm doomed.

CHAPTER FORTY-SEVEN
Aubrey

"Give me a second."

"No."

"I need to pee!" She chases me into the bathroom, catching the door when I go to close it. "You're pathetic."

"I've been worried. It's past midnight."

"It is not." Is it really? I know we spent a long time talking at the diner and the drive was a little far, but after that we only drove around for a half-hour. Maybe an hour.

Shit. It must really be after midnight. I finish peeing and try to ignore her. It doesn't work.

"Seriously, I was worried."

"I'm sorry. I didn't know I had a curfew." I wash my hands vigorously and try to breathe through my anger. It's understandable that she would be worried but I had an amazing night and she's ruining it.

"You don't. I'm sorry." She looks at me in the bathroom mirror and gives me her best 'forgive me' smile. I smile back, never being able to stay mad at her. I'm way too excited to tell her everything about tonight, anyway.

We talk while I change into pajamas, pour myself water, and pack my gym bag for the morning. She barely interrupts me, which is a good sign. When I get to the end and tell her that kissing him felt like coming up for air, she squeals. Every time I stop talking, she prompts me to continue. "I think I'm out of things to say." I finally tell her. She shakes her head, sitting down on the corner of my bed.

"Are you going to go out with him again?"

"Yes." I don't even have to think about it. Not for a second. Tonight was perfect. It was incredibly comfortable and easy. It was like eating dinner with a friend who I'm also attracted to. Insanely attracted to. Like, want to jump his bones attracted to. "I'm seeing him tomorrow but it's not a date."

"Oh, right. The pay per view thing?"

"Yeah." Now that I think about it, it'll be awkward making Jason a third-wheel. I wonder if he'll mind. He's usually so laid back.

Just thinking of tomorrow gives me goosebumps. I'll get to see Caden twice. Myla leans in for a hug and I let her. It makes my chest hurt but I count to five before pulling away. When I do, she stands up and smiles at me.

"Bree. I'm happy for you. Tonight was huge."

"Yeah. I guess it was."

"I like him." She announces, hands on her hips as if the authoritative stance makes it official.

"You barely met him." She's walking towards the door and stops when she hears this. She turns around and stares at me, a look of wonder on her face.

"Your smile tonight. I haven't seen that one in a long time." She nods. "I like him."

CHAPTER FORTY-EIGHT
Aubrey

Elliot is sitting across from me. His tattoos wrap around his arms and his messy curls invade his forehead. I want so badly to push them back but for some reason I know I shouldn't touch him.

He leans forward and puts his elbows on the table. Where are we? It looks oddly familiar. Pink booths and tiled floors.

"You're happy."

"I am." I lean forward as well, feeling brave. Why do I feel brave? Am I safe here? There's no way.

"I tried to make you happy."

"Maybe at first." I push my curled hair off my shoulder. I'm in a dress. Are we on a date? He stopped bringing me on those. "You stopped trying to make me happy a long time ago."

"Yeah. I guess I did." He dips a french fry into a milkshake. This feels wrong. Very wrong. He's not supposed to be here. I feel panic welling up in my chest. "I miss you."

"I miss you too." I pause. "Well, I miss parts of you."

"You're supposed to love your boyfriend for all the parts. Didn't anyone ever tell you that?" I sigh and something like anger flashes across his face. "He'll hurt you too."

I cross my arms. "He won't."

"He will. You don't deserve to be happy." He looks up at me and his face has changed. He's someone I recognize.

I shake my head. I don't want to hear these things from Caden. Wait. Elliot. Wait. I can't tell. Everything is fuzzy and those words just keep ringing in my ears.

You don't deserve to be happy. You don't deserve to be happy. You don't deserve to be happy.

CHAPTER FORTY-NINE
Caden

Aubrey's hair is still curled, pulled into a loose ponytail. Black yoga pants hug every curve, and her purple tank top dips down just enough to show her sports bra underneath. It took a lot of strength to walk away from her last night, and it's taking more now. She's sexy as hell.

I force myself to look away while she drops her bag and starts to stretch out. The last thing I need is to study her flexibility.

When she finishes stretching, I hear her clear her throat. I glance over to find her looking up at me, as if she's expecting something.

Oh, right. I'm supposed to train her.

"I figured we could mess around in the ring, today." Her face blooms with excitement and I backtrack. "Just sparring."

I grab my gloves and watch her do the same. The pout she gives me is adorable.

"No real fighting?"

"Not yet." I feel bad when disappointment registers on her face. Honestly, I don't think Jason would even be okay with us sparring, but it's a risk I'm willing to take.

"You know, I'm not really a fighter if I don't fight."

"Yeah, well." I head toward the ring and she follows. "I won't tell anyone if you don't."

She scoffs but she's smiling. It feels good to be messing around like this, as if nothing has changed. It's exactly what I needed to happen. The one thing I didn't want was for things to grow awkward between us at the gym.

I push open the gate and settle in the middle. Being here feels amazing. She stops a few feet away from me and takes in her surroundings.

While she looks around, I look at her. Her gloves are already on, adjusted and ready to go. I think those gloves are sexier than lingerie. Possibly. I'm not properly educated on the issue yet.

"First things first. I have five main rules of fighting." Like she's channeling Caitlin, her eyes roll.

"We aren't even fighting."

"We're in the ring. It's enough." I put up my first finger. "Never move back in a straight line. Always move side to side."

"That one, I knew."

"Okay. Number two, never set too long." She scrunches her eyebrows, so I elaborate. "Never stay in one place for too long. Always be moving, hopping, adjusting."

"Easy enough."

I put up the third finger. "Use your opponent's energy against them. Always redirect. We'll practice that one a lot, because it's much easier said than done."

She rubs at her eyes. "This is a lot at once."

"I'll write them down. Next one is pretty obvious. Know how they fight. Football and basketball players watch game tapes, and we study too. If a fighter is good on the ground, keep them on their feet. If they do bring you on the ground, steal their confidence. Use their own tricks on them."

"Can we practice that one, too? That one doesn't even sound easy."

Her bright blue eyes are wide open in confusion. I laugh at how damn adorable she is. "We can practice all of them. Here's the last one, then we can get to the fun stuff."

She gives me a stiff salute. "Pay attention to habits. Just like poker players have tells, so do fighters. Learn them, then play them to your advantage."

Now that the final rule is done, she's impatient. I watch her pace back and forth inside the ring. "Someone excited?"

"Yup." She hops a little and comes forward, offering me her right glove. I tap it with mine. Then I tap it again. On the third one, she blocks and throws a punch. It's got too much heat for a sparring session but she immediately hops back and readjusts. We go back and forth until her shin catches my calf. It barely hurts but I call it for a breather. She puts her gloves on her hips and exhales.

"Feel good?"

"Yeah." She looks up at me through her eyelashes. "It felt great." The words are breathless and airy, like she just told me a dirty confession.

"Good." I step forward. It's been killing me not to touch her. Not to kiss her. The gym won't be empty for long, we probably only have ten or fifteen more minutes. I gauge her reaction and take another step forward when I see that she's smiling.

She moves like a magnet toward me until she's wrapped in my arms, but it's clear by the way her breathing shifts that she's not comfortable there. I back away, giving her some space to breathe and settling my hands carefully on her hips.

"I'm going to kiss you now." I don't know why I tell her. Maybe because I'm afraid last night was a fluke. Maybe because I'm afraid to push her too far. Maybe because her ex probably never respected her enough to do so.

I duck my head down and catch her lips with my own. They stick, then move gently against mine. She tastes like toothpaste and cinnamon sugar. Weird combination, yet perfect.

When I go to pull away she wraps one arm around my neck to keep me there. Her glove hits the back of my head but I don't mind. Without meaning to, I'm pulling her into me so our hips are flush against each other. She doesn't panic, just kisses me harder. I push my lips harder against hers and moan. I need to stop this before we get caught, but it feels so good. Finally, she proves to be stronger than me and pulls away.

The gym doors creak open and we push away from each other, both out of breath and shaking. Jason stops short, clipboard in one hand and his bag in the other. My chest cavity feels like it's about to crack open from how hard my heart is beating.

This could go two ways. He could have seen that we were just kissing, or he could have missed it, and just be mad that we're in the ring together. Either way, my head's on the block.

"Am I interrupting?"

"No." Aubrey's voice cracks. She stares at me like I'm supposed to hold the answers. I mean, he is my best friend and she's my, well, something.

I walk over to the edge of the ring and lean my weight on the corner post. With a forced nonchalance, I cross my forearms and smile over at him. All he does is raise his eyebrow at me, unimpressed.

"What's up, man?" I challenge him. He glances at Aubrey before looking back at me.

"You tell me?"

"We're sparring." I shift my weight to seem more relaxed. "Casually, of course."

"Of course." He glances at Aubrey, again, before looking back at me. "Can I see ya in my office?"

"Dude." I can see Aubrey shift uncomfortably out of the corner of my eye.

"Just really quick. Come on." He nods to Aubrey. "Why don't you go do some conditioning."

"Yeah. Okay." She takes her gloves off and exits the ring. In a hurry, she crosses the entire gym like she can't get far enough away from us. I glare at Jason.

"I'm not going to your office."

"I'd prefer if we talked in my office, Caden."

"No." I lean over the post to get closer to him. "We can talk here."

"I'd like to talk to you as a trainer, Caden." He takes a step forward and I'm not sure if I've ever seen him like this. He's furious. I can see the emotion bubbling beneath his skin. "I'd like to talk to you as the trainer who is training *that* girl, and I'd like to have *that* professional conversation in my office."

Shit.

"Alright." I walk over to the gate and start taking my gloves off. He leaves me behind, walking fast toward the stairs to his office. When I get through his office door he shuts it a little too loudly, then starts in on me.

"Alright. As your boss, this is extremely unprofessional." He sits down on the edge of his desk and crosses his legs out in front of him. His clipboard is still in his hands and I'm half convinced that he's holding it just to keep up the professional persona. "You can't train her and sleep with her, Caden."

"We aren't sleeping together."

"Alright. You can't train her and date her."

"I'm training her for free. I'm not employed by this gym. I'm not under a contract. I'm not sure what the issue is." Well, I'm sure I know, but technically he can't do anything. Not that I know of, at least.

"I know." He lets out a long sigh and it fills the entire office. "Don't kiss her here, okay? Here, she's your fighter."

"Understood."

"And when she starts actually fighting, I'm going to have to step in." I hate the idea of that but I know it needs to happen. It would have had to happen anyway. I don't fight, and when she's training for competitions she'll need to do more than spar.

"Understood." He stares down at the floor. When he looks up at me again his face has transformed. He's smiling from ear to ear and his eyes are dancing. He places his clipboard on the desk and puts his hands in the air like he's presenting something.

"You're happy."

"I am." I smile back at him and a weight lifts off my chest. Trainer Jason sucked but I'm glad to have my friend to talk to now.

"When did this happen?"

"I don't know. We had a few little moments and then she asked me out."

"Wait, wait." He does the windshield wiper movement with his hand. "She asked *you* out?"

"Yeah. I was going to but she beat me to it. I took her to Karen's." He lets out all the breath inside of him and stares at me. The smile is still there but it's more shocked than happy.

"Karen's. That's big, man."

"I know."

"You like her."

"I do." I push my hair off my forehead. "Jace, I like her a lot."

"Damn. That's awesome." He grabs me, trapping me in a bear hug. "I'm really fucking happy for you."

"Thanks, man." I pat him on the back and pull away.

"Well, I don't want to hold ya back. Go be with your girl."

My girl. I like the sound of that.

CHAPTER FIFTY
Aubrey

It's too good to be true. I'm training at a real gym, going to school for a degree that I love, living with my best friend, and dating a boy that treats me like all the movies and the books used to promise I would be treated. I don't know if I'm going to ruin it, or if he will, or if Elliot will somehow; I just know it's too good to be true.

I tell Myla this as I sit on my bed in my pajamas. I'm not going to Caden's tonight because I have officially decided that this is all going to crumble. If I don't walk away now, I'll get hurt in the wreckage.

Myla doesn't seem to be listening to me. She's digging in my closet as I speak.

"Do you want to wear a sweater or a t-shirt?"

"Myla." She doesn't look at me. "Are you even listening to me? I'm not going tonight. Seriously, you can't be that distracted."

"I'm not." She turns to me, a light pink sweater in one hand and a faded t-shirt with the dance team logo in the other. "Pick."

"I'm not going."

"Pick." She throws both at me and turns to my dresser, rifling through until she finds a nice pair of dark blue jeans that will look good with both. They hit my face. "Pick."

"I'm wearing my pajamas, because I'm staying here."

"Get your shit together, Aubrey!" The words come out harsh. She puts her hands on her hips and stares me down. "Your life is not too good to be true. Like, I love you hun, but let's be real. You still have anxiety attacks and nightmares, you can't afford college, this supposedly great gym won't let you fight, and your own parents won't support any of your life decisions."

If this were anyone else talking, I'd punch them in the face. Since it's Myla, and she's the closest thing I have to family, I just huff at her. It doesn't faze her.

"You are going tonight. You are going to wear one of those damn shirts, you are going to put those damn jeans on, and you are going to go tonight. I don't even care if I have to bring you there myself." She rolls her eyes very dramatically. "Get your ass dressed. You only have an hour to get there."

I look up at her and wonder if it's worth the fight. I really want to be with Caden. He makes me crazy happy and comfortable and I haven't felt this safe in a long time.

I hate that. I hate that I like him, and I hate that Myla won't let me run from it.

"I'll wear the t-shirt." I hug the clothes to my chest and stand up.

"You should take a hoodie with you too, just in case his air conditioning is too high." I stare her down.

"Do not push it." I leave her behind to head for the bathroom, in need of a shower and a serious change in attitude if I'm going to do this tonight.

By the time I'm under the hot water, I'm panicking. Jason is going to be there tonight and I know Caden must have told him about us. They spent too long in that office today and when they finally emerged it was awkward. Jason kept making up excuses to talk to us and Caden seemed nervous every time he came around.

Plus, I have to meet his sisters. How will he introduce me? How much do they know? Caitlin is old enough to understand. Hell, she might be old enough to know who I am. Our town is small enough for a coincidence like that. Hopefully she goes to the other high school in town. I never thought to ask.

Myla knocks on the door, pulling me out of my anxiety spin. "If you're drowning yourself in there, I will not be impressed."

"I'm still alive." I shout, pushing a chunk of wet hair off my face. I wait for her to laugh but she's not in the mood. "I'll be out in just a second."

I wrap my hair in a towel and dry off with another one. Once I'm completely dry I pull my clothes on and start working on my hair. The blow dryer isn't in any of the drawers, so I emerge to go find it.

"Myla," She peeks her head out from the kitchen. "Do you know where the blow dryer is?"

"My room. Sorry." She leans against the doorway and looks me up and down. "You look good."

"Really?" I tug on my shirt.

"Yes. Very nice and casual. He'll have no idea that you just had a total meltdown." I roll my eyes and head towards her bedroom for the blow dryer. Since she follows, I try to think of a way to take the attention off me.

"What are you up to tonight?"

"I have a date." I pause at her makeup bin and dig in it for the blow dryer.

"Ew, not with gas station guy?"

"No, not with him. I met someone in my English class."

"Oh, no." I plug the blow dryer into her outlet. "That'll be awkward if it doesn't work."

"Yeah, well. You're dating your trainer." She smirks at me through her full-length mirror next to the bin. I stick my tongue out at her and turn the blow dryer on.

She must get bored at some point because she wanders off into the hall. By the time she comes back my hair is dried and hanging straight down my shoulders. I lean forward and add some eyeshadow and mascara. Myla suggests I put some lipstick on but I respond with an evil glare.

"Two nights in a row." She says casually, walking out into the hall backwards and winking at me. "Careful, Bree. You're starting to act normal."

I smile at her until she's out of the room before turning my attention to the mirror. My reflection catches me off guard. The girl in the mirror has gained a few pounds. She doesn't have any bruises or scratches. The dark circles that used to hang like nooses beneath her eyes are barely visible. She looks happy. Healthy. Normal. I never believed that was possible.

CHAPTER FIFTY-ONE
Aubrey

A girl just a few years younger than me answers the door. Her dirty blonde hair is in one long fishtail braid over her shoulder. Striking green eyes stare daggers into me. "I thought you were the pizza guy." I shift and try to look behind her, hoping someone will save me from this moment.

"Sorry." I put my hands up as if she needs proof that I'm not holding pizza. "I'm Aubrey."

"I know." She crosses her arms over her chest.

"I'm Caden's," I pause. I'm not sure if I'm anything. "I'm training at Elite."

"I know. You went to Jefferson, too." Every nerve beneath my skin catches fire. What does she know?

"I did."

"I watched you dance once, at an invitational with my school." Oh, thank God. She didn't go to Jefferson. The last thing I need is for her to tell Caden about all the rumors that went around about me my Senior year. I believe one of them was that I was quitting everything because I was pregnant. I wonder what those people think happened to the baby. "You were amazing."

"What?"

"At the invitational." She looks at me like she's trying to size me up. I hope I pass the test. "You danced a few times but your solo was by far the best."

"Well, thank you. Do you dance?"

"I used to. I stopped once I started high school. I didn't really want to do it to compete so I switched to volleyball."

"Volleyball is cool. I had a friend who played volleyball."

It's not totally a lie. Myla tried it for a season, but she hated the team captain who spoke in a nasally voice and thought she was Olympic bound.

"Caitlin. Do you need more money?" Caden's voice comes from the center of the house but Caitlin doesn't acknowledge it.

"Do you still dance?"

"No. I quit."

"Why?" Caden saves me by coming around the corner with his wallet in hand. His expression goes from relaxed to anxious in an instant.

"Oh, Bree." He shoves his wallet in his back pocket and comes to stand behind Caitlin. He mouths an apology to me before speaking out loud. "I thought you were the pizza guy."

"Common misconception." I gesture to Caitlin but she apparently doesn't find it funny. She slinks under his arm and walks away from the two of us.

He steps closer to me, anxiety rippling off him. "Did she say anything? I told her to be polite."

"She was fine." He shakes his head like he doesn't believe it. I put a hand on his arm to calm him and his entire body sags in relief. "She was just asking me about dance. She's seen me perform before."

"Oh. She never mentioned that."

"Maybe she recognized the face instead of the name."

"Maybe." He looks me in the eyes. "You're sure she was fine?"

"Caden. I can handle a sixteen-year-old." I laugh to lighten the mood. "Plus, she was nowhere near Myla."

I look around the house as he brings me inside. It's different than I pictured. Much less bachelor pad, and a lot more country living. It must have been his parents.

The room we are standing in has nothing but artwork on the walls. Most of them look like something Cassie would make, but some seem too advanced. Before I can get any closer, Caden grabs my hand and tugs me forward.

The living room is part of a wide open space that stretches across the whole house. From here, you can see the dining room and the kitchen clearly. All three rooms are lit up and Cassie is sitting at the dining room table reading. Caden sees me looking and smiles fondly.

"She started kindergarten and the teacher told me she could easily skip a grade, within the first week. I decided to keep her behind. She'll be the smart one, and she won't feel so odd in a group of kids her own age. She feels odd enough." He must sense that he's rambling. "Anyway, she likes to read."

"That's great."

"Cassie, say hi to Aubrey."

The little girl's head bobs as she looks up at me. Her eyes are the exact same as her sister's, but instead of accusing and angry, they're gentle and innocent. When she smiles at me, I see that her front teeth are missing. It's adorable. "Hello, Aubrey." She returns to her book, eyebrows scrunched in concentration.

Caden puts a hand on my back and turns me to face the living room. Jason is sprawled out in a big leather recliner, scrolling on his phone. His thumb is hovering above the screen as he smiles at me. "Hey, Aubrey."

"Hey." Caden drops me off at the couch and heads to the kitchen.

"Do you want anything to drink?"

"Non-alcoholic." Jason adds, not glancing up from his phone.

"Yes," Caden winks at me. "Non-alcoholic. We've got water, milk, juice, and some soda. There's some snacks too if you're hungry."

"Um, root beer if you have any?"

"And now it all makes sense." Caitlin mutters.

"What makes sense?" Jason asks.

"Our fridge is stocked for the first time in months and it's because of *her*." She doesn't sound angry so much as annoyed. I don't think she likes me, unless she's doing Myla's thing where she makes me fear her so I don't hurt her brother. If that's the case, I'm ashamed to say it may be working.

"Yes. I starve them." Caden tells me, his tone dripping in sarcasm as he hands me my soda.

I turn to face the television. Jason has moved his attention to the remote instead of his phone, fiddling with it. After a second he gets it to work and moves the channel to three guys talking about the upcoming fights. Caitlin dramatically sighs and shifts.

"It's fight night, Caitlin. I already told you to go upstairs if you don't like it." Caden warns.

"It's not the fight that's bothering me." She grumbles, giving me a pointed look before getting up and storming out. The doorbell rings and Caden turns to watch her go.

"Grab the pizza, please." She doesn't answer him but we hear the front door open and her voice drift across the house. Caden stands up. "I should make sure she has enough money."

I take a sip from my glass and look around the room. Jason is staring at me. I nearly jump out of my skin when I notice.

"As your boss, I should keep my mouth shut." I start tapping my foot lightly against the floor, trying to battle the anxiety head on. "As his best friend, I swear to God I will be so pissed if you're not serious about him. He's been through hell and back, and he has a lot on his plate. He's all these girls have and if you're fucking with him then I swear to God-"

"Pizza!" Caden announces, coming around the corner and placing the pizza boxes on the kitchen table. Cassie closes her book and claps her hands together.

I receive a final, warning look from Jason before he stands up and smiles at his friend. Him and Myla would get along. They could share tips on how to scare their best friend's love interests.

We both make our way to the table and settle on opposite sides of it. I didn't think this night could get any worse but here we are.

Yet, the night continues to decline. Caitlin continues her passive aggressive comments. Jason continues to give me warning glares. Caden continues to try and keep everything light and easy. By the time the preliminary fights begin, I'm exhausted. Everyone else is too.

"I'm sleepy." Cassie pads her way into the living room, rubbing her eyes with a tiny fist.

"Alright, sweetheart." My heart melts when he scoops Cassie up. She places her head on his shoulder, eyes drooping. "Tell everyone goodnight."

"Night." She says quietly. The whole room repeats the word and Caitlin stands up.

"I have homework." She pushes past Caden and Cassie, giving her little sister a smile. I watch as the three of them head upstairs. The air in the room feels as if it's a hundred pounds heavier, and Jason is staring at me again.

"What?" My tone is harsh and I don't care. At this rate, I'm feeling like I should have stayed home.

"Nothing." He turns the volume on the television down, making it clear that it is in fact not nothing. "It's just, I don't want him to get hurt."

"You've made that clear." I clench my fists. "He's a big boy."

"Trust me, I know. He's a very big boy. That kid is handling more things than most people handle in a whole lifetime."

"I know." He glances at me.

"Do you?"

"He told me about everything." I scratch at my knee even though it's not itchy. "He told me about his mom."

Jason sucks in a breath. "That she's dead?" His eyes dart anxiously at the stairway.

"No. That she's, well, in the hospital." I thought maybe this trust Caden has in me would win me points. Instead, Jason's entire body language shifts.

"Don't tell people that."

"I'm not! I just know that you know." I hate this so much. This is too hard. Putting myself out there after Elliot again has been bad enough. I can't handle this shit.

"Don't fucking hurt him, Aubrey."

"Jason."

"No, you listen to me. I really like you. And I really want to like you guys together. But he's my brother and I'm serious right now. Walk away if you can't do this." Something in his words makes me pause. If I can't do this. Does he know?

"He told you." I can't help that my voice shakes. "Did he tell you everything?"

"What?"

"He told you about," I try to get the words out but I can't.

"If you're talking about why you're angry and scared, no. He hasn't said a word."

"Oh." I bite my bottom lip to keep it from shaking. "Well he knows, and trust me, we both have equal amounts of baggage."

"Listen," he leans forward and puts a hand out like he's about to lecture. "He's happy. You make him really happy."

"Really?"

"Really." He smiles at me and it's finally warm. "I'm sorry for whatever you're going through, or have gone through. I'm glad you two have each other."

"It's fine." I give him a smile and it seems to make him comfortable again too. He settles back in his chair but then sighs.

"Listen, Aubrey. I want you to know that as much as I'd like to threaten you and make sure you never hurt him, your career at my gym will not be affected by your relationship with him."

"Good." The breath I didn't know I was holding escapes me. I feel a lot lighter.

"Although, when you start fighting I'm going to take over your training."

"Understandable." I wish I could get Caden to fight. I think it'd help him if he was willing to try it again. In the meantime, I just hope it doesn't take too long before I'm fighting. "When will that be exactly?"

Jason places a hand on his stomach and laughs, finding this hilarious. It goes on for a little too long and he lets out an exaggerated sigh at the end of it. "Oh, Aubrey. You're funny."

"I wasn't trying to be."

"I know." His smile fades. "You'll be fine, kid. Just keep working on your shit and the rest will come." He sounds like the old lady in almost every Disney movie.

"You remember that you're only twenty-three, right?"

"Yes. I'm reminded from time to time."

CHAPTER FIFTY-TWO
Caden

The current fight is starting to drag and I can feel Aubrey getting restless. When Jason hops up to grab a beer I propose a shift in activity.

"Want to play a few rounds?"

"Yeah." His voice is muffled from the fact that he's speaking into the fridge. "You want a beer?"

"I'll take one."

"Aubrey? Anything?" He yells, his head finally coming out of the appliance.

"I'm good." She glances at me. "A few rounds?"

"Of cribbage." Her face doesn't shift from confusion and I'm instantly disappointed. How did she grow up here without learning how to play? "Come on. You've played cribbage. You've had to have played cribbage."

"What is it?" My heart sinks into my gut. This needs to be fixed. Now.

I grab her hand and pull her up, leading her to the table. Jason puts down our beers and grabs the cribbage board that's hanging on a peg in the corner.

"It's a card game."

"But there's a board."

"Well, yes." I grab the board and place it in the center of the table so we can all reach it. She leans over to look at it, bringing a finger to trace the holes. "It's kind of a counting game. We can play a practice round."

She looks skeptical. Jason starts explaining the rules as he opens his beer. Her expression changes from unsure to downright confused.

She doesn't stay confused for long. By the time we're playing a real game, she's talking shit and counting her cards on her own. I find myself always watching her as she studies her cards, finding the way her nose scrunches when she's concentrating adorable.

With no idea, what to do with my hand, I throw a card in the crib and send up a prayer that something good will be cut from the deck. When I look up at Aubrey again, she's biting her bottom lip. It's too damn hard to concentrate with her doing that, because all I can focus on is the need to kiss her again.

For the rest of the game, I'm distracted. Jason has to keep reminding me of points I miss, thankfully letting me take them even though the rules say he can steal them from me. Before I know it, Aubrey is throwing her cards down on the table and giggling. "Sixteen. Read em' and weep boys." She moves her peg to the very last hole and rubs her hands together. Jason throws his cards at her.

"Beginner's luck." I spit out, throwing my cards as well. This just makes her giggle again. I glance at the television. There's still twenty minutes before the main event. Jason follows my gaze.

"I should probably take a piss before that starts."

"You really should." I let out a mocking laugh and point to Aubrey. "He missed Rhonda Rousey get knocked out because he had to pee."

"Hey, now!" His eyebrows are raised. "In my defense, she was supposed to last longer. I mean, come on. Who would have thought?"

"You never look away from a fight. We all know how fast those can end." He grabs my empty bottle, along with his, and brings them to the recycle bin. "That would be why I'm going to go to the bathroom right now."

"Alright." I leave the cribbage board in case we end up playing again. Aubrey follows me to the couch and settles down next to me. Noise carries in from the kitchen as Jason cleans before going to the bathroom. I try to forget that he's there, possibly watching us, and place my arm on the back of the couch behind Aubrey. It takes a moment, but she inches closer to me.

"Why are they doing that?" I look at the television to see what she's referring to.

"Um, they're taping his hands?"

"Right, but why like that?" This girl continues to blow my mind. How does she expect to get into this professionally? Does she even know how a true fight happens?

"They have to wrap their hands in front of the officials to prove nothing is inside the tape." I watch as one of the officials draws on the white tape with a sharpie. "They mark it to prove that they watched."

"Oh."

"Can I ask you something?"

"Sure."

"I get why you wanted to do self-defense, and don't get me wrong you're damn good, but why did you decide to start training for real?"

"I don't know. Jason made it sound good." I sit up straighter. That's news to me. I knew he recruited her but I always assumed she was actively looking for a place.

"Wait. You weren't going to fight competitively until Jason found you?"

"I was fighting competitively." She crosses her arms over her chest.

"You were fighting in a local gym with an audience of less than twenty people."

"That doesn't make it any less hard. Some of those girls were tough. And I even fought a guy once."

"You're right. I'm sorry."

She sighs. "Don't be sorry. I know where you're coming from. It was different with Rob."

"What happened there, anyway? How'd that all go down?"

"I needed help." Her small hands are shaking in her lap. Slowly, so she sees it coming, I grab them and hold them steady. When she smiles at me, it's full of relief.

"I found an advertisement at one of the grocery stores. It was after a really bad fight. I had never been so scared that he would kill me." Her voice chokes to a stop.

"You don't have to talk about it." She looks up at me, her blue eyes full.

"I'd like to. I've felt better, since telling you." A sense of pride wells up inside me. All I've wanted is to help her. "I found the advertisement and it was free. Rob knew almost right away. I was shaking like a maniac, and I could barely speak. All I could keep saying was that no one could find out."

"So, the defense classes started then?"

"It took some convincing. He had to make me believe that it was safe, and he offered to teach me outside of the classes so no one knew I was there. Then it was hard to do it, logistically. I usually didn't know when I was open until very last minute. By that point I had already quit a lot of my clubs and sports. I just had school, which I couldn't skip, and my every move was usually being watched."

"So how did you do it?"

"Well, you know I was left in the apartment alone pretty often. Rob was single and retired so I could call him unexpectedly and he'd let me come over."

"You weren't worried that your boyfriend would come back and see you were gone?"

"I knew him well enough. I knew how long it would take him depending on what he was doing. He didn't have a schedule but he was still pretty predictable." She tries to smile at me. "He came home once when I wasn't there."

I feel something churn in my stomach. Why do I get the feeling I don't want to hear this? "Did you tell him where you were?"

"No." She laughs like it's the funniest thing she's heard. The pent-up anxiety inside her pours out along with it, bubbling into a laugh that sounds like it could break into a cry at any moment. When she gets control over herself, she breathes and shakes her head. "Sorry, I don't know why that was so funny."

"It's fine."

I told him that Myla had something going on, a boy thing. He was irate and it wasn't pretty, but it was nothing compared to when he actually found out."

"Wait. He found out?"

"Um, yes?" She looks at me like I'm a bit of an idiot. Was I supposed to already know that?

"I could have sworn things ended because he got arrested."

"They did."

"So, things didn't end when he found out about Rob's?" I'm pushing her too far, I'm sure of it. She picks at her nails and takes a deep breath.

"No. He found out and he stopped me."

"How'd he find out?"

"He had some guy follow me." This dude is so creepy. I mean, I know that he was crazy and controlling, but to have someone trail her? If you're that worried about losing someone maybe you should reevaluate how you treat them. "He made me promise to quit and to never leave him."

"And you listened?"

"Yes." The word is the softest sound I've ever heard. When she glances at me, her eyes are full of tears and anxiety. Wherever this conversation is headed, she's worried about my reaction.

"Why? Why didn't you run?" It's a terrible thing to ask, I know, but I need to.

"Because I loved him. And because he would have killed me." She sounds ashamed. I'm more focused on the killing part, never having realized just how bad it was. "I didn't start fighting until after his arrest."

"And Rob knew everything?" Why didn't this guy report it? She was a minor for fucks sake.

"He did. There were times when he got me close to leaving, but I never got the courage. He threatened to call the cops once, but I think he was worried what would happen to me. When he came to the hospital to see me, he was devastated. He cried harder than Myla, even. I think he partially blamed himself."

Hospital? I try to wrap my mind around everything she's saying, processing it all. There's a million questions I need to ask but they all feel tangled together. Before I can pick one out she moves on, taking my chance of understanding with her.

"Jason still doesn't think I'm ready to fight. I get the feeling you don't think I should either, right?"

"It's not that. I'm not trying to be an ass, but this world Jason brought you into is different. You know so little and I just wanna make sure you actually want this lifestyle."

"I don't want the lifestyle. Like I said, this isn't my endgame. I want to be a social worker, and help people. It's not like I'm UFC bound." She looks at me and I try to keep my face straight. If she's not UFC bound, Jason and I are wasting time. Elite Gym is for dedicated fighters who want to go all the way. That said, I don't think either of us would ever be willing to let her go now.

"You may not want to go all the way, but you owe it to yourself to at least push toward the top. You're good, Aubrey."

She shrugs an apology to me. "I just want to fight."

"I know." I remember that feeling. It didn't matter what ring they put me in, or who was in front of me, I just cared that I was fighting. That changes though. Maybe it will change for her too.

She looks back at the screen just as Jason is walking back in. He rolls his eyes at us. "Look at you two lovebirds."

"You're just jealous you haven't been laid in months."

Aubrey waves her hand in the air. "Jason, don't let him make fun of you. He hasn't been laid either."

The serious conversation we just had feels years away. Jason and her burst into laughter at my sex life's expense, and I can't help but join in. By the time we're done throwing around comments and laughing, the fight is about to start.

As the announcer begins yelling into the microphone, she sinks into my side and rests her head on my shoulder. In that moment, I decide that I am very much so falling in love with her.

CHAPTER FIFTY-THREE
Aubrey

I break down and call my mother Sunday. She answers on the fourth ring with a clipped tone. "Yes?"

"Hey, mom."

"What do you need?" I can hear people speaking in the background.

"I'm sorry. Am I interrupting something?"

"I'm just at brunch." The word makes me cringe. I have wasted countless hours at my mother's brunches. "Do you need something, Aubrey?"

"I just wanted to check in. I've missed you." The words stick like hot goo to my tongue.

"Well, that's nice." I can hear someone yelling now. "You really don't have to call and suck up, Aubrey. Your tuition is not being paid."

"That's not-"

"Goodbye, now." She hangs up before I can think of a way to respond. My mother has always been cold but that was a new level. I expected her to continue the fight, not to just hang up.

I tackle some homework to get my mind off everything. Of course, it's easier said than done. My reading for sociology discusses drug culture and I'm thrown back into my own personal experience with it.

When I move on to my English reading, I start thinking about Elliot and Caden. The girl in my book is head over heels in love with a guy that's no good for her. I remember that feeling. It was scary as all hell, but it was also exhilarating. I thought I'd never feel that alive again. My body used to feel on fire when I was around him.

I decide to stop my homework for a while. I text Caden to see what he's up to and wait for an answer. To pass the time, I start cleaning. The kitchen is a nightmare and it takes me almost two hours to clean it. When I check my phone again, there's nothing.

"Look at you, Cinderella." Myla throws her purse on the counter and bumps her hip against me. I roll my eyes at her and pull my pink rubber gloves off.

"Where have you been?" I take in her appearance. She's in a red dress and heels. "You weren't here when I woke up."

"I wasn't here when you went to bed either."

"What?" I grab her arm and start to pull her into the living room. She giggles as we collapse into a hurried pile.

"I'm actually a little hurt that you didn't notice. I could have been lying in a ditch somewhere." I feel guilt for maybe two seconds.

"I'm sorry. I was so exhausted after last night, I pretty much collapsed into bed."

"How was it? Was it as bad as you thought it would be?"

"Shh, we can talk about that in a second. First, you need to spill." I grab the fabric of her dress and wave it to show what I'm talking about. She rolls her eyes but then smiles. It's mischievous.

"Alright, so a few girls from my History class were going out and they invited me along. Just a little clubbing, nothing fancy. And I met the most amazing guy."

Oh, here we go.

"Wait, I thought you had a date last night? With English guy?"

"Oh, I did. That lasted less than an hour. I skipped desert." Her eyebrows raise. "At a restaurant that's famous for their hot lava cake. Hot lave cake, Aubrey. I passed up hot lava cake."

"That bad, huh?"

"The worst. Complete worst. He was racist and sexist and totally full of himself. I wanted to poor my drink on him so bad."

"You should have."

"I was going to but I ended up sneaking out instead."

"You what!" I jump up and down.

"I told him I had to pee and I left. But do you see this dress? I was not going to waste this dress. And I curled my hair, which you know takes forever. So, long story short I hooked up with some friends and I met the most amazing guy."

"And you went home with him? A total stranger?" She raises an eyebrow at me.

"Don't act like that's totally taboo. I've had one night stands before." She sounds proud and I have to smile. The first time she had sex was just a few months ago. She had come to me after, all wide eyed and exhilarated. *Why did you never tell me how good that would be? You've been holding out, you bitch.* I can still remember the way she smiled at me when she told me that she would definitely be doing it again. And who can blame her? If it feels good, she should be able to. Guys do it.

"Anyway," she flips her hair over her shoulder, "He's a football player at the school. Totally gorgeous."

"What's his name?"

She sticks her tongue out at me. "Nathan."

"What's his last name?"

"Unless I plan on marrying the man, I don't really care."

"So, he's the most amazing guy you've ever met, but you don't see yourself getting married?" She throws her head back and laughs.

"Oh, Bree." She pats me on the knee like I'm an innocent child who just has no clue. It reminds me of how Jason laughed last night. Maybe they really would get along. "I said he was the most amazing guy, as in the most amazing guy at that club. He's not the most amazing guy I've ever met." She glances up at the ceiling. "Lord help me if I've already met the most amazing guy. Yeesh. Can you imagine?"

"You're a mess."

"I am, but shrug. At least I'm a mess who got laid."

Finally, my phone vibrates against the coffee table. I drop our conversation and grab it, eager to see what Caden said.

All he sent me is: *Sorry. At work.*

I drop my phone in my lap and sigh. I'm getting sick of just hanging out in the apartment. When I look over, Myla is lying back against the arm of the couch with hair strung across her face. She's not going to want to do anything today.

If I stay here I'm going to eat way too much junk food and fry my brain with Netflix. I should at least get some fresh air.

I hop off the couch and search for my running shoes, because I would feel much better about being lazy today if I at least workout first. My shoes are tucked under my gym bag and I pull them on. Myla doesn't even move as I walk around and I hope she'll be a little more fun by the time I get back.

CHAPTER FIFTY-FOUR
Caden

There was a massive party last night. Two people were rumored to have gone missing, only to be found a few hours later passed out in the woods nearby. Three people were arrested. Two of them were mine.

Jameson is slumped over in a seat in the conference room next to Officer Jones, the undercover working this case. They both have paper cups of hot coffee in front of them.

"So, go through it again." I stand up and walk over to the dry-erase board on the wall. There's a few words and lines already drawn on it but other than that our investigation is seriously lacking information.

"I told you. They wanted him to do drugs."

"So, you decided to get into a fist fight?"

"As a distraction." I stare my piece of shit informant down for a full thirty seconds before taking in the deepest breath I can. If I punch him, I will surely get in trouble. I keep this in mind as I take the cap off the marker.

"And you punched who?"

"His name is Kyle. He's in the main group."

"Why would you punch him?" I turn to look at him, not even hiding the expression on my face. I'm hoping he catches how stupid I think he is. "Wouldn't that look a little fishy, since he's supposed to be your friend?"

"Kyle was part of the reason I got arrested. He's the one who fucked up, and my buddy and I were the ones who took all the blame. I just kind of said it was about that. Everyone believed it."

"It's true." Jones looks up at me and shrugs. "One of the guys even told me to leave them be when I tried breaking up the fight. Said something about how they all knew it was coming, to let them hash it out."

"You could have blown your cover." I say through gritted teeth. The both of them are giving me a headache.

"No, me refusing to do their drugs would have blown my cover. He saved my ass."

"Okay." I write Kyle's name on the board, wondering if it's even important.

This case is starting to get stale. "So, the party last night got us nowhere?"

"I wouldn't say that." Jameson takes a sip of his coffee and closes his eyes to savor it.

"Elaborate?" I spit the word out at him and he opens one eye to glare at me.

"He met him last night." He points to Jones with a shit eating grin on his face. Jones sits up straight and looks at him like this is new information. Did Jameson not tell him? Of course, he didn't. He wants all the power.

"I didn't." Jones focuses his attention on me and shakes his head. "There's no way. Everyone I met there was too low on the totem pole. You could tell."

"No, you couldn't." Jameson scoffs and rolls his eyes. "I didn't want to tell you because I wanted it to be natural. He liked you, I could tell. You'll have to prove yourself to get in the group though."

"I don't need in the group. I need him." Jones leans towards Jameson and I wonder if he's about to hit him. That wouldn't be good, but I also wouldn't mind. In fact, I'd like to myself. Just one hit.

"You need him to sell to you, or to admit to you that he sells. He won't do those things until you're in the group."

"How am I supposed to prove myself?"

"Oh, I don't think I want to know." I mumble to myself as I make an X under the word 'party' to indicate that the target was there. Neither of them hear me.

"You'll have to do something for him, or for someone in the group."

"Well, we can't stress over that until you're approached." I put the cap back on the marker and sigh. "They aren't going to ask him to kill anyone, right?"

Jameson laughs hard and shakes his head. "You cops are so fucking dramatic. Not every criminal is willing to commit murder. They'll ask him to do the shit work, like clean up after parties and maybe scare a few druggies into handing over money they owe." He shakes his head again as if he still can't believe it. "And you totally clammed up last night at the party but use your head next time so I don't have to punch anyone. When someone offers you drugs, say you're on probation. Our story is that we met in prison, remember?"

"Sorry." Jones runs a hand down his face. Then he looks at me and grimaces. "Sorry."

"Don't be man. Nothing he's saying really goes with our training. You've just got to play it by ear."

I slouch down in the chair across from them and drink my now cold coffee. I glance over at my phone and notice that it's blue light is flickering. When I check it my stomach flips. Aubrey texted me, and now she probably thinks that I've been ignoring her. I send her a quick response and hope that I remember to text her again later. Before I can worry about it, Jameson starts speaking again.

"Listen, I have this friend that's still locked up. He's a good guy, and he has a girl that he never really got to end things with-"

"Relevance?" I ask, looking up at him and giving him a cold stare. He shifts in his seat uncomfortably.

"I just thought you could maybe offer him the same deal as me."

"We don't need two men for this. You know who we need to be introduced to, and you have the power to do it."

"I know, but he's a good guy."

"Right. I bet he is." I stop myself before continuing and Jones gives me a strange look. Jameson looks pissed but I don't care. All I can picture is Aubrey. The less guys like her's around, the better. "We can't bring another one of you in here. This is a sensitive investigation."

"Alright."

"And don't you start getting ideas into that guy's head. We don't need anyone finding out you're a rat." His face turns red at that last word but I don't care. It's what he is and if he can't get over that, then our investigation isn't going to be successful. "Back to the facts, please. When's the next time you'll see suspect X?"

CHAPTER FIFTY-FIVE
Aubrey

When I get back from my run I'm rewarded with three texts from Caden. All of them make me smile.

Sorry I couldn't answer earlier. Work has been crazy. I miss you.

I can't stop thinking about you. Your crazy beautiful face is going to get my ass fired.

I'm off at 2. Please tell me you're free tonight?

My fingers can't move fast enough as I tell him that I would love to see him. Myla is still sleeping on the couch so I quietly sneak past her and make my way to the bathroom. There's barely any towels left and I add laundry to my mental list of things to do, just now realizing how long it is.
 Maybe I shouldn't hangout with Caden tonight. I laugh at myself. Who am I kidding? I've been itching to see him and it's barely been twelve hours; I'm hanging out with him.
 The thought scares me. I don't like the idea of needing to see anyone. I've been doing just fine since Elliot. I let the warm water wash away all my doubts and try to relax.
 When my phone buzzes against the bathroom counter, I get soap in my eye trying to reach for it. After surviving the near-death experience, I squint at the screen and read.

Let me cook you dinner? It'd have to be at your place...

Myla is still sleeping on the couch when I enter, my hair wrapped in a towel turban. I shake her gently and she just groans. When I shake her again I'm met with a sleepy glare.
 "Tired." She states. I smile at her.

"Are you busy tonight?" She continues to glare at me.

"Dinner. Nathan." She blindly feels for something and huffs when she doesn't find it. "Phone."

"Your purse is in the kitchen." I hop up and run into the other room. When I come back she's sitting up and wiping at her face. She looks a little more alive now.

I hand her the purse and she digs through it, pulling out her phone. After a minute of silence, she confirms.

"Yes. I'm going to dinner tonight with Nathan." She winks at me. "You probably shouldn't wait up."

"Gag." I say. "Well, good. I think I'm going to invite Caden over."

"That'll be fun." She slaps me on the knee but I'm not so excited. Having him here is a step. A step I *think* I'm really to take, but I'm not sure.

"He wants to cook me dinner."

"Oh, gosh." She gives me a dreamy smile and looks up at the ceiling. "I wish I could find a guy that would cook for me."

"Maybe Nathan can cook." I offer this to make her feel better but she frowns.

"I doubt it. I'll have to ask tonight." Her frown disappears and she winks at me again. "I need a nap if I'm going to be up all night."

"I literally just woke you up from a nap." She sighs.

"That was my pre-nap. Wake me up by two." I throw a shoe at her, missing by a mile and hitting the hallway wall. I can hear her laughter as she heads to her room.

CHAPTER FIFTY-SIX
Caden

I have a good handle on how to cook. That said, I have no idea how to cook something meant for a date. Fancy food has never been an interest of mine. I can grill meat and cook my mother's casseroles, but I have no idea how to do the rest.

That's how I find myself watching tutorial videos on the internet. I read a few articles and decide on what's supposedly the perfect date night meal. It sounds easy enough.

Aubrey texts me just after five and tells me I'm safe to come over. I grab the meat that's been marinating in the fridge. Caitlin looks away from the television, tracking me as I move from the kitchen to the living room. "You're coming home tonight, right?"

"Of course I am." I try not to sigh or look too annoyed. It sucks that I'll probably never be able to stay the night with a girl, but I force myself to understand. It's not fair to Cassie and Caitlin. "I should be home in time to put Cassie to bed."

"I can handle it if you aren't." She shrugs and looks back at the television. Anyone who didn't know her would think that she's being rude, but that was actually a sweet thing to say. Just below a blessing. I'll take it.

"There's a frozen pizza in the fridge. It should be ready in five minutes." She glances at the Tupperware container of meat in my hands and makes a face. When she looks back at the television, she sighs dramatically.

"I guess that will do. Enjoy your chicken."

"I will." I mess up her hair and pretend I don't notice the smile tugging at her lips. "Do your homework and text me if you need anything."

I close the door before I can hear any snarky comment and make my way to my car. By the time I'm on the road, all thoughts of Caitlin are replaced by Aubrey.

She opens the door in a dress. It's deep purple and tight until it hits her waist, where it then gently flows out. It's sexy but innocent and I think I might die. Instinctively, I reach up and pull at the collar of my flannel. I should have worn something dressier.

"You look beautiful." She blushes and grabs the chicken from me.

"Thank you. Myla insisted I dress up." *Thank you, Myla.*

I look her up and down one last time before deciding that I could get used to her in dresses. Not that she doesn't look gorgeous in casual clothes, because she does. But this is for me, and the idea is sexy as hell.

"Myla gives good advice." This makes her laugh. She gestures for me to come in and closes the door. I notice the fact that she locks the door behind us. "Is Myla here?"

"Yeah, she's just finishing getting ready. She has a date."

"Nice." I only met Myla once, and it wasn't entirely the best experience. Hopefully, this time around she won't threaten any parts of my body.

"I'm not sure what you would need, but I can show you around the kitchen." I lift the grocery bag in my hand and smile at her.

"I've got everything besides equipment." She smiles and leads me into their small kitchen. When we arrive, she stands by the oven and presents it.

"Pots and pans are down here, and silverware is in this drawer." She points as she goes, her words a little too fast. "Mixing spoons and all that other stuff are in this jar." She taps a light purple mason jar with mixing spoons, spatulas, and ladles in it. Now that I'm paying attention, the dish towels and the coffee pot are purple too.

"You like purple." I wave at her dress and she looks down at it, blushing again. It's so strange that I make her this anxious outside of the gym. I like it, but I also want her to feel safe and comfortable.

"It's my favorite. Myla's too."

"I see that." I open the cabinet with pots and pans and laugh. All the handles are purple. She laughs too but it's nervous. She's not sure if she's doing this right. "Everything is great. You go relax."

"Oh, I can help." I give her a stern look. It makes her smile and I can't keep the look on my face for very long. Her smile is infectious.

"You can watch and keep me company if you insist. But you cannot help."

"Okay." The word comes out as a grumble and she walks around to the other side of the breakfast bar. She slides onto a stool and rests her weight on her elbows. I reach into the grocery bag and pull out two bottles of wine, causing her to arch an eyebrow at me. "I'm under contract."

"Not tonight." I wink at her. When she doesn't look convinced I soften my smile and place both bottles on the surface in front of her. "He doesn't enforce that rule unless you have a fight coming up. He seriously hasn't mentioned that?"

"No."

"Well, I swear you won't get in trouble."

"I'm under age." She pauses. "And *you're* a cop."

"Off duty." I lean forward so that my face is hovering in between the two bottles. "White or Red?"

"White." I smile.

"Good choice." It takes me two tries but I find the wine glasses. Surprisingly, they aren't purple. "Do you want ice?"

"Yes, please. Just a cube." I fill both glasses and plop some ice in them. She takes hers with a large smile, sipping as I start getting ready to cook.

I can feel her watching me as I move around the kitchen and I try not to let it get to me.

I'm unsuccessful, nearly cutting a finger off slicing the oranges when I glance over to see her licking her lips. By the time I have everything together, my mind is running wild with what I want to do with her once the food is in the oven. I respect her enough not to try any of them, yet, but it's still fun to imagine.

"So, what is that exactly?" She asks as I slide the dish into the oven and set the timer she showed me how to use.

"It's citrus roasted chicken. I've never made it before, so fingers crossed." She laughs, and it's such a beautiful sound. "It should only cook for thirty minutes, but I have to make the rice still."

"That's fine." She takes a sip of wine. "How was work?"

I cringe. "Terrible. I've been having to deal with this total asshole."

"Like, another cop?"

"No. A drug dealer." I pause. Too much information. Way too much. I look up at her and there's something cloudy in her eyes.

"Like, someone in prison?" I tread lightly. I don't want to make it seem like she got more information than she should have. I have to back out slow to avoid sending up red flags.

"He was. He's been stopping by for parole and crap like that. Grunt work for me."

She still seems off. "What's his name?"

"Oh, um." *Red alert.* "I'm actually not allowed to say that. Violates his privacy."

"Right. Duh." She runs a hand through her hair and smiles like she's not concerned. Her eyes say something different. Does she think she knows him? Everything inside me stills. *Shit.* What if she does?

"Your ex." I pause, trying to figure out the best way to approach the subject. "He's still in prison, right?"

"Yeah. He's got a few years left." I feel my anxiety vanish. Jameson's whole friend group knows he's out and I'm sure it would have gotten to her by now if she was his 'girl'.

Then my heart skips. Jameson has a friend. The one he wanted me to get out. A new wave of anger flushes through me. I take a gulp of wine to wash it down. I'd prefer beer or whiskey, but it does the trick for now.

CHAPTER FIFTY-SEVEN
Aubrey

The alarm won't stop. Caden is standing on a kitchen chair with a dish towel, waving it back and forth. I'm not sure how everything went so wrong. One minute we were laughing about the time I locked myself out of my car, and the next there was fire. Actual fire. I didn't know that happened in real life, and that's coming from someone who is a terrible cook.

"I'm so sorry!" He yells over the beeping, still waving the cloth. Myla comes running in from her room, her lips outlined but not filled in. The look she gives us is a mixture of amusement and annoyance.

"Take the batteries out!" She instructs. *Why didn't I think of that?*

Caden keeps waving the cloth. "What?"

"The batteries!" We scream in unison. He drops the towel and starts unscrewing the alarm. For a cop, he's not good under pressure. The beeping finally stops, leaving the apartment in an eerie silence.

"I'm sorry." He says again, his hands resting on his hips as he surveys the smoke. Opening the windows, I just laugh. This night couldn't be ruined, even by fire. He's too perfect.

"It's fine. Seriously."

"He almost burnt down our apartment." Myla screeches. When we both just keep smiling, she rolls her eyes and throws both hands in the air. "You people are gross and cute and I hate you."

When she's gone, we both look at each other and start laughing all over again.

"I swear; I've cooked rice like that before. It's supposed to make it go faster."

"Oh, it went faster alright." He playfully pushes me for teasing him. I wait for the panic to start, for my body to get triggered, but it doesn't. I'm nothing but comfortable.

We venture back into the kitchen, surveying the mess. I grab the roll of paper towel from the counter and start on the floor. He grabs a cloth and works on the stove. The rice is already starting to dry and stick to all available surfaces. By the time we're done, another problem is discovered. We forgot all about the chicken.

Caden takes the pan out of the oven with a frown. "Well, it's at least cooked."

I stare at the shriveled pieces of chicken. They've shrunk half in size, and the orange juice has turned into a blackened crust.

"How about I pay for Chinese instead? Is that still romantic?"

CHAPTER FIFTY-EIGHT
Aubrey

The smoke and Myla are both gone by the time the Chinese arrives. We sit at the perfectly set table, dumping our takeout boxes onto the fancy plates Myla bought us last month. I can't stop laughing.

"I'll never live this down, will I?" He asks as I cough to hide my latest fit. I shake my head, biting my lip to keep from smiling.

"Probably not for a while. Karen would be so disappointed." His shoulders sag but he's smiling wide at me. All the wine and laughter is starting to give me more confidence, and I think I really want to kiss him again.

Yes. That sounds like a great idea.

"I'm glad we got to see each other tonight. I missed your freckles." He blushes. I don't call him out on it, only because I hate my freckles and don't want to draw any more attention to the topic.

"I'm glad too. It's nice seeing you at the gym all the time, but this is different. Better."

"I can agree with that. There's something about the aroma of sweaty guys that just doesn't create the best ambience."

I laugh and take a sip from my wine. "Yes, that's true."

I stab a piece of chicken and plop it in my mouth. It may not be as good as what he was making but it does the job. When I look up at him he's watching me. I smile. "Yes?"

"Just looking. I'm sorry." He looks down at his plate and smirks. I feel so at ease with him, it's almost unnerving. I wonder for a moment if it's the wine, but I think it's just him.

A wave of guilt crashes into me. My dreams have been back, and stronger than ever. In some of them, I relive the happy memories with Elliot and I wake up missing him. Caden would hate me if he knew.

"Where'd you go?"

"Huh?" I jump, my fork clanging against the plate. He's smiling at me, but this time, it doesn't put me at ease. It's definitely the wine that makes me feel as if I owe it to him to tell him about my dreams. It has to be. No sane person would think that.

"We were laughing and then you kind of just went somewhere else." I feel my appetite slow to a bare minimum. This is literally the best segue if I want to tell him. It's now or never.

"I should tell you something." I put my fork down and finish my wine. He arches an eyebrow but doesn't say anything. "Well, I don't know if I should but I think I owe it to you."

"That doesn't sound good."

"I know." I try to breathe but my chest is aching. Just as I open my mouth he stops me, hand hovering in the space between us.

"I don't want to know. I can't." I feel the air get pushed out of me. He's not willing to listen to me? "If I wasn't a cop it'd be different, but whatever he made you do or you did with him, I can't know it. I can't have that on my conscience."

I sigh in relief. "It's not that. It's nothing illegal or anything like that."

"Oh. Well, shit. I'm sorry." He scratches his jaw. "Go ahead then. Sorry."

"It's okay. I just. Well. I have dreams. Almost every night. Sometimes they're nightmares about him coming to hurt me. Sometimes they're just me reliving memories, the bad ones and the good ones. Sometimes, after the good ones, I wake up and for a little while, I miss him. It's really messed up. It's like I miss the familiarity of the relationship. He would hurt me and threaten me and speak terribly to me but he was constant. And I loved him."

I don't care how school girl it is, I bury my face in my hands. My chest feels heavier than it ever has before. He takes a moment and I can hear him breathing slowly, like it's taking effort. Then I feel skin against my fingers.

"Look at me, please." He softly pries my hands away. The look on his face isn't what I expected. He's smiling. "Of course you miss him, Bree." I shiver at the way my name sounds coming from his lips. And from the fact that after what I told him, he's still using my nickname.

"I just-"

"He was like a drug to you. He knew exactly how to push you. Exactly what to say and when to stop. He took you higher than you've ever felt before. Don't feel guilty for that. Don't feel broken. Don't give him that power. Don't you dare. You loved him and that's okay. You're going to miss him sometimes. Bad people aren't always bad. It doesn't make you messed up. It makes you human." He squeezes my hand with his and gives me a smile. "You're sober now, right?"

"Yes." I don't even have to ponder that. Elliot could be kind, but I also used to have a different mindset. He had the advantage of being my first relationship. The first man I ever loved.

In just a few weeks, Caden has showed me what a relationship is supposed to be like. Caden is actually kind, whereas Elliot was just making up for what he had done to me. He was kind so I wouldn't leave. Caden is kind because he thinks I deserve it. I feel every inch of my body warm. "I'm not only sober, I'm starting to feel less and less like an addict. I know it's silly and metaphorical but every time we're together, I forget a little bit more. I let go a little bit more."

"Good." His chest puffs out with pride. "I feel the same way. I'm finally doing something other than going through the motions."

I smile at him, giving him a final squeeze of the hand before letting go. He stands up and grabs the wine bottle from the counter. I watch him as he pours the last of the bottle between our two glasses. My mind can't get over something, though. "How did you know that?"

"Know what?"

"All of that? That whole speech?" He pulls at the front of his hair.

"I've picked up some of it from what you've told me. And I'm a cop. I've talked to enough domestic violence victims. I also did a specialized course at the academy on women and children victims." He pauses and his eyes go wide. "You're not a victim though. I'm not saying that."

"It's alright." I know I am, but he's right to backtrack. The word is too much for me right now.

"It's not. You're a survivor."

try to think of something to say. Am I? Is this surviving? It feels like it, I suppose. Especially in the last few weeks. Especially with Caden. It feels like more than surviving.

"I just don't want to push you into a stereotype. That speech was probably stupid." He continues to ramble, his blue eyes scared.

"Caden. It was amazing." I have to bite my tongue not to tell him I love him. Because I don't. There's no way I already do. That'd be silly.

I finish my chicken and try to stop smiling. It's really hard. I give up after a few bites and find comfort in the fact that he's smiling too.

CHAPTER FIFTY-NINE
Aubrey

Somehow, we end up cuddling on the couch. I make him watch the news even though he complains the entire time. We talk about politics and he ends up laughing so hard he wheezes when he tries to pull in a breath. It's probably the best thing I've ever heard. It makes me laugh too and I end up snorting. By the end of it we're a breathless mess.

No, but." I try to catch my breath. "But, I can't believe you'll actually vote for him."

"Shh, no more politics."

But-" He interrupts me by catching my lips with his own. His hands slowly come up to my waist and settle there. This kiss is gentle compared to our frantic first one. Although, if I remember correctly, that kiss started this way too.

His hands start traveling, fingers clawing their way under my shirt. I nip at his lip and lick it better.

"Shit." He whispers under his breath, leaning further into the kiss. Before I know it, I'm climbing into his lap, his hands resting on my hips.

I grind against him and it feels good. I was never on top with Elliot. I like having the control. I like feeling powerful.

I shudder and push Elliot out of my head. He doesn't deserve to be here. Not now.

"You're gorgeous." Caden whispers, his big hand cupping my cheek. I lean into it and kiss his thumb. I'm not sure if I like being complimented but, coming from him, it's something I could get used to.

"Thank you."

Mmm," he hums low in his throat and smiles at me. This is a new smile. It's slow and sexy, like he's imagining what he could do to me. His eyes look at mine, then dart to my mouth. "I want to kiss you again."

"I think you should." I can't believe how breathy my voice sounds. It's strange.

"Bree." His voice is just as breathy as mine. He hangs his head like he's ashamed. I grab his chin with my pointer finger and lift it up. "I don't think I can stop if I start kissing you again. You're addicting."

I smile like I've won a prize. "Who says you have to stop?"

He wraps his arms around me and pulls me against his body. I kiss him hard without an invite. He doesn't seem to mind. We move against each other for a few minutes and when we finally pull apart again, it's because he's shaking his head.

"What?"

"This is good." He whispers. I laugh and lean back so I can look at him, cupping his face like he was doing to me earlier. With the tip of my thumb, I graze his long eyelashes, then run it over his cheekbone. It makes him shiver.

"I should go." The words spill out of his mouth and I frown.

"No. No, you shouldn't."

"Bree."

"Come on. You don't want to leave."

"No. I don't want to, but I should." He rests his head against my chest for a moment like this is very difficult for him. Then he pulls away and smiles up at me. "The girls will wonder if I don't come home soon. And we shouldn't move this fast."

"Ouch." I move to climb off him. I've never been rejected before. Elliot was my first and he always *took*. Always.

"Hey, stop." Caden's fingers dig ever so slightly into the skin of my hips to keep me still. I freeze and breathe through the sensation. This is a different kind of restraint. I'm fine. "I just don't want to push you."

"I know what I can handle." I crinkle my nose at him and climb off.

"I had a really great night tonight." He mumbles, trying to fix what he broke.

"I did too." I lean into him and kiss him gently. We stand there for a moment, and then he's kissing me again. It's over way too soon. "I'll walk you to the door."

"Alright." When we get there, he ducks his head down so he's on the same level as me and brings his lips to mine. Our lips barely touch before he's pulling away. I want to chase them but know I shouldn't. "Goodnight, beautiful."

"Goodnight." I can feel my heart in my throat and I try to swallow it, hoping the word doesn't sound choked.

I open the door for him and he gives me one final smile before walking out. The door makes a loud sound when it clicks shut. I deflate against it and close my eyes. I can't remember the last time I was this happy. It's exhilarating.

CHAPTER SIXTY
Caden

I walk to my car and stare at it for a full minute. My entire body feels like it's been lit on fire. I want her so damn bad. We barely know each other but it's already killing me to leave her. I turn away from my car and head back into her apartment complex. I only make it halfway up the stairs before I realize that I shouldn't go up. I turn around and walk back down.

She's gorgeous. Her hair is so damn soft and her eyes are so blue. I don't think I've ever experienced that deep of a color. I can drown in them. And her lips. *Jesus.* Before I know it, I'm climbing back up the stairs. I stop on the top one and try to breathe.

My hand shakes as I knock. What if she's already sleeping? Or showering? What if she's glad that I left? What if she really isn't ready? My thoughts are interrupted as the door swings open. She's still in her dress but her hair, which was pinned half up before, is now loose along her shoulders. I try to think of something but my mind is blank.

"Bree." It feels like a relief to say her name. I wrap my fingers in her soft hair and tug, pushing her back into her own apartment and kissing her like she's my oxygen. I slam the door closed with my foot and she moans against me. "I don't have a condom. Do you have any?"

She shakes her head, pulling mine along with the movement. She speaks against my lips. "On the pill. Don't need it."

"Okay." I stumble after her, picking up the intensity of my kiss.

"Caden." She pulls away and looks up at me, her hands settling on my chest to keep me steady. I breathe. This is it. She's not ready. I'll respect that, of course. I'll leave right this minute.

I don't want to though.

"I'm scared."

My heart has broken before. This moment is another, now added to my list. I kiss her and she melts into my arms. I'm pretty sure I'm all that's holding her up but I don't want to test it by letting go. She pulls away from my lips and starts frantically unbuttoning my flannel. She misses a few and I wish she would just rip the damn thing off.

"Bree." I stop her shaking hands and hold them. She's scared. I need to respect that. I need to acknowledge that. "Baby, look at me."

Her eyes snap up to me at the order and I wonder if it bothered her. Me ordering her around. It bothered me.

"Baby?" Her lips come up at one corner.

"Yeah. That okay?"

"Very." She's breathless and still shaking. I cup her face with both my hands and try to think of something comforting to say. My mind is in the gutter and I yank it out.

"What are you afraid of?" Her eyes search mine.

"I don't know." She sucks her bottom lip into her mouth and chews on it. I feel something stir and I try to ignore it. This is a time where I need to concentrate. "Not you. Not of you."

"Good." I smile at her and hope it calms her. "We can stop. I can go home, or we can watch a movie or something."

"Something." She whispers, pulling her shaking hands out of my grip. I let go of her immediately and she starts on my shirt again. This time she's successful and her lips start dragging across the skin of my chest. I moan.

Game on.

I push her back. I have no idea where her room is but I hope we find it soon. Her fingers are working on my belt now.

I push her towards one of the doors and she groans.

"Myla's." She says against my frantic lips. She grabs my belt loops and tugs me towards what I assume to be her own bedroom. When we get there I barely notice. I'm focused on the fact that she's now unzipping my jeans.

"Slow down, baby." I whisper. I don't plan on our relationship coming to an end anytime soon. I'm completely wrapped around her. With that in mind, this night will be important for us. I know that's usually the girl thing to think about but I promised myself to take care of her.

"No. Not slow." She laughs at me. "I'm not a virgin."

"I don't care." I grab her face with my hands again and hold her still. With her like this, I can visibly see how hard she's shaking. "Breathe, Bree."

"I'm fine. Just nervous."

"I know." I turn her around slowly and kiss the back of her neck. Her dress is clasped at the top and I undo it, kissing the now open spot. Very slowly, I unzip her dress until the zipper is resting at the base of her spine.

"Beautiful." I whisper, running my fingertips over her bare skin. Her shoulders are covered in freckles. If I thought her face was a galaxy, then her body is the universe. I can't wait to uncover more.

"How about we get you out of this dress?" She nods and I start pushing it down her arms. It falls to the ground when it passes her wrists, pooling at her feet. My breath catches at the base of my throat.

Holy shit. She's in nothing but a pair of powder blue lace underwear. No bra. There's something on her ribcage. *Does she have a tattoo?*

I keep my eyes moving, not wanting to dwell too long. She's not in heels, since we were inside, and I find this even more appealing. There's something about her being barefoot in front of me, naked and vulnerable..

I kick my own shoes off. I expect her to turn around to finish undressing me but she doesn't. She's still shaking. I gather her hair in one hand and pull it to the side. Her head tilts with the movement and I kiss the exposed neck.

"I'm falling in love with you." I whisper quietly against her skin. Her shaking stops. Her breathing stops. I wait for her to say something. Anything. After a moment, she turns around and looks at me, a smile spreading across her face.

I think I'm falling in love with you, too." I feel a warmth settle in my chest. Against it too. I have to force myself not to look at the breasts that she's pushing into me.

"Is that why you're scared?" I brush a strand of hair away from her cheek, using the movement to rest my palm against her.

"Maybe a little." She admits in a whisper. I lean down and kiss her soft smile.

"Don't be afraid. I'll never hurt you."

"You can't promise that."

I can. I'm just that good." I arch an eyebrow at her. It receives the giggle I was hoping for.

"Well, now that that's established." She giggles again, going back to what she started with my jeans. I push her back on the bed and center us. She practically melts as I start touching and kissing her. I feel like I'm playing with dough, molding and forming it in the best way.

I slow down right when I'm about to enter her. She's shaking again.

I pull away and start moving down the bed. She groans in frustration but it's quickly replaced by a relieved sigh when I reach my destination.

Within seconds, she's arching her back, her blue eyes screwed shut. I slide a finger into her and circle it, waiting for her to climb higher. It doesn't take her very long and with one very unladylike swear word, she falls over the edge.

Before she has time to recover I'm sinking into her. Both legs wrap around my waist but she's barely moving with me, her head resting against the pillow with her eyes still closed. I chuckle at the sight of her. She cracks one eye open and glares at me. Without warning, she pushes me away and turns so that I'm on my back.

I can tell almost right away she's never been on top before. When she climbs on, she's shaking again. I help her get in place and watch as she slowly lowers herself. It's mind numbingly good. We start to move together and I have to smile.

She's not shaking anymore.

CHAPTER SIXTY-ONE
Caden

"Wow." She breathes the word into the open air between us. I'm lying on my side, propped up on an elbow. She's lying on her back staring up at the ceiling. I drag my fingertips along her bare skin and stop at her tattoo. It's a tree, dead and mangled, with two boxing gloves hanging from it like a noose would. I trace my fingers along it slowly, making her shiver. "Wow."

A low chuckle escapes me. "You've said that already."

Her smile is lazy. "Yeah." The smile disappears as she bites down on her bottom lip. I know her well enough to know that she wants to say something.

"What's on your mind?" Her eyes dart to mine, then back at the ceiling.

"I never knew it could be like that." Her voice is hoarse.

"What?"

"Sex." She pauses and looks back at me. "I didn't know it could be that gentle." I feel like I've been slapped in the face. I tugged her hair a few times and bit her lip, on purpose. Towards the end, I even got a little rough since we were both so close.

That was gentle? I mean, it was. I made sure to take care of her, but I don't want to know what her past experiences were like. Something thick and heavy settles in the bottom of my stomach.

"I'll always take care of you."

"You took care of me alright." She gives me a mischievous smile.

"What does that mean?"

"Nothing." Her cheeks flame bright red as she goes back to staring at the ceiling.

"Noooo. Spill." I dig my fingers into her ribs, tickling her into a confession. Her laughter comes out breathless and choppy.

"Okay! Okay!" I let up and wait for her to catch her breath. She hides her face with her hands when she says, "I just never did that before."

"What?"

"You know. *That*." She peeks at me through her fingers. "Like, you know, coming or whatever."

That heavy feeling in my stomach gains an extra ten pounds. I want to rip that asshole limb for limb. "I'm sorry."

"For what?"

"That that's your past. That that's what you thought love was. Love isn't supposed to be like that, Bree." I pause, and she looks at me like she's waited to hear this all her life.

"So, what's it supposed to be like?"

I give her my best smile. "Let me show you."

CHAPTER SIXTY-TWO
Aubrey

Caden doesn't leave until almost midnight. I love every minute together. I've never felt so taken care of and it was amazing. Before tonight, I had never had an orgasm. It blew my mind that that could even happen. I thought they were something magazines used to sell more copies.

Sex was more Elliot's thing, and he never really cared about me in the matter. I always assumed that was normal. I suppose there might be a few things that I used to think was normal.

I take a shower once he's gone. Not because I feel dirty or ashamed, but because I'm sweaty and my curled hair is tangled and matted in the back.

Something happens under the stream of hot water. The shaking from earlier comes back and I feel everything inside of me start to crumble. Before I know it, I'm sitting on the floor of my shower sobbing into my hands. I'm not sure how long I spend sitting there but eventually Myla comes in and finds me.

"Bree?" She pulls the shower curtain back and gasps. "Aubrey." She falls down to her knees and turns the water off. There's a towel hanging on one of the hooks and she grabs it. I don't move as she wraps it around my shoulders. I don't even think I washed my hair yet.

"I can't." The words are thick as they tumble out of my mouth.

"You can't what?" She puts her hands on my upper arms and pulls me to my feet. Then she helps me get out, one step at a time. Even with the towel around me, I can't stop shaking. Obnoxiously loud sobs are coming from my mouth and I'm not sure how to stop them. I'm not sure how to do anything anymore. "Bree, calm down. Breathe."

"I can't." I drag my fingernails across my chest like I'm trying to claw something out. I want it to be lighter. I want the pressure to go away.

"Breathe. You're doing it. You're talking, so you're breathing. Just focus on breathing." She's rubbing her hands up and down my arms like she's warming me. I want to tell her that I'm not shaking because I'm cold but I can't get the words out. I start to fall and she controls it so I land on the closed toilet seat. It's cool against my skin but I don't care.

"I can't." I bury my face in my hands and the sobs continue. She kneels in front of me and pries my hands away.

"What did he do to you?" I want to tell her nothing, but it's not true. He did things, they were just things I wanted. So why am I crying? Why do I feel like my mind is spinning out of control? "I'll fucking kill him."

She leaves me, and I'm not sure where she's going. I worry that she's going to go find him but realize that's silly. I laugh at the idea and the feeling rolls into something bigger. Before I know it, I'm laughing hysterically instead of crying.

Myla comes back into the room with a glass of ice water and some clothes. I snort as another wave of laughter washes through me and she gives me a sad look. This is what happens when I get too stressed out or sad. She calls it 'breaking'. It's rare, but when it happens, it *really* happens. "Great. He broke you. Drink this when you can." She places the glass on the bathroom counter and helps me stand up again. I would be embarrassed as she dries me off and dresses me, but I'm too busy laughing.

"I can't. I can't." My laughter dies down and suddenly I feel extremely serious. My smile droops down into a frown and it feels like my face is melting. *Weird.*

I grab the water and take a long drink, then wipe my cheeks clean. I feel empty. I know Myla jokes when she says that me acting like that is 'breaking' but it's how I feel.

I feel broken.

"You can't what? Speak full sentences." Now that I'm dressed I sit back down on the toilet and try to breathe. I stare down at the tiled floor and it starts moving. That's the exhaustion kicking in.

"We had sex." My voice is gross and scratchy. Myla sits down on the floor and leans her back against the tub. She's frowning, but she wants to smile too.

"Did he hurt you?"

"No. It was amazing." I take in another breath. It's getting slightly easier.

"I think I'm in love with him. Or really close to it."

"Wow." Her lips twitch up for a second. "That's big."

"It is." The pressure on my chest comes back again. "Too big."

"Yeah?"

"I don't know." I pick at the strings attached to my shorts. "It wasn't at the time. I loved it, My. He was so sweet and it was amazing. It was so much better than it ever was with Elliot and I really do think I'm in love with him."

"So, the problem?"

"I don't know." I wipe my eyes and try to think of what started the panic attack. I was replaying the night over, and all the other times he's made me feel safe or happy. I felt like I was walking on air and then suddenly I was shaking. I don't understand.

I tell her this and she gives me a devastated look.

"Can I make a suggestion?"

"Yeah."

"You're happy." Her smile transforms into one of relief, like she's been waiting for this moment. "You're finally happy and I think it's freaking you out that you could lose that. That, once again, a guy is making you happy. I think that scares you."

"No." Even as I say the word I know it's a lie. She's right, but how embarrassing is that? I mean that would pretty much prove I'm broken. Who gets scared of being happy?

"I think you are." She stands up and sighs, like her work is done. "Don't run from him. I know that look in your eyes and you're two seconds away from panicking. Well, you already panicked, but you're two seconds away from doing something stupid. Don't."

"I'm happy." I stare at her as I try out the words. They're foreign and heavy. I'm not sure if I like them. "I'm happy."

She smiles. "Yeah. I think you just might be."

CHAPTER SIXTY-THREE
Caden

I don't start worrying until she's twenty minutes late. By thirty minutes, I'm starting to fully panic. I pace the gym and stare down at my phone. I've already called her three times, and any more would be too much. She never skips practice. If she's not here it's because of me.

My phone vibrates in my hand after another five minutes go by and I look at it. It's just a text from Jason.

Shit. Where the hell is she? I go back to pacing and decide if she's not here in another five minutes, I'll go to her place.

The gym doors open and I snap my attention to them. A girl is standing there, but it's not Aubrey. This is a bad sign. She looks around the gym before closing the door quietly behind herself. After she sees that we're alone, she starts towards me. I feel like I want to hide in a corner.

"You said she was safe." Her words are cold and hard. I stuff my phone into the pocket of my shorts and try to look tough. I don't think it works because she smiles like she's amused.

"She was. She is." I can't help but still feel panicked. Myla is pointing a finger at me and her face is starting to match her hair color.

"You can't leave her after something huge like that! She had a fricken breakdown."

Breakdown? "She was good when I left her. Said she was going to take a quick shower and go to bed."

"Well, that's not what happened." I start to panic. What does that mean? What happened to her?

"Is she okay?" She runs a hand along one of the weight machines, and I wonder if she's thinking about bashing my head in with a weight. "She's sleeping. I turned her alarm off."

I'm not sure if that's a good or bad thing, but my body seems to relax. She didn't skip practice on purpose. That's good, at least. It doesn't mean she knowingly decided not to see me. "Is she okay?" I repeat.

"Yeah. She kind of freaked out last night. It's not your fault, so I'm sorry for yelling at you. I'm just frustrated." I wonder what to say to that but she doesn't stop long enough for me to come up with anything. "She's going to want to run and push you away. I'm here to tell you not to let her."

"Oh?" This is a new twist. I thought for sure she was going to be chopping something of me.

"It's none of my business, I know, but she's happy and she's safe with you and I don't think I've ever felt so relieved. I honestly thought she was done. Like shut down and never trust again, done. But then she met you." She smiles, and I realize her tone has softened. Everything about her has.

"I'm not going to hurt her."

"Not intentionally, but shit happens. This isn't a romance novel. Life is messy and you make her happy and I think she's scared of losing that. She's been sad for too long."

"That's something we can both agree on."

"Good." She laughs, and I want to ask what she's thinking about. I don't though. If she wanted me to know she would tell me. She seems like the kind of girl who you don't have to pry for information. The kind of girl who gladly throws it in your face. I can't help but think, despite the inappropriate timing, that Jason would really like her.

"I think I'm going to like you." The words pull me out of my thoughts and I smile at her.

"Ditto."

"Good." She claps her hands together once, like it's solved. "She's taking the day off. She needs it."

"She needs to be here." She rolls her eyes and I step forward. I place my hand out in the open air between us and start my small lecture. "She needs to be here because it's a coping mechanism for her. Her career and all that bullshit aside, she needs to be here to work through all the shit in her head. She's angry and afraid and she can't run from that."

I want to tell Myla that even if she's sleeping, she could still be in hell, but I have a feeling she knows what I've just recently found out about Aubrey's dreams. She lives in the same apartment with her after all.

"She was up until two last night, freaking out. She was exhausted." Myla places her hands on her hips. "I'm dragging her to therapy today. Don't expect to hear from her until she's calmed down. There's stuff she needs to work out."

"Okay. I'm glad you were there. I should have stayed."

She fixes a stare on me that could probably petrify a weaker individual. "Next time, you will. Aubrey is not the type you bang and leave."

"It's a little more complicated than that, but trust me, I know. If I could have stayed, I would have."

"Okay." She seems to take my word for it, her glare turning into a slight smile. "Now the only thing I have to complain about is the fact that you ruined one of my pots last night. No amount of soap or scraping is getting that burnt rice off."

I give her my best attempt at an apologetic smile. "I'll buy you a new one. It'll even be purple." Myla nods like I've passed the test.

I watch as she exists without a goodbye and pull my phone back out. I know it's silly, Myla just left, but I don't want to miss Aubrey's call. I'll just have to be glued to this phone for the rest of the day.

CHAPTER SIXTY-FOUR
Aubrey

"I'm dragging your ass to group." Myla announces as she pours coffee into our travel mugs. Green eyes lift to look at me, a dare to argue. There's no reason to. It's time.

"If you're holding me hostage, do I at least get a list of demands?"

"Sigh." The travel mug is warm when she hands it to me. It's comforting, like I could curl up in a blanket and read. I'd give anything for a lazy day like that. "You get three demands, Miss Crab Ass."

"I pick the music." I slip my feet into my shoes and grab my purse from the hook on the wall. The emptiness in my stomach is from a lot of things, but one of the major issues is hunger. "We stop at the gas station for snacks, too."

With a sharp salute to the forehead, she follows me out the door. "You wanna drive?" She jangles the keys like I'm a grumpy cat whose trust she's trying to gain. I suppose that's not too far off.

"No. You go ahead." I start by plugging my phone into the radio, scrolling through my song list. With Robert Plant's voice filling the car, I feel much calmer. I know it won't last. The group I go to is almost an hour away. Plenty of time for my anxiety to swell.

Once we're stocked with combos and licorice, we head north. We listen to song after song, Myla groaning but still singing along. As much as she complains, I think she secretly likes my music. Not better than her annoying pop artists, but it's a step in the right direction.

When we're five miles out, she turns down the music. She's lucky it's just Journey, or she'd get the same lecture as Caden.

"You still have a demand left."

"Sure do." I pop a combo in my mouth, chewing extra loud just to annoy her. "I want you to come in."

Her grip tightens on the wheel. She's been going with me since the first meeting, starting the day after I got released from the hospital. Yet, she's never come in. Instead, she spends her time at the library across the street.

"Why would I go?"

We both know the answer to that one. Myla didn't go into foster care until she was twelve. All twelve of those years would be worth discussing in a group like mine.

"That's such a waste of a demand, man." She slides the car into a parking spot and breathes through her nose. Red hair hides her face from me. I'm in the dark as to what she's thinking.

"Fine. But I'm not talking."

I reach for her hand. "Deal."

CHAPTER SIXTY-FIVE
Aubrey

Group is full of familiar faces. The only person I don't recognize is a boy to my left, clutching a Styrofoam cup hard enough to make it crack. Myla sits to my right, knees bouncing.

"Good morning, survivors." Emma's maxi dress sways as she gestures to the room. Her kind eyes settle on me and she smiles. "Aubrey. Welcome back."

"Thanks." I squeeze my fists as everyone turns to look at me. The cuffs of my sweater are crumpled and damp in my hands. It's been over a year since I came. Just after Elliot's trial finished and college was starting. The nightmares had slowed, the panic attacks were manageable, Rob had a gym looking to train me, and I was moving on.

When I finish telling them all this, Emma gives me a sad smile. "So, what changed?"

Everyone in the circle is leaning forward. We all dream of moving on. Surely, they want to know what I did to ruin it.

I tug at my cuffs again. Myla's knees are finally calm now that she knows the attention isn't on her. When the silence gets too much, I finally tell them. "I found a guy."

The announcement is met with an equal mixture of cat calls and groans. Emma just does that annoying nod and smile that means she understands. "Being with someone for the first time is hard."

Izzy, a twenty-three year old that used to be married to a financial advisor that saw her as a ragdoll, raises her hand. "Izzy, do you have something to add?"

"When I met Michael, oh, wait. Aubrey, I met someone too! While you were away." She smiles wide. "Anyway, when I met him, the triggers all came rushing back. It felt like starting from day one." She fiddles with her brand-new wedding ring.

"The worst part is that I still sometimes miss him." I bite my lip. "No. Actually, the worst part is how much I'm learning. Like, I knew I was abused or whatever, but Elliot was my first boyfriend, ya know? I didn't know what normal felt like. How good it could be."

"It's like getting abused all over again. I'm just now realizing how bad it really was, because there's something to compare it to." I brush my cheek against my shoulder to get rid of the stray tear rolling down it.

The entire room sits in silence. Then the boy beside me coughs and leans forward. "So, we're better off just being alone?"

"No." Izzy, Emma, and I all say at once. I look at the boy and give him a firm head shake. "I used to think that too, but I was so wrong. Being with someone again is hard, and messy, but it's also amazing."

He rolls his eyes down to his empty, broken cup. That's when Myla speaks. "Plus, staying alone? No thanks. Being alone sucks."

"What does that mean?" Emma asks Myla. "And what's your name and story, if you don't mind?"

"Sucks being the new kid." The guy teases, probably excited he isn't the newest here anymore.

"Oh, um." Myla's knees return to bouncing. "I'm Myla. I, uh." She looks at me in fear.

"You don't have to." I whisper.

She nods and slumps forward, arms wrapping around her waist to hold herself together. Despite the defensive position, she still speaks. "I'm a survivor, I guess? Um, sexual and physical child abuse."

Everyone calls out to her in variations of greeting. She smiles at me, proud that she did it.

"So, Myla. What did you mean about being alone? Are you happily with someone?"

"No." She laughs at this. "I'm a firm believer in one night stands and not getting attached. Guys suck."

Everyone gives Emma a nervous look. This is usually an issue she tackles head on. Her favorite thing is teaching us how to have healthy relationships and trust again.

This time, probably because Myla is new and she doesn't want to scare her off, she just smiles. "Everyone copes differently. Hopefully, when you're ready, we will work on changing that."

Myla just shrugs, and the group turns its attention back to me. "So, what do I do? I don't want to sleep around." I stick my tongue out at Myla. "No offense."

"None taken."

Have you opened up to this new guy about your past?" Emma asks.

I nod. "Yeah. He's been great."

"Good. Then all you can do is what, everyone?"

The group says, "Keep coming back," in a jumbled cheer.

I sigh. "For how long?"

Emma gives me a sad smile. "For as long as it takes."

CHAPTER SIXTY-SIX
Caden

"I really think we should go."

"No. I'm not going. It's stupid and it's not a part of this investigation."

"It is. Jessica is friends with Heather, who's friends with Kyle. And Kyle-"

"Larson." Jones looks up at me, his eyes pleading. I turn my attention away from my phone and sigh.

"If he thinks you should go, you should go."

"It's a birthday party." He says this like it's dirty.

"It's a birthday party where you'll get to interact with X again." I'm slightly annoyed. Jameson is doing a great job remembering to call X by his codename. It would make our lives easier if he would just slip up, and he knows that.

"What's the point of interacting with him when I don't even know who he is?"

"Because he needs to come to you, or he'll know that someone in the group gave him away. You can't act suspicious and you can't act interested in him. Only a few of us even know that he's the one running things."

I let out a dramatic sigh and stare at my phone. This is giving me a headache. Why do I even have to be here for this shit? I feel like a glorified babysitter.

"Larson."

"Jones." I roll my eyes in his direction and he seems to second guess himself. I make it easier for him. "His reasoning is sound. You'll go to the party."

"But-"

"You guys have to stop coming here all the damn time. You have to handle these things yourself." I stand up and collect my stuff, dismissing them without saying so. Just then, my phone starts to vibrate.

I don't care that I'm not alone or that I probably come off too eager, I answer on the second buzz. "Hello?"

"Hey." She sounds relieved that I answered, and maybe a little nervous. An image of her lying naked across her bed flashes in my head and I push it away to focus.

"I missed you this morning."

"I know, I'm really sorry. My alarm got turned off."

"Yeah, Myla stopped by the gym and told me. Wanted to make sure you wouldn't get in trouble."

I wait for her to answer. It takes a moment. "What else did she say?"

"You had a rough night." I wonder if she's okay. I really hope so. "I wish you would have called me. I could have talked you through it."

She gives me a breathy laugh. "You didn't want to be talking to me. I was in a bad place."

"Bad place or not, I'm still here."

"That's," she pauses, and I think I hear her sniffle. "That means a lot."

I turn around and see that Jones is gone but Jameson is still sitting there, playing with a pen. Aubrey sniffles again. I just want to hold her. "We can work out tonight if you want? I'm not off until six and I'll have to bring the girls with me but I can do it."

"I actually have a ton of homework to do. I could come early tomorrow to catch up?"

"Yeah, that works." Jameson is staring at me now, his eyes cold. "I actually have a random day off tomorrow. We could do two sessions?"

"Yeah, um." There's a bang in the background and she curses under her breath. I smile at how cute she is. When she speaks again, she sounds out of breath and possibly in pain. "Sorry, I tripped."

"Over what?"

"Oh, um." She laughs. "Myself."

"Where are you?"

"Walking to class." I have to stop myself from laughing when I picture her walking with her little backpack and tripping. She's adorable. "I have two today. Not as busy as Wednesday, because of the extra-long class in the morning, but still busy."

"What's your schedule like for tomorrow?"

"I just have one on Tuesday and Thursdays. At eleven."

"We could do our morning workout, then grab a late lunch after your class? Then workout again later, at some point." I smile to myself and lower my voice. "Maybe the second one could be in bed."

"Mmm. That sounds tempting." Someone yells in the background and I wonder if it's at her or someone else. Hopefully someone else. She's had a hard-enough time as is. "There's this great little restaurant by campus. I'd like to show you it."

"Sounds perfect." Jameson stirs in his chair and gives me a strange look. I turn so I can pretend he's not there. "I can't wait to see you."

"I can't either."

"You're okay, yeah?"

"Yeah." She exhales and it sounds cleansing. "I'm actually really good."

"Alright." I have to hide my smile. I don't want Jameson to see it. "I'll see you tomorrow then, bright and early."

CHAPTER SIXTY-SEVEN
Aubrey

My phone vibrates three times before falling off my bedside table. I grab it and answer it, still half dreaming about a strange grocery store where everything is chocolate.

"Hello?" I glance at my alarm clock and groan. I need to be awake in three hours, so whoever is calling me better have a damn good reason.

"Bree?" My name sounds foreign, yet so familiar, in his husky voice. The room collapses around me, the weight of it crushing my chest and leaving me breathless.

"It's me." I finally say.

The sheets are tangled in between my legs. I kick them away, as if they are the rubble that's causing me to suffocate. It doesn't work. I still can't breathe.

"I thought you would have changed your number." I should have. I meant to. He never called from prison and I thought I was safe. If he was calling from prison, I should have had to accept the call. Doesn't that happen in all the movies and shows?

My head feels so damn heavy. "I miss you."

"Oh." *Is that really the best I can do?* I should tell him that I don't miss him. I should tell him to leave me the hell alone. I should go get Myla. I should hang up and call Caden right now.

"Are you still mine?" The words are thick and heavy. He sounds drunk. *How can he be drunk in prison?* He sounds sad. My heart aches for him and my hands start shaking. I can't do this. I can't be speaking to him. "Bree?"

"Elliot." His name is like a grenade falling from my tongue. Every memory, every hit, comes rushing back.

Does he know where I live? Is he here?

"I shouldn't have called." He hangs up, leaving me to cling to the phone and wonder what the hell just happened.

My entire body is shaking and the room is spinning. The combination leaves me nauseated. Sure enough, I find myself stumbling to the bathroom just in time to spill the contents of my stomach into the toilet.

I brush my teeth after the dry heaving stops. My reflection tries to get my attention in the mirror but I openly ignore it. There's no time for soul searching right now.

My skin starts to crawl as I search my room for clothes. It feels like I can't get dressed fast enough.

I can't be here anymore. I can't be anywhere.

My bedroom door creaks as I open it. I cringe, but don't hear Myla stir. I'm not sure if that's a good or bad thing, because maybe I want her to stop me. Maybe, I want her to fix things this time.

Am I really doing this?

CHAPTER SIXTY-EIGHT
Aubrey

The gym is dead silent. I meant to leave town, I really did, but this place was too hard to leave. Almost as hard as the idea of leaving Caden and Myla.

I start searching for some spare gloves, since I obviously didn't bring my own. I know I've seen them before, but can't remember where they are. As I'm searching, I realize that Caden will be here soon for his own workout, and I have no idea what I'll say to him. I have no idea what I'm going to do at all.

Now that I'm thinking clearly, I know for a fact that I would have had to accept that call. He's out of prison and I don't know what to do about that. I want to ask Caden how that could happen, but I don't want him involved. Our relationship, or whatever it is, is new and fragile. It's complicated enough as it is without adding a psycho ex on the loose.

"Look who's early." I jump out of my skin and whip around to look at the door. Caden is standing there with a lazy smile on his face. It freezes when he notices my reaction. "Shit, didn't mean to scare you."

"I'm fine." My voice trembles. He takes in my jeans and sweater, eyes scanning every inch of me before returning to my face. He shakes his head.

"No, you're not." He starts towards me and I involuntarily step back. He reaches a hand out to me like he's approaching a scared puppy. "What happened?"

"Just a bad dream." I cross my arms and shake my head, hoping to clear it. I wish this was a bad dream. It sure feels like one.

"Yeah?"

"I told you about them."

"I know." He takes a step toward me. I do the same, closing the gap between us. I'm not afraid of him and the realization makes him visibly relax. He drops his hand but keeps the careful smile. "Why do I have a feeling that this is different than that?"

"Because it is." My hands are shaking and I clasp them behind my back to hide them. That way makes me feel defenseless and vulnerable, so I pull them back to my front and cross my arms against my chest instead. Really, I'm just stalling, because once I say it out loud, it's real.

"He called me last night."

"Who?" His body stiffens and he closes his eyes for the briefest of moments. It's like he's composing himself, trying to push off a wave of anger. It breaks my heart. I shouldn't have gotten him involved in my mess. He's dealing with enough.

When he's calm, he asks, "How?"

"I don't know."

"When? What time? Last night? Did he call your cell phone? Why did you accept his call? You could have turned it down. He wouldn't have been able to do anything." He runs a hand through his short hair and looks around the gym like the answers are suspended in the air. "He shouldn't have been able to call you last night. Was it last night? Phones turn off at eight. Shit, what prison is he in?"

"Caden."

"What's his name? I'll get his privileges–"

"Caden." My voice breaks at the end of his name and he finally stops. I try to remember all his questions. "He called last night, well this morning, really. Just an hour or two ago."

"On your cell?"

"Yeah." I hear his words in my mind, *I thought you would have changed your number.* I'm such an idiot. I thought I was safe. How could I think that? "I didn't have to accept the call. I had no idea it was going to be him until he spoke, but I don't think he was in prison."

He stares at me, eyes wide open. "You mean, he's out?"

"I'm assuming." I thought it would be harder to talk about this, but Caden being here helps. I should have gone straight to him. "How can that happen?"

"The President is releasing a shit ton of drug offenders. He believes it's the solution to overcrowding. They're apparently the least terrible out of everyone." He clearly doesn't agree. His anger is palpable. I feel like I could reach into the air around us and touch it. "You need to give me his name. I need to find out what's going on."

"No." I look him right in the eyes and shake my head. "Absolutely not."

"Why?"

"Because I'm smart enough to know that you'll get in trouble if you start looking into something you're not supposed to. And I know you well enough to know that you'll do something pretty stupid if you find him."

I can practically see him agree with me, the way his head nods and his shoulders lift into a shrug. But his eyes look defeated. "I can't help you if you don't tell me about him."

"I can tell you about him." I take in the deepest breath possible and let it sit in my chest for a minute before puffing out my cheeks and exhaling. "I can tell you everything. I just can't tell you his name."

"Fine." He stares down at the floor.

"Not yet, though." His eyes snap up to mine and they search my face. I can feel the electricity between us, and it's why I want to wait. I don't want to lose this. I just want to kiss him.

I step forward and he smiles when he realizes what I'm doing. He wraps his arms around my waist and pulls me in tight against his chest. Our lips come together easily and I shiver. When he pulls away he rubs his nose against the tip of mine and smiles.

"I just want to keep you safe, baby." I close my eyes and savor the moment. I'm falling so damn hard for this man.

"You are. I just want to go through with our normal plans today." I sigh.

"He didn't sound like he was going to hurt me."

"What did he say?" He pulls away slightly to look at my face, but his hands stay on me. Protective. I used to feel suffocated by that feeling, but now I can't stop smiling.

"He told me he missed me and asked if I'm still *his*." I can't look at Caden while I say this. For some reason I feel guilty, like I cheated or something. "Then he said he shouldn't have called and hung up."

"Alright."

"He sounded drunk." I don't know why I offer this. Maybe because it scares me. He was always so much worse under the influence.

"He shouldn't be drinking if he just got out. His offenses would lead to a no drinking clause."

"I'm just saying what it sounded like." My chest aches. "How could he already be out, Caden?"

"I don't know, baby. I would have to look at his case. I would have to see the charges and if there was a plea deal or something. I don't know." He rests his forehead against mine and lets out a long sigh. "Just tell me his name."

"No." I kiss him and he smiles against my lips. I stay there for a few seconds before slowly pulling away from him. His fingers tense but let me go without a fight. It's hard for him, but he knows me well enough to know I can't feel pinned down. Especially today. Especially right now.

"We should workout then. You've got class." The words sound like he's upset and dismissing me but his tone is different. It's soft and meaningful, like he understands exactly what I need right now. He glances at my clothes. "Did you sleep last night?"

"No. Not really."

"Is Myla home?" I nod. Knowing her, she's probably still fast asleep. "Okay. I'm going to drive you home, you can leave your car here."

"No, you'll have to go to work and I'll need my car for class. It's okay. I'll be okay."

He huffs at me, obviously annoyed at my stubbornness. "Fine. I'm walking you to your car, at least. Then you're going to go home, lock the door, and get some rest." He pauses. "Please."

"Okay." I frown. "Are we still on for lunch and hanging out later?"

"Of course." He beams at me, his hands stuffed in his pockets. I have a feeling it's so he doesn't grab me again. "He doesn't get to ruin our day. He doesn't get to ruin anything for you anymore."

I don't know how he knew, but that's word for word what I needed to hear. I have come so far. Too damn far.

CHAPTER SIXTY-NINE
Caden

I slam my bare fists into the bag, over and over. The muscles in my back are aching and my arms are damn close to giving out, but I continue to throw my weight into every punch.

I can't see straight. I don't even know how I'm hitting the bag right now. My vision is red and blurred.

My fist slides across the bag and runs off, sending me stumbling forward.

"Fuck!" People quiet down when I yell, but I don't give them my attention.

I hang my head and try to breathe. Try to concentrate. I only have an hour to pull myself together before work. An hour to stop my mind from spinning out of control.

"Caden." Jason comes up behind me, his hands stuffed in his pockets. I ignore him, already back on my feet and ready to go again. "Caden."

"What?" He's standing beside me now and I glare at him.

"Wanna talk about it?"

"No."

"Caden."

"I want to fight." I don't know why the words tumble from my mouth. I know that I can't fight anymore, it's not an option, but before I can take them back he smiles.

"Are you angry?"

"Yes." I don't know why he even has to ask. My anger is so thick in the air, I can barely breathe. I expect him to shoot me down because of it, and I'm not sure how I feel about that. It's better for me to walk away, but now that the idea is blooming, I can't stop thinking about it. I want to fight. I want to fight so damn bad.

"My heads straight. I wanna fight."

"Meet me in the ring. And get a pair of fucking gloves on, you moron." He walks away from me and heads toward his office. I watch him, frozen in shock and fear. What if I can't walk away when we're done?

I grab my gloves and try to breathe normally. Jason comes out of his closet with his sweatshirt off and his gloves in his hands. He heads towards the ring without looking over at me. The familiar magnetic pull tugs at me as I approach it. Tremors run through my body as the excitement builds.

"Sparring or fighting?"

"Fighting." I crack my neck.

"Stay out of your head." Jason taps his head with his glove. "Focus on the fight. Focus on me." I nod and try to breathe. I trust him. Not myself, but him.

He hops up and down a few times and I start doing the same, trying to get over my excitement and nerves. I look around the gym and people are staring. This might be a bad idea. I shouldn't do this. What if I can't stop?

"Ready?"

I jump.

"Huh?" I expect him to roll his eyes or get annoyed but instead he smirks, tapping his glove against his head again to remind me of what I'm supposed to be doing.

Stay in your head. You can do this.

"You ready?"

"Yeah." I come toward him, my glove out in the open air. Jason steps forward and hits his glove against mine. We both retreat to our original spots and nod in acknowledgement.

For a moment, I panic that I won't remember what to do. Then Jason comes toward me swinging, and my muscle memory kicks in. The moment we collide, I feel like I've stepped back into my own skin.

How did I not see it before? This is where I need to be.

CHAPTER SEVENTY
Caden

I finish my bottle of water and close my eyes, resting my head against the back of the couch. The leather is cool against my overheated skin. Jason lets me stay that way for a while. I hear papers rustling and the clicking of his keyboard. I assume he's working.

My muscles start aching and I open my eyes. When I look at him he's sitting in his chair, leaning back and staring at me. I groan. I don't want to talk about it.

"You good?"

"Yeah." I put my head back against the couch and close my eyes again. I don't have the energy for this. I still need to shower and get to work.

"How'd it feel?"

"Good." I let out a breath. "Really damn good."

"Good." He shifts and I open my eyes to see what he's doing. He comes around the desk and leans against it, his legs kicked out in front of him. He's about to lecture me.

"You were textbook in there, man. You stayed in the ring the whole time. I could feel your anger, especially when you were doing your combos, but you never went into your head. I never lost you."

I think of a way to respond. What he's saying is true, but that almost makes it harder. I stayed in control and I fought well. I kicked his ass in there. And it felt so damn good. It felt so familiar and comfortable. *How do I walk away from that?*

"You should start doing it again."

"Doing what?" I ask, already knowing the answer but needing to stall.

"Fighting." He ducks his head like he's trying to get me to look at him.

"I can't." Not only is it not appropriate to bring that around the girls, but the lifestyle doesn't make room for being a parent. I can't fight and take care of them. I already feel like I'm stretched too thin.

"You don't have to go big time or anything. But you should at least be fighting, even if it's just with me. Even if it's just training the guys here, getting them prepared. Even if it's just small fights around town." He takes a breath, his head shaking. "You belong in that ring."

"I know." I've never known anything more than I've known that. "I'll think about it."

CHAPTER SEVENTY-ONE
Aubrey

I choose a seat in the back corner, glancing at the clock and seeing that I'm early. The waitress brings me a water and I let her know that I'm waiting on someone. With a wink she leaves me be and I pull out my flashcards for History, hoping to cram in a few minutes of studying before Caden arrives.

"How the hell are you concentrating?" Caden slips into the seat across from me, shouting over the music. One of the things I love about this place is how unconventional it is. The brightly colored walls are lined with crazy bumper stickers and pictures of what I've always assumed are the staff. The best part is the music though. They're always playing really good music, usually classic rock, at the perfect volume. Loud enough to create an atmosphere but just quiet enough to be able to talk. Well, slightly yell.

"I always study with music." I yell over Jimmy Page's guitar solo. He smiles at me, the corners of his eyes crinkling.

"Of course you do." He looks around, his eyes lighting up as he takes in our surroundings. When he turns his attention back to me, he's amused. "This place is amazing."

"I know." I beam at him. "I found it when I first toured campus. It's like it was made for me."

"I think it was." He laughs and shakes his head.

"I'm glad you like it."

"Of course I do." His eyes are bright. "Thank you for showing it to me."

The waitress comes up as the new song begins and we order coffee. Once she's gone, I grab two menus from the center of the table and hand him one. His eyes bulge as he starts reading.

"Everything comes with so much food."

"A ton." I nod, scanning the menu even though I know what I want. I've been craving it for at least a week. When I see him put his menu down I follow suit. "What'd you decide on?"

"The pulled pork sandwich. You?"

"The cheese curd burger." The waitress shows up with our coffees and takes our orders. When we're left alone I lean back and start listening to the music, losing myself in it for a moment. When I look at Caden, he's smiling ear to ear. "What?"

"Nothing. Just happy." He takes a sip of coffee and smiles again. I feel all my anxiety from today leave me. If he's happy, that means I didn't ruin us with my news about Elliot.

"Good. Happy is good." I pick at the corner of one of the menus and try to think of something to say. Thankfully, he jumps in quick.

"What were you studying?"

"I have a History exam next week. Just trying to get a head start." I can feel myself blushing. I'm a total nerd and I wait for him to call me out on it. He doesn't.

"I can help you. Quiz you sometime."

"That'd be awesome." I have to push the image of Elliot away, throwing my textbooks at the wall and screaming. He hated when I studied or put too much time into school projects. He knew if I got into Brown, I would succeed at escaping him. He refused to let it happen.

"What's it on?" Caden pulls me out of my thoughts and I'm thankful for it. I dive into the topic of next week's essay, losing myself in how passionate I feel about the civil rights movement. By the time I'm finished, out of breath and embarrassed by my rambling, the waitress is bringing us our food.

"How's work going so far?" I ask him, before taking a bite of my burger.

The look on his face is not pleasant. "Terrible. I'm bogged down with paperwork."

"Boo. That's no fun." I watch him eat a french fry, studying the way his lips wrap around it. If we weren't in a restaurant, I would be kissing him right now. Which reminds me, "So, tonight. We're working out at your place, right?"

"Right." He points his fork at me. "And I know I promised sex, but you've skipped two workouts, so training first."

"First, huh?" I wink at him. "Does that mean sex, after?"

"Hmm." He licks his lips. "If you're lucky."

CHAPTER SEVENTY-TWO
Aubrey

Myla is waiting for me when I get home. She plays it off like she's not, flipping through a textbook and humming softly to herself, but I know better. She always studies at the table, not on the couch, and she always has a notebook nearby in case something important needs to be written down. Her notebook is nowhere to be seen.

"Hello." I place my backpack on the floor and give her a forced smile.

"Oh, hey. Didn't notice you there." Her eyes linger on the book for another second before meeting mine.

I'm not in the mood to ignore the lie, so I call her out. "You were waiting for me."

"No. No, I wasn't. I was just studying because-"

"Shut up." I flop down on the couch next to her and turn sideways so we're facing each other. "You were waiting for me."

"I was." She scrunches her nose at me. "Sorry."

"You're good."

"I just woke up to pee this morning and you were gone. There's no way you were working out that early, and I was worried."

I pause and take a breath, preparing myself for the outburst to come. "Elliot called me last night."

"What?" She sits up straight, her textbook flying to the floor. Her hands gravitate to mine. "Explain."

"I don't even really know how to explain, honestly. I woke up to my phone ringing and answered." My voice starts giving out and I gulp all the emotions down. I really don't want to cry. "It was so awkward. He kept saying my name and he asked if I was still his. He sounded drunk."

She pauses, pondering what I just said. I give her the time. I kind of hope that she can solve it, because I've been trying all day and I'm exhausted.

Eventually she sighs. "And it was Elliot? You're sure?"

"Definitely."

"So, he's out then."

"I guess so."

"Well, shit." I feel my phone vibrate against my leg, just once. We both stare at it for a few seconds.

"It's probably just Caden." She assures me.

"Yeah." I grab it, not sure if I want to look. "Yeah, you're probably right."

"Look." Her voice is a whisper, like we're sharing a secret. "Come on, it's killing me."

I roll my eyes but listen to her. The screen lights up with seven words, all from Caden. My shoulders sag in relief. "It's Caden."

"Oh. Good." She glances at the phone in my hand. "Um, we should go through the call log. Call him back or something."

"What, take back the power?" I snort. It's an absurd idea. I'm not chasing him. I'm not asking for trouble. Hopefully, after last night when he realized he shouldn't have called me, he'll never call again. "I don't want to talk about this anymore. I need to change and get going."

"Where are you going?"

"I have another workout with Caden." She follows me into my room.

"Does he know? About Elliot?"

"Yes." I pull my shirt over my head and go over to my closet. The fact that I'm getting naked doesn't throw her off the least bit. She plops down on my bed and continues firing questions at me.

After I assure her that I'm good, that I know Caden would help but I don't want him to, and that I promise to tell her if he calls again, she leaves me alone.

It's the first time I've been alone since the morning. I don't like it.

CHAPTER SEVENTY-THREE
Caden

I'm not sure why I'm so nervous. The girls have met Aubrey before, but it wasn't like this. This is different. Less casual. Caitlin has pointed this out three times now. I have a feeling she likes the fact that I'm nervous. I have no idea why I invited Aubrey for dinner. Well, I kind of do. We're doing the workout in my basement gym and it's just more convenient.

"Can I help?" Cassie climbs up on the counter, her little legs dangling. I hand her the bottle of Italian dressing and wink at her.

"Squeeze all of that in here." I lift the Tupperware container with the four chicken breasts in it.

"Why?" Her head tilts like it's the most serious question.

"When the chicken soaks in it, it tastes really good." She gives me an uneasy look but does as she's told. It must be entertaining for a four-year-old because she giggles as the dressing pours into the container.

When she's done, I put the cover on and stick it in the fridge. She hops down and smiles up at me.

"All done?"

"All done." I mess up her hair. "Why don't you go play for a little while. If you need me, I'll be in the basement."

"Working out?"

"Yes."

"I work out too?" I can't help but smile. I usually let her hangout downstairs with me when I use the gym. The most she does is bounce on the exercise ball and do silly little dances in the mirror. It's adorable.

"Not tonight, sweetheart. Aubrey is coming, remember?" I cringe at my own words. I shouldn't be taking away from Cassie so I can give to Aubrey.

That's not what I'm doing, right?

"Okay." She shrugs her shoulders and skips off before I can worry too much about it. Caitlin wanders in and glances in the fridge, shaking her head. My patience is thin at the moment, so I snap.

"What?"

"Nothing." She continues staring and sighs.

"What, Caitlin? I'm not in the mood."

"I was just hoping we would eat something other than meat, that's all."

Fire crawls into my chest. "What's wrong with chicken?" She doesn't look at me or say anything. I watch her bite her bottom lip for a minute, trying to breathe. "You're a vegetarian again?"

"Is that a problem?" She turns around, letting the door to the fridge slam shut. I breathe, in through my nose and back out. It's not nearly as cleansing as I need it to be.

"Nope. Not a problem. I will make you something else." Before she can say anything sarcastic, or before I can raise my voice, I storm out of the kitchen.

Since my life has great timing, the doorbell rings.

CHAPTER SEVENTY-FOUR
Caden

Within seconds, I have Aubrey pinned down on the mat in my basement. She taps out too fast, not even fighting to get out of the chokehold. After she calms down, I approach her. It's a relief when she doesn't look at me like she's scared.

"Sorry." She stares up at the ceiling in total frustration. I stand up and offer her my hand.

"Don't worry about it. Just something we need to work on." She wraps her fingers around mine, letting me pull her up to a standing position.

"Yeah. Can we just, um." She runs a hand down her face. "Can we take a break from that?"

"From what? Ground work?" She nods. "But that's what we're working on today."

"I know." Her blue eyes look right at me. They're filled with anxiety. I have to force myself to remember that right now, I'm her trainer. I need to push her.

"We can take a water break but you need to be able to work on the ground if you're serious about fighting."

"I know." She crosses her arms, defensive now. Her ponytail swishes dramatically behind her with the movement.

I choose to ignore her, still channeling my inner trainer, and go grab my water bottle. She does the same and we drink in silence. I try to give her enough time to calm down but after five minutes I tell her to get back on the mat. She hesitates, then moves forward.

The exercise starts off simple enough. I begin with straddling her and she smiles up at me, wiggling her hips seductively. I squint at her like I'm angry and she giggles. "Bring it on, baby."

Her blue eyes light up and I can't help but smile at her. She takes advantage of my moment of weakness and bucks her hips, throwing me off. I slip down into a half guard position and she kicks her right foot, just a little too far. I find my opening and put her in submission, settling the crook of my elbow under her chin. Her arm is scooped up over my shoulder and she immediately taps out again.

"Come on." I raise my voice without meaning too, pulling away from her and hitting the open mat with the palm of my hand. She jumps, holding her throat as she moves.

My eyes travel up her hand to her mouth and I notice her bottom lip is shaking. My temper immediately disappears. "Shit, Bree. What's wrong?"

"Nothing. We can go again."

"No. We can't." I inch forward on the mat and reach for her. She waves me off and gets back in position.

"Come on. Let's go."

"No." I climb back on top of her and she flinches. Despite the reaction, I settle my weight on her, bringing my hands up in the air like a surrender. "Look at me."

She gives me a quick glance before looking away. I wave my hands and repeat myself. "Look at me. Please, Bree." The plea seems to melt her and she sags against the mat, bringing her big blue eyes to focus on me.

"I'm fine." Even as she says it, she shakes her head. She's nowhere near fine.

"What happened?" She shifts herself under me and I lift so she doesn't feel weighed down.

Realization hits me like a brick wall. "Shit, you can't be held down, can you? That's why you tap out?"

"I guess." She clamps down on her bottom lip. "I don't panic until you get a firm hold on me."

"Like when I choke you?"

"Yeah. Especially then." I have to fight the urge to scold her, swallowing everything Jason ever drilled into my head about working on the ground. As a trainer, that's all I know to say. As a boyfriend, I have no idea. Hell, I don't even know if I'm a boyfriend.

"Then I won't choke you, for now. We'll work on it." What a terrible thing to say in any other circumstance. At the same time, it's not like she can realistically avoid ever getting brought to the ground, and when that happens she will get pinned and choked. It's inevitable, and we need to eventually train for it. "Let's try again. I won't go too hard. We can just run through the motions."

I'll give her credit. As long as my arm doesn't come near her neck, she does okay.

On our fourth round, she turns the tables on me and I'm pinned underneath her before my mind can process. I bring my knee up to change dominance but stop short when her lips pass over mine. Once. Twice. Three times. She catches my bottom lip between her teeth and tugs. I shiver, bringing my hands up to tangle in her hair.

I can't think straight. I'm not sure who initiates it, but suddenly we roll so I'm straddling her instead. I grab her shorts and tug them down, making sure to pull her underwear with them. She digs her fingers under her sports bra and takes it off while I sit back on my heels and push down my shorts. We're naked within a minute, both sweaty and panting on the sticky mat.

She's almost frantic now, her fingers clawing at every inch of my bare skin. Before she can even grab me, I'm hard. There's nothing patient in the way she moves. I chuckle, the sound wrapping around the both of us, but I can't get myself to ruin her fun.

We line up easily, as if we're made for each other. I sink into her and settle my weight onto my hands, my face hovering above hers.

Her lips reach up to meet mine and I start rocking, swallowing the little sounds that escape her. I move three times before stopping, cursing under my breath.

"You feel too good. I need a second."

She bucks up to meet me. "Impatient, are we?" I whisper into the crook of her neck.

She shivers and moves faster. At this rate, I'm not going to last very long. I think back to the last time we were together, wanting to make her come that hard again. I lean back on my heels and grab her hips with my hands, lifting them to adjust the angle. She throws her head back, eyes rolling.

"Shit. I'm not going to last." I try to slow down again but she won't allow it. I watch in amazement as she moves herself against me.

"I don't care. Just don't stop." She says frantically. I feel bad, but if she's not going to let me stop I might as well make it good while it lasts. I lean forward again and pound into her.

I need to reach up with the hand that's on her hip and cover her mouth, muffling her tiny screams. The way she looks, with her legs wrapped around me and her bright blue eyes wide, sends me over the edge. I spill into her before collapsing against her sweat soaked chest.

"God damnit." I breathe. "I love you."

CHAPTER SEVENTY-FIVE
Aubrey

"I love you too." I tell the ceiling with a smile. His body is heavy against me, weighing me down. I wait for the anxiety to settle in but it never does. All I feel is comfortable.

I lift my hand up to start running my fingers along his sweaty skin. He hums low in his throat and smiles down at me. He places a kiss on my shoulder, neck, chin, and nose, before rolling off me and propping himself up on one elbow. His big hand sprawls out along my stomach and his fingers start doing what mine were earlier, tickling circles along my skin.

"You're very addicting." He's not looking at my face, instead concentrating on the movement of his fingers.

"Is that a good thing?"

"Yes." He chuckles, his eyes traveling up to mine. "Can I tell you a secret?"

"Sure."

"I've never been in love before." His words come out low and steady, like he's been thinking about saying it for a while. Like he's calculated the risk. It makes me smile.

"I kind of like that."

"Good." He kisses my bare shoulder, dragging his lips along the skin. "We should get dressed. I need to feed the girls. And you." He taps me on my nose before sitting up. I follow suit, reaching over to grab my shorts.

Once his shorts are back on, he glances over his shoulder at me. "What?" I ask, adjusting my bra so it's more comfortable.

"Nothing." He looks away from me quickly, staring at the very empty wall. I walk over to where my zip-up sweatshirt is, pulling it on and yanking the zipper up to the bottom of my bra. I hear him clear his throat and glance over at him. The wall remains his focus.

"I fought today."

I freeze, my hand still on my zipper. "You what?"

"I fought today. With Jason."

"Wow. That's great." My mind reels. Did the thing with Elliot drive him back in the ring? Is that a good or bad thing, if it did?

"I guess." He walks towards me, circling his arms around my waist and pulling me to him. "I'm not sure how I feel about it. It was so good, you know?"

"I know." I remember the feeling.

"God, I forgot that I missed it. It felt so fucking good, Bree." He rests his forehead against mine like he's exhausted. "Sorry, I know you understand. It's just hard because I walked away from it myself, ya know? For you, it's Jason holding you back, but for me it's just my own willpower."

"I know." I cup his face in my right hand, running my thumb along his cheekbone.

"I'm sorry we aren't letting you fight." He sounds defeated. I don't want to take away from how big of a thing this is for him, because he's right. He walked away himself, so the fact that he got into that ring again means something.

"It's fine." The image of him on the twenty-sixth comes to mind and anxiety crawls inside me. "Do you mind if I ask you something, though?"

"Go ahead."

"I don't want to take away from your big moment or anything, but the last time you got in the ring it wasn't very good."

"True." He cringes, but keeps his eyes on me.

"Was today like that?"

He rubs his nose against mine. "No. Surprisingly enough, it wasn't. I thought it would be. I started out so angry. I didn't even realize I wanted to fight until I said it out loud to Jason. Everything after that fell into place. It felt right. I stayed in my head the whole time even."

"That's great." His eyes are on fire talking about it. I wish I could have been there to see him. "I'm really happy for you."

He shrugs and pulls away from me. "It's nothing, really. I'm not going to do it again."

"What? Why not?"

"I can't." He looks at me, big blue eyes seeping with sadness. "We should go upstairs. The girls." Before I can respond he moves towards the door, opening it for me. His eyes fix on the doorframe instead of me as he waits.

I take a breath and walk through it. When I move past him, I swear I hear him mumble under his breath, "I can't," as if he's convincing himself instead of me.

CHAPTER SEVENTY-SIX
Aubrey

Cassie is adorable. She's a tiny ball of energy in a pink, glitter tutu and a ninja turtle shirt. I listen to her ramble about school, her coloring books, and dancing. When she finds out I used to be a dancer she goes ballistic, bouncing up and down while firing a million questions at me. Caden has to ask her to calm down twice, but I assure him it's okay. It's much better than Caitlin.

The sixteen-year-old sits in her chair, staring down at the grilled asparagus and chicken. I overheard her telling Caden right before that she refused to eat meat and I'm fairly certain he said something to her about making her own damn meal. Apparently, that wasn't a good enough option because here she sits, with a scowl and meat on her plate. She hasn't looked at me once, even when I mentioned that she had seen me dance before to Cassie.

"Can you help me dance better?" Cassie asks. Caitlin rolls her eyes at her plate but remains silent.

"I would love that." I try to ignore the girl across from me and give Cassie all my attention. She beams over at Caden.

"Did you hear that? I'm gonna be the best!"

Caden raises his eyebrows in excitement. "That's awesome."

"Yeah, it's great." Caitlin stabs her chicken with her fork and scoffs. "Maybe if you didn't spend so much damn time at the gym, or fucking around with-"

"Language!"

"-girls then you could actually put her in the dance classes she used to love."

"Caitlin." Caden barely raises his voice but it sends a chill up my spine. He sounds just like a dad.

"Just saying." She pushes away from the table and Caden immediately stands up.

"Caitlin Elizabeth Larson!" Caitlin pauses, her hand resting on the back of her chair. When she turns her gaze onto him, she's sending daggers.

"What?" The word is spit out into the open, awkward air. I can't help but glance at Caden. His face is perfectly calm but his fists are clenched.

"Apologize."

"No." She squares her shoulders. The corner of his mouth twitches.

"Apologize." I watch him fight for a deep breath, his chest expanding slowly. They stare at each other for a long time.

I hear a little noise to my right. When I glance over at the smallest occupant of the table, my breath catches. She's crying, wiping at her cheeks quickly like she already knows at the age of four that she should hide it.

"Caden." I reach up and grab the fist nearest to me, squeezing it. He looks down, then follows my gaze to Cassie. His stance completely shifts when he sees her. Very calmly, he sits down and smiles.

"I think you'll have a lot of fun dancing with Aubrey."

I plaster a smile on my face. "Heck yeah. I'm better than those silly classes anyway. No annoying little girls who can't dance." I wink at her and she giggles, wiping another hand down her face.

"I was the best in my class." She informs me.

"I believe it." Out of the corner of my eye, I see Caden stand up and walk away from the table. I keep my focus on Cassie, the smile remaining. "By the time Caden gets you back into classes, I'll have you dancing so good you'll be better than the teacher."

"Awesome!" Her eyes are wide open and completely dry now. I glance at her plate and notice that all the chicken is gone while the asparagus is untouched. I grab a spear and turn my attention back to her. She watches me sniff it and make a silly face.

"These taste good but they smell gross."

"They taste gross too." She sticks her tongue out and shakes her head. I giggle.

"Try one."

"No way."

"I promise, they're delicious. My favorite, actually." It's a white lie. I do like asparagus, but it's not my favorite. She watches me apprehensively, her little eyes in slits. Then, very slowly, she grabs one spear and brings it to her mouth. I watch her take a tiny bit and chew way too long. Then she takes another and smiles at me.

"It's good!"

"I told you."

"Wait a minute, are you eating your veggies?" Caden slides back into his seat and smiles over at the two of us. Cassie nods and lifts her asparagus up to show him before focusing her attention on it. I look at Caden and wink at him. He leans in and kisses the hair above my ear.

"Thank you."

CHAPTER SEVENTY-SEVEN
Caden

It takes me less than a minute to get an apology from Caitlin. I knew it was an act for Aubrey but I honestly didn't expect for her to change course so fast. Before I even closed her bedroom door behind me, she was apologizing.

We agreed that she'll stay in her room and cool off, but I remind her that she's more than welcome to join us for a movie or something later. The automatic eye roll gives me a clue that I won't be seeing her.

When I come back down, Aubrey and Cassie are giggling together, eating their asparagus. I haven't been able to get her to eat vegetables unless they're doused in cheese or cooked inside a dish. That fact, along with seeing Aubrey change Cassie's tears into a smile, makes my heart melt.

I lean into Aubrey and give her a kiss against the side of her head, whispering a little thank you. She scrunches her nose the way she always does. Cassie eats four more spears before announcing she's done. Aubrey agrees and together, the three of us clear the table. I take Caitlin's food and push it into a Tupperware container before plopping it in the fridge. Aubrey promises Cassie that they can start dancing in a minute and Cassie skips out of the room, singing a song from her new favorite movie. Once she's gone, Aubrey rests her hip against the counter.

"What was all that about?"

"She's adjusting." I shrug but she doesn't look convinced. "We have good days and bad."

"Are the bad days when she decides to be a vegetarian?"

I can't help but laugh, air blowing through my nose. "Usually, yes." This reminds me that Caitlin does need to eat something. I reach up into the cupboard and pull out the peanut butter. "Can you grab the jelly from the fridge? Should be on the door."

Once I'm done making the sandwich, I plop it on a paper plate and sigh. Aubrey kisses my shoulder, her lips making me shiver despite the cotton of my shirt.

"Maybe she'll want some chips." She points around the kitchen and raises an eyebrow like I should tell her where they would be. I point to the cupboard next to the one with the peanut butter. She grabs the Doritos and pours some onto the plate next to the sandwich. Then she totally throws me off. "Do you mind if I bring it to her?"

CHAPTER SEVENTY-EIGHT
Aubrey

I knock on the door three times and hold my breath. A sixteen-year-old girl should not be this intimidating.

"Can I help you?" Her eyes shift from the plate back to my face. I think I might see some sort of twitch in her expression but I'm not sure.

"Caden wanted you to eat." I offer her a smile. "No meat."

"Funny." She reaches out for the plate and I hand it to her. We both stare at each other for a few seconds, neither of us knowing what to do now.

At the same time, I say, "Well," and she says, "Do you?"

I nervously smile. "You first."

"Do you want to come in?"

"Oh, yeah." She moves out of the way and waves a hand at her room like she's presenting it to me. It's nothing like I imagined. I figured it'd be full of depressing stuff, maybe a lot of black. The room doesn't match her at all. It makes me wonder who she used to be before her life got flipped. "It's nice."

"I guess." She stands by her bed, picking at the corner of one of her pillows. "My mom picked most of it out."

"Yeah, my mom used to do that too. She had terrible taste though." I laugh at the memory of my room growing up. It changed at least twice a year, always whatever my mother wanted it to be. I started decorating my closet my own way because she never thought to repaint in there, and it was a small act of rebellion. At least until she found it when she went to hang up my dry cleaning one morning.

"I liked it at the time." I look at her and notice that she's staring at the paint on the wall like it's disgusting. It's a medium shade of purple. My favorite color.

"We could paint it." She smiles over at me like it's the craziest idea.

"I doubt Caden would approve."

"Oh, he's a grump, but I think he'd be okay with it." I put my hands on my hips like I'm approaching a new mission. I suppose I am. *Operation bonding.* "You know what would look cool? A chalkboard wall."

"A what?"

"Oh, come on. You've probably seen them online. You use chalkboard paint and then you can draw and write with chalk on the whole wall." I wave my hand in the air as if I'm painting the wall in front of me. She stares for a moment, her eyebrows crinkled. Then she nods.

"That'd be sweet." I do a small circle, taking in the whole room before pointing at the wall across from her bed.

"It'd probably look best if you did that one. That way you don't have to work around the door, or the window. And the wall behind your bed wouldn't work because you'd get chalk dust all over your bedspread."

She laughs and picks up the bright pink fabric. "That might not be the worst thing."

"Right." I laugh with her. "We can replace that too."

"That'll cost money." The words are laced with both anxiety and guilt. Despite how much she gives Caden a hard time, she obviously understands what he's going through.

"We'll figure something out." I watch her fight with herself for a minute. Then she shakes her head.

"I can't." Like brother like sister, I suppose.

CHAPTER SEVENTY-NINE
Aubrey

The rest of the night unfolds easily. We watch Cassie's favorite movie all the way through, even though she falls asleep fifty minutes into it. I tell Caden it's because I've never seen it before, but it's really because I want to torture him. He figures this out when I start singing one of the songs along with the movie, calling me out on my lie. Since we're alone, this earns me a fake glare followed by a heated kiss.

"Spend the night." He whispers as his hand travels up my back.

"What about the girls?"

He gives me a smirk that's full of mischief. "I'll sneak you out."

"Okay." I pull away from him, earning a pout from him. "I just have to call Myla and let her know."

"Oh, alright." He stands up and makes his way to the spot on the floor where Cassie is lying. She's passed out with her hand still in the bowl of popcorn. "Meet you here in five?"

I nod. He picks his sister up carefully, cradling her in his arms. I can't help but study the way his muscles ripple with the movement.

I'd be okay spending the rest of my life trying to memorize his perfection. His flaws too.

The charger where my phone is plugged in is across the room. When I get there, I see that I have three missed calls, all from Myla. I groan and call her back. She answers on the third ring.

"I was about to send out a search party." Her voice is full of humor, but anxiety is right underneath it.

"It's not that late. I told you I was at Caden's."

"I know, but with everything, I was worried."

"I'm sorry." It's understandable. The nice thing is, even though she's been worrying about it, for a few hours I nearly forgot.

"Don't worry about it, I'm just being a dweeb." She sighs dramatically. "When will you be home?"

"Um," I smile innocently, hoping she can sense it through the phone, "Tomorrow?"

"Tomorrow, huh? Tsk tsk." I can tell by her tone that she's joking. "You're such a slut."

"Shut up. I'll see you for breakfast."

"Yeah, yeah. Goodnight." She hangs up and I stare at my phone for a moment. I've been avoiding checking my email, just waiting for the inevitable moment when I'm officially kicked out for not paying. Caden still isn't back. Now is as good a time as any.

The first email catches me completely off guard. It's a confirmation that my tuition has been paid. As in, money, somehow, made its way into my school account.

"Hey, you." I jump, my phone clattering to the ground.

Caden picks it up and hands it back to me. "I really need to stop sneaking up on you." When I don't laugh, he drops his smile and asks what's wrong.

"Someone paid my tuition."

"Maybe your mom?"

"No way. She would have called to rub it in by now, I promise." He stares at me and I can see his mind working as fast as mine was. His smile slips.

"You think it was him?"

"If he's dealing again, he would have the money." I shrug. "Actually, either way he probably had money stashed places. It could for sure be him."

He lets out a low whistle. "I don't know. That's a decent chunk of change."

"He was part of something really big." I see his expression change from slight amusement to deadly serious. His stance changes too.

"How big?"

"I don't know. Big enough." He used to launder money through a local business, he bought a brand-new challenger with cash, and every time I needed anything, he gave me at least a hundred dollars. The people at McDonalds were not impressed when Myla and I showed up with a one-hundred-dollar bill just to buy two milkshakes.

If all that doesn't add up to enough, there's the fact that he was part of something big enough to make people disappear. To need to have conversations with people about dead bodies. To have someone trail his girlfriend twenty-four-seven, handing in official reports.

"What was his name?"

"Caden."

"No. Tell me." He runs a hand through his hair and looks at the wall. When he turns around his face is full of grief. His lips move but he doesn't speak. I can't tell him. He's proving that right now.

"I don't want to talk about this, okay? Maybe it was someone else. Maybe it was-"

"What's his name? Tell me now." The words are cold and disconnected. I don't like the way they sound coming from him.

"Please don't speak to me like that." I hear my voice tremble but I keep my chin up. He immediately softens.

"I'm sorry." He runs a hand down his face. "I'm sorry. I'm just worried about you."

"Don't be. I'm safe." I walk towards him and wrap my arms around his waist. "I'm spending the night. Is this really what you want to do?"

He leans down, wrapping his lips around mine. He shakes his head and mine follows suit. I let out a nervous giggle. "That's what I thought."

CHAPTER EIGHTY
Caden

She stops to pee on the way to the bedroom. The moment she shuts the bathroom door, I head to my safe and take out my loaded glock. All it needs is a bullet in the chamber.

I stick it in the first drawer of the bedside table and head back downstairs, double checking that everything is locked.

When I return to the room, Aubrey is in nothing but one of my flannel shirts, the buttons undone in front of her chest so I can see just a peak of the flesh underneath.

All my anxiety about her ex disappears as she climbs onto the bed and lifts herself up to her knees. "What took ya so long?" Her words are taunting, fingers dragging slowly up her bare thigh.

"Sorry. Checking-" I don't finish my sentence and I'm pretty sure she doesn't care. She just gives me a knowing smile and waits patiently for me to come to her. It doesn't take long.

We collide at the edge of the bed and I quickly push her up until her head is resting on my pillow. I take a moment to stare at the image before me. Her dark brown hair is a wild mess against my soft white sheets and my flannel is pushed up under her armpits now, exposing her bare stomach. I start kissing there and work my way down.

"Caden?" My name is followed by three little knocks on the door. If I don't answer in the next ten seconds, Cassie will just come in.

"I'm coming, sweetheart." I rush to the door in panic mode, hoping Aubrey has enough time to cover up. With a deep breath, I swing the door open, revealing Cassie with the hair on one side of her head fluffy and her blanket dangling from her fingers. "Nightmare?"

She nods, her bottom lip trembling. She's been having them ever since we lost my dad. My mother told me it happened about once a week but Caitlin claims it happened more. Apparently, Cassie learned my mother wasn't the one to go to, since she went through stages where she was convinced my dad was fine. Everything was fine. Cassie having nightmares would shatter the illusion.

"I don't," the words are thick with emotion and she chokes on them, her big eyes watering. "I can't lose you." She starts sobbing, and for a moment I forget that she's only four. It's easy to do when looking at a girl who's been through so much.

"You won't baby." I pick her up and cradle her head against my shoulder. Her tiny body shakes every other second as she violently cries. This doesn't happen as often as the nightmares. Usually she calms herself down before needing to come to me. "I swear. I won't ever leave you."

I turn my body so I'm facing Aubrey instead of Cassie. She's sitting on my bed, the blankets pooled around her breasts. She looks beautiful and, more importantly, sympathetic. Most girls would be totally over this situation right not. I mouth a thank you to her and she waves me off. I love that most about her. She's been through shit too. We're messed up together.

"Why don't you go potty, and then you can come to bed with us?" Aubrey asks Cassie. I stand still, facing the empty wall. There's no reason I deserve someone so damn perfect. What other girl would let a four-year-old crawl into bed with her when she's supposed to be getting laid?

Cassie runs to the bathroom, little bare feet slapping against the hardwood. The moment she's gone, I dig in my drawer for a pair of shorts and a shirt for Aubrey to put on, then get in some myself.

When Cassie comes back, we look like two normal people, ready to go to bed. Well, besides the fact that I'm still hard and Aubrey keeps biting her lip, I'm pretty sure on purpose, to drive me wild.

The three of us settle in, Aubrey reaching over to turn the lamp off. Cassie burrows under the blankets, one hand clutching her small blanket and the other resting on my arm. "Caden?"

"Yeah, Cass?"

"I love our family, even though it's smaller now." It takes me a moment to respond, the emotion making my throat feel tight.

"I love it too, Cass."

"Aubrey?"

She shifts to look down at Cassie. "Yeah?"

"We have extra room, if you wanna be a part of it?" It's the most innocent, yet loaded question I think I've ever heard. I feel Aubrey shift again. When I look over at her, I see that she's staring at me above Cassie's head. In the dark, I can't tell her expression.

"Yeah, Aubrey." I whisper. "I think we can squeeze you in."

Her hand reaches across the tops of the pillows to rest in my hair. I reach up and hold it there. "That's the best offer I've ever gotten, Cassie. Count me in."

CHAPTER EIGHTY-ONE
Aubrey

The stack of textbooks is intimidating, but the glass of wine Myla places on top of it helps.

"I think I'm going to fail." I accept the wine and chug half of it. "Whoever came up with the idea of midterms should be burned at the stake."

"Preach." She drinks her own wine and grabs the first book from the stack. It's a biology book, and its presence makes me cringe. Myla will be an amazing teacher, but whoever is willing to study math and science past high school is a sadist.

"So, Halloween tomorrow." She peeks over her wine glass at me. "Are you going out with me?"

"No, I'll probably hangout with Caden. Maybe do stuff with his little sisters, too."

She perks up. "Wait, I just got an idea."

"Oh, no." I wave a finger at her. Any idea that spawns from the mention of little kids on Halloween is a bad one for Myla. She's been waiting for years to be able to acceptably participate in the cute Halloween activities again. "You're going to the bars, aren't you?"

"Uh, yeah? At night."

"That'd be up to Caden." I decide to tell her this because Halloween is only a day away, and she won't be seeing him before then. This way, I can avoid her craziness being around his sisters, and I can avoid her finding out about his family situation. I'm not sure how Caden would feel about her knowing.

I pour us more wine and bring the focus back to our textbooks. "How about one more hour of studying, and we can reward ourselves with takeout?"

"That sounds perfect." She raises her glass to me. "Here's to passing!"

"C's get degrees." I drink to the toast and open my psychology book. Someone knocks on the door, making both of us freeze. "It's probably just the landlord or something."

"Yeah." She carefully puts her wine glass down. "Or, ya know, Elliot."

We both stare at the door. Whoever it is knocks again. I jump.

243

"It's not Elliot." I stand up, wiping the sweat off my hands and onto my jeans. "He wouldn't come here, right?"

She just shrugs. I tip-toe to the door and peak through the little hole. I've never felt so relieved. "It's Caden." I tell her before letting him in. He's smiling wide, two pizzas in one hand and a bottle of moscato in the other.

"Shit, yeah!" Myla cheers.

"No!" I point my finger at her, then at Caden. "We haven't earned it yet."

"Don't be a party pooper." He plants a kiss on my forehead and kicks the door closed. I lock it for safe measure. "Fuel for the brain, right?"

Right." Myla gives me a thumb up. "He's a cop, Bree. He knows what's best."

I scoff but give in. What could a little study break hurt?

This is my mistake. There are three things that Myla loves more than life herself, at least in her own words. These are: puppies, wine, and Holidays. Caden has given her one already, and is on his way to being pressured into a second.

"So, Halloween." Myla says, giving him an intense smile. She looks insane.

"Yeah." Caden scratches his chin. "Tomorrow."

With eyes full of mischief, she inches closer to him. "You have sisters, correct?"

"Um, yeah." He gives me a nervous laugh, eyes begging for help. "Two sisters."

"Any chance they'd want to hang out with you for Halloween?"

He shrugs. "I don't know about want, but they will be, yeah."

Myla claps her hands together. "Oh, great. Aubrey and I want to come too."

"Oh?" Caden gives me a look, as if I should have told him about this before.

I shrug. "It was her idea, but I wouldn't mind."

"Great, it's solved." Myla pours herself more wine and grabs a slice of pizza. "So, there's a harvest festival we should go to. It's got pumpkins and mazes and games. We could eat lunch at the little shop at the farm after. Oh, does the little one nap? She could nap, and then we could go trick-or-treating!"

"Yeah." Caden takes in as much oxygen as he can. I understand the feeling. Myla can be quite suffocating. "Alright, guess that's what we'll be doing."

I mouth an apology at him. He just raises a pizza slice to me and takes one for himself, giving me a playful smile. After all the crazy in our lives, I suppose Myla's Holiday excitement isn't too much.

CHAPTER EIGHTY-TWO
Aubrey

"You're cheating!" Caden points at Cassie, who is on Jason's shoulders and can clearly see how to exit the maze. His mock horror makes her explode in giggles.

"Run, Jason!" She orders, her little finger pointing in the opposite direction of her brother. Jason crouches down and sprints away from the group, making airplane noises as they go. Even out of sight, we know where they are by the sound of Cassie's laughter.

Myla links her arm is mine. "You've got a good thing here."

"Yeah." I smile at the scene. Caitlin and Caden have joined in, the sixteen-year old laughing so hard she's snorting while her brother hoists her on his shoulders. They take off after Jason and Cassie, leaving us behind.

"They're his, aren't they?" The question catches me off guard.

"What? No."

"I overheard Jason and Caitlin when we were by the pumpkin patch. He was asking her to let up on him because he's doing the best he can to take care of them and keep everything together. He said she has to remember that he lost them too."

"Oh." I give her a pleading look. "Please, My, don't mention it. I'm not sure how he'd feel about you knowing."

"I get it." She squeezes my hand and leads us through the maze. A gust of cold wind blows by, and we both burrow into our jackets. I'm going to need a mug of hot apple cider after this.

"Now." Myla bumps her hip against mine and pulls us toward the rest of the group. They reached the exit already, since they cheated, and the guys are now spinning in circles with the girls on their shoulders. Myla points her finger at Jason. "Tell me about that one."

Oh, no.

CHAPTER EIGHTY-THREE
Caden

We pick out pumpkins and bring them back to my place, promising Cassie she can help carve them if she takes a nap right after. Caitlin volunteers all her finished crossword puzzles from the newspaper to cover the table, and Jason grabs the carving kit that Myla showed up with this morning.

Caitlin and Cassie work on their own pumpkin, and Aubrey and I pair up to work on another. Jason and Myla are too busy flirting and whispering to carve anything.

"Don't make it too scary!" Cassie tells Caitlin. She's sitting on her knees so she can see better, her chin settled in both hands. If anyone else was paired with Caitlin, they would have gotten sarcasm, but Cassie always has a knack for just making Caitlin smile.

It's Myla's idea we have a contest. We line up all the pumpkins when they're done, Myla and Jason finally getting together to create, well, something. I'm not sure what. If you squint, it resembles a smiley face.

Obviously, Caitlin and Cassie win.

Cassie goes down for her nap in euphoria. She doesn't even get upset when I tell her she can't wear her costume yet. Everyone else is left cleaning up the pumpkin guts.

When I get downstairs, Jason is chasing Myla around the kitchen in a fit of laughter, throwing pumpkin seeds at her. There are a few stuck in her hair, and the sexual tension is uncomfortable.

"Let's get out of here." I whisper in Aubrey's ear, arms snaking around her waist.

Caitlin throws the last of the newspaper in the garbage and, with a final look of disgust at Myla and Jason, stomps up to her room. Aubrey nods. "Hey guys, we're, um, going to nap too."

Myla and Jason stop what they're doing and stare at us. "Yeah, right."

"Go ahead, get laid." Jason waves us off. "We'll finish cleaning."

"Yeah." Myla winks at me. "Maybe we'll nap too."

"You're disgusting." Aubrey turns to me and shakes her head. "We aren't leaving them alone."

"Fine." I glare up at Jason, sending him a loving death threat through the air. "Well, I doubt Cass will nap for more than an hour. She's way too excited, today."

"Cribbage?" Jason raises an eyebrow. "We could do teams."

"Yes!" Myla does a shimmy. "Jason and I will kick your asses."

Jason and her. I give Aubrey a nervous look. When did that happen, and why does it make me nervous?

CHAPTER EIGHTY-FOUR
Aubrey

Myla leaves halfway through trick-or-treating, needing to get ready to go out. When the rest of us return to Caden's, we find Caitlin on the couch with a boy, in a somewhat compromising position.

Cassie drags her pillowcase full of candy through the living room, dumping it out on the rug with a big smile. She's the only one in the room who isn't shocked into awkward silence. Surprisingly enough, Caden plays it off very cool. "Hey, Cait. Who's your friend?"

"This is Adam. My friend from school."

Jason snorts from behind me. We're all thinking the same thing. Friends don't straddle each other and make out like these two just were.

"I thought you were staying home to handout candy because it's too cold?"

"I was. Adam was keeping me company."

"I see that." Caden rocks on his heels, eyes focused on Adam instead of Caitlin. "Does Adam come over often when I'm not home?"

Caitlin says, "no," right as Cassie says, "yes."

Adam stares up at Caden with eyes blown wide. His shirt has two pumpkins over his chest and the words 'show me your pumpkins' beneath them. If I wasn't fearing for the boy's life, I would laugh.

"I should go." Adam says this to Caitlin, but he's still staring at Caden in terror.

"Nope." Caden crosses his arms against his chest. "You'll stay, Adam. I'd like to get to know ya."

"Oh, um." Caitlin shakes her head, smart enough to know this won't end well. Jason plops himself in between her and Adam, putting his arms around both to make it purposely awkward. Caitlin's cheeks burn bright red.

Cassie lays on her stomach and begins sorting her candy into piles, finding the drama irrelevant. "Can we watch Charlie Brown Pumpkin?" She begs, little feet waving in the air.

"Oh, please no." Caitlin grumbles. This earns her a shit eating grin from Caden, one eyebrow arched.

"Oh, yes. You and Adam will just love it."

This is not the case. Caitlin and Adam do not love it the first, or second, time we watch the movie. Thankfully, for all of us, Cassie ends up passing out in a sugar coma before we can watch it a third time.

Caden still wants to play it again, but I squeeze his bicep and shake his head. "Get the cutie in bed. I'll find a grown-up movie." I give him a pleading smile. "Please. I can't watch any more Charlie Brown."

"Fine." He plants a kiss on my lips before going to grab Cassie from the floor.

The moment he's out of the room, all three people on the couch sigh in relief. Jason snaps his fingers at me and points at the floor. "Hey, Aubrey, toss me that candy bar by your foot."

"Get up yourself, lazy!" He gestures to Caitlin and Adam.

"I'm being a buffer." I reach over and grab the candy, throwing it hard at his head. He catches it with a cocky smile. A jumbo tootsie roll catches my eye across the floor. I slide off the couch and head for it. When I return, candy in hand, I catch my phone ringing.

"Hello?" There's loud music coming through, covering whatever it is Myla is trying to say. I put a finger in my open ear and try to listen. "Hello? Myla?"

The call ends and I frown at my phone. "What's up?" Caden asks, now back in the room and looking at Netflix for a scary movie.

"Nothing. I think Myla butt dialed me."

We decide on a cliché clown movie because they're Caitlin's biggest fear, and Caden is still mad at her. Jason is cuddling Adam, arms wrapped around his waist. Every time Adam gets the courage to bring it up, which has only been twice so far, Jason just says he's scared. Caden's entire body is shaking from how hard he's suppressing his laughter.

Perfectly timed with the moment a girl is walking around an empty house, just waiting for something to jump out at her, my phone rings again. Every person jumps, even Caden, and Caitlin screams.

"Hello?" I sneak out to the kitchen so I'm not bothering anyone.

"Bree?" The sound is less of a coherent name and more of a sob. My years of trauma experience don't help me keep calm. "What's wrong? What happened? Where are you?"

"Bree? Are you there?"

I yell into the phone. "I'm here. Myla, what's wrong? What's going on?"

"I don't want to be here." She's sobbing into the phone, harder than I've probably ever heard from her. "I'm scared."

"Where are you?" I try to remember the bar she was at. It was somewhere with a costume contest but that doesn't narrow it down on Halloween. Jason and Caden come into the kitchen, resting against the breakfast bar as they listen.

"I don't know. I'm at a house, locked in the bathroom. It's on the same street as the building we took our psych class in last year. Um, Geoffrey."

"Okay, stay calm. I'll be there right away."

I hang up and start searching for my keys, then remember Caden picked me up.

"What's going on?" Caden grabs me by the arm so I stop pacing. I can't differentiate between the anxiety from him grabbing me, and the anxiety that Myla could be in danger. It's all just one big pool of panic.

"Myla's stuck in a bathroom at a party. She sounds super freaked out. I don't know." My heart is racing. "Can I borrow your car?"

"Yeah, um."

"I'll go get her." Jason looks up at me, his brown eyes full of anxiety. He just met Myla, why would he care so much?

"You don't have to do that."

"Well, you aren't going alone, and we can't leave those two on the couch alone."

"Yes, we can," Caden says. "The three of us can go. We have no idea what we're walking into. Let's just tag team it."

Caitlin comes into the room, with Adam cowering behind her. "What's up?"

"Aubrey's friend from earlier needs help. We'll all be back in a few, okay?"

She must see how anxious we all are, because she doesn't say anything sarcastic. She just nods. "Adam can go home," she offers.

"No. He can stay. Just lock the doors." He leans over and kisses her forehead. It's not usual for them. He must be worried.

I hope he has no reason to be.

CHAPTER EIGHTY-FIVE
Caden

The house is full of idiot college kids, stumbling around half naked. I wade through the bunny ears, police uniforms, and one strangely accurate representation of Willy Wonka- the Gene Wilder version. That kid is not getting laid tonight.

We find the upstairs bathroom with the help of a vampire. Jason and I need to push our way to the front of the very angry line, no one willing to give up their spot. From the comments we hear, it sounds like Myla has been locked in there for a while.

"Myla?" Aubrey knocks on the door until it opens to reveal Myla, her red hair matted and a big, blue towel wrapped around herself. I'm not sure I want to know what she's hiding underneath.

Aubrey grabs her and holds her tight. Everyone who was bitching at us earlier, quiets down. They obviously see that it wasn't just some girl hogging the bathroom to fix her makeup.

"Get me out of here." She all but whimpers, wiping at her mascara stained face with the corner of the towel. Aubrey helps guide the way to the door, Jason and I trailing behind them for backup.

Right when we get to the exit, a guy standing with a group of assholes yells at Myla, "Way to ruin everyone's night, stupid slut."

Before I can react, Jason has the guy by his throat and against the wall. I can't hear what he's saying to him, but whatever it is seems to scare the shit out of him.

Aubrey and Myla make it through the front door before Jason lets him go. I come up and clap him on the shoulder, ready to get out of here, when a different guy from the group speaks up. "That bitch sleeps her way through campus. She was fucking asking for it."

We both wind up at the same time, but Jason is closer. His fist collides with the tip of the guy's nose, sending blood through the air and onto the first guy's face. Jason takes a step back as the guy he hit falls straight to the floor, knocked out cold.

"No girl is ever asking for it." Jason yells, before spitting on the guys face.

He storms out of the house, leaving me behind. When I catch up, he gives me a dirty look. "I don't need a comment about anger. I get that I was just a hypocrite."

"Shut up, man." I offer him a closed fist and he bumps his against mine. "That was fucking awesome."

"Yeah." He grins. "It was."

CHAPTER EIGHTY-SIX
Aubrey

In and out of consciousness, Myla tries to cooperate with all of Caden's questions. She tells him that, no, she was not raped. That it didn't get past kissing. That there's no need for a rape kit. That she was not drugged, she just went a little heavy on the tequila.

After he asks again if she wants to go to the hospital, she gives him a dirty look and informs him that if he doesn't shut up, he will be punched in the face.

We all sneak back into the house, or at least most of us do. Myla sort of stumbles in, giggling her way through the process of removing her heels. Caitlin is asleep on the couch, with Adam nowhere to be found. Caden shakes her awake and sends her up to her room, then helps me clean up all the candy.

"Myla, you want the spare room?" Caden asks, turning around to look at my best friend. She's already passed out on the couch, the towel falling to reveal a mermaid skirt that's ripped all the way up to the hip.

"She'll be fine there. Although, she wasn't being dramatic about the puking things. I'd get her a bucket."

Shaking off what I believe to be a gag, Caden heads into the kitchen and grabs a blue bucket from below the sink. He sets it beside the couch and motions for us to hold on while he runs upstairs.

In the meantime, Jason asks if he can stay with Myla. "I feel like she shouldn't be alone, ya know?"

"Yeah." I smile at him. If it was any other guy, I'd think he had other motives, but Jason is genuinely worried. "Don't stay because you think she'll be alone, though. If you go home, I'll stay here with her all night."

"No." He shakes his head, eyes catching sight of Caden coming down the stairs with clothes in his hands. "I'll just go home and worry, plus I'm pumped full of adrenaline after punching that guy. I'm fine here. You guys get some sleep."

Caden nods at him, picking up on the conversation and agreeing. He hands me the clothes, both men turning away while I help Myla into them. She doesn't cooperate at all, the only interaction being a sound that's half snort, half giggle.

By the time Caden and I are in bed, I'm exhausted.

Caden comes onto the bed and kisses me. "Have I mentioned that I'm in love with you?"

My breath catches. "Once or twice."

"Well, Aubrey Pierce, I am completely in love with you." I hum low in my throat, appreciating the way that sounds.

"I love you too." The words don't seem as big or important coming out of my own mouth. I hope they sound different to him, because I mean them. I mean them too much.

He shifts on the bed and pushes me up so my head is resting on the pillows. I let myself sink into the mattress as his mouth lingers on my belly button, fingers tracing circles on the skin of my thighs. The touch is barely a whisper but I can feel it in all sorts of places.

His mouth travels lower and I close my eyes, reminding myself to be quiet. He must notice the way I clamp down on my bottom lip because he chuckles. When he finally reaches his destination, tongue circling around me, I grab the pillow from his side and bury my face in it to stay quiet.

He sends me crashing through two orgasms, each as intense as my first the other night. When he finally sinks into me, I'm so sensitive that I cry out.

"You alright?" He pulls back, hovering. His eyes are worried, and I love him for that. Elliot would have gotten off on the noise I made. Would have wanted me to make it again.

"I'm perfect." I reach up and cup his face in my hands. "Just sensitive."

"Sensitive?" He chuckles, the sound deep in his throat, and I decide it's my new favorite sound. It's so sexy, like he knows a dirty secret he's about to share. He leans down so his face hovers above mine. "Oh, baby. You will be."

CHAPTER EIGHTY-SEVEN
Aubrey

"Aubrey." He yells my name in a sing-song voice. I can hear his heavy boots making their way through the apartment. Then something smashes, most likely his bottle of whiskey. Good. At least he can't drink anymore.

"Aubrey!" The second time isn't nearly as playful. Myla is sitting on my bed, our chemistry notes in her hand. She looks at me, eyes wide, and I wonder what to do.

I shouldn't have invited her here. He said I could, but he was sober when that happened. I should have known that going out to dinner with a client would mean this. I should have known what he meant when he said be up waiting for him. I should have known. I should have anticipated. I'm so stupid.

"It's fine." I tell Myla quickly, gathering all her stuff and shoving it into her open arms. She tries to cling to everything but one of the papers falls to the floor. We both ignore it.

"Bree." She's scared, I can tell. I haven't told her anything; what's there to tell? It's not like Elliot has hit me. He would never hurt me. But Myla knows he can get angry and she's seen him grab me a little too hard once. He was just upset, and it hasn't happened since. Why can't she get that? Why doesn't she understand that the longer she stays here the angrier he'll be?

"Aubrey!" He's screaming now. Myla and I both jump and she gives me a look. "You're scared of him."

"Am not." I push her towards the door. "Please just leave."

"It's a school night. You should come too." I roll my eyes.

"My parents are gone all week. I'm staying here." The expression on her face makes it clear that she thinks that's a terrible idea. She's probably right.

I push her towards the door again anyway, and this time she goes. We pass Elliot in the living room, pacing and talking to himself. Myla gives him a final look before pausing at the door.

"Bree. Come with me. Please. Stay at my place. You can't be here." Her words are rushed and low so he can't hear them. I shake my head.

"He'll be fine, I swear. I'll be fine." I shut the door, on my best friend, and I only have a second to feel bad about it before his hands are on me. I jump at the contact and look up at him. His green eyes are incredibly bright against the bloodshot red.

"What were you two doing?" His breath reeks of alcohol and I try to pull away from his grip. It's too tight.

"We were just studying." I gently move my wrist around in his hand. "You're hurting me."

Usually, that's plenty. Usually, he'll back right off, run his hands through his hair, and apologize. Usually, he'll beg me to forgive him, which is always an overkill. People grab people when they're upset. I grab Myla sometimes to get her attention or to tell her she's getting on my last nerve. And people yell. It's okay.

This time is different. His grip tightens and he passes right by my words. "Studying, huh? So you can leave me? You two think you're better than me? Better than some lowlife drug dealer?"

I lift my chin to hide the fact that I'm scared. "I don't really care that you deal drugs." It's not true. I only found out a week ago and my world still feels like it's spinning.

He studies me for a second. "You're not going to break up with me?" I think about that for a second. I should. I'm pretty sure he's bruising my arm.

"Of course not." His lips crash against mine with the conformation. Two strong arms wrap around my waist, lifting me. My wrist aches from where he grabbed me but I focus on his lips, making sure mine are still moving with him. I don't want to upset him. I hate when he's upset.

We arrive in his bedroom and he drops me on the bed. I bounce once before settling in a fluffy section of his blanket. His hands are greedy, grabbing every inch of me. My jeans peel off with no problem. My shirt, which is made of tiny buttons along the front, is another issue. He ends up ripping it off, letting the fabric bunch along my ribs. I remind myself that that sort of thing happens in the movies all the time. He's just full of passion, that's all.

Before I can fully grasp the change in situation, he's on top of me. His jeans are hanging off his ankles, falling off slowly as he pushes me up the bed. My entire body is shaking, but I want to show him I can handle all of this. I can handle him. I can, right?

I love him.

I'm not focused and he pulls a condom out from somewhere I can't see. "Wait." The word is barely a whisper but he pauses. I can feel my entire body writhing against the bedding from how hard I'm shaking. It's exactly like the first time I drank, when I woke up early the next morning with the cold sweats and nausea.

Losing your virginity isn't supposed to feel like that. At least, I think it's not.

"You're just nervous. It'll feel amazing." He finishes putting the condom on and licks his finger before sliding it into me. "See, you're already wet. You want me." I believe him, even though I don't feel wet. His finger kind of hurt. But I smile and bring my lips up to kiss him. I'm just nervous. I'm just being silly.

"You're right. I want this." I look him in the eyes, trying to ignore the bright red surrounding the green. "I want you."

It's all he needs to hear before he's pushing into me. It hurts, pinching in a weird place. He doesn't let me adjust like guys always do in the books I've read. I suppose I can't hold that against him. This isn't a romance novel.

Eventually, the pain eases and in its place comes a warmth. It's strange but not uncomfortable, and as he moves I decide I like it. I even start bucking my hips with him. Too soon, he stills. I wait for something to happen and wonder why he's not moving.

He rolls off of me, taking the condom off and throwing it in the trash beside the bed. He doesn't look at me or speak and I find myself wrapping my arms around my waist, trying to disappear.

"Did I mess up?" I can't help that my voice shakes. He looks over at me.

"No way. That was amazing."

"Oh." Was it? I mean, it felt good. It felt unfinished, but maybe that's normal. Maybe I'm expecting way too much.

"I just have to piss. Be right back." I stay exactly where I am, wondering why I feel nauseous. Wondering why I want to grab my things and run straight to Myla. I've almost convinced myself to do it when he returns, crawling into bed with a warm smile on his lips.

"I am so in love with you, Aubrey Pierce." Something sparks in me and I forget what I was just thinking about.

"I love you too." He turns the lamp off and brings me to him, burying my face in his sweaty chest. It's too hot and I feel suffocated. When I go to move he holds me there, pinning me to him. I try to remind myself that, despite the feeling, I am breathing. I am getting oxygen.

That's how I fall asleep. Not a virgin anymore. Smelling of sex, sweat, and whiskey. With the boy I love. Fighting for air.

CHAPTER EIGHTY-EIGHT
Caden

I wake up to her screaming. When I turn the lamp on, I see that she's clawing at her own throat, a lone tear trailing down her chest. "Bree." I reach out and touch her, my left hand resting on her shoulder. She screams again, her leg coming up and kicking at the open air. It misses by a few inches and she whimpers. The sound makes me cringe.

I change my approach, now understanding she doesn't want to be touched. "Bree." I move to get off the bed, giving the mattress and my knees some space. "Bree." I raise my voice to get through to her but it seems to make it worse. Her whimpering gets louder and her head starts moving back and forth against the pillow. I've never felt so helpless.

Before I can talk myself out of it, I decide to just rip it off like a band aid. I lean forward and rest both my hands on the tops of her arms, giving her two hard shakes. "Wake up!"

She sits up with a gasp. Our foreheads bump against each other and I get an instant, radiating headache. "Caden?" Her voice is hoarse. She brings a shaking hand up to her throat and winces. The light from the lamp is dim but I can see some scratches across the skin beneath her fingers.

"Yeah, it's me." I want to touch her but hold myself back. She's looking around the room like she's lost or out of place. Like she's not supposed to be here. I wonder where she just was, in her head. If it was with him. I'm not jealous or anything, it just upsets me that she has to keep going back there.

"You okay?" I ask after another minute of her being too quiet.

She squints under the light and looks up at me. A frown settles on her lips. "Yeah. I'm sorry." Her voice gives out as she buries her face in her hands. I grab at her fingers and gently pull at them, revealing two watery blue eyes underneath.

"Don't be sorry. Don't you ever be sorry, Bree." I let go of her hands so mine are free, then cradle her face with them. I don't want to push her but I need to know she's okay. Slowly, so my intentions are clear, I lean in to her. She falls into the kiss easily, maybe even a little too easily. I can feel how desperate she is as she moves against me, like I'm the only oxygen supplier around town.

I let her do whatever she wants, giving her the reigns. The last thing I want is for her to feel out of control with me. She pulls away slowly and rests her forehead against mine. We stay that way for I don't know how long, just breathing each other in. A comfortable silence wraps itself around us. I can almost feel the warmth of it. She takes in a shaky breath and whispers, "I love you." It's not just three words. It's a battle cry.

"I love you, too." She looks up at me, relief washing over her features.

"Thank you."

"For what?"

"Everything." She tries a smile but it shakes and falls. "For loving me."

"You act like it's hard." My words do something to her. She shrugs and drops her head so I can't see her face. A rush of anger passes through me. I grab her chin with my thumb and finger, pulling at it. When she's finally looking at me I give her what I hope is a meaningful stare. "It is not hard to love you, Aubrey Pierce. Not even a little bit."

"Caden."

"No. Don't do that. Don't brush it away." I cup her face again, holding her steady so I can study her. Memorize her. Her eyes remind me of the night sky, just after a storm. The dimness of the room makes her freckles seem to blend together. I watch as her bottom lip begins to tremble. She pulls it between her teeth and tries to get it to stop. I wish she wasn't so upset right now. I wish I could think of a way to make her laugh.

I think of her laugh now, and her smile. The way she crinkles her nose. The way she can lose herself in a song. The way her hair falls out of her ponytail. The little dances she does when she thinks no one is watching. Was he just too high to see those things? Was he too busy? How could someone ever look at this girl and hurt her? "He didn't love you."

The thought forms and bursts before I can really think about it. Even so, I know in this moment that it's true. It has to be. I stare at her and wait for a reaction. It comes slowly, both sadness and anger blooming in her face. The air between us feels incredibly empty, like there's miles of distance between our beating hearts. I start to ramble, hoping to fill some of it.

"The problem was with him, not with you. Maybe he did love you. Fuck, I have no idea. I didn't know him, but if he did then he didn't do it right. Love isn't like that. You don't do the things he did to people you love." I pause, searching her eyes for some sort of sign of what to say or do. There's nothing there. "It's not hard to love you, Bree."

Finally, the blankness on her face morphs and she starts crying. She wipes at the tears quickly. When she pulls her hands away I see that she's smiling. "Thank you."

I have to laugh at her. This is how the whole damn conversation started in the first place. Her and her stupid gratitude. "Shut up." I shake my head at her, my lips cocking in a crooked smile. She laughs and I move forward, capturing the sound with my mouth and swallowing it. I can't help but think I'm saving it for later. We fall back against the pillows and she moans.

I want to see her so I pull my lips away from hers. I watch her blink a few times, each time her eyelids taking longer to come back up. "You're exhausted." She gives me a guilty smile and nods. I hum low in my throat, content with just being next to her.

Her smile melts back into a frown and I feel mine do the same. "What?"

"I just don't want another nightmare." She looks ashamed. She has nothing to be ashamed about. That anger from earlier returns and I want more than anything to know his name. I bite my tongue. I won't take advantage of her vulnerability right now by asking.

"I'll stay awake. You'll be safe, I promise." My words send a shiver through her and I can't help but wonder when the last time was that she fell asleep feeling safe. Especially now that she knows he's out wandering the streets.

"Thank you." I roll my eyes but she's not paying attention, already letting her body melt into the mattress. Reaching over, I turn the light off before wrapping myself around her, my hand resting at her hip and pulling her in. She flinches and I push away, giving her space. Her body doesn't move and I can tell she isn't breathing.

"What just happened?" I kiss her hair to show her that I'm not angry, just concerned.

"Nothing. I'm sorry." Her response is instant. I wish she would stop apologizing.

"Please don't pretend you're fine when you're not." Desperation thickens my voice as I speak. I move away to give her more room and she turns, settling herself on her back instead of her side. I watch her stare up at the ceiling for a while. When she finally speaks, she squeezes her eyes shut. It reminds me of a child watching a scary movie, waiting for the bad part to come.

"Sometimes I get a little claustrophobic. I know you won't hurt me but, I don't know." It makes perfect sense after everything she's been through, but her words still send a jolt to my heart. It hurts that she can't be held. It's not fair to her.

I've never hated someone. I don't hate my mother, even after she almost killed Cassie. I don't hate the driver who crashed into my father, even after finding out he was drunk. Accidents happen, I get that. People make mistakes. But I hate him. I hate this nameless piece of shit who took her life apart.

"Are you mad?" I cringe. I was so wrapped up in my own head I forgot to respond. To tell her it's okay. I'm such an idiot.

"Not at you, baby. Just upset that you have to go through this shit." I wipe a tear from her cheek, streaking the moisture across her freckles. One day I'll have to count those. "It's late and you're exhausted. Try and get comfortable, okay?"

She nods, arranging herself so she's on her stomach. Her arms are tucked underneath her pillows, her face towards me. I stroke the long strands of hair that run down her back, straightening them out piece by piece. She hums in appreciation at the touch, her eyelids fluttering shut.

"You're perfect." It's cheesy but it needed to be said. She crinkles her nose exactly the way I like and I wonder if she knows how that gets to me. I plant a kiss on the tip of it and it relaxes back to normal. "Are you comfy?"

"Yup." Her voice is already quiet and sleepy.

"Alright." I rest my head on my own pillow, leaving an inch of space between us, and place my hand on the small of her back. "Is this okay?"

"Yeah. 'S perfect." Her words come out slurred, her lips barely moving to make the sounds. Her body relaxes into the mattress under my touch. I feel a warmth running through me. If she's this sleepy, she must feel safe.

"No, you're perfect." I say again, teasing. Her smile is slow and soft and I can tell she's already on the edge of a dream. I keep my hand where it is. I don't care what she dreams about, but I'll make damn sure it's a good one.

I watch her for the longest time, falling more in love with her with every exhale.

Overtime her breathing steadies and I finally close my eyes, ready to fall asleep myself. Then her phone rings.

"Shit." I roll off the bed, praying she doesn't wake up. This girl deserves some fricken sleep.

I find it on the floor next to her bag. My fingers move to silence it but my sleepy mind catches up to me. It's an unknown number. *It's him.*
It's a terrible idea. All I will be doing is poking a sleeping bear. Then again, he's not really sleeping, is he? He's asking for it.

"Hello?" My voice comes out in a harsh whisper. I hurry over to the door and enter the hallway. Despite the twenty or thirty seconds it takes to quietly get a safe distance away, the line remains silent. If I was unsure before, I know now. It's him.

"She doesn't want to speak to you. It's in your best interest to stop calling." Nothing. I glance at the phone but he hasn't hung up. I give him a few more seconds before my anger gets too heavy in my chest and I burst. "Do you hear me, you son of a bitch? You *will* leave her alone. I will fucking end you. I swear to God; you have no idea who you're messing with. I'll make-"

I swallow the rest of my words, seeing in my peripheral vision that the phone screen is lit up. I glance down at it and frown. He hung up. His cowardice is flashing across my screen in big black letters.

Fuck. I was so close to finding out who he was. So close to getting him to leave her alone. I hope he stayed on the line long enough to get the picture, at least.

Not wanting to go to bed this upset, I stay in the hallway and try to breathe through my anger. My mind won't stop racing with all the ways I could kill him. All the ways I could ruin his life, at the very least. To calm myself, I look at her phone, wondering if there's a game or something I could play for a minute.

The number is still on the screen, giving me the option to call it back. That's when it hits me. It's familiar. Why is it so familiar? I feel like I just saw it recently.

I sneak back into my room and find my jeans, digging in the pocket for my own phone. I only type in the first four numbers before it appears, digit for digit the same. My blood runs cold.

No. Fuck no.

CHAPTER EIGHTY-NINE
Caden

It takes me an hour to come to a decision. It's almost five in the morning by the time I grab my clothes and get dressed. I reason with myself that it's the right thing to do. I need to make sure he never comes near her again.

I try to step light as I make my way down the hall, slipping a bright pink scrunchie on Caitlin's doorknob. We came up with the system when we realized waking her up at three in the morning to tell her I have to go to work wasn't working.

Now, if Cassie has a nightmare she sees the scrunchie and knows to go to Caitlin. Caitlin will know that Cassie is her responsibility once she wakes up and sees it. I've only used it twice, both times for something less important than this.

I don't know what I'll tell Aubrey. Lying to her is the last thing I want to do, I've only ever lied to her once and that was about my mother being dead. It was before our relationship too. I shove my feet into my shoes and decide I'll tell her it was a work emergency if I need to. Fingers crossed that she sleeps through this whole disaster and never has to know.

As I drive, I realize a few things. First, I left my gun. This is something that could get my ass killed, if he pulls out the gun I'm sure he illegally has, or something that could save my ass because right now, in this moment, I want to kill him.

I'm also in nothing but a hoodie and workout shorts, my beat up running shoes not even tied on my feet. I wish I was in uniform, for the intimidation and dominance, but since murder has already crossed my mind I suppose that's a good thing as well. A cop killing someone is one thing, a cop in uniform but off duty is just a whole other problem. Not that I'm going to kill him. *I'm not going to kill him, right?*

The last thing I didn't consider is whether or not he lives alone. I had his address in my files but he could have a roommate. He could be waiting for me. He could have recognized my voice. He could have a whole group of guys ready to jump me. He could, like thought about earlier, have a gun.

None of it matters when I pull up to his apartment building. It all just melts away. I stare up at the brick exterior. It's the same apartment he had when he got arrested. According to the landlord we interviewed a few months ago, he paid extra on top of rent to hold it. He said it was for *his girl*. The thought makes me sick.

How many times did I hear him talk about her without knowing? How many little comments? Everything is clicking into place. When he was arrested, there was blood on his clothes and his knuckles were split open. They said he had been in a fight, and he kept asking for his girl, but we never connected that the person he beat up was her. How did we not see that? How did I not see it?

Aubrey said she was in the hospital, and this son of a bitch is who put her there, the same night we dragged him in. The guy I've been desperate to know has been sitting in front of me for months.

I get out of the car as quietly as I can, not wanting to tip anyone off. I take the stairs two at a time, my mind racing with all the different ways this could go. None of them are good.

When I reach my destination, I start pounding against the door, right below the number eleven. A woman comes around the corner, bouncing a toddler on her hip. Her eyes open wide when she sees me. I must look crazy, pounding on the door at this time of day. She probably thinks I'm some junkie in need of a quick fix. Honestly, I feel like one.

"Good morning." I say quietly, my voice low and steady. I move slowly and pull out my badge. I got it when the investigation started, even though I'm not detective yet. This is my first time using it and I'm off the clock. *Great*.

"CPD, nothing to worry about." Her body relaxes when she sees my badge but she still hurries past me, tucking her child's head against her shoulder. I want to chase her, ask her if she lived here last year. If she heard anything. Why she didn't help.

I take my anger out on the door, pounding again. "I'm coming. Jesus." I hear a bang and a little chuckle, like it's funny that he knocked something over. I glance up and smile at the fact that there's no peephole. I have the upper hand.

The second the door opens, I charge. My hands collide with his chest, my fingers balling up the fabric and holding tight. He swears, the word coming out with a sucked in breath. I keep my feet moving until he's against the wall. The door, like it understands, swings shut from the force of being pushed back. No one can see us. This must have been how Aubrey felt. The idea makes my fingers itch to hit him. It takes everything in me to keep my hands where they are, pinning him underneath a canvas painting. I find myself wondering who picked it out, him or Aubrey.

"Caden."

"Officer Larson." I correct him, my focus shifting back to the moment. He's looking at me with wide, clear eyes, but they aren't confused. Scared, yes. Desperate, for sure. But not confused. He's already calculating. He knows exactly why I'm here, and why wouldn't he? Aubrey told me he had her watched, and I'm sure it never stopped. He's known all along who I was to her.

"Listen, man." I pull my fist back and snap it forward. His nose shatters underneath the blow and I come alive. All that anger and frustration pools inside my chest, seeping its way down my arms. I hit him again, trying to ease the feeling. If anything, the anger grows.

"Stop!" The word is accompanied through the air with a glob of bloody spit. It lands on my cheek. Now I'm livid. I release him and take a step back, wiping my face and cringing. He takes the opportunity to speak again, changing his angle from defensive to offensive. *Bad move.*

"She's mine!" The words seem to shake his entire body. I can see that he's furious, and that he's trying to warn me off. The words don't affect me, because I'm not at all worried about her being his.

I stand back and let him ramble, digging his own grave. "She's mine. She knows it. She'll come back to me because she's in love with me. She's just afraid of what people will think. Of what Myla will think, and her mother." He wipes the blood from his face with one hand, giving me a stained smirk.

"She's only dating you to get to me. You think I didn't know? You think I haven't been following her? Watching her at that silly gym, trying to make herself feel safe again. Watching her walk to class. Watching her at your house."

He laughs, but there's no humor in it. It's wild. Just on the edge of control. Is this who she knew? Is this how he used to act? "I don't care that she feels safe. I really don't." He puts his hands up in surrender. "I'll let her feel safe for now, even if it means letting her act like a fucking slut." The last word echoes in my chest and I lunge.

I don't yell or tell him to shut up. I don't want him to think he's getting in my head. Instead, I carefully bring my right hand to the base of his neck and start to squeeze. Did he ever do this to her? *Who am I kidding?* Of course he did. She was clawing at her throat just this morning, trying to get away.

I have to fight to keep my words calm and controlled. "She is not a slut." He laughs again, even though my fingers are starting to cut off his oxygen. The sound pushes me over the edge and I tighten my grip, feeling better when I see his eyes flash with fear. "You will leave her alone."

"Make me." The words are choked but clear. Will I really make him? Am I willing to lose everything? My job? My reputation? My girls? The answer petrifies me.

"Are you forgetting who holds your future in his hands? One bad drug test, one lie, one slip up, I could have you arrested so fast." Now I'm the one laughing. I let go of him, smiling as he gasps for air. "Hell, one little tip to your home boys that you're a rat and BOOM, they'll handle it themselves."

"You'd lose your job!" His entire body is trembling. *Good.* He deserves to feel fear. To experience what Aubrey experienced. To have his life crumble in the hands of someone else, someone who couldn't care less.

"Where's the proof?" I gesture around the apartment. "You've got nothing on me."

"I'll tell them you threatened me. I'll tell them about Bree." *Bree.* A new wave of anger washes over me, sending my fists flying. God, that feels good.

"Don't say her name." My fist lands again and again until his legs give out. I step back and watch him crumple to the floor. I continue to speak, keeping my voice low and controlled. "What will you tell my boss, huh? I threatened you to stay away from the girl you used to beat? The girl you used to do this too?" I crawl on top of him, easily slipping into a chokehold. The one move Aubrey still can't do. The one that might bring down her career. I hear him sputtering and tighten my grip.

"I'll ruin you." I remind him. He starts fading, his body weight sagging against me. I immediately relax. I won't make this easy for him. I readjust so I'm straddling him. One of his eyes is already swelling. *Fucking amateur.* "What, you can hit girls but you don't know how to fight back against someone your own size?"

I spit on him and he bucks his hips. His hands remain at his sides. He's smart; he either knows not to hit an officer or knows my past as a fighter. Fine by me. No marks means no explaining on my end. I hit him one more time for good measure.

"When your people ask, you'll say you got into a stupid bar fight. When Jones asks, you'll say some old client got on your ass." I grab his throat again. "Stop following her. Stop calling her. You will leave her the fuck alone."

I stand up and kick him in the ribs. He gags and rolls over. I watch him dry heave for a second before rolling my eyes. What a pussy. As he sputters, I look around the apartment, surveying the area. I find what I'm looking for immediately. It's sitting on a small table, surrounded by stacks of vinyl records. It only takes four steps to reach it. My arms wrap around it and I slam it against the floor as hard as I can, smiling as I watch it break.

I pause and take in the rest of the place. This is it. This is where her life fell apart. This is where she goes to every night. Where she's still trapped.

All of the anger inside of me is replaced by a sudden need to be with her. I walk to the door, not acknowledging him as he struggles to sit up. When I reach it, I rest my hand on the knob and look back at him. I know I should leave but I just need to say one final thing. "She's not yours. She's not mine either. You don't own people, especially people you love."

He doesn't say anything but his coughing stops. I slam the door and leave him behind. I should have killed him. Jason would be proud.

CHAPTER NINETY
Aubrey

I wake up to an empty bed. My arm reaches out to double check, one eye squinting open. The bright sunlight pouring through the bedroom window burns. Then the fact that it's a weekday registers in my mind and I bolt upright. We missed a workout, and I'm going to miss school.

Caden's flannel from last night is still on the floor in a puddle. I grab it and wrap it around myself, starting the search for my phone. I remember specifically leaving it next to me in case Myla called. It's not there anymore.

I find it on the side table next to where Caden was lying, which is strange. I press the home button and groan. My first class starts soon. I look around for some sort of note since my phone has no texts but there's nothing. The anxiety of him not being here doesn't last long. There are plenty of reasonable explanations.

Hoping both girls went to school this morning, I pad down the hallway in nothing but my underwear and his flannel. There's noises coming from the first floor. I follow them, absentmindedly buttoning up the shirt as I walk.

When I get into the kitchen I see Caden standing by the stove, shirtless. A pair of grey workout shorts are hanging loosely from his hips. I study him for a moment as he stirs whatever he's cooking, memorizing the way his back muscles ripple. I take a step forward, wanting to get closer to him, and the floor creaks.

His muscles stiffen at the sound, his shoulders lifting up in defense. He relaxes when he turns around to look at me. "Morning beautiful." A warm smile spreads across his face as he opens his arms. I move to him, letting him wrap himself around me.

"Good morning." My words are slightly muffled by his chest but I don't mind. The contact feels good. "Why didn't you wake me up earlier? I have class soon."

"I know, I'm sorry, but you needed sleep." I can't argue with that. Even after I fell back asleep last night, I still felt restless. Almost like I was sleeping alone.

"It's okay." I groan before pulling myself away from him. "I have to get ready for school."

"Don't go." His words come out rushed and desperate. I can see in his eyes that he's anxious.

"I don't like missing school."

"I know. You're a nerd." He offers me a playful smile and I stick my tongue out at him, giving him a swat on the butt.

"So, first dinner and now breakfast? I feel pretty special."

"You are." He turns around and lifts me, placing me on the counter like I weigh nothing. I watch him as he goes back to stirring what I can now see are eggs. He moves on to some food on the counter and my mouth starts watering. He's coating french toast in crushed cereal.

"Is that Karen's french toast?"

He smiles over at me, his eyes lighting up with humor. "Sure is." He cocks an eyebrow. "That okay?"

"I don't know." I tease. "Can you really measure up to Karen?"

He feigns insult but quickly drops the act, replacing it with a carefree grin. "It won't be as good, but it is her recipe." He taps the homemade cookbook on the counter, filled with cramped handwriting that isn't his own. I feel a sudden emptiness when I realize it must be his mother's. The emptiness grows when I see the hand he pointed with has bruised knuckles and a few cuts. They weren't like that last night. "Plus, she's who taught me to cook so there's that."

"I trust you." I can hear how monotone my voice is but I don't care. All I can focus on are his knuckles. I do trust him, don't I? I want to ask about them. If it was Elliot, I wouldn't dare ask. It'd be none of my business. That's what decides it for me; Caden isn't Elliot. "What happened to your hands?"

He cringes, not meeting my eyes. Instead he focuses on the french toast, carefully coating it despite the fact that his hands have started to shake. Finally, he drops the toast into the pan and looks up at me. "I did a workout this morning."

I haven't been with him long enough to know when he's lying but the no eye contact and shaky hands aren't comforting.

"Without your gloves?"

"I needed to get some stuff out of my system. It's always better against skin." It's true, and I can't help but feel responsible for him needing an outlet. Between all my little freak outs, the fact I won't tell him Elliot's name, and now the nightmare last night, he's probably totally overwhelmed. I feel a stab of guilt at the thought that I'm adding more to his already top heavy plate.

"Well, wake me up next time. We can work out together." He looks up from the pan and offers me a kiss. I take it fast, holding onto it for a while. When I finally pull away he sighs.

"I'll wake you up next time, of course. I'm sorry." He flips the french toast, his eyes losing focus on the pan for a moment too long. Before I can read too much into it, he snaps out of it and smiles again. "I have to go to work soon anyway. Want me to drop you off at class?"

"Yeah. That'd be great." I have a car but there's something comforting about having him drive me. "So, anything interesting happening at work today?" He jumps and I wonder if he forgot I was here. Before I can ask, or even tease him about being a scaredy-cat, he slides back into the conversation. "Yeah. Big day for me. Promotion on the line." His words come out thick.

"Well, I think it'll go good." He shrugs and I feel myself deflate. Elliot used to do this. He'd walk around with a cloud over his head and make me fix it. Nine times out of ten, it always turned into a guessing game. I hated guessing games. I always lost, and the consolation prize was never shiny. I won't do it with him. "Caden. What's wrong?"

"Nothing." The answer is sharp and comes way too fast. I want to let it go, I really do, but like I said earlier he's not Elliot. I won't stick a band-aide on the conversation and hope he's better later. It doesn't feel good.

"I don't want to fight, but I really don't appreciate you treating me like an idiot. I thought we could be open with each other. I thought you trusted me." He winces, like my words physically hurt him. It takes a moment for him to say anything, him keeping his focus on putting our food on plates. Finally, he settles his hands on my thighs and explains.

"I'm worried about you. I don't like that your ex is out and trying to contact you." He looks me in the eyes for the first time and I can see the anxiety there. "I'm not trying to be controlling, I would never control you, but just be careful okay?"

"Okay." I lean forward and kiss him, hoping to take some of the anxiety away. We can carry this weight together. "I'll be careful, I promise, and for what it's worth I really think today will go well. At work, I mean. You seem great at your job."

"Thank you." He kisses me again, this time feeling like himself again. It's the first time this morning that it hasn't felt like an obligation. "I'm sure you're right. Everything will be fine."

It's clear he's convincing himself, not me.

CHAPTER NINETY-ONE
Caden

Everyone goes on alert when he walks into the room. His eyes immediately find mine before focusing on the bruised knuckles wrapped around my disposable coffee cup. Jones speaks first.

"What the hell happened, man?" I wait for him to name me, or at the very least to make a meaningful comment. Instead, he scoffs and looks away.

"Ran into an old client. Asshole still had an issue with me." He starts pouring coffee like this is just another morning for him. I have to hide my smile.

"Are you alright, though?" Does he actually care? I hope not. I hope he just cares about the job. As if to answer me he continues. "You can still handle this, right?"

"Yeah." The answer comes instantly, followed by another pointed glance to my knuckles. He's trying to make me uncomfortable. It won't work.

"Good." I stand up and stare at him until he awkwardly takes a seat next to Jones. Once he's settled and all focus is on me, I go into the little speech I've been practicing in my head since dropping Aubrey off at class.

Throughout the overview of the investigation, my mind drifts. I thought I'd be able to put distance between the investigation and my hate for Jameson, but every time I glance at him my insides start to bubble. To avoid losing my job, I keep my eyes focused on the Chief. He smiles when I finish, nodding his head like he's impressed.

"Sounds like you're handling your new position quite well, Officer Larson. Well done." I feel my throat constrict. New position? I have to sip my coffee to hide my shit-eating grin. "Do we have an estimate on time?"

The question is directed at both Jones and Jameson. It's great watching the piece of shit squirm under pressure. His discomfort grows as Jones glances at him as well. I watch him open and close his mouth like a damn fish twice before stepping in.

"Shouldn't be more than a month, Sir. Jones is climbing the ladder fairly fast."

"Yeah." Jameson sits up straight like he just discovered his voice. "The crew really likes him. They think it's hilarious that he's a prissy straightedge."

"Well, that's good." The Chief gives me an uncomfortable smile. He hates Jameson. I half believe it's the reason he handed the investigation to me. "I think we're ready for the final phase."

Jones and Jameson both nod. The Chief smiles and focuses his attention on me. "Officer Larson?"

"Yes, Sir?" I clench my fists behind my back so no one can see my fingers twitching.

"Your investigation." He offers me his hand, giving me a meaningful smile. I take his hand and shake it hard.

"Thank you, Sir." He leaves the room and the attention shifts to me. I puff out my chest.

"You both feel comfortable?"

"Absolutely." Jones smiles. Jameson gives me one tight nod, which is good enough.

"Great. I think we're set then. You guys know what to do? I can let you loose?"

"Yeah." Jameson stands up, obviously impatient to leave.

"If we talk protocol or emergency plans one more minute I think I might kill myself." Jones mumbles, standing up as well. I can't help but laugh at this. It's true.

"Alright. Let's catch some bad guys, then." A weight settles over the entire room. The final phase is always the most dangerous. Always the hardest to pull off. Even the best plans can end up messy.

I start to lead them through the station towards the door, the three of us silent as we walk. When we get outside the sunlight soaks us in warmth. I have to fight the urge to scan the parking lot. If Jameson's crew is still tracking him or Jones, I can't make it worse. For good measure, I wave them off and yell across the few feet of distance.

"Sorry for the inconvenience boys, but at least you passed."

"Don't worry. Ill pee for ya anytime, officer." Jones says with a cocky fake salute and a smirk. Jameson, like usual, says nothing.

CHAPTER NINETY-TWO
Caden

I change out of my uniform and check my phone when I get home. Three missed calls and two texts. Almost all of them are from Aubrey, but one is from a number I'm growing tired of seeing. I answer Aubrey first, letting her know I'm free tonight. I'm anxious to see her and hold her. After today, I just need a little reassurance that she's safe.

I take four very deep breaths before calling the other number back. He answers almost immediately, like he was waiting with his thumb hovering above the screen. "Can we meet?"

"Sorry, not into booty calls." He scoffs on the other end and I bite back a remark. There's no reason to stir the pot when we just launched the final phase. "What do you want, Jameson?"

"Why don't you call me Elliot?" It's so off topic, I actually answer.

"Because you're not my friend."

"I'm not an officer, either."

"Hence why I don't call you *Officer* Jameson." Annoyance drips from my words but I really don't care.

"But you don't call Jones *Officer* Jones."

"Because he's under cover and it's a poor habit to get in. Plus, he's my friend." This conversation is driving me nuts. I storm over to the fridge and grab a beer, cracking it open on the bottle opener screwed into the wall. After a long gulp, I sigh. "What the hell do you want?"

"I already told you; I want to meet up."

"No." I take another long drink and ponder whether or not I should see him. Could I get him to leave Aubrey alone? Could I get some answers, like if he's going to hurt her and if he's paying for her college? Maybe I *should* see him. "Why do you want to see me?"

"You know why." Now it's his turn to sound annoyed. I fiddle with the label of my beer before giving up.

"Not at your place. Somewhere public." I'm hoping this throws him off. It must, because it takes a few seconds before he responds.

"It can't be anywhere someone will see us."

"Then I guess we aren't meeting."

"No. It's fine." I smile at how rushed and desperate he sounds. "There's a used bookstore downtown, next to a pawn shop. It's usually pretty empty and I doubt anyone on my end knows it exists."

"I'll be there in fifteen." I hang up and text Aubrey to let her know something came up. It worries me that she hasn't answered my text from earlier yet but I assure myself that she's probably just busy.

Sure enough, my phone dings as I get to the door.

That's fine. I'm hanging out with Myla, anyway. She needs some girl time. No rush. I love you!!

The message gives me the strength to follow through with this stupid plan. I'm doing it for her, after all.

CHAPTER NINETY-THREE
Aubrey

Myla's hangover has disappeared and she's ready to take on the world. "I want to go to group. There's one in an hour, then I thought we could do some shopping therapy?"

I'm exhausted, and just found out that my professor decided adding an essay on top of midterms would be a good idea today. That said, I can't tell her no to therapy. She has refused to open up to me about whatever freaked her out last night, but whatever it is should be confronted.

We drive to group in awkward silence, listening to her kind of music instead of mine. It's a sacrifice I'm willing to make.

"So, Jason brought you home last night?" I ask, turning the music down. We're rolling into town and I only have a minute or two left before we'll be at group.

"Yeah. That was nice of him."

"He didn't take advantage of you, right?" I glance at her. Jason is nice, and he's Caden's best friend, but I don't know him that well. It makes me nervous that I trusted her with him, especially when she was obviously going through something.

"Of course not." She huffs like this is ridiculous. "He pretty much helped me puke my guts out all night."

"He stayed over?"

"Yeah, he slept on the floor." She brings her knees up to her chest and rests her cheek against them. "He was nice."

"Good."

"Don't worry, Bree. I'm not going to screw things up for you by banging him."

I feel my cheeks burn. That's not where my mind was going at all. "I wouldn't care if you slept with him, My."

"Well, I won't. I'm done doing that." She lets out a long breath. "Thanks for coming with me."

I park the car and look over at her. "You go, I go. No matter what."

She reaches across the car and hugs me, burying her face in my neck. We stay there for a while, both holding each other as if our lives depend on it. By the time we come apart, we're running late.

Emma has already done the opening part of group when we show up. She welcomes us in and asks us to take a seat. Myla heads toward the coffee first, filling up a cup for each of us.

"So, does anyone want to speak today?"

Myla hands me my coffee and raises her hand, taking a seat to my left. The crabby boy isn't here today, and I hope he hasn't stopped coming.

Emma smiles at Myla, and I get the feeling she already knows what's about to happen. Emma is good like that.

"Myla, go ahead."

"So, last night, it was Halloween, and I went as a slutty mermaid." She gestures to her hair. "Ariel, obviously."

This gets the group to laugh, and Myla's shoulders relax. "I got really drunk and I met this guy at the bar. He convinced me to come back to his place, which I usually don't do. I usually hook up where I feel in control, at my place, or in like a bathroom or something. But I went with him, and it ended up being a house on campus with a big party. I rolled with it and we drank some more, and then things started getting weird."

Emma smiles patiently for Myla to continue, but the room remains in silence. "Would you feel comfortable explaining what you mean?"

"Yeah." Myla reaches for my hand and I inch our chairs closer so she can hold it. "His friends kept giving each other weird looks, and they all kept making comments that sounded like they were in on this joke that I wasn't. Then the guy asked if I wanted to go upstairs with him, and since his friends were weirding me out, I told him sure."

She chugs her coffee and starts playing with the empty cup, picking off pieces of foam. "It was fine at first. We were making out and it was normal, but then his friends came in. I was expecting him to yell at them for interrupting but he just kept going and told me to ignore them. We weren't having sex so I sort of just went with it, but then they locked the door and the guys started getting undressed and I freaked out. They, um."

She starts crying, clinging to my hand for support. "He started holding me down and telling me to relax. And one of them was saying that I sleep with everyone, so why not knock a few out at once." She shrugs, like he had a point. I want to punch whoever this guy is in the face. My only hope is that he was the guy that Jason knocked out.

"I screamed and someone on the other side of the door started jiggling the knob and asking if I needed help. It freaked them out long enough for me to get out of there, but it just brought me right back." She closes her eyes, tears falling freely down her cheeks. "I was there all over again, my dad inviting his friends to see his special little girl."

She chokes on a sob and my hand begins to lose feeling. It's worth losing the hand if it means Myla is finally talking about this.

The group stays quiet while she cries. After a minute, she gets calmed down enough to talk again. "I don't want to sleep around anymore. I thought it was a way to feel in control of myself, but it's not working."

"You want to know a secret?" Emma asks. Myla nods, wiping at her face with both hands. I take my hand back and discreetly shake it out, hoping to get some blood back in it. "You being here, is taking back control. It's the first step."

"Okay."

"I want you to do some homework for me. In the next week, I want you to stay away from men. No dates. No sex. Nothing. Just work on yourself. Find other ways, healthier ways, to feel in control."

"I can do that." She sits up straight. "Then what?"

"Then you come back." She gestures to the group. "What should she do, everyone?"

"Keep coming back."

CHAPTER NINETY-FOUR
Aubrey

We decide to go shopping back home, since Myla has a coupon for one of the little shops downtown. It helps, being out with her and just having fun. The last time we did this was before school started, back when the boy drama was much lower.

She picks out a cute dress for Thanksgiving, sticking true to her Holiday loving self. The top is a deep red but it slowly fades to a white skirt. It's sophisticated but flirty, which was the goal. Myla drapes the garment bag over her arm and steps into the fall air. It's cooler than it was this morning, the sun playing peekaboo behind the clouds.

I wrap my arms around my waist, wishing my sweater was thicker.

"We could stop by the bookstore." Myla's voice is nothing but casual as she gestures across the street at the little used bookstore. I practically grew up there. The owner used to call me when something would come in that he thought I'd like.

But that's where I met Elliot, right where the Young Adult Romance novels merge into the Thrillers. A perfect metaphor of what was to come. I haven't been there since his arrest.

"Maybe another time." I stare longingly at the rows of books through the windows. It's the only good bookstore in town. I've been having to buy overpriced books from a chain store.

"No." Myla scolds me like I'm a small child. "Not another time. You haven't been in there in way too long, love." The little pet name is what does it for me. She always calls me 'love' or 'hun' when she's concerned, and I don't feel up to a long lecture today. Plus, I do really want to go in there again.

"Fine," I say, my feet already moving me across the street. Myla hurries to catch up, rambling in excitement.

"Oh, good. You should buy something too. I know money's tight but-" I stop listening to her, all of the blood in my body turning to a numbing temperature. Through the window, I can see Elliot leaning against a bookcase, casually smiling. His tattooed arms are thicker than they used to be, and his hair is cut short. There's not a doubt in my mind that it's him, though. I'll always have him memorized.

Unfortunately, there's not a doubt in my mind of who he's talking to, even with his back to me. I was wearing that flannel this morning. I ran my fingers through that hair last night.

"Bree." Myla's voice is low and I can hear both the concern and the warning in it. "Let's go."

"Caden." It's the only think I can get past my heavy tongue. The only thing floating around my stunned mind.

"What? You want me to call him?" She shifts beside me, obviously freaking out. I shake my head and point to the window, repeating myself. She must understand because she gets closer to the window and squints. As if he can sense that she needs a different angle, he walks over to a set of books so we can see half his face. Myla gasps.

The ground below my feet starts to give in and I don't care that I'm falling. All I can focus on is the tedious task of replaying all the conversations. All the moments. When did Elliot get to him? When did it stop being real? Was it ever? Was he another spy?

"They're coming." Myla hisses, grabbing my arm and pulling me up and over to a cubby where a door to a law office is tucked away. I don't know how I'm standing or breathing, but I'm sure it's only because of Myla. I'm too numb to understand any of this.

Elliot is laughing as they walk out. I can feel the sound deep in my bones. He turns to Caden, who has his hands stuffed in his pockets. "We good then?" Elliot asks, his smile sarcastic.

"Yeah." Caden squints up at the sun and I know he's pondering something, rolling it around in his mind. I think I might start to cry. Actually, I may be crying now. "It's almost over, anyway. Just a few weeks."

"I'll hold up my end, don't worry." Elliot laughs again. End of what? End of a deal? Between them? I remember Kyle following me, and reporting back to Elliot. Is that what this is, or is it so much worse?

"We don't need to see each other again, alright? Not until it's over." The way Caden stands, the way he speaks, makes it feel like he's the one in charge. I can't decide if that's good. Myla's hand slips into mine, squeezing.

"Fine by me." Elliot smirks. I recognize it and know instantly; he got whatever he wanted. Of course he did. He always does. "Pleasure doing business with ya, buddy."

He backs away, towards his car. I feel Myla's hand pulling at me. I think she's saying something but I can't hear it. None of it makes sense until I realize I've gotten closer to Caden. I've moved.

His eyes land on me at the same time Myla catches up to us.

"You should leave!" She shouts, putting her small body in between us. Caden's face crumbles and I can't help but feel better at that. I hope me finding out ruins all his stupid little plans. His deal.

"Bree." He looks over Myla's shoulder, pleading with me. I cringe at the sound of my name and take a step back, putting more space between Myla and I. When I speak, it's without thought. As the words tumble out I feel wall after wall being repaired and put back up inside myself.

"It's Aubrey." Caden steps forward, his arm reaching for me, but Myla blocks him. I don't stick around to see the scene unfold. I don't stick around to hear any bullshit excuses or crazy explanations. Myla starts yelling, her hands bunched in the fabric of the softest flannel I've ever worn, holding him back. I feel nothing. Then, all at once, I feel everything. My chest collapses and I can't breathe.

I know I should fight. I should let him have it the way Myla is right now. I can hear Rob's voice in my head, egging me on. I can see Jason telling me to channel the anger and use it. I can hear Elliot. *Hit me, Bree. Come on.* I can even hear Caden, his *I love you*s echoing in my mind.

None of it matters. I don't want to fight. Not ever again. So, I run.

Made in the USA
Columbia, SC
06 January 2018